Dani Atkins was born in Hertfordshire and has lived there all her life. She worked for many years as a secretary in London, and books were her constant companions on the daily commute. She never let go of her secret dream that one day she too might become an author.

A long and happy marriage, two children and a great many much loved pets later, Dani wrote **FRACTURED**, which became a best-seller in 2013. **THE STORY OF US** is her second novel. Dani still has to pinch herself to realise that she is now, quite literally, living her dream.

Dani Atkins

THE STORY OF US

HEAD
of
ZEUS

First published in the UK in 2014 by Head of Zeus Ltd.

9 7 5 3 1 2 4 6 8

A catalogue record for this book is available from the British Library

Paperback ISBN: 9781781857144
Ebook ISBN: 9781781857120

Typeset by Palimpsest Book Production Ltd, Falkirk, Stirlingshire

Printed and bound by CPI Group (UK) Ltd,
Croydon, CR0 4YY.

Head of Zeus Ltd
Clerkenwell House
45-47 Clerkenwell Green
London EC1R 0HT
WWW.HEADOFZEUS.COM

To Kimberly and Luke, for holding my hand.

And to Ralph, who holds my heart.

THE END

PART ONE

You'd think that the day your whole life changes would be marked in some way. Bells should be ringing (well, I guess they would be later). Maybe there should be lightning bolts or a thunderclap or two? I looked through the window, but all I could see was a bright autumn morning, with a handful of russet leaves tossed by a breeze, floating past like amber confetti.

I could feel the nervous tension inside me flipping my stomach like a pancake. My hands were shaking so much that I was sure to make a mess of my make-up, which was lined up on my dressing table like surgical instruments in an operating theatre. I smiled at my reflection. Not too bad. I took a deep breath and forced myself to relax. That was better. It was natural, of course, to feel this way. What woman wouldn't feel nervous on a day like this? A drink might have helped, but the last thing I needed was to turn up at the church with the smell of alcohol on my breath. Although I knew how hilarious he would find that.

'Not going to happen,' I told my reflection. As I carefully applied my make-up, I found my eye drawn to the elegant dress hanging in a protective covering on the wardrobe door. I'd known it was the perfect choice as soon as I'd seen it, and I really wanted to look special for him today. Not that he cared how I looked... well, not in clothes, anyway. Honestly, Emma, I chastised my reflection, while a range of highly improper and graphic images came to mind. Talk about inappropriate!

A knock on the front door got me to my feet, but before I was halfway across the room, I heard the sound of it opening and the rumble of voices in the hall below. The house was full of family and friends, some of whom had travelled a long distance to be here today, so there were more than enough people to handle door duty. In fact, was it really ungrateful of me to wish I could have got ready for today without the distraction of them all around me? Surely that was normal?

I could hear various family members getting ready in the bedrooms next to mine, and I knew I should probably be dressed and done by now. If I didn't move faster, perhaps they'd go without me? I gave a small laugh at the ludicrous thought and stepped over to the window to check out who'd just arrived. A small white florist's van was parked in front of our house, and the flowers we had ordered were being carefully lifted and carried inside. Okay, I really was late now. Just time to do my hair and get into my dress.

I'd dithered over whether to go for an up or down style for today. But then I thought of his hands running through the long reddish brown strands, twisting them around his fingers like reeds, to pull me closer towards him. No contest. Leave it down and let it sit on my shoulders as usual. Before shrugging out of my silky dressing gown, I peered at the mirror and suddenly swept back the fringe from my forehead, exposing a faint scar which was still visible at my hairline. I ran a finger over the white, slightly raised skin and briefly closed my eyes in memory of how it came to be there. That night had marked us all, and while I might be the only one who still bore a visible reminder on my face, nothing had ever been the same for any of us from that moment on. So many lives had been changed that night, so many futures had been rewritten.

I let my hair fall back into place, as the mirror caught and bounced a comet-bright reflection of my engagement ring, bathed in a beam of autumn sunshine. Of course I'd been wearing a different

2

ring on that finger on the night of the accident, but that one had ended up at the bottom of a ravine. Long story. It was unfortunate, but not as unfortunate as falling in love with a mysterious stranger had been. I'd read every wedding magazine and book going, but none of them seemed to cover that particular thorny issue. What do you do when, a fortnight before your wedding, you suddenly find yourself in love with two different men?

THE BEGINNING

CHAPTER 1

Despite the obvious assumption, it was definitely the deer that caused the accident and not the daiquiris, and it *most definitely* wasn't due to Caroline's driving, because she hadn't touched anything stronger than lemonade all night.

As hen parties go, mine had been a fairly subdued event. Nothing tawdry; no strippers, no L-plates, no drunken antics that come back to haunt you in the months to follow. At twenty-seven I felt I was perhaps a little too 'elderly' for the nights of raucous partying which had been a signature note to my university days. Not that we hadn't all had a great time, mind you. A group of ten of us had spent an indulgent 'girly' day at a luxury spa hotel, and then, pampered, massaged and moisturised to within an inch of our lives, we'd moved on to the hotel bar which (allegedly) served the best cocktails this side of Manhattan. I'd never been to New York, but if that was what the locals drank, it was certainly worth a visit in the future.

We'd only had one round of drinks when Sheila, my soon-to-be mother-in-law got to her feet. 'Oh, don't say you're leaving already?' I cried in disappointment.

'I have to,' she said with a regretful smile. 'Poor Dennis has been on his own all day. I've just called a cab; it'll be here in a few minutes.'

I got to my feet with a smile. 'I'll walk you out,' I said,

picking my way over an obstacle course of legs and handbags. With my arm linked through hers, we wove across the bar and headed towards the hotel foyer. Our route took us past my close friend Amy, who was sitting on one of the highly polished bar stools, ostensibly ordering more drinks. However, from her body language and low provocative laughter, I suspected she was looking for more than just a round of daiquiris from the good-looking young barman. With his floppy blond hair and perfect white teeth – which I could virtually count from the wide grin he was flashing at Amy – he looked more boyband member than bartender. I almost felt sorry for him, the way you'd feel sorry for a marlin just before it's hauled from the sea. He didn't know it, but he didn't stand a chance.

The foyer was eye-dazzlingly bright after the discreetly lit bar, and my eyes watered a little in adjustment as we walked to the revolving doors. 'Thank you so much for coming today, Sheila,' I said sincerely. I'd initially been rather surprised when Richard's mum had accepted my invitation to join us. Of course, she was already like family to me, even before she officially became my in-law. Our mothers had been friends for years; it was how Richard and I had first met, although as we were only two years old at the time, I really don't remember it much.

'I wouldn't have missed it for the world,' Sheila replied, pulling me towards her in a real motherly bear-hug of an embrace. I felt the pinprick of impending tears, as she softly whispered the thing we'd both been thinking all day, 'It's such a shame that your mum wasn't here with us.'

I nodded into her shoulder, enveloped in a fragrant cloud of Chanel No. 5, not entirely sure I could trust my voice to reply. She let me step back, squeezing both my hands tightly. 'It's all going to be fine, Emma, you'll see.'

I watched her walk to the cab and waved as she climbed inside, but as the car pulled off the hotel forecourt, the smile on my face slowly slid away. Her words echoed in my mind. Mum *should* have been with us today, indulging in the lavish spa treatments and then pretending to be shocked at the bawdily named cocktails. My eyes began to water again, and this time it had nothing to do with the lighting.

At that moment the door to the ladies' room opened, and Caroline, my third musketeer, emerged and saw me. She crossed the foyer in rapid strides, her face a picture of concern.

'Emma, what's wrong?'

'Nothing. I was just saying goodbye to Sheila.'

I gave Caroline an admittedly wobbly smile, and then almost lost the feeble hold I had on my composure, when her arm went comfortingly around my shoulders. She didn't need to hear me explain why I was suddenly overcome with emotion. She knew without asking, in the way that only your very best friends who've known you for ever can do.

She steered me gently from the door and back to the place she had just come from. Every woman's sanctuary in a crisis: the ladies' toilets. She paused just once at the entrance to the hotel bar, and waited until Amy glanced our way. Caroline semaphored a message with a vigorous nod of her head and a meaningful glance at me. To the untrained eye it might have looked as though she had some sort of nervous complaint, but to the final member of our trio, it was as clear as if she'd just shouted through a megaphone across the room. Amy jumped lightly down from her stool and left the barman without a backward glance.

They listened with matching faces of sympathy and understanding as I told them why Sheila's words had affected me. They allowed me just a few tears of self-pity before springing into action like well-rehearsed mechanics at a pit stop. Caroline pulled a handful of tissues from the chrome wall dispenser, while Amy rummaged in her bag for mascara and powder to fix the mess I'd made of my make-up.

They waited patiently as I repaired the damage, their teasing banter gradually pulling me back from my moment of darkness. 'Feel better now?' asked Amy, giving me a brief hard hug when I handed back her make-up bag. I nodded and turned to face the reflection of the three of us in the wall of mirrors. They both smiled back at me in the glass, and wound their arms around my waist. I'd known Caroline since we were at primary school, and Amy almost as long. And although there had been a period of time when we had drifted apart, in the year since I'd moved back to Hallingford, we had picked up the dropped stitches of our friendship and sewn it back together, almost seamlessly.

Our bond was a real and tangible thing, a golden and unbreakable cord that tied us to one another, every bit as strongly as it had done in childhood. I hadn't known a second's hesitation when it had come to choosing my two bridesmaids. They'd both been in training for the role for over twenty years. No one had my back better than they did.

'So, shall we go?' urged Amy, clearly anxious to return to the bar.

I just knew Caroline wouldn't be able to resist.

'You're in an awful hurry. Wouldn't have something to do with that hot guy serving the drinks, would it?'

Amy gave an impish smile. 'Maybe. I think he goes off duty soon.'

Caroline glanced down at her watch, then gave me a small wink. 'It figures. He won't want to be up too late... not with it being a school night, and all.'

'No, it's not. It's Saturday,' Amy corrected automatically, before the penny dropped and her face twisted in a wry smile. 'Ha, ha, very funny.'

At just after twelve people decided to call it a night. Some of my guests faced a long journey home, and I'd be seeing everyone again in just two weeks' time, on the day of my wedding. I felt a familiar shiver run through me at the thought, part nerves, part excitement, part... something else. I shivered again as we stepped into the cold March night air of the hotel car park, wrapping my arms around me in an effort to combat the biting wind, slicing with grim determination through the thin material of my sleeveless dress.

Caroline jumped into her car and started the engine, while I over-enthusiastically hugged the assortment of female friends who'd shared the day with me. They were an eclectic mix from long-past schooldays, university and work, and although most of them had started the day as strangers to one another, they were ending it as deepest friends. Or could that just be the cocktails talking?

When the last of the waiting cabs or good-natured other-halves had collected everyone, I ran lightly across to where Caroline's car was ticking over as she waited for me. I saw that Amy had already joined her in the vehicle, shot-gunning the passenger seat. She swivelled around to look at me as I opened the rear door and slid gratefully into the car's warm and cosy interior. 'You don't want to sit here, do you?' she asked with typical guileless charm. I looked down at the very tiny space Caroline's seat left for my legs in the rear section of the car. I'm no giant, but I had to be at least fifteen centimetres taller than my old friend. 'It's just I might get car sick if I sit in the back,' Amy continued.

'Daiquiri-sick, more like,' corrected Caroline. Flicking off the car's interior light and fastening her seat belt, she gave us both a tolerant grin. 'There's a thirty-pound surcharge if you puke in my car.'

'Drive on,' Amy commanded, and then turned again to stage whisper to me, 'She's such a *grump* when she hasn't had a drink!'

It was a forty-five minute drive back to the small market town where I'd grown up; the town that I'd happily escaped from to go to university, that I thought I'd never return to after I got my first job in London, and that I'd had no choice but to move back to just twelve months earlier.

The country roads that we travelled along were largely deserted, but then it was getting late. I still found it so very different from the buzzing traffic that had continually hummed past my small London flat, no matter what time of the day or night it was. For a girl born and raised in the country, I was a real city-lover.

A fine rain had fallen earlier in the evening and in the headlights' beams I could see a glittering reflection on the black tarmac as the roads began to freeze. It was the beginning of March, but it still felt very much like winter. I really hoped the weather was going to warm up before the wedding, or I was going to need thermals under my strapless bridal gown.

In the front seat Amy and Caroline were debating whether it had been poor judgement on Amy's part to give the bartender her phone number. No prizes for guessing which one of them thought it was a bad idea. Caroline had been happily settled with her own partner Nick for... well, for ever it seemed, and I knew she sometimes took a dim view of Amy's more adventurous love life. My own relationship with Richard was much more to Caroline's liking: childhood sweethearts; separated for years and now happily engaged to be married. Real story-book stuff, she claimed.

'Any man – no, boy – who spends the entire night trying to look down the front of your top doesn't deserve your number,' Caroline declared scathingly.

I sniggered, but had to admit the barman *had* spent a great deal of time talking to Amy's chest and not her face.

'I feel sick,' said Amy, in a small shamefaced voice.

'With humiliation?' I asked jokingly.

In reply Amy gave a small heaving sound.

Caroline flicked her eyes from the road to her passenger. Even in the darkened car, on a road with no street lamps, it was obvious to see that Caroline's humorous prediction had come true.

'Jesus, Amy. Hang on, I'll pull over in one second. The road's too narrow here.'

'Can't wait,' Amy gurgled back somewhat unpleasantly.

'There's a carrier bag on the floor by your feet,' Caroline advised.

That was the last normal moment the three of us would share.

After that, everything happened really quickly and really slowly, all at the same time. Before I had the chance to tell her not to do it, Amy had unclipped her seat belt in order to reach for the bag. Caroline, her attention split between the road and her imminently vomiting friend, rounded a tight bend and there, immediately in front of us, illuminated in two piercing beams of light, was a large stag standing in the middle of the road.

Someone swore, possibly me, but the sound was lost in the cry of screeching rubber as Caroline slammed hard on the brakes, and jerked sharply on the wheel to avoid the animal, which even as we approached still stood straddling the white line, as though he had all the time in the world to get away. Perhaps it's like that for animals too, those final moments before an accident: the moments when you seem to have an endless amount of time to see exactly what's going to happen; think about it, do something, do nothing, and *still* wait for the impact. That's what it seemed like to me.

I saw Amy straighten up in her seat, a totally different sick look on her face; I saw the deer growing larger and larger directly in front of us, and then the animal was suddenly replaced by a view of the steep grass bank which ran alongside one edge of the road. A bank we were heading towards far too quickly.

The moment we hit it everything speeded up again. The car bounced back violently from the impact, and although Caroline had frantically tried to steer us back on to the road, there was nothing that could be done to avoid the collision. I felt the biting jerk of the seat belt cut across my body, as I was thrown forwards and then backwards in my seat. I heard the bang of an explosion which heralded the mushrooming bloom of the airbag, which suddenly obscured everything out of one half of the windscreen. But Caroline's car was an older model and only had protection on the driver's side, and sometime during the seconds when we hit, when my eyes were screwed tightly shut in terror, it happened. When I opened them again, Amy was gone.

And still it wasn't over. Like a nightmare you just can't wake up from, I felt the car flip into the air. One minute the road was beneath our wheels, and the next the car was on its roof, torpedoing and spinning out of control across the road in a cloud of bright orange sparks. The scrape of metal on tarmac was deafening and didn't stop until the very last moment when the car eventually left the icy surface behind and crashed, rear-end first, into a steep ditch on the opposite side of the road.

I didn't lose consciousness, and I'm still not sure if that was a blessing or not. I felt the flaring burn of pain as the side of my head collided with a sharp piece of metal which had once been part of the car's roof. The car was crumpled around us like an old tin can a giant had finished drinking from. We were wedged so tightly in the ditch that all I could see on both sides were thick walls of mud and twisted roots. It actually wasn't easy to see anything at all, as the only light around came from one remaining headlamp which – God knows how – was still working, but due to the angle of the car was now illuminating the inky-black sky. It sliced into the dark, like a spotlight to the fallen.

From the seat in front of me, which had collapsed backwards and was now painfully crushing both my legs, I heard the terrified sound of Caroline moaning and crying. I tried to reach out my hand to her, but the driver's seat had me pinioned where I sat. 'Caro? Are you okay? Are you hurt?'

More crying and a long wailing moan, which I actually thought for a second was an animal. Was the deer down here in the ditch with us? Had we hit it after all? Then I heard the hitching breaths between the moans, and realised it was my friend's voice – well, something like her voice – because it was plain to hear that she was in shock.

'What happened? Where are you?'

'I'm right here, Caroline. I'm in the back seat. Are you hurt?'

She sounded genuinely confused at the question. 'Hurt? No. Why? What happened?'

I was no medic, but this was most definitely shock.

'We had an accident, Caro,' I said, surprised my voice sounded so calm and controlled. 'There was an animal in the road and we... we crashed.'

'We've crashed?'

I paused before answering. I didn't know what to say to her, because I had a feeling that hysteria was really only a moment or two away, and I needed to ask her something really, really important.

'Caroline. Can you see Amy? Is she there beside you?' I felt, rather than saw her move in her seat, and then scramble up on to her knees and crawl over to the passenger seat, as though to confirm what her eyes were telling her. The only good thing that proved was that Caroline could still move around, so probably wasn't that badly hurt. 'She's not here! She's not here! Where's she gone?' Her face suddenly appeared in the small gap between the two headrests. Her eyes, frantically darting in their sockets, raked the rear of the car. 'Is she back there with you?'

I bit my lip and swallowed noisily before answering, trying all the while not to look past Caroline at the Amy-shaped gaping hole in our shattered windscreen, which looked to be ringed with something dark and dripping.

'I think she got thrown out, Caro. She'd just undone her seat belt before the crash—'

'So she's okay? She wasn't in the car when we crashed, so she's okay, right?'

It was like talking to a five-year-old. Was it just shock, or had Caroline hit her head? I looked at the windscreen, or what was left of it, bowed out in a funnel shape from the accident. I looked at the hole and tried really, really hard not to look at Amy's blood which was still trickling in places over the shattered screen.

'Caroline, you have to get out of the car and find Amy.'

'No,' protested my friend, shaking her head to emphasise her words. 'I can't. I shouldn't. You mustn't move after an accident.'

How on earth had that little gem stayed in, when all other good sense seemed to have temporarily been lost?

'I know, I know. But you've already moved a bit and Amy's hurt. She's gone thr—' Something stopped me from making this too graphic, given Caroline's current state of mind. 'She's not in the car any more. So you need to find her and check she's okay. Can you do that for me?'

Caroline looked back at me, her face a picture of terror. I was terrified too, not just from what had happened, but for what she might find waiting for her out on the road. 'You're coming too, aren't you? We'll look together.' She clearly hadn't seen, or perhaps just couldn't comprehend, the mangled driver's seat that was crushing both my lower limbs and imprisoning me in the car.

'I can't get out,' I said, and although I thought I was being so brave, I was suddenly aware that the whole time I'd been talking to her, tears had been falling down my face. I heard them now in my voice as I spoke. 'The seat's trapped me here, *you* have to do it. *You* have to find Amy and get help. *Please*, Caroline.'

Something in my desperation pierced through the cushioning haze she'd been enveloped in since we crashed. She nodded fiercely like a child. I looked at the front doors of the vehicle and saw that, like the rear ones, they were wedged tightly in the ditch. There was only one way in and out of the car. 'You have to climb out through the windscreen and then crawl up the bonnet until you can grab on to the grassy sides of the bank. Can you do that?'

It was a lot to ask, it was a lot to do, but until help in the form of the emergency services reached us, Caroline was our only hope. She turned wordlessly and stared at the hole in the windscreen, then placed her hands on the dashboard for purchase.

'Wait!' I commanded, reaching in the mangled remains of the back seat for the jacket Amy had thrown in earlier. 'Put this around the bottom of the hole before you crawl through, or you'll cut yourself to pieces.' *Just like Amy must have done*, a horrible voice intoned in my head. *Stop it!* I couldn't think like that. I couldn't let the panic take over.

Caroline actually managed to accomplish her exit from the car and climb up the bank with remarkable ease. Without another word she did everything I had asked of her, and scrambled from the tip of the bonnet on to the side of the bank, using an exposed tree root for a handhold. And then she was gone.

The wait seemed interminable. I knew how hard the task I'd given her was. The light from the headlamp was uselessly illuminating only the sky, and the moon was covered with scudding clouds. It was virtually pitch-black out there, and Amy could be anywhere on the road. Caroline could literally walk right by her and never know it. I heard her calling Amy's name, the sound getting increasingly fainter as she moved further away from the car. Amy was unconscious, I told myself. Amy couldn't reply because she was unconscious. Any other reason for the lack of response was unthinkable.

As the moments passed I struggled yet again to free myself, shoving both hands against the back of the seat and pushing

16

with every last ounce of strength in my body. It was no use. The seat wouldn't budge and I couldn't pull my legs free. I began to feel sick from the effort, and the wound on my head, which I'd been doing my best not to focus on at all, began to bleed even more profusely, dripping down my forehead and into my eyes.

I hadn't heard Caroline's voice for a minute or two. 'Caroline, are you okay? Have you found her?' I called out. No answering reply came back. And I could only pray that a shocked and confused Caroline hadn't wandered completely off the road and into the surrounding fields, and was now too far away to hear me.

Then an answering scream split the night, horrible and terrified, just one high-pitched strident cry of a name.

Caroline had found Amy.

I don't know what we'd have done if he hadn't come along just then. I certainly hadn't heard the approach of a car, but suddenly the night was filled with sounds: Caroline screaming, and then a long shriek of brakes as a car attempted to come to an emergency stop. I tried to imagine what was happening on the road: Caroline, kneeling beside Amy's prone body, and then the two of them caught like rabbits in the headlights, as a car rounded the corner and ploughed straight into them in the darkness.

Thankfully, it didn't happen that way.

I strained my ears and heard the sound of a car door opening and a deep voice speaking rapidly with words I couldn't make out, and then Caroline's (probably incoherent) response. But at least someone else was here now, someone who could help. I struggled to hear more, but a really irritating sound coming from the front of the vehicle kept distracting me. Actually, the noise had been there for several minutes I realised; a sort of intermittent crackling. I leaned over to one side, as far as my trapped legs would allow, and waited for it to come again. I only had to wait for a few seconds, and then I saw a small yellow glow flickering briefly like a trapped firefly, coming from behind the smashed dashboard. But no firefly I've ever heard of makes that weird arcing and shorting electrical sound. I edged back in my seat, my eyes riveted to the dashboard as though it was a coiled cobra.

It was frustrating not knowing what was happening on the road, but I didn't want to distract the new arrival with my own situation. Amy, and to a lesser extent Caroline, were of more pressing importance just now. The crackling, crisp-crunching noise came again, this time accompanied by the brightest flare of a spark so far.

I could only hope that whoever had just arrived had telephoned for help, because my phone was with Caroline's in our bags in the boot of the car. And Amy's... well, I guessed Amy wasn't going to be able to tell us where her phone was for a little while. *Or ever.*

'Shut up!' I cried to that evil voice, not realising I'd said the words aloud at the precise moment that a face came into my field of vision. Someone was looking down at me from the edge of the bank.

'Hello there.' The voice belonged to a man who appeared to be in his mid-thirties, a man with dark wavy hair and a face whose calm expression belied the gravity of our situation. He *had* to be concerned and worried to have three wounded accident victims suddenly becoming his instant responsibility, but you'd never have known it from the tone of his voice, or the gentle smile he gave as his eyes darted over the car and me, quickly assessing the situation.

'Hi,' I replied in response.

He lifted his hand and raked a powerful flashlight beam over the car's interior and then over me, from my head to my legs, which disappeared from view at about knee level behind the collapsed seat. He frowned a little when he saw the bleeding head wound, then a lot when he saw my legs.

'You're hurt.' It was a statement, not a question. I raised my hand to my forehead, all the while shaking my head in denial.

'It's nothing. My friends? Have you called for help? One of them went through the windscreen. How is she? Is she okay? And Caroline... I think she's in shock.'

'They're okay,' he said reassuringly, and I didn't challenge the obvious lie. 'Help's on the way, it'll be here soon and your friend... Caroline... is looking after the other girl—'

'Amy,' I provided, knowing full well that Caroline was currently in no state to be looking after anyone. Why wasn't he out there helping Amy?

'Please, just go back and take care of them,' I urged, as I saw him assess the steep-sided bank and the angle of the car and realised what he was intending to do. 'I'll be fine here until someone else comes.'

He smiled back at me as he swung himself down from the edge of the bank and landed lightly on the bonnet of the car. Nevertheless the mangled metal groaned loudly beneath his weight. It was hard to tell from this angle, but he looked tall, possibly well over six foot and broadly built.

'I don't think so. I think we should try and get you out, right now. I'm Jack, by the way,' he completed and it was only then that I heard the soft burr of an American accent.

'Emma,' I replied automatically, and then for no good reason that I can possibly think of, I added, 'I'm getting married in a fortnight.'

'Congratulations,' he responded, winding Amy's jacket around his hands to protect them.

'We were on my hen night.'

He gave a small nod, his attention fixed on the windscreen. 'Cover your eyes.'

I looked up at him blankly. Perhaps Caroline wasn't the only one in shock.

'I need to punch out the glass so I can climb in and help you out.'

'It's no use, my legs are stuck behind the driver's seat. I've tried, but I can't get out.'

Just then the entire dashboard was illuminated by a huge spark from the car's damaged electrics. Jack's forehead crumpled into a frown, but the gentling smile never left his face. 'Let's just see, shall we? Cover your eyes.'

I did as he said, so can't say exactly what he did next, but I heard several loud thumps, a grunt or two and then suddenly I was being showered in a shrapnel rainfall of broken windscreen. It fell over and around me like lethal hail, landing in my hair, settling on my face and even sticking to the bloodied wound on my forehead. I went to brush the pieces off my face, but was stilled by his shouted warning. 'Don't touch it, just shake your head.' I did as he suggested, and most of the pieces fell away.

He gave another smile. 'Can't have you ruining that pretty face for the wedding photos,' he said, sliding through the aperture which had once held the windscreen. The moment he entered the car his demeanour changed. He froze, half-crouched on the front passenger seat, and inhaled. I couldn't see what was worrying him, until I did likewise. Petrol. Really strong petrol. Why hadn't I smelled it before? The odour was everywhere, the car was permeated and bathed in pungent fumes. More crackles from the front dashboard caused both of us to turn in that direction. We looked back at each other with identical expressions.

'Let's just get you out.'

I shook my head angrily. 'Just go. You won't be able to do anything, and if this stuff ignites, there's no need for both of us to be in here.'

He carried on as if I hadn't spoken. He reached down to one side and released the lever to recline the passenger seat, and pushed it back as far as it would go. A moment later he was beside me on the cramped remains of the back seat. He was a big guy and seemed to totally fill the space. His face was only centimetres from mine.

'Hi,' he grinned, as though we weren't in the middle of a life-threatening crisis.

I gripped his arm with an urgency that I just couldn't see in him. 'You have to get out of here. Now!'

He just shook his head, as though I'd said something totally ridiculous. 'You first, then me.'

Who was he, this American stranger who was risking his own life to save mine?

'Now tell me,' he continued in a tone of voice that sounded as casual as if we were chatting at a dinner party, 'are you hurt anywhere else besides your head? Can you feel your legs, move your feet okay?' I wriggled my ankles, as much as I could, and winced a little with the pain.

'No. All good,' I reported back.

That earned me another smile.

'Let's just have a look at this seat, shall we?' asked Jack, leaning forwards and across me to examine it closely, pushing experimentally at several points along the back of the frame. He did this a few times, more strenuously, grunting with the effort. My field of vision and lap was entirely full of this kind (but clearly misguided) accidental hero, who was making my rescue his current mission.

'I'm sorry, I'm going to have to get a little personal here,' he said, placing both his hands on my bare legs and running them down what was accessible of my limbs, until they disappeared under the seat, presumably to see if there was a way of pulling them free. There was an unhurried air to his exploration, even though I knew that a very deadly clock was ticking. 'I apologise for that,' he said again, straightening up until he was once more beside me. 'I know how fond you Brits are of your personal space.' How could he sound so light-hearted at a time like this?

Suddenly a small muted puffing sound came from the front of the car, followed by a long thin snaking white trail of smoke, which began to meander out of one of the vents. Jack glanced at me, all humour gone. For the first time he looked worried.

'Please go.'

He shook his head. 'I think I might be able to push on the seat hard enough to give you enough room to wriggle your legs free.'

He was strong, I could tell that. His forearms were muscled, and with his shirt sleeves rolled up to the elbow, I could see his well-developed biceps straining against the fabric as he braced his arms and pushed on the frame of the seat. The entire back of the car seemed to vibrate with the effort and force he was expelling. Suddenly a dull tearing noise interrupted the low growl Jack was making from the effort. And then his arm just disappeared into the back of the seat through a gaping hole in the material.

'Fuck! That hurt!' he exclaimed. 'Sorry,' he apologised

ludicrously. He withdrew his arm from the hole and it was covered in blood flowing from a long deep cut which ran along the inside of his foreman. The unyielding metal of the frame had sliced viciously back in retaliation. That did it.

'For Christ's sake give up. Now *you're* hurt.'

He looked down at his dripping arm. 'What? This? I've cut myself worse than this shaving.'

'You shave your arms?' He grinned at that. 'Jack, please,' I implored, using his name for the first time. I kind of liked the way it sounded. 'The fire engines are on their way. They'll have all the proper equipment to cut me out of here. They'll have those Jaws of Death thingies.'

'Jaws of Life,' he corrected.

'Whatever. I can hang on until then. I'll be okay as long the petrol doesn't seep into the car and ignite.'

He looked at me intently, and I wondered whether I should have paid more attention to those chemistry lessons at school, after all. From the look on his face, what I thought I knew about combustible fuels was completely and utterly wrong. 'What? Isn't that right?'

'It's not just the *gas* that can ignite, Emma. The *fumes* can too.'

I didn't need it spelling out any more clearly. The car was full of them, and they were getting stronger by the minute.

I nodded at the seat. 'Try again.'

He turned his body slightly, and braced his back against the side of the car.

'Let's try a new position, this time, shall we?'

Despite everything that was going on, there was a cheeky double-meaning in his words, which I didn't doubt was deliberate. It was there in the twinkle of his eye, as he brought

23

up his legs and positioned one large booted foot on either side of the seat's frame.

Absolutely anyone could have been driving the car that stopped to come to our rescue; it could have been a woman, a wimpy stick-thin man, or even a coward. I'm just eternally grateful that instead it was a big, strong, athletic man, with a curiously over-developed hero complex. I knew it was going to work, even before the seat began to move. I knew that that level of steely determination, the grimace of concentration and the extraordinary strength and effort, were going to succeed. He would have it no other way.

The seat didn't give much, but at the first small protesting moan from the metal, I got ready. Then, when finally I felt the smallest of movement and lessening of pressure, I whipped my legs up, and suddenly I was free. Amazingly, apart from cuts and the kind of bruises so horrible you end up taking photographs of them, my legs were intact.

Almost as though the car, hungry for my blood, knew I was about to get away, a shower of sparks flew out of each of the vents on the dashboard. The world's smallest and deadliest fireworks display.

'Go,' he urged, gripping hold of my upper arm and manhandling me over the reclined seat and into the front of the car. I clambered through the front windscreen cavity and crawled on all fours up the slippery incline of the bonnet. Jack was following close behind.

'That gas is going to blow, stand on the edge of the hood, I'll push you up.'

'Petrol and bonnet,' I corrected.

'You are one very bossy woman,' he replied, pushing me up the car with a hand placed quite unashamedly on my backside. He hauled me to my feet on to the bumper and then had to catch and steady me when I tried to apply weight on to my legs, which were still numb and tingling from their ordeal. I hung on to his arm and looked up at the sheer sides of the ditch in concern. I hadn't actually realised how deep it was; the road had to be at least three metres above my head. How on earth had Caroline managed to climb up it so easily?

'I don't think I can—'

He was way ahead of me. He dropped to his knees at my feet as though he was about to propose. 'Stand on my shoulders.'

'I'm too heavy.'

There were sparks flaring almost continually from the dashboard. We didn't have long.

'Are you fishing for compliments? Because I really don't think this is the time. Now get up there.'

I placed my hands in his outstretched ones to gain balance and placed one bare foot on each broad and solid shoulder. He got to his feet so easily, you'd think he did this every day of the week. I tried to help, grabbing on to whatever roots or foliage I passed for a handhold, as the top of the ditch came into view.

I was almost there.

I looked down at the man who I was literally standing on to secure my safety. 'What about you? Can you get up here?'

'Don't worry about me. I'll be right behind you.'

I was still crawling away from the ditch on all fours, when the sparks and the fumes stopped their teasing courtship and made their first and final deadly encounter. Caroline's car exploded like a bomb in an inferno of flames.

CHAPTER 2

The blast knocked me flat on to the road, and in its wake I felt a hot wave crest across my body. I glanced back over my shoulder before crawling once more on to my knees. There was certainly no problem in seeing anything now. The fire from the blazing car lit up the surrounding area almost as brightly as daylight. I felt a hand cup my elbow and raise me to my feet.

'Are you all right, are you hurt?'

I shook my head dumbly, wondering why everything sounded *wrong*, then realised the explosion had left me with a muffled ringing sound in my ears. I looked up gratefully to face the tall – I'd been right – man standing in front of me. Had it not been for him, the explosion would have left me dead! Mild tinnitus was a small price to pay.

'I'm fine. Thank you for... for everything.'

He shrugged as though it was nothing, which we both knew was untrue.

'Amy and Caroline. Where are they?'

In answer, Jack took hold of my shoulders and turned me around, so I was facing the direction we had been driving from, and there, about forty metres back down the road, I could just make out two silhouettes in the shadows. I hadn't realised our car had travelled so far after the impact. Jack held out his hand and I placed mine in it, unthinkingly. 'Come on.'

From a distance I had thought that Caroline, kneeling beside Amy on the side of the road, had actually been praying. As we got closer I could see that wasn't the case; she was in fact rocking back and forth on her knees, moaning. Not good. Not good at all. We covered the final metres at a run, but when we were just a little short of the place where Amy had been thrown from the car, Jack pulled me to a halt. 'Emma, you need to know, Amy's injuries are pretty... severe.' I nodded back dumbly, and then pulled away from his hold and covered the remaining distance alone.

I knew he was trying to prepare me, I got that. But he might as well not have bothered. *Nothing* could have prepared me for what I saw when I looked past Caroline at the third member of our trio. Suddenly I was very, very glad that the light was poor, because what I *could* see made my heart lurch and my stomach drop. Her face, her poor face.

I fell to my knees beside Caroline, gripping her hand and squeezing hard. I don't think she even knew I was there. But it wasn't Caroline who needed me now, anyway.

Amy's injuries were so bad; I literally wouldn't have known it was her. I tried to stifle the cry of despair that seemed determined to force its way out through my lips, especially when I realised that she wasn't unconscious. She turned her face slowly and painfully in my direction.

'Mmmemma?'

I nodded, unable to trust my voice, then realised her eyes, virtually swollen shut into bloodied slits, probably couldn't see me.

'I'm here, Ames, I'm here.' I reached for her hand, hesitating when I saw the raw and angry cuts and abrasions that covered almost every inch of visible skin. I took it anyway, she needed the contact. 'Don't try to speak,' I urged as I saw her cut and distended lips struggle to formulate words.

'You... kay?'

That's what started me crying. She was lying there on the cold road, with injuries so horrible who knew how long it would take her to recover from them, and the first thing she asked was if I was okay. 'I'm fine, just fine.'

She gave a small nod, her head cushioned on a makeshift support of a folded leather jacket, Jack's, I guessed. He had joined us by then, walking around to the other side of Amy and hunkering down near her head. 'You doing okay, kiddo?' he asked with a smile, and I recognised the tone he had used on me in the car. For just one stupid, unthinking moment I felt jealous. He reached down and laid his hand comfortingly on her shoulder. 'Help's on the way.'

Amy's face contorted as a spasm of pain ripped through her, and I looked up at Jack in desperation. 'Did they say how long? She needs to get to a hospital.'

There was a look I didn't like in his eyes when he answered solemnly, 'I know,' but nevertheless he got to his feet and pulled his mobile out. 'I'll call again.' But before he had dialled even the first digit, a distant sound of a siren cut through the frosty March night air.

Amy's eyes had flickered shut, so I reached down and gently touched her face. 'Listen, Amy, they're coming. Can you hear them? They're almost here. Just hang on.'

'Hurt...'

That had to be the understatement of a lifetime. I couldn't even begin to comprehend the level of pain she must be in. 'I know,' I crooned, 'but they'll give you something for the pain. Just stay with us for a minute or two more, they're almost here.'

28

I had hoped to console and comfort her, but my reply seemed to agitate her further. She shook her head violently from side to side and opened her mouth in a moan of despair. I tried not to let the fact that almost all her teeth were broken show in my face as I looked back at her.

'Hurt... you.' She was confused, and with very good reason.

'No, Amy. I'm fine.' I looked across at Jack, and saw the naked sympathy on his face. 'This kind American man got me out of the car. I'm not hurt.' *Not like you*, I finished in my head. But still my words didn't satisfy her.

'Good fren... you forgave. So... so... sorry.' She was rambling and getting distressed, so I did the only thing I could think of; I pretended her weird comments made complete and absolute sense. I was good at doing that; I'd had more than enough practice.

'Absolutely, Amy. Don't worry, everything's good. Rest now, please rest.'

She gave one last small nod, as though a heavy burden had just been passed on, and I swear I felt some of the tension relax from the bloodied hand which I still held in my own.

They sent just about every type of emergency vehicle they had. They arrived in a siren-blaring cavalcade: a fire engine, two ambulances and several police cars. The relief that professionals could now swing into action and take charge had the opposite effect on me to the one I was expecting. As I got to my feet and stepped out of the way of the two paramedics who had briskly flanked Amy, I felt my knees buckle beneath me. Jack caught me instantly, taking my entire weight. I began to shiver violently in his arms, like someone in the throes of a raging fever. He pulled me closer against his chest, to warm me with the heat of his body. By now my teeth had begun to chatter uncontrollably.

'It's just shock,' he soothed, his hand stroking my hair from the back of my head to the nape of my neck, as though I was a frightened animal that needed to be pacified. That wasn't far off the mark.

It seemed to take them ages to attend to Amy and get her in a stable enough condition to be transported. The longer it took, the more agitated I grew. 'Why don't they just put her in the bloody ambulance and get going?' I said in a voice that probably wasn't quiet enough not to be overheard by the intently working paramedics. I saw the apologetic look Jack offered the two medics, before he gently guided me further away from them.

'Let's just give them some space to work, shall we?' he questioned equably.

It was easy for him to sound so calm. We were, after all, total strangers to him. He had nothing invested in the outcome of this night, in us. Nothing at all.

Jack steered me over to his car, which he'd brought to a stop halfway across one lane of the road. I didn't want to get inside the vehicle, even though I was still shivering violently. If Amy was out in the cold, then I should be too. Strangely, Jack seemed to understand this very twisted logic and came beside me, leaning back against the bonnet. We watched the paramedics hard at work as a drip was inserted into Amy's arm, an immobilising neck brace applied, and then finally a wheeled stretcher was brought from the back of the ambulance.

Without asking permission, Jack put an arm around me, and I gratefully allowed myself to be held closely against the side of this total stranger. 'I'd give you my jacket... but there was a prior claim on it.'

30

I nodded, my attention fixed now on Caroline, who was currently in the care of one of the paramedics from the second ambulance and two police officers. When I saw one of the policemen produce a breathalyser kit for her to blow into, I pushed rapidly away from the car. There was absolutely no need for that! I could testify that she'd been stone-cold sober. There was *no way* she was the one who caused all this. If they had to blame anyone, blame the sodding deer! It was only Jack's restraining hand that stopped me from launching into the fray with a loud and noisy protest.

'They're just doing it by the numbers. It's not an accusation. Don't go charging in there like a prizefighter.'

He was right. I knew that. And in normal circumstances it wouldn't occur to me in a million years to be this aggressive. I settled back against the front of his car with obvious reluctance, still disgruntled.

'Are you always like this, or have I just caught you on a bad night?'

I gave a small humourless laugh that turned into a sob. 'One of my best friends is about to be stretchered into the back of an ambulance, the other looks set to be taken off in a Black Maria. I've known better evenings.'

'Black Maria, eh? Just how old *are* you?'

'Twenty-seven,' I answered automatically, totally missing his sarcasm at first. Then I got it, and gave a wry half-smile. 'I watch a lot of old films.'

'Me too,' he confirmed companionably, and it struck me that if we'd met in any other circumstances than these, I would really have liked this man as a friend.

'Now then, my love, can we take a little look at the pair of you?'

I'd been so distracted by Jack's diversionary tactics, I hadn't even seen the paramedic approach us with her bag in hand. Slipping on a clean pair of latex gloves, she raised my face to examine the injury on my forehead. There were still bits of windscreen glass stuck to the wound, which had thankfully almost stopped bleeding by this point. 'We're going to have to leave cleaning this up until we get you to hospital, my lovely, and get it X-rayed too. Are you hurt anywhere else?'

I shook my head, and beside me Jack made a small hissing sound. 'Her legs were trapped by one of the car seats. She's got some pretty bad bruising on both of them.' The paramedic dropped to a crouch, while I gave Jack a small glare; it seemed wrong for them to be spending any time at all looking after me, when Amy was in such greater need.

'My colleagues are three of the best in the county – they'll look after your friend,' the medic reassured, following my worried gaze to the flurry of activity beside Amy's stretcher. 'Your boyfriend is right; we need to look after you now.'

'He's not my boyfriend,' I corrected automatically. The paramedic got to her feet and took in Jack's protective arm, which was still holding me close to his side, and then her eye fell to the large diamond solitaire on my wedding finger.

'Sorry, your fiancé,' she amended.

'He's not—' I gave a weary shrug, it was suddenly too exhausting to bother explaining. Let them think whatever they liked. There were far more important things to be concerned with just then.

'And you, sir,' continued the paramedic, balling up the rubber gloves and slipping on a clean pair before reaching out her hand for Jack's wounded arm.

'Me? No, I'm fine. I wasn't involved in the accident.'

'Then how did you get that?'

All three of us looked down at the bloody gash on Jack's arm.

'Shaving,' I supplied succinctly.

The paramedic eyed me suspiciously as though perhaps she hadn't assessed my mental state accurately enough. But Jack interceded before things got even more confusing.

'I just caught it on a bit of metal in the car when I was helping Emma get out.'

Just? Like it was something you could dismiss that casually. Suddenly it was important that everyone should know precisely what he'd done. 'He saved my life,' I declared solemnly.

Jack looked embarrassed.

'Did he now? Well then, it's even more important that we get him properly taken care of, isn't it?'

'Can't we just stick a plaster on it? Just something to make sure I don't bleed all over my hire car?'

'Nonsense,' the paramedic replied, clearly horrified at the suggestion. 'We need to clean the wound and it looks like it'll probably need a few stitches. And then you'll probably need to have a tetanus injection too.'

Jack sighed, sensing resistance was going to be futile. Our conversation was halted briefly as the ambulance bearing Amy finally departed from the scene, its sirens like a town crier, ringing out the severity of the patient within.

'Scared of hospitals, are you?' I challenged, desperate to divert my attention to any topic I could latch on to, any topic which didn't involve the fate of my friend.

'I think I might be more scared of *you*,' Jack played along. 'I was right, you *are* bossy.'

There wasn't enough room in the second ambulance for all three of us. Jack walked with me to the rear steps, and smiled

33

at Caroline, who was looking much calmer sitting on one of the beds in the back of the vehicle. She gave us a slightly woolly look, and I guessed they had given her something to calm her down. The paramedic climbed into the ambulance and reached out her hand to help me in.

They had wanted to summon a third ambulance to transport Jack to the hospital, but he'd been absolutely insistent that he was able to drive his own car. So they'd just put a temporary bandage on his arm, and accepted his assurances that he would follow us. I eyed him suspiciously from my position on the second bed.

'You *are* coming, aren't you? You're not going to do something stupid like just drive off and not get yourself checked out?'

He saw my concern, heard it in my voice, and although I knew it was probably the last thing he really wanted to do, he gave a small nod and a smile, repeating the phrase he'd already said to me once before that night, 'I'll be right behind you.'

The hospital was busy and chaotic, in a way you somehow never expect in the early hours of the morning. In the windowless Accident and Emergency Department it could easily have been the middle of the working day and not three o'clock in the morning.

Like a well-oiled machine, the medical staff had sprung into action, wheeling, assessing and processing us with practised speed, separating Caroline and me almost instantly. I'm not entirely sure where they took her, but I was wheeled into a triage area for further assessment and then, after that burst of initial activity, was left for what seemed like for ever, for the arrival of the duty doctor.

As the minutes ticked by, my agitation, a small thing at

first, grew into a hard angry knot lodged somewhere in the pit of my stomach. I appreciated that they were busy, that much was obvious from the flurry of activity I could hear beyond the cubicle curtains. But surely someone could spare just a minute to tell me what was happening with Amy? It was the question I'd asked every member of staff who'd come within a few feet of me, one of whom I was pretty sure was actually a cleaner, who didn't even speak English.

I was also aware of an ever-pressing need to phone both home and Richard and let them know I was all right. It was really late, and my dad had started worrying about me like a teenager out past curfew since I moved back home. It was irritating, infuriating and completely understandable, so I lived with it. There were bigger issues to concern him and I'd moved back to lessen not *add* to them.

Richard too would surely be worried by now. We'd said we'd phone each other at the end of our respective hen and stag nights, and I wasn't entirely sure what happened when you dialled a mobile that had been reduced to molten plastic in a fiery inferno.

When a shadowed silhouette paused just beyond the curtain, I called out in a tone even I could recognise as annoyingly demanding. 'Excuse me, could you please come in here and see me?'

There was a grating sound of old metal rings scraping on the pole, as the curtain was drawn back and Jack's large form stepped into the cubicle, making it suddenly feel matchbox-small.

'There you are,' he announced, as though he'd been on some sort of quest to find me. *Had he?* 'I thought I recognised that imperious tone.' I flushed at his rather damning but, let's be honest here, entirely accurate comment.

'Sorry, I thought you were a nurse or someone.' His look quickly changed to one of concern. 'Is something wrong? Are you in pain?' I shook my head, and he seemed to relax a little. 'What is it you need? If it's anything other than a bedpan, I'll see what I can do.'

He had a curious knack of being able to make me smile in situations where no humour should exist. 'A phone would be good, better still would be some information about Amy. I've no idea what's happening with her.'

He nodded understandingly and drew his mobile out of his pocket.

'I don't think you're meant—' I broke off as the screen lit up, and as he passed me the phone I noticed the large red stain on the temporary bandage swathed around his forearm. 'Has no one seen that yet?' I asked, nodding at the wound which was clearly still bleeding.

'I told you, it's nothing. And the ER has been kind of crazy over the last half-hour, with ambulances arriving every five minutes. I overheard someone saying there's been a fire in an old folks' home.' That explained the activity and the lack of attention. 'But *you* should've have been looked at by now, you have a head injury. It could be affecting you in all sorts of ways.'

'Nah. I'm pretty much like this all the time.'

He smiled. 'Then he's one courageous guy, your fiancé.'

God. Richard. I was meant to be calling him and not exchanging pleasantries with my new-found rescuer friend. Jack was on my wavelength instantly. 'Give me the number and I'll dial it for you.' I recited my home number first, willingly letting him key it in; I didn't think I was up to handling an unfamiliar mobile. It actually took three attempts before I got the number right, which was the first real indication that I was still far more shaken up than I'd realised. How could I not know my own home number? Jack was calmly reassuring, saying it was just another symptom of delayed shock. I nodded back weakly – he wasn't to know how forgetting something, *anything*, freaked me out these days.

The phone was answered on the second ring. I took a deep breath and smiled broadly before speaking, hoping that might take the tremor out of my voice.

'Hi, Dad.'

'Emma?' Not a bad guess, since I was an only child.

'Yeah, Dad, it's me. Did I wake you up?' I heard grappling about, and knew he'd be reaching for the alarm clock on his nightstand.

'Emma, it's half past three in the morning. Where are you?'

Pause. Think of the best way to say this without causing panic, I told myself.

'I just wanted to say first that I'm fine, absolutely fine, but that I won't be back for a little while, we've had a bit of an accident.'

I saw Jack's eyebrows rise several centimetres at this gross understatement.

'Are you all right? Are you hurt?'

Damn. Even lying through my teeth hadn't stopped the panic from threading its way into his question. I heard a second voice then, and felt my concern ratchet up another notch.

'Is that Emma? Is something wrong? Where is she?'

'I'm good. Tell Mum I'm just running late, then I'll tell you properly.'

I waited patiently while he repeated the lie to my mother, keeping my gaze firmly fixed on the weave of the hospital

37

blanket covering me, rather than meet Jack's eyes. It might be his phone, but that didn't mean I had to explain myself to him.

'Okay.' My dad's voice returned on to the line.

'Don't say anything at your end, or you'll start her worrying again. Just listen, okay?' He gave a deep sigh, but he understood why I was being this way.

'Okay, love.' There was a false cheeriness to his tone.

I related it as succinctly as I could. 'We had a car accident. I'm okay, just a little scratch on my forehead.' I *did* look up then, and saw Jack's eyes widen and the eyebrows rose, if possible, even higher than before. 'Caro is fine, but Amy was hurt quite…' there was a quavering in my voice, that no lie could wallpaper over, '… quite badly. I'm not sure what's going on with her. No one will tell me.'

'Where are you? I'll be right there.'

There was some more muted questioning in the background, and I realised that we were doing a pretty poor job of keeping the tone of our conversation calm enough not to panic my mum.

'No, Dad. That's not necessary. I'm going to phone Richard, and he can come up and be with me. If you left now, who would you get to sit with Mum at this hour?'

He was silent for a long moment, realising I was right.

'I don't like the idea of you being there on your own.'

I looked up at Jack and gave a small smile.

'I'll be fine, Dad. I'm not alone. I have a friend with me.'

There was a long moment of silence after I pressed the disconnect button on his phone. Jack broke it first. 'So, compulsive lying? How long have you had that little problem?' I shrugged. This was one conversation that I just wasn't getting into with him. Annoyingly he wouldn't let it go. '"Bit of an accident"? "Little scratch"?'

'Yeah, then I went for a major whopper and called you my friend.'

His face softened then, as though he suddenly recognised not to push me on this matter. 'No. That one was true.' His hand reached across the blanket, and gently laced his fingers through mine. I felt the pressure of my diamond solitaire press into the skin of his palm, and wondered if that was why he released my hand almost as quickly as he had taken it.

'Okay, let's ring that fiancé of yours,' he commanded, and there was a distance in his voice that I swear hadn't been there a moment before. 'And this time, tell the *truth*.'

The phone rang for five minutes in Richard's flat before I hung up. Surely he had to be home by now? And the phone was right there in the bedroom. He couldn't have slept through its constant ringing, could he? I glanced at my watch. Almost four o'clock. He'd told me it was going to be a low-key stag do, just a couple of teachers from the school where he worked, and a few guys from the rugby club. Nothing wild. I thought of the look Simon, his best man, had given him, when he'd overheard Richard describing the plan for the night.

I sighed and punched Richard's mobile number into Jack's phone. The blare of loud music was the first thing I heard, that and a loud background buzz of a noisy bar or club.

'Richard?' More noise, a raucous shriek of laughter, and the clinking of glasses. The stag party was obviously still in full swing. 'Richard, can you hear me?'

'Who is this?' Not a good start.

'Richard, it's Emma.' There was a long pause, which sounded like it needed filling. '*Your fiancée.*'

'Emma,' he repeated, as though the name might just be a little familiar to him. I heard another voice I recognised then, speaking in what he must have thought was a whisper. I couldn't make out all the words, but I definitely caught the phrases 'checking up on you, mate' and 'ball and chain'.

'Richard, something terrible has happened. We've been in an accident and we're all at the hospital.' My words were more effective than throwing a cold bucket of water over him would have been, just not as satisfying.

'Emma, are you okay? Are you hurt?'

'Nothing major.' I looked up at Jack who was waiting with poorly concealed interest to see how I was going to finish my sentence. 'I have a nasty cut on my head, and my legs are badly bruised, but Caroline and I got off pretty lucky. But Amy...' I suddenly couldn't finish as my throat had constricted and the only thing coming past my lips were gulping sobs.

'Amy? What about Amy?' Richard's voice sounded completely sober now. 'Emma, calm down, tell me everything.' But I couldn't, the words were lost in the tangle of fear and panic that I thought I had managed to escape from, only to find it was just lying in wait to enmesh me all over again. I shook my head helplessly at the phone, knowing I could say no more.

The handset was gently prised from my grip by its rightful owner, and a calm and controlled voice spoke for me. 'We're at Queen Victoria Hospital. Just get here as soon as you can.' Jack looked about to disconnect the call, without ever identifying himself, but stopped to add just one last comment. 'Get a cab, man. Don't even think about driving.'

Jack held me while I sobbed, and it never once occurred to me how strange it was that I was leaning so heavily upon someone who I really didn't know. He could be anyone. He *was* anyone. Chance or fate had just put him on the right road at the right time. Had he not have been around, both Richard and my dad would have been getting an entirely different type of phone call by now. The thought made me sob even harder.

'Better?' Jack asked eventually, when the tsunami had petered out to just a small flow. He passed me a box of sandpaper-rough tissues, and I tried to mop up as best I could. There was nothing ladylike or genteel about the nose-blowing, though. He waited patiently until I was once more able to converse sensibly.

'Where's the buck's night? Has he got far to travel?'

'You should come with subtitles. That's an Australian term. It's called a stag night over here.'

He gave a shrug and a smile, and surprisingly I found my lips still remembered how to return it. 'I'm not from around these parts, ma'am,' he said, mimicking the words I'd heard in countless old western movies.

'I kind of guessed that. What *are* you doing in the UK, if you don't mind me asking?'

'I'm an author, with a publisher's deadline and a novel I have rather foolishly set in the English countryside, so I thought I should spend a couple of months here doing some hands-on research. I'm renting a cottage on the coast near Trentwell.'

In different circumstances I'm sure I'd have been intrigued enough to ask more, but there were other much more important issues on my mind right then. For someone who didn't know me, it was a little disconcerting to find Jack was able to read me like a crystal ball. 'Why don't I go and round up one of those doctors and see if I can get you an update on Amy and Caroline?'

41

After he'd gone, the cubicle seemed much more spacious, but curiously bland and colourless. He was the kind of man whose presence filled all the available space around him. And it wasn't just a matter of his good looks or charm, which even on a night like tonight were undeniable. He was probably going to have to utilise both of those to full effect if he was going to get any information about Amy, because I was pretty certain they only gave out details like that to close relatives or immediate family. But damn it, we *were* Amy's family, Caroline and I. Well, not in an actual sibling sense, but in a deeper more enduring way that bound us closer than blood ever could. I imagined the police would have called Amy's parents by now, but as they'd moved out of the area several years ago and lived four hours' drive away, until they got here Caroline and I were all she had.

I decided to go out and find Jack for myself – I spotted him walking down the corridor in deep conversation with a nurse. She turned to me first. 'What are you doing out of bed?'

'That was going to be my line,' said Jack.

'I've found out Caroline is about to be discharged and Amy's in surgery,' he informed me, as we walked back to the cubicle. He held out a hand to assist me back on to the hospital bed. I pulled the blankets back over my damaged legs and let Jack's worrying news sink in.

'Surgery? For her face?'

He shook his head sadly. 'No. I think she has some internal injuries, but I couldn't find out what specifically.' I felt a blast of cold fear run from the base of my neck right down the length of my spine, hitting every vertebra on the way. Internal injuries sounded like a hospital euphemism for *really, really badly hurt*. Nothing else Jack could say or offer in consolation could get me beyond that dreadful terrifying phrase.

42

Fortunately he appeared to be the kind of man who valued silence over mindless conversation-filling, which was lucky because I wasn't able to concentrate on anything except the nightmare we were currently living through. I'd even needed his help completing some hospital forms which a nurse had given to me on a clipboard. My hand was trembling too much to write even my name and address, so I gratefully allowed him to take the pen and board from my hands and complete the form in sure bold lettering as I dictated my details.

At my request he'd left the cubicle curtains open, as though somehow news would reach us quicker without that thin barrier of fabric holding it back. We watched a continual stream of medical staff pass by our bay, some rushing with purpose and haste, others just idling by, some mindlessly chatting away, apparently oblivious to the fact that the road leading to our future was about to be altered beyond all recognition. When I overheard two nurses deeply engrossed in a discussion about a ludicrous plot twist from some television show, real and genuine anger flooded through me. *Television?* You had to be kidding me? They should be saving lives, doing CPR on speedily pushed stretchers, or barking out unintelligible orders that ended in the word *'stat'*, not discussing some TV programme, for Christ's sake! Jack saw my agitation, and patted the back of my hand understandingly. 'It's just another day at the office for them.'

'Not for me.'

'I know,' he replied consolingly.

Richard arrived in a tornado of panic, concern and alcohol fumes. His footsteps preceded his arrival, slapping noisily against the tiled floor, as he ran the length of the triage area, calling my name. He burst into the cubicle, and Jack immediately got out of the chair he'd been occupying beside the bed. I'd thought I was done with crying, thought I'd already wrung myself dry in Jack's arms, but apparently not. Just one sight of Richard's familiar face, suffused in worry, concern and love and suddenly the Sahara was replaced by a mini Niagara. Richard held me against him, rocking me like a child, and even though he smelled more like a distillery than a person, it felt good to be in his arms.

'Hush, hush,' he soothed against my hair, and I tried not to notice the faint but still discernible thickened slur in his voice, and the aroma of stale cigarette smoke he appeared to be kippered in. He'd been out on his stag night, and it was totally unjustified of me to feel angry that while we'd been crawling through debris and flames on the side of the road, he'd been in a bar, getting drunk. But I felt it anyway.

'What on earth happened, Emma?' he asked, apparently not noticing my wince of pain as he sat down on the foot of the bed, and rested one arm against my lower legs. Jack swooped in like a hawk, removing the arm from my shins and earning an annoyed glare from my fiancé. He looked up at Jack as though he'd only just noticed he was there.

'Her legs are badly bruised,' Jack explained succinctly and even though Richard looked abashed and apologetic, something told me that, first-impression-wise, he'd just failed a major test.

'And your face…' Richard continued. 'It looks really bad.'

There's not a lot you can say to an observation like that. Fortunately I didn't have to.

'She cut her head when the car flipped over, before it crashed into the ditch, and trapped her in the wreckage. After that, it burst into flames.' Jack's statement of what had happened, although accurate, was deliberately harsh and cuttingly shocking.

'My God, Emma. You could have *died*. I could have lost you.' There was such vulnerability in his voice, I could only hold out my arms to him. For a moment I was so absorbed in the reversal of our roles, I almost didn't notice Jack was about to exit the cubicle.

'Wait!' I called to his retreating back, and for a moment I thought he wasn't going to turn around.

'You're going?' I asked incredulously, knowing I had no right to be surprised, but feeling it all the same. He'd already gone far beyond the role of Good Samaritan with everything he'd done that night. Why on earth should he remain here, now that Richard was here? Yet still, I felt something akin to panic at seeing him go.

Jack's eyes met mine, and I knew a moment of real dread as I realised I would probably never see him again. Could he read that feeling? Maybe. He'd been pretty intuitive at knowing what was going through my head all night. He paused, then took a decisive step back towards the bed. We both ignored the confused look Richard was giving us, as his head turned from me to Jack, as though trying to fathom out a complicated plot in a play he'd missed the start of.

Jack smiled gently down at me and picked up one of my hands, holding it carefully in his own. 'It's time for me to go now. You're going to be fine. I really hope everything works out for your friend.'

I nodded, my throat suddenly too full to squeeze a word past the lump that was lodged within it.

'Look after yourself, Emma,' he said softly, bending down and kissing me gently on the forehead.

'What—?' Richard exclaimed, swivelling around to follow

Jack's tall shape as he strode quickly out of the cubicle. 'What the hell...? Why did that bloody doctor just kiss you goodbye?'

Two strong black coffees later, Richard could probably have passed a basic sobriety test. By the time he'd accompanied the entourage of nurses and orderlies who wheeled my bed to the X-ray department, he was at least capable of holding a coherent conversation. Not that I'd have recommended putting him in charge of anything mechanical or operating equipment of any kind, not after watching his torturous attempts to send my dad a text to let him know what was happening.

Of course, he did turn a very unpleasant shade of green when they cleaned up and sutured the wound on my forehead, but that was more due to a basic weak constitution and a phobia of needles, rather than alcohol. In the end, someone had stuck a moulded plastic chair behind him, which considering the way he'd been swaying on his feet, was probably a good call.

As the morning inched ever closer, he stayed by my side, refusing to leave me even when I was eventually moved to a small single room, where they insisted I was to remain under observation for the rest of the night. He left my room only to make regular trips to the nurses' station to ask for updates on Amy, and was repeatedly given the same standard reply.

'Still in surgery,' he reported back to me at some time after six. The lights in my small side room were turned down to their lowest setting, presumably to encourage sleep, but nothing had ever felt less likely to happen. No night I'd lived through had ever felt this long.

I knew at once when he'd received different news. I swear the door handle opened strangely; his shadow fell in a peculiar way through the gap when the door slowly swung open. He stood awkwardly, and there was a look I have never seen before on his face. I prayed to God that nothing would ever happen in our lives, that I'd ever have to see it again.

He stood immobile and silent, and I just *knew*.

'No,' I protested, shaking my head in denial of something that hadn't yet been voiced. 'No, no, no.'

His eyes began to fill, yet still he never moved.

'It can't be true. I don't believe it. I *won't* believe it.'

He moved then, taking small unsteady steps towards me.

'About ten minutes ago,' he said hoarsely, reaching for my hand. I could hardly see it through my tear-blurred vision. I think he may have said something else then, something about them having done all that they could, or was it something about the gravity of her injuries? I just don't know. I couldn't get beyond the screamingly awful headline to the news.

Amy, one of my best friends for over twenty years, was dead.

CHAPTER 3

Numb. *Novocaine* numb. Ice-water numb. And not in a good way, more the kind of numb you feel when you have frostbite, right before you start losing your digits.

Richard and I had sat in total silence for what felt like hours, trying to assimilate and absorb something so gut-wrenchingly terrible that it was almost beyond acceptance. Amy, the most vibrant and alive person I'd ever known, had turned her own philosophy of living each day as though it was your last, into a prophecy.

The news had clearly shocked even the hospital staff, for I swear we were treated differently after it had broken. It was there when the nurse who came to take my blood pressure had given my hand a long hard squeeze, after removing the cuff from my arm. It was even evident with the registrar on morning rounds, who had finally told me I could go home. He had patted my shoulder, in a slightly awkward and uncomfortable way, and although nothing had been said there had been a look of sympathy and condolence on his face, which I had a feeling I was going to be seeing quite a lot of in the days to come.

After the hospital team left my room, Richard had helped me to get changed out of the starchy gown they'd put me into, and back into my suddenly highly inappropriate short party dress. I cringed when I felt the fabric brush against my bare skin, because there were several dark encrusted stains splattered on it, which I knew had to be blood. I just didn't know whose. Mine? Jack's? Or was it Amy's? What difference did it make? It was going to go straight in the bin the moment I got home.

To save time, Richard volunteered to go the hospital pharmacy and fill the prescription for the painkillers I'd been given. 'I won't be long,' he promised, kissing me briefly below the large white bandage on my forehead. 'Will you be all right while I'm gone?'

I shook my head sadly and all he could do was nod back in understanding. It felt like nothing and none of us were going to be all right ever again, we both knew that. And I strongly suspected that the moment we left the confines of the hospital, it was going to get a whole lot worse.

A light knock on the door was followed by a young nurse who opened it just wide enough to slide her head through the opening. I assumed she was there to tell me the cab we'd ordered had arrived, but she surprised me instead with the words, 'You have a visitor, Miss Marshall. It's not our regular visiting hours… but given the special circumstances…' There it was again, that VIP treatment reserved for those whose tragedies transcended the usual. I didn't want to be a member of this club.

The nurse stood to one side to allow my visitor to enter the room. Jack stood for just one moment without saying anything, then his first words were my undoing. 'Emma, I am so, so sorry.'

I tried very hard not to lose it. I nodded my head, acknowledging his sympathetic words, but I could already feel my lip beginning to tremble, like an opera singer about to sing an aria. With a sound that started like a hiccup and ended like a dog's yelp, I was once again being held in his arms, while the tears, which hadn't fallen when Richard had been there, finally found the crack in the dam.

I am actually not much of a crier, I never have been. So it was even *more* astounding that this American stranger, who I'd known less than twelve hours, had now comforted me in was arms while I wept like a child more often than my fiancé had done in the last twelve years.

I didn't hear Richard enter the room, even though I was starting to regain control by then. So the first I knew that we weren't alone was Richard's rather cool enquiry, 'Emma?'

Jack looked up, but kept his arms firmly around me. His hold was innocent and intended only to comfort, but I saw a challenging light spark in his golden-brown eyes at Richard's tone. This was definitely something I didn't need right then. I struggled out of Jack's embrace, and his arms instantly fell from around me. He extended his hand to Richard. 'Jack Monroe,' he announced. 'I'm sorry, we never got a chance to be formally introduced last night.'

Richard took a moment too long in raising his hand to shake Jack's. Then, just before the situation tipped from slightly discourteous to downright rude, he placed his palm against the other man's. There was no warmth in the handshake, or on either of their faces.

'Richard Withers,' supplied Richard baldly, 'Emma's fiancé.'

A small muscle twitched on Jack's face.

'You've not been here all night too, have you?' I queried, failing to notice until I'd finished speaking that Jack was in different clothes and had clearly washed and shaved since I'd last seen him.

'No. I got fixed up and then went home.'

I noticed then a much smaller bandage on his forearm, just

visible from beneath the rolled-up sleeve of his dark shirt.

'So what are you doing back here?'

I glared at Richard, because there was no way to gloss over such blatant rudeness. His returned look said *what?*, but he knew exactly what.

'I phoned this morning to find out how Emma was doing, and to ask about Amy. They gave me the news and I just... well, I just felt like I should come back to see you.'

'That's very nice of you,' said Richard, although his voice said he actually meant the exact opposite.

'Yes, it really was,' I added, with a great deal more sincerity.

'However, as you can see, I'm about to take Emma home, and she really needs to rest up properly. So thank you for coming and all that, but we have everything under control here now.'

Under control? Nothing, *ever*, had felt less like being under our control; but dealing with Jack, being beholden to him for saving the woman he loved, was just one pressure too many for Richard to deal with at that moment, and I knew that, rightly or wrongly – and I really knew it was *wrongly* – I had to side with him.

'Thank you for coming. It means a lot.' My voice said *Goodbye, please go now*, even if my words didn't.

'I just wish it wasn't under these circumstances. I just wish there was more I could have done. For Amy.' I felt the last two words were added to prevent Richard from jumping in with some smart-mouth comeback about having done more than enough already. As ludicrous as it sounded, it was almost as though he resented Jack for saving me; as though not having been the one to do it himself belittled or emasculated him in some way. It made no sense. He should have been grateful, but all he sounded was petty and jealous.

'Are they discharging you now?' continued Jack. 'Can I offer you a ride somewhere?'

'No thanks. We have a cab waiting downstairs,' jumped in Richard, so speedily I think he was worried I'd been about to accept. As if on cue, the same young nurse knocked on the door to inform us our cab was outside.

Richard placed an arm around my waist and steered me firmly to the door. I turned to look at Jack, whose face gave away so little emotion I honestly couldn't tell what he was thinking. I gave a small sad smile of goodbye to the man who had risked his life to save me. Leaving him there felt like unfinished business, or a debt that hadn't been repaid. When you owe someone your very life, perhaps it always does.

I didn't think to challenge Richard on his behaviour during the cab journey home. There were bigger and more devastating things to deal with and the enormity of this seemed to hit us both like a wrecking ball the closer we got to home. When the cab pulled up beside my parents' house, I laid a hand on Richard's arm as he pulled out his wallet to pay the driver.

'Why don't you go back to your flat first, and wash and rest up and then come over later?'

'Surely it would be easier if I just came in with you now?'

I shook my head sadly, and leaned over to kiss him gently, hoping he understood my reasoning. 'It's not going to be easy whichever way we do this. Just come back in a little while, okay?'

They were both waiting for me at the kitchen table. My dad got to his feet as soon as I walked in, his arms going around me in a bear hug of fatherly relief, concern and love. I'd already spoken to him on the phone from the hospital, so he knew about Amy. I saw his red-rimmed eyes and knew it had hit him hard. Amy and Caroline had been frequent visitors to the house for over twenty years.

'Do you want some tea? I don't suppose that hospital stuff was at all drinkable.' His voice was gruff with emotion, and although I wasn't fussed about the drink, I knew he needed some time to compose himself.

'Thanks, Dad.' I pulled up one of the pine chairs and positioned it next to my mother. I saw the balled-up tissue held tightly in her fisted hand and when she turned to face me, there was a matching look of grief on the features that so resembled mine, that looking at her was like staring into a magic mirror of my future. That used to give me comfort and a sense of continuity, now it just scared the hell out of me.

My glance flicked across to my dad, and he gave an almost imperceptible nod. I felt a small wave of relief. It was, iron-ically, one of her better days, though quite possibly my very worst.

'Dad told me,' she confirmed sadly. 'I can hardly believe it. Poor, poor Amy.' I nodded dumbly, feeling the hot prickle of tears escaping down my cheeks. Her eyes fell on my band-aged forehead. 'Your head? What happened?'

'It's a small cut from the accident. It's nothing really. The plaster makes it look worse than it is. Don't worry about it, Mum.'

She nodded, and just that ready acceptance of something that should have concerned her so much more, would have told anyone who had known her before, that this was no longer the same Frances Marshall.

'I can't imagine how Linda and Donald must be feeling,' she continued, and my Dad and I both exchanged a surprised look. Even I might have struggled to remember the names of Amy's parents, but despite not having seen them in years, my mother had recalled them instantly. There really was no explaining what this disease decided to rob you of, and what it let you retain.

We sat drinking our tea in a sad silence. My head was starting to feel too heavy for my neck, and I kept rubbing my fingers against my eyes, which felt like they were filled with hot gritty sand. 'Why don't you go upstairs and try to take a little nap, love?' my dad had finally suggested.

I shook my head. 'I can't, Dad, there's so much to do. So much that we have to think about. I should check on Caroline, I've no idea how she is doing, and then I should go and see Amy's parents. And then there's the wedding. We'll have to postpone it—'

'What?' questioned my mother sharply. 'You're postponing the wedding? Why? Have you and Richard argued?'

I looked at her in confusion. 'No. Of course not. But we can't go ahead with it now. Not after Amy...' My voice trailed away. Surely she could understand? I looked across at my dad who was studying her with an intense expression, as though willing her failing brain synapses to function properly. It was a look he wore often.

'Oh, yes. Of course. She's your bridesmaid, isn't she?'

I nodded. That should have been *was* and not *is*. Everything about Amy was now in the past tense. No future for her. The thought sliced me like a sabre.

'There's time enough to think about everything later,' my dad said, turning his attention away from my mother, who was completely unaware she had just passed a small unspoken test. 'You won't be able to help anyone with anything if you make yourself sick. Go and get some rest now.'

It felt wrong to allow myself the luxury of sleep, and with it a brief welcome escape from reality, but I knew he was right. If we were going to postpone the wedding, and I couldn't think of getting married now, then there was a hell of a lot to sort out, but I was incapable of functioning or even thinking straight by then. I got shakily to my feet. I bent and kissed his forehead and then did the same with my mother. Her face scanned mine in concern.

'Just a couple of hours,' I cautioned my father. 'Don't let me sleep any longer than that, okay? Richard will be over later, and I don't want to still be in bed when he gets here.'

'Richard's coming round?' said my mum, and the pleasure in her voice should have alerted me. 'How lovely.'

Her parting words came as I reached the door to the hallway, and successfully ensured that rest would be a long time coming. 'Emma.' I turned back to face her, and the confusion on her face said it all. 'What's happened to your head? Why is it bandaged up like that?'

Not one of her better days after all.

From the dark circles beneath his eyes, it looked as though Richard had been as unsuccessful in catching up on sleep as I had. Every time my eyes had closed I'd seen again, in horrible, graphic detail, the events of the night before, like a spooling trailer for a film you never wanted to see.

Feeling restless and edgy within the confines of the house, I'd wandered out into the back garden, bundled up in an old comfortable cardigan to combat the late afternoon chill, and sat on a wooden bench beneath a leafy tree. I watched unobserved through the glass patio doors as Richard entered the cosily lit lounge. I saw him go across to my father, and felt a fledgling smile tug at my lips as I watched their handshake greeting turn clumsily into a brief and uncharacteristic embrace. His greeting to my mother looked considerably more natural. He'd crossed straight over to her armchair, crouching low to speak to her. I don't know what words were exchanged, but I saw him patiently nod his head and take hold of her hand as she spoke. He was more than good with her, he was amazing, and in a natural and tolerant way, that was never patronising or impatient. As hard as I tried to emulate him, I was nowhere near as good with her as he was. Perhaps, like he suggested, I was just too close, and losing her piece by piece like this was so damn hard and unfair.

I saw my dad point in the general direction of the garden, and Richard's answering nod. A few moments later he was beside me on the bench, sliding an arm around my shoulders and drawing me up against him. I fitted against the familiar contours of his body, like a jigsaw piece completing a puzzle. I could smell the spicy aroma of his shower gel and aftershave and for the first time in almost twenty-four hours I felt a slight lessening in the tension that had knotted around me like a garrotte.

We didn't speak for a long time, there was no need. A virtual lifetime spent in each other's company meant we were pretty intuitive at knowing what the other person was thinking. But this time, when I finally broke the silence, I genuinely had no idea how he was going to react. 'We have to postpone the wedding, Richard.'

For a long moment he said nothing, and I twisted slightly in his hold to study his impassive profile. A gentle breeze ruffled his dark blond hair, and the impossibly long eyelashes of the same colour fanned his brows as he stared down the length of the garden with an expression on his face I simply couldn't name. Whatever images were running through his mind, he certainly wasn't seeing the neatly trimmed lawn or the flanking shrubs and plants. The silence stretched like elastic, and just when I started to think that surely it was going to twang and break with a painful and noisy protest, Richard gave a deep and sorrowful sigh, and gave me his answer. 'I agree.'

His words pierced and deflated the argument I had waiting in readiness. I'd been so sure that he was going to disagree, I was completely taken by surprise. Irrationally, I felt a moment of disappointment that he'd not tried harder – or at all – to dissuade me.

'It's the right thing to do,' I said, parroting the script I'd prepared in my head.

'It is.' He reached for my hand then, and gently fingered the diamond solitaire on my ring finger. It had only lived there for three months, and I was still almost constantly aware of its weight and presence.

'Just for a while,' he agreed, lifting my hand to his mouth and grazing the knuckle gently with his lips. 'Postponing, not cancelling.' His eyes were locked on mine. I nodded back, unable to trust my voice.

Despite the protests from both Richard and my father, I insisted that I wanted to see Caroline that evening. I'd phoned several times during the day, but had only spoken to Nick, as Caroline had worryingly refused to come to the phone. With each call I could hear the base note of desperation growing in her partner's voice.

'If you don't want to go then fine; I'll drive myself,' I said stubbornly, putting Richard in an impossible position. I knew he sided with my father, who thought the only place I should be going was back to bed, but there was a steely determination in the glare I gave my fiancé.

'Caroline needs me, I *have* to go. And come to that, Nick could probably do with some support from you too.' It was a winning argument. My mother had watched the three-way stand-off, as though she had a front row seat for a very interesting foreign play. 'Are you going out?' she asked mildly, as Richard held out my jacket and I shrugged my arms into the sleeves.

'Just for a little while, Mum.'

Caroline and Nick lived on a new housing estate on the far side of town. They were the first from our circle of friends to climb on to the property ladder. I suppose it was an inevitable outcome, what with Nick working in a bank and Caroline in an estate agents. The crescent where they lived was model-village neat and tidy, peopled with like-minded young couples. Caroline, who'd been putting things away in a 'bottom drawer' about a century or so after that notion had died out completely, was a natural homemaker and couldn't understand why neither Amy nor I had shared her enthusiasm for home décor catalogues or DIY superstores.

We pulled on to their familiar drive and Richard tucked his car neatly into the space behind Nick's. The one Caroline's car used to occupy. We turned to each other and shared a long regretful look before reaching for the car door handles and then walked hand in hand up the path.

I don't think I've ever seen anyone more grateful to receive visitors than Nick, who answered the door almost before the pealing chime of the bell had finished echoing in the oak floored hallway. He held me gingerly in a welcoming embrace, trying very hard not to focus on the white bandage on my head as he spoke. 'She's in the bedroom.' I gave a nod and a smile which I hope said *I've got it from here*, slipped off my jacket and draped it over the newel post on the stairs.

'Caro, it's me. I'm coming up.'

As I got closer I heard music coming from the bedroom: it was a band the three of us had been obsessed with about a decade ago. Interspersed with the soundtrack of our youth were noisy gulping sobs, which were heartbreaking to hear. I gave a soft knock on the wood-panelled door and went in.

Caroline was a mess, and even more tellingly her *room* was a mess, which if you knew her even a fraction as well as I did, was a definite sign that things were far from right. Her short blonde hair was sticking out at weird angles from her head, and her face was red and blotchy from crying. She was kneeling in the middle of their double bed, on a beautifully embroidered white duvet cover, only you couldn't see the fabric at all, for the entire surface of the bed was covered in a sea of photographs. Dressed only in pyjama shorts and a strappy vest, my friend sat on an island in the duvet, surrounded by just about every snapshot that had ever been taken of the three of us.

'I just can't believe she's gone,' said Caroline, her voice choked with pain. She ran her hands along the mattress, sweeping over the many photos, pieces of Amy, which were all we had left now.

I gave a cry which sounded alien and anguished. 'I know.'

'Why her? Why Amy? When there are so many terrible people in the world, why was *she* the one who had to go?' Even through my tears, I could see the question in Caroline's eyes, because it was the same one I'd been asking myself all day: *Why Amy and not me?* Survivor's guilt.

I cleared a pathway and crawled on to the bed to reach her, my arms going around her, and hers around me, like Hansel and Gretel lost in the woods. We cried for a long time, clinging together but saying nothing, because sometimes the pain is just too great for words to be of use, and the only thing you can do is hold on tightly to someone you love, until it stops trying to rip your heart out through your chest.

I groped among the photographs for a buried tissue box, which was protruding from beneath a pile of pictures of us at primary school. I plucked one up and looked at it nostalgically. It was a photograph I hadn't seen in almost twenty years, and had been taken after a school nativity play. Amy was in the middle of the frame, looking adorable in a long blue gown, the perfect Virgin Mary, until you panned down and saw she was holding the baby Jesus doll upside-down by its ankle. To her left stood Caroline, wearing a pair of large donkey ears fixed to a hairband on her head, and a goofy smile on her face. On the other side of Amy was me, bizarrely wearing a weird tinfoil contraption on my head, for if memory served me correctly I'd been cast as The Christmas Alien... I felt Caroline's chin come to rest on my shoulder, as she too studied the photograph in my hands. Three faces, each so different, except for the undisguised look of happiness and friendship. I didn't need to examine the hundreds of other photos I was surrounded by to know that I'd find that same look on virtually every one. It had been there too on the snaps we'd taken just the night before, at my hen party. Three heads squeezed together, while Caroline held the camera at arm's length to take the shot. There might be make-up replacing the freckles, and styled hair instead of pigtails, but the same friendship had still shone from our eyes. And now those last photographs, which we'd thought were recording just one more milestone on the road, actually marked the final moments of Amy's life. I reached for the tissues again.

By my left knee a photograph I didn't recognise caught my eye. I plucked it up and held it closer to the light. I guessed it must have been taken three or four years ago, for although Amy and Caroline looked much the same as they did now, Caroline's hair still hung down to her shoulders, and she hadn't worn it that way for some time. The photograph had obviously been taken in summertime, for the subjects were all in shorts and T-shirts and were sitting in what looked like a beer garden of a pub, four bicycles propped up against a tree beside them. Nick and Richard were on one side of the bench, with long draughts of lager in front of them. On the other side of the table were Amy and Caroline, laughing crazily at whoever had been taking the photo. I was not in the picture.

'Where was this one taken, Caroline?'

She took the snap from my fingers and a small smile curved her mouth at the memory. 'Oh yes, that was the day Amy persuaded us it would be fun to cycle to Brownleigh, over fifteen miles away, on the hottest Sunday of the entire summer. I swear we nearly died from heatstroke. It must have been three, no maybe four years ago.'

A strange feeling squirmed somewhere inside me as I took the photograph back from her. That was during the period of time when I'd temporarily lost contact with the girls. To begin with my job in London had taken up so much of my time, and weekends, that I'd hardly come back to our home town at all, except for brief family visits. Then, after two years of working in the capital, I'd been given a fantastic opportunity to transfer to the company's Washington office for eighteen months, which I had absolutely adored. I'd never really given much thought to what had happened to the group of friends I'd walked away from. It was unsettling now to realise that they owned a past history and shared memories about which I knew absolutely nothing. It shouldn't have bothered me – of course my friends had been entitled to be happy in the years when I'd not been around – but suddenly it did.

Richard and I had been apart for almost five years, and in that time neither of us had found a relationship that matched the one we had left behind; the relationship we'd managed to rediscover just one year ago.

A tentative knock on the door made us both look up, as Nick poked his head nervously around the edge of the frame. 'You two girls okay?' He wore the classic look of a man who was extremely uncomfortable around feminine tears.

I looked at Caroline and reached out to squeeze her hand. 'No. But we will be.'

I eventually persuaded Caroline to come downstairs with me and have something to eat, which according to Nick were two things she hadn't done at all in the last twenty-four hours. If I achieved nothing else, that alone justified the visit.

Nick and Richard had opened a bottle of wine, and when we joined them in the welcoming kitchen, Nick reached into the cupboard for two more glasses. I was still on painkillers and definitely shouldn't be drinking alcohol, and I'd noticed a small brown bottle from the hospital pharmacy beside Caroline's bed, so I guessed that neither should she. Both of us took the wine.

Inevitably the conversation was unable to stray far from the event that had exploded our world into smithereens. 'Has anyone spoken to Amy's family yet? Has anything been said about… Do they know when the…?' Richard was clearly struggling with the word 'funeral', and with good reason. That word belonged to old people, to sick people, to people who had achieved everything they had wanted to do and see in life. Not to a beautiful, funny and loving twenty-seven-year-old woman, whose life had hardly begun yet.

'They phoned to speak to Caroline this afternoon,' supplied Nick.

'They *did*?' Caroline queried, swivelling in her seat to look at her partner in surprise. 'Why didn't you tell me?'

Nick's face wore a look of caution, as he tried to find a reply that didn't sound condemning. 'I did, honey. But you wouldn't come to the phone. In fact, you used some fairly colourful language when you sent me away.'

Caroline got out of her seat and crawled on to Nick's lap, and his arms went around her. 'I'm sorry,' she whispered into his neck, and suddenly I felt like Richard and I were intruding. I might have dragged Caroline back from the edge of an abyss, but it was Nick she needed now for the strength to get up on to her feet once again.

'Shall I call them tomorrow?' I suggested, and Caroline gave a small nod of thanks, as a task she hadn't felt strong enough to face was lifted from her shoulders. 'Where are they staying?'

Nick gave me both the name of a hotel in town and an extremely grateful smile. We left a short while later, and I was grateful for Richard's supporting arm around me as we walked to the car. Apparently there's a very good reason why they tell you not to drink while on medication.

CHAPTER 4

As soon as I gave their name at the reception desk of the country house hotel, I sensed a shift in attitude. The professional demeanour of the black-suited receptionist softened, and a look of empathy replaced the diamond-hard glaze in her eyes. 'They're in our Garden Suite,' she said, and I noticed that even the tone of her voice had softened when she realised that I was a player in the tragic drama being enacted in their establishment. 'Are they expecting you?' I saw her glance down at a pad on the desk and run a perfectly manicured fingernail down a list of names. My own sat in the middle, below that of one of the town's undertaker firms and above a local florist.

'Yes, they are. Emma Marshall. That's me.'

Their suite was on the ground floor, in a wing which overlooked the impressively kept hotel grounds. I didn't suppose either of Amy's parents had so much as glanced out of a window since their arrival. Although I'd known them for almost my entire life, Caroline was actually closer to Amy's family than I was, so it was startling to be enveloped in an all-encompassing embrace by Amy's father the moment the door had opened. He had always seemed a rather distant and aloof figure, and Amy had never fully explained what he did for a living, other than to say it was 'something in the City'. It was obviously time-consuming and demanding, as he had frequently been absent from school events and even from some of her birthday parties. Consequently, I'd always thought of him as a rather cold and remote individual. So it was a shock to see the tears running down his face when Donald Travis eventually relinquished his hold on me. That was what did it. To see his open and unashamed heartbreak, and know there was nothing I could ever do or say that could possibly lessen his pain, was like a stiletto stab wound in my chest. He gripped my hands so hard it hurt, and still his tears kept falling, and he did nothing to brush them away. A torrent like that was going to have to run its course, and it was nowhere near spent yet. I found myself thinking of all those times when teenage Amy would berate her absent father, who she claimed always prioritised his job over his family. *Can you see him now, Amy? Can you see how he's grieving?* I really, really hoped that she could.

Linda Travis was in pieces. She was one of those women who always looked as though she had just stepped out of the beauty salon or the hairdressers. Among the jeans- and trainers-wearing mothers at the school gates, she had stood out like a diamond in a jumble sale, with her immaculate clothes and designer heels. Amy was the child who had always appeared to have it all: the big house, the fancy cars and the glamorous parents. But beneath the TV-advert-perfect mum was a woman who had clearly doted on her only child. It was hard to recognise her in the dishevelled woman curled up on the chintz-covered settee of the suite. For a start she looked about thirty years too old to be Amy's mum, and broken, in a way I didn't think would ever be fixed. I went to her side, and could find no words that could offer even a moment's solace. Instead I just picked up her hand and

65

held it, much as I had held her daughter's two nights earlier.

When I had phoned that morning, to arrange this meeting, I'd been unsure of how they would receive me. They had, after all, contacted Caroline and not me in the first instance. Was it possible that they blamed me in some way for Amy's death?

'If there's anything I can do to help... with the arrangements...' My voice trailed away. It seemed I was just as inept as my fiancé at getting the words out. Fortunately organisation was Donald Travis's forte, and in a strange way I sensed that having a funeral to arrange would carry him through the next ten days, until the time came to bury his child.

'There is just one thing...' Linda began hesitantly.

'Anything. Please name it.'

She gave a sad ghost of a smile. 'The undertaker has asked us to pick out an outfit, and I really don't think I could—' The words were lost in an avalanche of tears. Amy needed something to wear for the burial, and Linda, who had accompanied her daughter on countless shopping trips for the perfect dress, couldn't bear the thought of choosing this final outfit. What mother could?

Planning our wedding had been joyous and uplifting, so it really wasn't surprising that having to pull it apart piece by piece was depressing, demoralising, and also incredibly sad. Of course I could have made the cancellations by phone or email, but there was something fittingly sombre in physically retracing the footsteps I had taken a couple of months earlier when I'd booked the venue, the church, the florist and the caterer. Also, I felt driven by a burning need to keep busy and active, as though if I kept moving fast enough I would somehow be able to outrun the pain.

Many of the establishments I visited had been expecting

my call to cancel. It's a curious phenomenon that bad news seems to travel so much more effectively than good, but at least it saved me from the necessity of having to explain the reasons for the cancellation many times over.

As I drove home from my final appointment it occurred to me that unpicking our wedding plans was just one more example of how my life was moving backwards instead of forwards. Nine years earlier I'd left my home town, family and boyfriend for university and then a career and life in London, yet here I was at twenty-seven, living back at home with my parents, working in the very same place where I'd been employed as a Saturday girl. Even resuming my relationship with Richard could be seen as a retrograde step. I honestly believed our relationship had run its course when I had broken up with him many years ago. Yet now we were getting married, or had been about to, if I hadn't just spent the best part of the day undoing those plans.

I was feeling tired and miserable as I let myself into the house. I could smell the flowers even before the front door was fully open. Their fragrance filled the hallway, and as I shut the door behind me my mouth opened in surprise when I saw the display propped up on the hall table. The exotic blooms were artfully gathered together beneath a clear cellophane sleeve, in a stunning bouquet. 'Richard,' I said with a smile, as I crossed over to the delivery and prised the small white envelope with my name on it from the corner of the packaging. He'd only sent me flowers twice before this, and both times they'd been small bunches of white freesias, his favourite flowers. I was genuinely touched by the thoughtfulness of his unexpected gesture. I pulled the small white card from its envelope, and felt my smile freeze, then thaw and widen. There were just eight handwritten words in bold black ink on the card: *With deepest sympathy for your loss. Jack Monroe.*

I was still transferring the flowers into the tallest vase I could find, when Richard arrived. 'Are these yours?' he asked, kissing me briefly, his attention focused on the display. Just for one moment I considered lying, but decided instead to be honest. With hindsight, I should have followed my first instinct.

'Yes. They're beautiful, aren't they?'

'Hmm. Yes,' he replied distractedly, looking around for something, which, you didn't need to be Sherlock Holmes to work out, was the gift card. 'Who are they from?'

I took a deep breath before replying, 'Jack Monroe.'

'Who?'

'Jack Monroe. The American guy, from the other night... the one who pulled me out of the car.'

The blank look on his face cleared, to be replaced by a small frown of displeasure.

'Why is he sending you flowers?'

'I don't know. As a gesture of condolence? Because it's a nice thing to do? Who knows?' Perhaps it was Richard's look of undisguised irritation that made me add, 'Actually, I thought they were from *you*.' He had the grace to look a little embarrassed and uncomfortable, but not enough good sense to know when to drop the subject.

'So, why did you give him your home address?'

'I didn't.' Richard's attitude was really beginning to rankle, and was ruining the small lift receiving the flowers had given me after such a terribly sad day.

'So how did he know where to send them?'

I stopped sliding the blooms into place and turned to look at him. 'I have no idea,' I replied in a tight voice, which really

68

should have warned him against pursuing this any further. 'He's a writer, so maybe he's just good at doing research? Surely you don't have a problem with this?'

Richard looked flustered at the challenging note and I could tell he might already be regretting everything he'd said since he had arrived. Unfortunately his next comment wasn't much better. 'Still, it's kind of weird, isn't it? Him tracking you down like this, and sending this expensive display? It's all a bit stalker-ish, isn't it?'

I carefully laid down the sharp scissors I'd been using to snip the blooms before I answered. It's never wise to get angry while holding sharp implements. 'Well, I don't know, Richard, let me think. First he comes along and rescues me from the accident, then he saves my life when the car explodes, and now he has the nerve to just go and send me flowers. D'you know what, I think you're right. The guy's clearly deranged. Perhaps I should get a restraining order?'

'I was just saying—' he began, but I was quick to interrupt.

'Well don't.' I picked up the scissors and cut short a stem and the conversation in one decisive snip.

Six blooms later, I realised I had been unnecessarily short with him. I looked up and saw him watching me carefully, unsure of whether the argument had run its course or was just taking a breather.

'Sorry,' I said, breaking the deadlock, 'I may have over-reacted.'

'You reckon?'

I felt the tension running away like raindrops down a windowpane.

'And I might have been a jerk,' he admitted, holding out his arms.

'You reckon?' I replied, slotting against him and feeling some more of the nerve-jangling tension ebb away as his hold around me tightened.

'I've had such an awful day. It was so sad having to cancel everything for the wedding, and visiting Amy's parents and seeing them so torn up just broke my heart,' I confided into the soft fabric of his shirtfront. 'But that's no excuse to take it out on you. I'm sorry.'

'That's what I'm here for,' he soothed against my hair.

When I carried the vase with Jack's flowers to the table, I could still make out a lingering look of distaste on Richard's face as he surveyed the display.

'What is it you don't like – the fact that he sent me flowers, or him?'

'Him.'

His terse reply was really no surprise. 'But why? You don't even *know* him,' I reasoned.

Richard leaned back against the kitchen cupboards and gave a deep sigh. I noticed he didn't quite manage to meet my eyes as he admitted, 'I don't like how he makes me feel.'

Strangely, I felt exactly the opposite, but wisely didn't share that thought. Instead I went to stand directly in front of him, forcing him to look at me as I took both his hands in mine. 'What do you mean?'

Richard now focused his gaze over the top of my head, so that he appeared to be talking to the coffee maker as he reluctantly replied, 'He makes me feel guilty and inadequate. It should have been *me*; I should have been the one looking after you, rescuing you, comforting you, not some total stranger. But while the woman I love was going through the worst ordeal imaginable, where was I? What was I doing? Drinking, laughing, having a great old time.'

'You weren't to know. How could you? Can't you just be grateful that someone came along? Surely it doesn't matter who that someone was?'

He gave a small ghost of a smile. 'No, I guess not.' He pulled me back into his arms, and I really don't know if he intended me to hear the words he muttered softly into my hair. 'I just wish it hadn't been *him*.'

It took me ten minutes to get out of my car, and a further five to summon up the courage to slide the key Amy's parents had given me into the lock, and enter her flat. I'd volunteered for this task in order to spare her mother the pain of doing it, but I hadn't considered how hard it was going to be, being the first one to cross the threshold since her death.

I stepped on to a small scattering of post which had already begun to accumulate in the days since her death. I stooped to pick it up, noticing that most of it appeared to be credit card or store card statements. Despite the situation, I smiled. Amy's philosophy on credit had always been that if they didn't want her to have debt, the companies shouldn't keep on giving her cards. I placed the stack of bills on the kitchen worktop, next to a coffee cup ring that hadn't been wiped away. For some reason that struck me as incredibly sad, and I rubbed the brown circular ghost of the beverage away with my finger. The open plan kitchen and living area was quiet, except for the constant hum of the fridge in the corner of the room, and that's what felt wrong: the silence. Amy was *never* quiet. There was always music playing, or a blaring television, or frequently both. She was an extrovert, with enough confidence for ten people, yet still she had always hated being alone, hated the silence of solitude. I visualised her now, lying on a cold aluminium table somewhere in the dark and the quiet, and felt a body-blow of grief rock through me.

I looked around me at the one-bedroom apartment that was the very *essence* of Amy. There she was in the wall of framed movie posters, and the vivid mismatched scatter cushions on the settee, and of course she was easily found in the unwashed plates stacked up on the draining board and the pile of laundry heaped beside the washing machine. I looked sadly at the clothes that would never need to be washed, and it reminded me of the purpose of my visit. I grabbed a square of kitchen roll and furiously wiped at my eyes.

Looking for an excuse to put off searching through Amy's wardrobe, I set to work tidying up the kitchen, washing the dishes and wiping down the counter-tops with a thoroughness I suspected they rarely saw. This was all so much more Caroline's area of expertise than mine, but I knew that the third member of our trio was only hanging on by her fingernails, and there was no one else to lift this weight from Amy's parents, except me.

'Oh Amy,' I cried to the empty flat, loving her and hating her for leaving us in equal measure.

I found a roll of black bin bags beneath the sink and unfurled one, taking it over to the fridge. Amy wasn't one for eating at home, but even I was surprised at the scarcity of food. Aside from a punnet of grapes, some fancy-sounding cheese, whose name I couldn't pronounce, and a carton of milk, there was nothing in the way of fresh produce that I needed to dispose of. Of course, the six bottles of wine chilling in readiness on the shelves hadn't left her a great deal of room for actual food. I knew, without looking, that the freezer would be full of ready meals and the top drawer of the kitchen unit would be overflowing with takeaway menus. Caroline would have thrown her arms in the air in despair.

Eventually I ran out of tasks to keep me in the kitchen and walked slowly towards Amy's bedroom. The smell of her favourite perfume was detectable in the air the second I opened the door. I closed my eyes and savoured it; for an intoxicating moment it was almost as if she was there beside me. But when I stepped into the room the only reflection in the wall of mirrored wardrobe doors was my own.

Amy's shoes and accessories had spilled out of the wardrobe and each corner of the room held mini stacks of shoeboxes and plastic crates full of scarves, belts and handbags. I looked around me and felt a moment of despair. How on earth was I going to do this? Going through her drawers and cupboards was going to feel like a violation of her personal space and privacy. A sudden memory came to me, and it made me turn on my heel and return to the kitchen to unwind another bin bag from the roll. I was here to select an outfit for the funeral, but eventually Amy's mum and dad would be coming here to sort through her belongings, and there was something I needed to take care of before that happened. There were some things no parent should have to see.

I went to the bottom drawer of Amy's bedside cabinet and pulled it out and off its runners. Keeping my eyes deliberately focused elsewhere, I upended the contents of the drawer into the bag, hearing the items fall upon each other in a muted cascade. I remembered the night she had shown me her latest purchase, pulling it out of the self-same drawer I had just emptied into the refuse bag. Amy had waited until Caroline was out of earshot to show me the item, but we were both still giggling like school children when she had come back into the bedroom with a fresh bottle of wine to replenish the glasses we had drained.

'What's the joke?' she had asked, and instead of replying, Amy and I had just burst into another fit of adolescent giggles. She had looked at us both patiently, waiting for the laughter to subside, or for us to grow up, whichever was likely to happen sooner.

Eventually, I had composed myself enough to reply, 'Well, Caro, let's put it like this. You know how your bottom drawer is full of designer linens and towels...' Caroline nodded her head. 'Well, Amy has got one too...' Caroline began to smile in hopeful encouragement, until I finished, 'Except most of the stuff in hers won't work without batteries!' We had dissolved into the kind of laughter that is out of all propor-tion to the humour of the situation, and even Caroline had joined in, as we flopped back on the double bed, tears streaming from our eyes.

'You're impossible,' Caroline had chided Amy, only half joking. 'Who is that stuff for? You don't even have a regular boyfriend.'

'Duh. That's why I've got it,' Amy had teased, knowing Caroline would blush to the roots of her hair at her words. She didn't disappoint. 'When I get myself all fixed up like you two, I'm going to give it all to a charity shop!'

'Oh, I'm sure Help the Aged will be delighted!' I declared, and that had set the three of us off all over again.

I looked around the empty room as the echoes of the memory began to fade, and gave myself a mental shake. This was not getting the job done at all.

Amy's wardrobe was packed to capacity, with hangers

forced together so tightly that each garment had to be forcibly plucked out to free it from its neighbours. There was no division of style or category, so skimpy playsuits were hung between sparkly evening wear and work clothes. At least it explained why it had always taken her so long to get ready; she must have spent most of her time just trying to *find* her chosen outfit!

As I browsed through the rail, it began to occur to me that I might not find anything suitable. There were an awful lot of dresses and tops with quite low plunging necklines, or skirts so short that every time Amy bent over she was in danger of revealing the colour of her underwear. Only, there'd be no bending or moving in whatever I picked out that day. It was almost impossible to reconcile the idea of Amy, so vibrant and full of life in her sexy outfits, lying still and silent within a casket. I found the perfect dress and jacket squeezed in at the end of the rail. It was an outfit I didn't recollect ever having seen her wear. I pulled it out to examine it more closely, knowing even before I removed the protective cellophane sleeve covering it that it was going to be the one I chose. I recognised the name on the elegantly stitched label. It was one that featured in glossy magazines and was definitely not for sale in the high street. Whichever credit card this one had gone on must have taken a major hit with the purchase. The dress was classy and elegant and yet still sexy. It was tightly fitted and the neckline, although low, wasn't indecently plunging. The material was deep midnight blue, and I didn't need to check the label to know it was made of real silk. The outfit included a small tailored bolero jacket. It was the sort of outfit you bought for an incredibly fancy wedding or a really special occasion. I wondered if she'd ever even worn it.

It didn't take as long as I had feared to locate a pair of shoes to match the dress and jacket. Unsure of just how much I needed to assemble, I also found a set of designer underwear and a necklace for her to wear. For some reason it felt really important that Amy should make her entrance into the next world looking as good as possible. With that thought in mind, I wondered if I should get the dress dry-cleaned before delivering it to the funeral home. I carried it on its hanger to the window, to check for marks or stains that would need taking care of. Maybe I could just have it professionally pressed, I considered, then I could collect it later on today and drop it off at the funeral home, as arranged?

I ran my hand over the jacket, dipping into the two half pockets, to make sure they were empty. The first one was, but as my fingertips swept into the second one, I encountered a tiny square of folded paper, no bigger than a postage stamp. I pulled it out, and was about to toss it straight into the wastepaper bin when some curious instinct stopped me. Instead, I took hold of the tightly folded scrap and opened it. It was a piece of paper which looked as though it had been torn from the bottom of a notepad, for its edges were jagged and uneven. On the paper was a handwritten telephone number. A number I recognised.

I carried on packing up the items for the funeral directors, even throwing in a cosmetic bag, into which I put both her favourite shade of lipstick and her signature perfume. Yet all the time I was wondering why my best friend had my fiancé's work telephone number in her pocket. Why would she ever have had to call Richard at school? For a start, he was usually teaching, so it was virtually impossible to reach him. The number was a direct line to the Technology Faculty office

76

Richard shared with his colleagues, and I usually had to leave a message with one of them and hope someone remembered to deliver it.

All the way down to the car I could feel the small square of paper burning through the pocket of my jeans like an irritant. I wasn't concerned that Amy had Richard's work number in her possession, but I was puzzled. I was carefully reversing into a bay outside the dry cleaners when the answer came to me. That phone number wasn't just Richard's, it was used by *all* the members of his faculty. It hadn't been my fiancé who Amy had wanted to contact at all.

Caroline and I had spent much of the last year attempting to find Amy a new man. In Caroline's case this mission had become little short of an obsession, as she set Amy up on a string of blind dates with colleagues from her estate agent office and Nick's bank. Amy had gone on these dates good-naturedly enough, claiming that any man who wanted to buy her dinner was good enough company for an evening out. It wasn't the attitude Caroline had been hoping for, but it *was* typically Amy. Although Caroline and I had essentially been with our partners since our teens (give or take the five years Richard and I spent apart), Amy had always had a very different attitude to dating. With her looks and personality she had never been short of offers, but I don't think she'd had a single relationship that lasted longer than a couple of months. She claimed she got bored too easily, or felt too tied down, and in truth there was a moment you could recognise in each of her relationships, when the guy clearly wanted more of an emotional connection and commitment, and that was usually the point when she cut them loose. 'Like a fisherman, throwing them back to be free in the ocean,' she had described it, when

Caroline and I had despaired after one really hopeful-looking relationship had ended the same way as all the others. 'Being too damn picky is a more apt description,' Caroline had moaned, and Amy had just given that charming little shrug of hers. 'Anyway, he was kind of weird in bed,' she confided, knowing how much Caroline would hate having that fact for ever in her mind whenever she had to socialise with the guy, who was one of Nick's colleagues.

Not to be outdone, I had tried to persuade Richard to set Amy up with some of the single teachers at his school, but he'd been obstinately resistant. 'It's just too embarrassing to be pimping for your friend,' had been his excuse.

'It's hardly *pimping*,' I had countered, 'it's more like match-making.'

'Then that's worse.'

'How? Why?'

'It just is.'

And that had been the end of it, until a really good-looking teacher in his late twenties had joined the school last year. Richard's new colleague had passed by our group when we'd all been out for a drink, and even Amy – who was hard to impress – had to admit he was jaw-droppingly gorgeous. After much badgering, Richard had reluctantly agreed to have a discreet word with him and sound out if he was remotely interested in being 'treated like a bit of meat' as he had scornfully put it.

'Pot. Kettle. Black,' Caroline had succinctly said in response.

Now, having found the department's phone number in the pocket of Amy's fancy outfit, it looked as though something might actually have come of it after all. I wondered why she had never said anything about it, and what had happened. I realised, with incredible sadness, that I would never know.

CHAPTER 5

The church was packed to capacity, just as I knew it would be. We were in a pew not far from the front, and I was finding it extremely hard trying to look anywhere except at the waiting trestle stands positioned by the altar. It wasn't much better looking at the blown-up portrait of Amy that was displayed on an easel directly beside them. I don't know when the shot had been taken, but it was a lovely photograph, with Amy's skin sporting a soft tan and her hair blowing around her face like a honey-gold cloud. She was laughing at the camera and her eyes were shining brightly, and whoever had taken the picture had captured her in a way that was so achingly familiar that looking at the image was an actual physical pain.

It was inevitable, I knew, that the Travises would have picked this church for Amy's funeral. It was the local church, closest to where they had once lived, and it was the one where Amy herself had been christened as a baby. It was also the one where, in three days' time, Richard and I had planned to be married. I only hoped that my mother, who kept looking at Richard and me with such wistful sadness, would have enough restraint not to voice her regret at the cancellation to anyone today.

I turned around and surveyed the sea of sombre-clothed people behind us. So many of those present today had also been on the guest list to the wedding. How many of them were thinking of the very different ceremony they had been planning to attend? Bright-coloured clothes, with flamboyant hats, instead of black suits and ties; a choir singing out in celebration, instead of in sorrow; a service that produced smiles full of joy, instead of hearts full of grief. How many of them blamed Richard and me for being indirectly responsible for Amy's death? It wasn't a difficult equation: no wedding, no hen party, no crash, no funeral.

I swallowed the lump in my throat, which felt almost golf-ball sized, and stared intently at the column of late arrivals snaking in through the large oak doors. The pews were full, so I guessed most of them would have to observe the service from the rear of the church. I scanned the row of those already standing up against the back wall, my head going from left to right. The shock at seeing him there was so startling that I actually heard the small bones in my neck crick as I whipped my head around to check that I hadn't just imagined it. Standing tall and immaculately suited against the wall of the church was Jack Monroe.

I knew he'd seen me, had probably even noticed my look of wide-eyed surprise, but the only acknowledgement he gave was the merest inclination of his head. After a moment's hesitation, I nodded back. I turned around, about to mention it to Richard, but caught one look at his face and decided against it. Richard was not doing well. I knew from the moment he had picked me up that morning that he was only just holding it all together. There was a tightness around his mouth, as though every facial muscle was being held in rigid paralysis, lest it give away any trace of emotion. Once we were alone in his car, I had questioned anxiously, 'Are you all right?' He had looked at me bleakly.

'Not really. Are you?' I shook my head, yet still I was surprised at his reaction. 'I just don't do well at funerals,' was his eventual explanation, and as I'd never been to one with him before, and hoped not to again for a very long time, I had to accept his answer.

As much as you think you are ready for it, nothing prepares you for that moment when a shuffling silence descends on the church, the organist begins to play the first straining notes, and the pall-bearers begin their slow procession up the aisle. I reached down for Richard's hand and gripped it with ferocious intensity, trying to focus all my attention on the bones of our entwined fingers and skin, instead of on the shiny black casket with the gleaming silver handles, being held aloft on the shoulders of the six men, walking slowly past Amy's friends and family. One of them was Nick, and seeing his usual jovial expression replaced by one of such solemn concentration tugged at my heart. I wondered if Richard was regretting his decision not to be up there beside him. I had been surprised when Donald Travis had asked both men to be part of the funeral procession; and even more surprised when Richard had sorrowfully declined. Looking at him now, and feeling the tension rippling through his body as he surveyed the casket as it slowly passed by, I had to concede he'd probably made the right decision. He scarcely looked capable of holding himself upright, much less of carrying such a precious cargo. His comment that he didn't do well at funerals was an understatement.

After the casket was carefully lowered by the bearers on to the stand, I found it impossible to look anywhere else. I know there were prayers said, and hymns were sung, and I guess I must have stood up and sat down at the appropriate moments, but the whole event felt disjointed and unreal, as though we were caught up in the world's most vivid mass nightmare. It was an effort to stop myself from scrambling to my feet and shouting out my objection, that there'd been some dreadful mistake, and that Amy couldn't possibly be lying stiff and cold inside that shiny black casket. But it's only at weddings where you get the chance to object to the proceedings; at funerals you're just supposed to keep quiet and accept it all, however terrible it might be.

Donald's eulogy to his daughter was heartbreaking, loving and brave, and that he got through it at all is testimony to an inner strength I doubt many people possess. I didn't need to look around to know that pretty much every woman in the church had been moved to tears by his words; you could hear it in the rustle of tissues and the discreet sniffing. The men present weren't immune either, and even though Richard hadn't raised his head from the moment Amy's father had begun to speak, the occasional tremor in his shoulders gave him away. I was deeply touched that he was so moved, because I honestly didn't think I had ever seen him cry before. He wasn't given to public displays of emotion. Even when I had wept like a lost child when I'd broken up with him five years earlier, Richard's eyes had stayed stonily dry. Seeing him now, so openly vulnerable, was both unsettling and unfamiliar. I linked my arm through his and drew myself closer to his side, uniting us.

Finally the service was over, and the congregation got to their feet in a collective daze as Amy was lifted and carried away for her final journey. Richard and I joined the shuffling queue of mourners preparing to exit the church. Amy's parents were positioned just outside the main doors, to receive anyone wanting to offer some words of condolence or comfort, none of which would probably penetrate the white noise of their grief and pain. From the length of the line, it was going to take us a good ten minutes to reach them.

'I'm just going to have a quick word with someone,' I told Richard, giving his arm a brief squeeze. He nodded distractedly, not even looking around as I slipped away and began to weave through the pews to the rear of the church. Some of the mourners had already left by a small side exit, and initially I couldn't see him. Had he already gone? I mumbled 'Excuse me' repeatedly, as I squeezed past small clusters of people gathered around the exit.

'Emma.'

I turned, and found he was right behind me. He was much taller than I had remembered.

'Hi,' I replied, feeling an unexpected nervous flutter, somewhere at the back of my throat. I swallowed it down, and tried again. 'Hello, Jack. This is a surprise; I wasn't expecting to see you here today.' It wasn't exactly the most welcoming of greetings, but he didn't appear to take offence.

'I bumped into Caroline in town the other day and she mentioned when the service was. I wanted to come; it felt like the right thing to do. I hope that was okay?'

It wasn't my place to say either way, and if some might have questioned why he felt the need to be present, *I* understood totally. Around us were people from all areas of Amy's life, who undeniably had known her better, and for longer than Jack had done. But a connection had been forged on the roadside that night, one that tied him to me and Caroline, and to Amy. In a strange way he had even *more* right to be there than the mourners who hadn't seen Amy in years. I was just surprised that Caroline hadn't mentioned that she'd seen Jack again.

There was a look of genuine regret etched into his

handsome features. 'I just wish that I'd found you all sooner, or had been able to do something more…' His voice trailed away, and without stopping to consider whether it was appropriate or not, I reached over and grasped his hand in mine.

'I don't think finding us sooner would have made any difference to Amy. You did everything you could. More than most people would have done. If it weren't for you, I wouldn't be here today either.' The debt I owed him could never be repaid, and just saying 'Thank you' didn't even scratch the surface.

'How *are* you doing?' he asked gently, in a tone I recognised from the night of the accident. As he spoke, his eyes searched my face and I knew he wasn't looking for the visible scars, which were already much less prominent, but for the deeper ones, the ones which were going to take far longer to heal.

'I'm fine, just fine,' I replied, in a stupid knee-jerk response, like the one you give to a doctor when you're really sick and they ask how you are. I looked around at where I was, and then back up to meet his eyes, which were still studying me intently. There is something intrinsically wrong about lying when you're standing in the middle of a church. 'Actually, that's not true. I'm not fine at all. I'm bloody terrible, in fact.' You probably aren't meant to swear in church either, but fortunately both God and Jack seemed prepared to overlook it.

'It will get better,' he reassured me, giving the hand I hadn't realised he was still holding a gentle squeeze. 'I know it doesn't seem like that now, but trust me, it will.'

As crazy as it might sound, I *already* trusted him, even though I knew almost nothing about him. And because of that, I wanted to believe him, nearly as much as I wanted to continue holding on to his hand, which felt strongly comforting around mine, but that was wrong on so many levels that God was *never* going to let that one go. I carefully withdrew my fingers from his, and he instantly released me.

'Today has just felt like this enormously difficult and painful mountain we've all had to climb. I'm sure next week, when I'm back at work, things will be better.'

He nodded understandingly. 'Where is it that you work?'

'Just a bookshop in town,' I replied, and then felt struck by a double dose of guilt: for sounding dismissive of the job my boss Monique had generously created for me, and for talking about something as trivial and banal as work at Amy's funeral. What on earth was I thinking of?

'Just keep focusing on the future,' Jack advised, his eyes soft and warm as they looked down on me. 'Your wedding must be soon and—'

'It's cancelled,' I replied, hearing my choice of words and wondering what Freud would have made of the slip. 'I mean *postponed*. It's postponed.' I looked around sadly. 'Actually, it was going to be here. In three days' time.'

There were two expressions on his face at my words: one was sympathy, and the other one I couldn't identify at all. 'I'm sorry,' he replied eventually. 'That must make today even harder, for *both* of you.' His deliberate emphasis wasn't lost on me.

'Anyway, I should be getting back,' I said, glancing over my shoulder and noticing that Richard, Caroline and Nick had almost reached the huge oak church doors. 'Thank you again for coming today. You really *are* a good person.'

He smiled wryly, but said nothing. I turned to go, and had actually taken two steps before I remembered my slate still wasn't wiped clean with this man. 'I'm sorry, I almost forgot.

Thank you for the beautiful flowers, Jack. It was really thoughtful. I would have contacted you to thank you when they arrived, but I didn't know how to reach you.'

'I'm glad you got them all right,' he replied, before glancing over at Richard. 'I hope sending them to your home was okay? I didn't want to cause you any awkwardness.' Clearly he was referring to Richard's less-than-hospitable attitude when they had last met.

'No, no, no,' I refuted, aware I had used at least two too many noes to sound convincing. 'We *both* thought they were a really lovely gesture.'

I thought I saw a slight twitch of his lips when he heard my lie, but he did nothing to challenge it. For the first time I began to feel awkward.

'Well, goodbye then,' I said, and because just walking away felt wrong, I stepped back to him, leaned up and swiftly kissed his cheek, trying hard not to be aware of the aroma of his aftershave or the slight bristle of his skin as my lips grazed across it.

I walked back quickly to my fiancé and friends, and Caroline, who was the only one facing in the right direction to have seen my brief encounter, opened her mouth to say something as I approached. I darted a meaningful look at Richard and shook my head almost imperceptibly, before resuming my position in the queue, beside him. Caroline obediently closed her mouth on whatever she'd been about to say, while a look of understanding lit her eyes. Friends do that.

Loss is a funny thing. It was a word I heard a lot in those early days, from just about everyone I spoke to. 'I'm sorry for your loss' seemed to be the go-to phrase, followed by a good deal of arm patting, after which people started to look vaguely uncomfortable and unsure of what to do or say next. That's the trouble with death, there's no etiquette book on the protocol for grief or condolences. No one really knows how to react; also no one wants to get too close to the raw gaping wound that's visible on those left behind, as though – who knows – it might just be catching.

The dictionary defines loss as *the state of no longer having something because it has been taken from you or destroyed.* I guess that's fairly accurate. Except ever since the night of Amy's death she wasn't lost at all. She was everywhere.

She was in the silver bangle bracelet I wore every day, her gift to me on my eighteenth birthday. She was in the fast-food wrapper carelessly discarded on the floor of my car, when she'd insisted we pull into a drive-in for burgers after shopping for wedding shoes. She was in the mirror when I slipped earrings through my ears, because it was fourteen-year-old Amy who'd persuaded us to get them pierced, while Caroline had timidly refused to even enter the shop. She was the first name on the directory of my mobile phone, and I was *never* going to be able to delete that.

Amy wasn't gone at all. She was omnipresent, which was sometimes comforting, and could sometimes make me smile, but more often just made the pain of losing such a bright and beautiful flame the very worst tragedy I could ever imagine.

Someone who *was* lost, however, was Richard. Well, not in the real and physical sense, but definitely missing. In the days before the funeral, when I was still off work, he had come straight from school to our house each afternoon, and I could chart the change in him like the world's most depressing graph. It was as though a doppelgänger Richard had invaded our lives. The person who sat at our table for dinner each night, or beside me on the couch as we stared unseeingly at the television, was not the same man who had slipped the diamond ring on my finger on Christmas Day. Although I'd unburdened my grief in Richard's arms many times since Amy's death, I felt as though he was holding back from me. For the first time in our relationship, past and present, I couldn't get to the source of the problem. 'What does he say when you ask what's wrong?' Caroline had asked, setting down two mugs of coffee on her kitchen table – and a plate of biscuits, that neither of us would touch. Appetite, that was something else we both seemed to have lost since Amy's death, and in consequence a fair amount of weight. My wedding dress would probably hang off me now, I remember thinking, and then braced myself against the onslaught of grief when I thought of the two midnight blue bridesmaids' dresses, hanging in their cellophane shrouds in our spare room.

'Emma?'

I'd shaken my head, trying to jostle my thoughts back to Caroline's question. Attention deficit. Another loss. 'Sorry. My concentration is shot to pieces these days. I think it must be lack of sleep.' Loss of sleep, the list just kept growing.

'Richard says nothing is wrong,' I had replied eventually. 'He says it's just his way of dealing with things.'

The solution to the problem came from an unexpected source, when a teacher at his school had fallen ill, leaving them without a leader for a skiing trip.

'Of course I said no when they asked if I could stand in,' he explained.

Richard was the obvious person to have asked. He and his whole family had skied for as long as I could remember.

'Tell them you've changed your mind, that you'll do it.'

He'd looked shocked at my suggestion. 'But I can't go. I can't leave you now. You *need* me here.' But behind the protests there had been a look in his eyes like a prisoner who'd seen an open jail door, which was slowly closing shut.

I reached for his hand, curling my fingers through his. 'Go. I think you need to get away. I'll be fine. I'm back at work next week and I have Caroline and Nick and Mum and Dad. It's only ten days.'

He had pulled me towards him and kissed me with more enthusiasm than he'd shown in several weeks. That alone told me I'd just done the right thing.

Working in a bookshop can hardly be termed as arduous, but apparently the simple task of standing behind a counter and interacting with the general public was still too much for me to cope with – according to my employer, that was.

Monique, my boss, had been on the second rung of a small stepladder, filling shelves with glossy hardback books when I walked into the shop on my first day back. She swayed a little alarmingly on the ladder, and I instinctively dashed forwards. She batted away the hand I held out to her, but stepped down to envelop me in a massive hug. She wrapped her short plump arms around me, the voluminous sleeves of her kaftan billowing around us like massive floral sails. Her dangling shell earrings caught in my hair, and I was grateful that by the time I had disentangled myself, the tears her greeting had generated were almost gone.

'Now why the fuck have you come back so soon?' There were two things I loved about Monique: that despite living in the UK for over forty years she still had a thick French accent; and that she swore like a sailor. To hear them both in her opening sentence had been a double treat.

'I need to keep busy. Being at home gives me too much time to think,' I confessed. I smiled sadly at the woman in front of me. She was more than just my employer; she was a confidante and friend.

She nodded, and the shell earrings clattered like mini percussion instruments. 'Your fiancé called me before he left on his trip, did he tell you that?'

'Richard phoned you? Why?' Her words were surprising, for it was a poorly kept secret that they didn't particularly like each other. Monique was the only person who had looked less than delighted when she heard I had accepted Richard's proposal.

'Ah ha! I suspected you did not know this,' my boss declared, sounding like Poirot and looking like Miss Marple. 'He said that I should look out for you and not work you too hard. Pwah! As if I am an imbecile who had to be told these things.'

'I think his meaning may have got lost in translation,' I suggested, instinctively springing to Richard's defence.

Monique gave me a long hard look and I realised again how many people underestimated this woman with her apparently broken English and heavy accent. I knew only too well she had perfect command of my native tongue as well as her own. I'd seen her reading highly complex English literature with complete understanding and knew that long ago, for reasons she chose not to disclose, she had decided to conceal this fluency.

She softened then, and I saw the sympathy shining brightly in her hazel eyes. 'Take time to heal, my Emma. All will be well, but it will take time.'

I nodded dumbly and with no conscious thought tumbled

into her open arms, as she held me against her pillowy bosom in the way my own mother hadn't been able to do, with any real meaning, for the longest time.

It was midday on Thursday and I had already drunk my fourth cup of coffee and was starting to climb the walls with boredom and caffeine overdose when Monique entered the back room, making a big show of mysteriously shutting the door behind her.

'Tell me the truth, Emma, are you in trouble with the law?'

I looked at her blankly for several seconds. 'What? No, of course not,' I replied, trying to think if I'd even got as much as a parking fine in recent years. 'Why do you ask?'

'Because there is a man in the shop asking if you work here. He looks extremely serious and actually rather 'andsome. But he is American, and wearing sunglasses on a dull day, so I figure he must be FBI.'

My heart inexplicably began to beat faster, and it wasn't because I was afraid I was about to be apprehended as an international felon. 'What did he say, exactly?' I asked, already getting to my feet and stepping out from behind the desk.

'I already told you. He asked if you worked here. I said yes. He said could he speak with you. We didn't make the chit-chat.'

I went to open the door that led to the back of the shop, pausing at the small mirror hung by the coat hooks on the wall. I smoothed down my hair, making sure the newly cut fringe covered the scar on my forehead, and ran a finger under each eye to check for smudged mascara. Monique watched with open interest and fascination.

'What?' I challenged, as her scrutiny transformed into a knowing smile.

'Nothing. I say nothing at all,' she replied with a very Gallic shrug of her shoulders.

He had his back to me when I entered the shop, with Monique only two steps behind. Not for her the discretion of leaving us alone for a moment or two of privacy. She was far too curious to see who my visitor was. It would serve her damn well right if he *had* come to arrest me; and her too for harbouring a criminal!

'Jack,' I said in greeting, pleased to hear that my voice sounded relatively normal.

He was smiling as he turned, and I could easily see how he had earned Monique's ''andsome' classification. He was dressed casually, in jeans and a plain white shirt, with the sleeves rolled up to reveal arms that I had good reason to know were every bit as strong as they looked. I was suddenly glad that the bruises on my legs had faded enough to allow me to wear a dress to work that day, even though I'd thought the only person who would see it was my slightly eccentric French employer.

Sometime during Monique's absence, Jack must have pocketed the sunglasses, for it was easy to see the warmth in his eyes as he left the display stand he had been studying, and walked up to the counter.

'I remembered you said you work in a bookshop, and as I have some research to do for my novel, I thought I'd try and source a book on the subject.'

I could have questioned why he hadn't used the internet, which surely would have provided him with whatever answers he needed to find, but that would have sounded like I wasn't pleased to see him. And I was. Perhaps more than I should be.

'Well you've definitely come to the right place,' I said with a smile. 'For books, I mean... we have books here.' Dear

God, I was actually babbling. I cleared my throat and tried to sound a little more professional. 'Are you looking for any book in particular?'

'What? Oh yes. Something on local lakes, if you have one.'

I stepped out from behind the counter, extremely glad that I'd worn heels and not flats, when I stood beside him. He was so tall he actually made me feel petite, which was quite a pleasant novelty.

'Are you writing a book about sailing?' I enquired politely, walking over to the stack which held our local geographical volumes.

'No. Actually, it's about a murder. I need a lake deep enough to hide a body in.'

'Of course,' I replied smoothly, shooting Monique a furious glare at the small eruption of laughter that escaped from her lips. She was making absolutely no pretence at being other-wise occupied, and had settled herself on the stool behind the counter to observe us, as though watching an episode of her favourite soap.

'Do you write crime thrillers?' I asked, because that's what I *would* ask him, if I hadn't already Googled him extensively, checked out the catalogue of titles he had released, and was actually awaiting delivery of a copy of his first book. I blamed Monique for that, leaving me alone with the internet and not enough to do to keep me busy.

'Mostly, yes,' he confirmed, moving to stand beside me at the rack of books. I could smell again the distinctive after-shave he wore, not in an oppressive wave, but as a subtle undertone to a smell that I guessed would be called 'manly' if we were in a trashy romance novel. The thought sobered me. I wasn't a character in a novel. And it really didn't matter how handsome or mysterious Jack might appear to me,

Monique, or anyone. I was engaged to someone else, and I had no business thinking the kind of thoughts that kept coming unbidden into my mind whenever he was around.

'We have a couple that I think might be suitable,' I continued, pulling two large colourful hardbacks from the shelf and passing them to him. He scanned the front covers for a brief moment, and scarcely even glanced at the blurbs on the back.

'This one will be fine,' he said, passing me the more expensive of the two. It was, actually, probably the best choice for what he was looking for, but he couldn't possibly have realised that from such a cursory glance. He followed me back to the counter, and must have seen the meaningful glare I threw Monique, when still she didn't move from her stool-top sentry post and actually forced me to squeeze behind her to reach the till. She smiled beatifically at Jack and then me. I rang up the purchase, took the notes he held out, and was extremely careful that I counted back the change into his outstretched palm without once touching his skin. I passed his book across the counter, wrapped in tissue paper and nestled within one of the shop's distinctive colourful bags, hoping Monique hadn't noticed that I'd stretched out the entire transaction for just a minute or two longer than necessary.

'It was really nice seeing you again,' I said truthfully.

'And you,' he responded with a smile that did an anatomically improbable thing with my stomach. 'Actually, I was wondering if you had time to join me for a bite to eat.' He glanced at the expensive-looking watch on his wrist. 'What time is your break?'

'We don't usually stop for lunch,' I explained sadly. 'As it's only the two of us, we tend to just work through.'

'No, we don't,' corrected Monique, deciding now was the moment to join in the conversation. I couldn't actually call her a liar out loud, but the look on my face screamed it as though from a megaphone. She blinked mildly back at me. 'All of the employees must now take a one-hour lunch break – it is something the unions require.' Oh. My. God. Could she be even the *slightest* bit less obvious?

'Really?' I asked. 'Strange that I didn't know this, considering the only employees here are you and me, and neither of us belong to a union.'

Monique made a highly distinctive French noise which was somewhere between a dismissive spit and a cough. 'You cannot argue with the unions.'

I shook my head at her bald-faced interference. I'd always known she disapproved of my relationship with Richard, but openly encouraging me to go to lunch with another man was something new. However, she had left me with no option but to accept Jack's invitation. 'I'll just get my jacket,' I said, disappearing into the back room. By the time I emerged, Monique was busy serving a new customer, so thankfully could add no further meddling to the situation.

Jack held open the door for me, and the moment we were outside I turned to him in apology. 'I am *truly* sorry about that. Monique can be quite opinionated at times.'

'She *does* seem to be quite a character,' Jack admitted with a grin. 'Have you worked there for long?'

'Since I was sixteen,' I replied, 'on and off.' He looked puzzled. 'It's a long story.'

'Then you will have to speak fast,' he advised, 'because I hear the union is only giving you an hour for lunch.'

We walked past a parade of shops before Jack gently asked, 'So how have things been with you, Emma?' I bit my lip on the automatic 'Fine' rejoinder that I seemed to give to everyone who asked me that question these days. His golden brown eyes held me prisoner, and I knew instinctively that I couldn't lie to him; he'd see through me in an instant.

'Hard. It's been hard. And painful. Some days are better than others...' My voice trailed away and he smiled gently, reaching for my hand and squeezing it briefly. I knew then that he saw through my protective shield as though it wasn't even there.

'Let's make this one of those then, shall we?' he suggested gently, and my heart gave a ridiculous skip and skittered weirdly within my chest. 'So, where do you recommend we go for lunch?' His abrupt return to the mundane was a welcome relief. 'Is there somewhere here in town? If not, my car's just around the corner.'

I glanced up and down the high street. There were several places where we could eat. But it was a small town, and people loved to gossip, and even though I had nothing at all to hide, I still didn't want to be the object of idle speculation. Speculation that could easily get back to Richard and hurt him.

'There's a nice pub about five minutes' drive away. The ploughmans there are delicious,' I suggested.

'I have absolutely no idea what you just said, but as long as it doesn't involve me eating some poor farm worker, then let's go.'

'So is your thriller going to be set in Hallingford?' I asked, as we wove along the narrow country lanes. Jack handled the large car skilfully, pulling up on to the bank to allow a tractor to pass.

'Not specifically, but getting a feel for the area will definitely help.'

'Well, I've lived here for most of my life, so if there's anything you want to know, you can always ask. About the area, I mean, not my life.' I was babbling again and I could hear the nerves in my voice, even if he couldn't. Why had I agreed to have lunch with him if it was making me feel so guilty? I think I knew the answer to that, and it was largely tied up with how Richard would react if he knew where I was right now. Perhaps a better question to have asked was why was *Jack* here? What was his reason for seeking me out?

Jack took his hand briefly from the wheel and clasped mine, which was nervously plucking some invisible piece of lint from my dress. I visibly jumped at his touch. What was the matter with me?

'Relax, Emma. We're not doing anything wrong here,' he said, surprising me, as usual, by being able to read me like an open book. 'We're just a couple of friends having lunch, that's all.'

His words seemed to be patently underscoring that he had someone special in his life, someone important. Well that was good, because I had one of those too.

'Oh, I know that,' I assured him, because I really didn't want him to think I'd read more into this invitation than there was. 'I think Monique's meddling just got me a little rattled. I guess she's more against Richard and me as a couple than she's ever let on.'

'Interesting,' Jack mused, negotiating the large hire car into a minute parking space at the pub with great accomplishment. 'You really *will* have to talk fast today to tell me everything.'

In the end we scarcely touched on any topic that crossed the borderline into personal territory, or the tragedy on the night we'd met. Perhaps I could even tell Richard about this meeting, knowing I'd not said or done anything that would cause him a moment's worry. That was how everything appeared on the surface, at least. On a separate lower level, I was experiencing some pretty unsettling sensations that I knew I couldn't share with him. Like the way the skin on my back had burned like fire as Jack steered me through the crowded bar. Or how my heart began to beat faster when he studied my face as I spoke, or how something warm lit up inside me when he laughed at some small quip or joke I had made.

I had just finished recounting some crazy and embarrassing story about Monique, and Jack was still laughing as he leaned across the table for his drink and his hand brushed mine. That was the moment when the crowded pub and the noise of its patrons faded away, and for just a second it felt as though the air itself had been sucked out of the room, in the way a raging fire can draw oxygen from a space. His eyes met mine and suddenly there was no laughter. He looked as shocked as I was. Fire was a good analogy here, as was heat. They were both present in abundance, and playing with them was dangerous, only a fool didn't know that.

I was the first to speak. 'Well, it's getting late. I really should be getting back, or they'll kick me out of that union... or something.'

He gave a smile of understanding, and I know he too had felt something, and knew why I was running away before I was scorched. 'Let's get you back then.'

In the mirror of the ladies', I saw the flush on my cheeks and the dilated pupils in my eyes. There was no point in denying the unexpectedly powerful connection I felt with Jack, but I was certain it was just a natural by-product of the intense situation when we'd first met, and because he'd saved my life. It was unique and extreme, and it was really dangerous and stupid to confuse it with any other type of attraction. There were probably books written on the subject, about how your whole life and perspective changes after a near-death experience. And when a total stranger puts their life in jeopardy to save yours, that has to forge some kind of intense bond between the two of you, doesn't it? I resolved to check it out on the internet as soon as I got back to the shop.

Jack pulled up directly outside the bookshop, leaving no awkward or ambiguous privacy to say goodbye. As I turned to release my seat belt, I noticed two large carrier bags on the back seat of his car, each bearing a logo from Monique's competitors in town. Without asking permission, I reached over and pulled them both into the front. Jack said nothing to stop me, but his face bore a small wincing expression as though he was preparing for a blow. I pulled out a book from the first bag and instantly recognised it as the exact same one I had sold him just over an hour ago. I reached into the second bag and withdrew its contents, the same book. I said nothing; I let my cocked head and raised eyebrows do the talking.

'Well, who knew there were going to be *three* bookshops in a town this small?' he eventually supplied. I felt a smile starting to unfurl and bit down on my lip to stop it.

'And the books?'

'Ah well, I actually *did* want that particular volume about the lakes. So when they told me in the first shop that you didn't work there, I thought the least I could do was buy the book from them.'

'And the second shop?'

'Likewise,' he said, with a small guilty grin.

It was no use. There was no way I could get that smile under control. 'And you never thought to ask for a *different* book, in shop number two or three?'

He looked even more shamefaced at that one. 'That *would* have made more sense,' he conceded, 'it just didn't occur to me. Lack of imagination, I guess.'

'That's got to be a major disadvantage in your profession,' I lamented, releasing my seat belt and getting out of the car. I could still hear him laughing as he pulled away from the kerb.

THE END

PART TWO

The tea in the cup beside me had grown cold. There were now several unattractive dark splotches floating on its surface. I wasn't usually so easily distracted.

I thought about going downstairs to make a fresh one, but the kitchen of my family home was already full to bursting with our visiting guests and relatives. Besides, was anyone supposed to see me until the church ceremony? I couldn't remember the etiquette. I put the cup back down on my bedside table. There would be more than enough to eat and drink at the hotel reception. The caterers had come highly recommended and the menu they had suggested for today was perfect. That, at least, had been one less thing we had had to plan.

I had a fleeting moment of panic when I glanced at the clock and then an even greater one when I turned back to my dressing table mirror. My hand flew to my throat and I gasped, because suddenly it wasn't my own familiar image staring back at me, but that of a much older woman, her face softly lined, her skin no longer firm and smooth. There were grooves fanning from the edges of her eyes and time had scored etch marks beside her mouth, which was open in shocked surprise. It was my mother. I was so startled by the vision of her that I actually turned and looked over my shoulder to see if she was standing behind me. But the room, of course, was empty.

I looked back into the glass and reached out my hand to its surface, my fingers longing to trace the shape of her face, the sweep of her hair, still rich in colour, but when I made contact with the mirror she disappeared, and I was back there in her place.

CHAPTER 6

I knew that something was wrong as soon as I pulled into my parents' drive that evening. And if the front door flung wide open, despite the pelting rain, wasn't enough of an alert, then hearing my father's frantic shouts as I raced towards the house confirmed it.

I opened the driver's door almost before the handbrake was fully engaged, and although I knew I was moving at speed, everything seemed slowed down and dreamlike. The illusion shattered as my dad burst through the front door like a charging bull. His hair was dishevelled and wet, so I knew his search had already extended beyond the interior of the house. His eyes were what scared me though; wild and desperate, as though he was already tumbling down into a steep well of panic. I tried to force myself to breathe calmly and evenly, but it wasn't easy. Panic is as infectious as the plague, and just as deadly.

'What's wrong?' I asked, grabbing hold of both of his arms and forcing him to stop his headlong charge back into the rain, to look at me. It was a stupid question. I knew exactly what was wrong, so hastily amended it. 'How long has she been missing?' He shook his head so hard that little droplets of rain showered down from his hair. 'I don't know. Fifteen minutes... twenty... maybe even longer. Oh God, I just don't know.'

'Calm down, Dad. Breathe. Just tell me what happened.'

'It's all my fault. She was fast asleep in the armchair, she nodded off during her programme, you know how she does?' I nodded, impatient to cut through the details that would do nothing to help us find her. 'I had a couple of letters that needed to catch the post. And she was so soundly asleep that it seemed a shame to wake her to come with me, so I just thought, it's only five minutes to the post box, I'll be back before she knows I've even gone. But then I bumped into that Debbie woman from the chemist, and you know how she likes to talk… and then, when I got back here the door was wide open…'

'It's all right, Dad. We'll find her. We always do.' *Until, of course, the time comes when we don't*, a voice whispered in my head. 'Have you searched the house?'

'Yes.'

'Every room?' He gave me a withering look. 'Sorry. Of course you have. All right, we'll split up. You take the street and then if you don't find her there, try the path that leads down to the forest for that walk she likes, okay?'

He pulled himself together with a visible effort. 'I'm sorry, Emma.'

I gave him a quick hard hug. 'It's not your fault, Dad. You know that. You can't watch her twenty-four/seven. It's just not possible.' There was a granite-like determined glint in his eyes, which I knew meant he totally refuted my words, but now was neither the time nor the place to rehash the argument we'd been having on and off for almost all of the last year.

'I'll try the school first,' I told him, already turning to go, 'and if she's not there, I'll call you and we can work out where to look next.'

'Do you think we should phone the police?'

I shook my head. 'It's too soon for that, Dad. It's not even been half an hour. Let's try all the likely places first and see where we go from there.'

I turned on my heel and raced back to my car. Phoning the police was extreme, a last resort, and hopefully a totally unnecessary option. *This* time. But there was going to come a day when we didn't find my mum walking around, lost and confused somewhere near her home. It was just a question of when.

It was difficult driving so slowly on the route to the school, when every instinct was telling me to put my foot to the floor and get there as fast as possible. But I knew from experience that I needed to keep my attention on not just the road ahead of me, but also on the pavements and even the front gardens of the houses flanking either side of the street. The last time I had found her in someone's garden, sitting on a child's swing, idling swaying backwards and forwards, without any comprehension or idea of the panic her disappearance had caused. But at least Richard had been driving on that occasion, so it had been much easier to scan through the hedges and bushes that hid the properties from view.

As satisfied as I could be that she wasn't in any of the gardens I had driven past, I turned left on to the main road and headed for one of the places which drew her like a magnet. I shuddered as a van overtook me, sending a cascade of muddy rainwater down my windscreen. This was my nightmare, my real dread. That she would just walk out into the road. While this illness was busy robbing you of your personal identity and memories, did it bother leaving you the rather vital instinct of self-preservation? How far down the slippery slope did you have to tumble before you didn't know any better than to step out in front of a speeding vehicle?

My hands gripped the steering wheel like talons, as the fear I hadn't let my father see coursed through me like a virus. And I was angry too, not at Dad, never at him. All he was trying to do was hang on to Mum for as long as he could; I knew that better than anyone. No, I was mad – way beyond mad – I was *furious* with myself. I'd been so absorbed in myself recently, I hadn't been paying attention where I should have been. These 'episodes' that Mum had normally came with a set of warning signs. She'd become even more woolly or forgetful and emotional and if nothing else, it at least made us all even more watchful. But I'd been so distracted with the accident and losing Amy, worrying about Richard's strange behaviour, and the disquieting feelings – which I was trying to ignore – that I was feeling for Jack, that I'd taken my eye off the ball. Big time. And now here was the wake-up call. Hopefully, please God, not too late. I shouldn't be giving head space to things I couldn't change, and certainly not to some pathetic schoolgirl crush. *This* was real. *This* was what I'd come home for, to help.

I pulled into the school's sweeping forecourt and instantly let out a grateful cry of relief. I stepped on the brakes and pulled my mobile from my pocket. 'She's here, Dad. I've found her.'

There was a long moment of silence, which I knew he was using to compose himself, and when he eventually spoke his voice was unusually gruff. 'Thank God. Just bring her home. And Emma... drive safely.'

Anxious not to spook her, I slowed my car down to a crawl and pulled into one of the parking bays beside the Art

Department. The rain was still pounding down with vicious intensity, and Mum had no coat on. I pulled a plaid picnic blanket from the back seat and got out into the driving rain. She looked up at my approach, and I covered the last of the distance between us with deliberate nonchalance. I knew how to play this.

'Hi, Mum. What are you doing?' Unfortunately the casual tone I was striving for was lost when I looked down and saw she was still wearing the pink bobble-front slippers I had bought her for Christmas. Only now they looked like sodden and squelchy furry road-kill. And *that* was what started me crying – not the Alzheimer's that had stolen my mother from me, not the fear that I felt every time she went missing, but the stupid ruined slippers. I brushed the tears away angrily with the back of my hand, hoping she would think it was raindrops I was wiping away.

'I've lost my keys, Emma,' she explained, indicating the upended handbag, whose contents were scattered in a metre-wide circle on the tarmac. It reminded me of that game that we used to play at children's parties, Kim's Game I think it was called, where you memorise a whole load of inconsequential items. The one with the best memory won the game. Guess there were no prizes for working out who today's biggest loser would be?

I dropped into a crouch and began to gather up the random belongings housed in Mum's bag: purse (with no money in it, because she never went shopping alone); a wallet full of credit cards (all cancelled, just in case she did); her favourite brand of perfume (which still reminded me of my childhood and being held close in her arms whenever I smelled it); and a dozen other bits of handbag paraphernalia. I scooped all of it into the already waterlogged bag. The only thing I *didn't* pick up were the keys she had been looking for, the keys to the Art Department. Because she hadn't had those for over three years, since she stepped down from being Head of Art and then from teaching altogether, as the symptoms of her illness became harder to ignore. She hadn't worked here for a very long time indeed. But sometimes she forgot that.

I was very glad the Easter weekend offered me time to do some serious thinking and prioritising. And priority number one, which I sadly realised I had been neglecting recently, was my mum. That my father and I had both had a bad night's sleep was obvious by the matching dark circles beneath our eyes the following morning. But when Mum had gone for her morning shower and I tentatively tried to raise the topic, I was met by his usual resistance.

'Dad, you have to see that we can't go on much longer like this,' I had begun cautiously, once I knew she was definitely out of earshot.

There was a dangerous obstinacy in his eyes as he raised them to mine. That's where I got my stubborn streak from, or so Mum used to tell me, before she lost the key to the treasure trove of a lifetime's memories.

'Emma, I am not getting into this again. I am *not* going to put your mum in a home. Not while there is still breath left in my body.'

'No one is saying that, Dad. But there are other options out there: day care, carers, organisations who understand what we're going through. You can't do this alone any more. No one could. I know you think you're protecting her, but what you're really doing is risking your own health. I worry about you, I don't want you making yourself ill again.'

His eyes clouded at my words, as we both thought back to the incident twelve months earlier, the one which had prompted my return home. I could still see him, grey faced and drawn, wired up to monitors at the local hospital as we waited to learn if his collapse had been due to a heart attack. That time it had just been angina, brought on by stress. *Just*. Next time he might not be so lucky.

'I know you're worried about me, and I love you for it, and for the way you put everything on hold to come back and help me. But this decision isn't yours to make. It's mine.'

I sighed, and stirred the cooling coffee in the cup before me as I struggled to find an argument I hadn't already attempted a hundred times before. 'But if we found a really good place that could take her for just a few days a week? Just to give you a break when I'm not living here any more?' I suggested, already knowing he would shoot down the idea before it had taken flight.

I was right. He couldn't have looked more horrified if I'd proposed he run off with one of the neighbours for a dirty weekend. '*What?* And just leave her there, like she was a dog we were dropping off at the kennels, because we want to go away and enjoy ourselves?'

I pushed the coffee cup aside and reached for his hand, noticing obliquely how much more pronounced the wrinkles on the back of it were, than just a short while ago. He was aging faster than he should, and his retirement was now totally occupied with his unplanned new role as a twenty-four-hour carer for the woman he still loved with all his heart.

'When it all gets too much, I'll let you know,' he advised, trying to temper his words with a grateful smile. 'And having you and Richard around to help has made everything so much easier. And you won't be that far away, even after you're married.'

There was a noise in my head, and it sounded an awful lot like a steel prison door clanging shut, but I didn't let it show on my face as I gave my hopelessly optimistic and loving parent an answering smile. 'No, we'll be right here,' I promised.

Mum's illness had all started so innocuously. Such a silly little incident, that I had no way of realising its foreboding significance. I had just returned from Washington and had come down from London to spend the weekend at home. I'd been looking forward to a quiet family meal, but actually what I got was a full-scale intervention, masquerading as Sunday lunch. 'What, no fatted calf?' I remember joking, as I opened the oven door and saw the enormous joint of beef roasting in its tin. 'Christ, Mum, there's only three of us for lunch, you and Dad are going to be eating leftovers for days.' She had looked a little abashed then, as she'd gathered up an armful of cutlery from the drawer. That should have alerted me that it wasn't just us for lunch. 'Actually, I've asked the Withers to join us too, to celebrate your return.' She'd made a very hasty exit to the dining room, and with good reason. My face had probably been a very eloquent picture of just how I was feeling. It was too much to hope that she hadn't included Richard in the invitation. Of course she would have. I wondered if Sheila, Richard's mum, was in on it too? Neither of them had been shy about expressing their regret when we'd broken up, but this degree of matchmaking was taking things to a whole new level. I recall wondering if Richard was as much in the dark as I had been. Oh, this was going to make for a *delightful* lunch, I had thought.

Then I'd heard my mum's sharp cry of distress from the dining room. I dropped the oven gloves I'd been holding and ran to her aid, all anger gone. As I dashed across the hall, horrible visions of injury or heart attacks ran with me. But what had met me wasn't the sight of my strong and capable mum physically debilitated. Instead, she had been standing at the head of the polished dining room table with the cutlery scattered in front of her, like a shiny silver mountain.

'Mum, what is it? What's wrong?' I'd asked, crossing quickly to her side. I remember feeling terrified because her face was contorted in anguish and confusion, and tears were coursing down her carefully made-up cheeks in fast-flowing rivulets.

'I can't do this,' she wailed in fear and despair.

I looked around the room in confusion. 'Do what? What can't you do?' I could see nothing in the familiar dining room to cause her this level of distress. Everything looked absolutely normal, except for my mum, of course. Nothing normal there. Nothing at all.

'I can't do *this*,' she sobbed again, this time waving a hand in front of her to indicate the waiting cutlery. 'I can't lay the table,' she cried and looked up at me with eyes as lost and helpless as a child's. 'I can't remember how to lay the table. It's gone… it's just gone.'

Of course we'd laughed it off. We had to. I had calmed her down, and laid the table myself, and once the task was done she had seemed to pull herself back together and had appeared almost normal again. I think we even made a silly joke about it, *unbelievably*. I suppose if we'd done anything else, we'd have been opening the door to the demon even sooner than we had to. But he was on his way, and it wasn't long before he became an all-too-frequent uninvited visitor at our house. It had begun.

As frequently happened after one of her episodes, in the days following my mother's pilgrimage to her old place of work, she appeared much more settled and connected with the present. She even expressed a desire to paint, and as he set up the easel, canvas and brushes, the tools of her former trade, my father had given me a look which eloquently said, *See. Everything is fine now.* I wondered if he actually believed that.

Richard, at least, was able to offer his support, even if it was only via a lengthy late-night conversation on our mobiles, which we'd probably both regret when next month's bills came in.

'We just have to go along with what your dad thinks is best,' he had said reasonably.

'I know,' I sighed, 'but what if I *hadn't* found her? What if next time she gets lost, or hurts herself... or worse? He'd never forgive himself if anything like that ever happened.'

There was a silent buzzing on the line, and for a moment I wondered if we'd been disconnected. Then, when he eventually spoke, there was real sadness in his voice. 'You can't live your life like that, being afraid of the *what ifs*. You can't predict the future; you just have to make the most of what you have, while you've got it. Everything can change so quickly...' His voice trailed away, and I wondered if he was suddenly regretting the path our conversation had taken. It was inevitable that his words would make us both think of Amy. But he was right. Amy had embraced that philosophy as though it were a religion: live for today, tomorrow will take care of itself.

Talking to Richard left me feeling more grounded and settled than I'd done in days. He was right about so many things: about my parents; about not worrying about the future; and also, about us.

'I don't want to wait a long time before rescheduling the wedding,' he had said.

'But won't people think it's wrong, or disrespectful, if we do it too soon?'

'Screw what anyone else thinks. This is about you and me. And let's be honest, would it have worried Amy? Well, would it?'

I shook my head, which was a stupid thing to do on the phone, but suddenly there was a tightness in my throat, as I could almost hear her voice saying the very same thing that Richard had done, except perhaps even *more* colourfully.

'Okay. Let's talk about it when you get back,' I agreed.

I sat at the kitchen table the following morning, turning the small brown package over and over in my hands, cautiously, as though it contained an unexploded bomb. I gave an impatient snort at the ludicrous thought. It was a book. Just a book. I dealt with hundreds of them every day of the week. I was being ridiculous.

If I had managed to figure out nothing else over the Easter weekend, one thing at least was clear: for some reason – and I'm really sure it was due to how we met – I found Jack strangely compelling, and that connection drew and repelled me like the poles of a magnet. So the *last* thing I needed to do was get him even further into my head by reading his book. I should just throw this unopened package into the kitchen bin, have no further contact with him, and allow all these confusing feelings to just fade away. Simple. So why then did I hear a small tearing noise and find that my fingers – following their own separate agenda – had ripped open the parcel?

It was a hardback edition, with a shiny glossy black cover and eye-catching artwork. I flipped it open and read the front blurb, which told me nothing about the novel that I hadn't already gleaned from the internet when I'd ordered it. I went to the back. My breath caught in my throat as I looked at the picture of the man who had saved me. It was a smiling, relaxed, outdoor shot of him leaning up against a tree. Behind him was a ranch-style fence, and his casual clothing of jeans, open-necked shirt and boots all completed the general 'cowboy' outdoorsy image, which I imagined the photographer had been striving for. Jack looked younger in the portrait, and his hair was a little longer, and possibly the small creases that fanned from his eyes when he smiled weren't quite as pronounced as they'd been the other day when he was looking at me, but otherwise— I snapped the book shut with a noisy smack, as though a coiled serpent had just reared up from its pages. And *this* is why I should just bin the book, I thought grimly, because for whatever reason, being around Jack – even looking at a picture of him, apparently – was as intoxicating to me as a drug. And just about as dangerous. I needed to kick this irrational addiction before it took an even stronger hold, and concentrate on the things that were really important in my life: my family; my fiancé and my friends, and trying to return to some sort of normality after losing Amy.

As though just touching the book was harmful, I carried it across the kitchen holding just one corner, so not surprisingly it slipped from my fingers and landed on the kitchen floor. I stooped to retrieve it, noticing it had fallen open at the dedication page. I must have remained in a half-crouched position for quite some time, long enough at least for the muscles in my calves to begin to protest. Yet still my eyes remained riveted on the three lines of writing on the open page before me. *To Sheridan, my friend, my lover, my inspiration and my wife. For ever, Jack.*

I spent the Bank Holiday with Caroline and Nick, and the first thing I noticed when I pulled on to their drive was the smart and shiny brand new car parked next to Nick's. I don't know much about cars, but I guessed this new upgrade must have cost a great deal more than the insurance pay-out on Caroline's old model. I bent down and peered at the interior as I walked past it to reach their front door. I counted at least five airbags embedded into the leather panels. I knew Nick well enough to know this high safety spec would have been at his insistence. And understandably so. It posed one achingly sad question: if *this* had been Caroline's car on the night of the accident, would things have ended the way they did?

I was still looking over my shoulder at the new vehicle when Nick opened the front door and kissed me warmly on the cheek.

'Very fancy,' I said before the car disappeared from view as he closed the door.

'Yes, it is,' Nick commented a little bitterly. 'Shame I can't get her to drive it, isn't it?'

There was genuine concern behind his words, and I automatically dropped my voice to a whisper which I knew couldn't be heard from the kitchen, where Caroline was certain to be waiting. 'She still won't drive?'

He shook his head, a worried expression furrowed upon his

kind face. 'No. She can just about cope with being a passenger for a short journey. But honestly, Emma, I don't know if I'm *ever* going to get her behind the wheel of a car again.'

He was concerned and frustrated, I could understand that, but I understood even better Caroline's incapacitating fear. I'd experienced just a small taste of it myself on those first few terrifying journeys on the road after the accident – that had to be nothing in comparison to what Caroline was feeling. 'Just give her time,' was the only advice I could give. It was the one platitude everyone kept offering to me: just give it time. It was, without doubt, the single most well-meaning and useless piece of advice you could give a person.

There was a delicious smell of something cooking in wine coming from the oven as I made my way into the kitchen. Caroline turned to greet me with a wide smile, looking as composed and in control as ever, until I went into her outstretched arms and felt her hold on to me for just a second or two longer than normal. But that wasn't just her, it was me too.

As it was just the three of us, we ate in the kitchen, but even so the absence of two of our regular group was noticeable in the vacant chairs on one side of the rustic pine table. I rearranged the serving dishes as I laid the table, trying to cover the spaces where Richard's and Amy's placemats should have sat.

'So how is Richard enjoying Easter skiing down a mountain with eighty fifteen-year-olds in his care?'

I could understand Nick's gentle sarcasm. The thought of the extra responsibility Richard had willingly volunteered to take on made me realise even more just how badly he had needed to get away. I only hoped it was the situation he'd needed to escape from, and not me.

'He's doing much better,' I replied, spooning up the last delicious mouthful of something laden with cream, pastry and about a thousand calories from my plate. 'He's sounded much more like his old self on our last few conversations. Much less troubled.'

'That's good news,' said Caroline with a smile, and I thought I saw something in her eyes as she took Nick's plate from his outstretched hand. Perhaps I did, for a few minutes later he excused himself and disappeared into the lounge, muttering something about watching a match on television.

Caroline waited until we were loading the dishwasher before attempting to casually drop in the comment she must have been sitting on for days.

'So, I heard that you and Jack Monroe had a lunch date last week?'

I paused mid-rinse of a dinner plate, before turning to face her.

'This town is absolutely *unbelievable*. Where did you hear that?'

She shrugged and chose not to comment on the way I had instantly bristled at her words. 'Hallingford is a small place. People talk. You know that.'

I could feel my lips drawing together in a tight line. 'It's things like this that make me really miss living in London, where you don't have to explain everything you do to people who have no business asking about it.'

Caroline continued to study me. My desire to leave our home town had been as much a mystery to her as quantum physics. She had everything she ever wanted in the place she'd lived all her life. To her, moving away was an unnecessary interruption in the rhythm of a perfect life plan. Our views were almost polar opposites.

'Do you still miss living there? Even though everyone you care about is here?'

I looked at her sadly. Not everyone. Not any more. 'I just don't like people sticking their noses into things that are nothing to do with them.'

Caroline arched one brow, forcing me to jump in and correct her. 'Not you. I just meant the town busybodies, spreading tittle-tattle. *And* getting it all wrong.'

Caroline arched the other brow. She really had perfected that one down to a fine art.

'It wasn't a date, nothing like it,' I corrected.

'But you *did* go for lunch together?'

She was beginning to sound a little like a prosecutor in a trial. And although I knew I'd done nothing wrong, I instantly felt guilty. 'Jack showed up at the shop looking for a book, and as it was lunchtime he suggested going out and grabbing a bite. That's all. End of story.' I deliberately omitted the interesting fact that he had sought to find me in each of the town's bookshops, because even I didn't know why he'd done that.

She looked at me carefully, her eyes probing the words out of me.

'He's happily married anyway, and I'm as good as. But I don't suppose the gossip mill decided to broadcast that little fact, did they?' Offence is usually the best type of defence, except when the other person knows you as well as Caroline knew me.

'So what did Richard have to say, when you told him?'

'As it wasn't important, I didn't even mention it to him.'

She looked at me for a very long time, and then reached over and took my hand in hers before saying gently, 'Be careful, Emma. Be very careful.'

As advice goes, it was almost as useless as *give it time*, and maybe already too late.

Why is it that as soon as you resolve yourself on a course of action, a really sensible and mature, well-thought-out course of action – like severing all contact with Jack Monroe – Fate wades in and upsets all your plans? For me, Fate arrived on the Tuesday morning just as I was leaving for work, in the form of a delivery driver wearing the distinctive red-and-yellow uniform of a well-known courier company. I had no choice but to get out of my car and greet him, seeing as he'd pulled in directly behind me.

'Emma Marshall?' he queried, consulting a small handheld electronic device.

'That's me,' I confirmed.

'Parcel for you. Can you sign here please?' He passed me the scanning device and I scribbled on the small screen. In return he passed me a large square brown paper parcel. I took it curiously, studying the unfamiliar writing on the label. It wasn't heavy, and it felt kind of squishy, as though it contained some type of fabric. I hadn't ordered anything recently other than Jack's book, but as intrigued as I was to find out its contents, it was exceedingly well-wrapped with what looked like the best part of a roll of brown tape, and I was already running late. I tucked the package under my arm and threw it on to the passenger seat beside me.

I was late for work, and Monique already had two customers in the shop, so I dropped the package on the shelf in the back office and went straight into the store to help her serve. It was a couple of hours later before I had reason to go back into the office, and the first thing I saw was the unopened parcel. While waiting for the kettle to boil, I grabbed a pair of sharp scissors and snipped my way into the package someone had taken great care to ensure arrived with me in one piece. The someone was Amy's mother. I knew that almost without having to read the note addressed to me, which was one of two lying on top of a leather jacket neatly folded within a dry-cleaning bag. The envelope on the second note bore no name, I guess because she had never been told it.

I opened my own envelope carefully, perching on the edge of the desk as I read the neatly handwritten note.

Dear Emma, I am so sorry to bother you with this, but I didn't know who else to ask. Among Amy's belongings which the hospital gave us, was the enclosed man's jacket. I think it must belong to the American man who stopped and helped you girls after the accident. I have had it cleaned, and I believe the stains have been removed. Someone told me you were talking to him at the funeral, so I am hoping that you might have his address so that we can return his property to him. I have also enclosed a letter of thanks that I'd be grateful if you could pass on to him.

Thank you, Emma, for all the support both you and Caroline have given Donald and me over this terrible time. You really were wonderful friends to Amy, and she was lucky to have you both in her life.

Please don't be a stranger. With all our love and thanks, Linda and Donald (Amy's Mum and Dad).

I cried at the bit when she thanked us for being Amy's friend, as if that could ever have been a hardship. And then I cried even harder when I read the bracketed words after the signature, because it hadn't been written to identify who they were (obviously, I knew that) but just to reaffirm that even though she was no longer with them, Amy was still their little girl.

'Did you go to Brazil for the fucking coffee?' Monique began, and then saw the small pile of used tissues and my exceedingly red nose, and was by my side in an instant. I passed her Linda's note and she scanned it quickly, her eyes darting back up to check on me after every sentence. She sniffed, grabbed a tissue and blew her nose loudly after handing me back the sheet of paper. 'We should put brandy in the coffee,' she declared.

I tried a small smile and found I almost remembered how to do it.

I drove cautiously along the twisting coastal road. Even with the windscreen wipers at full speed, it was hard for them to cope with the torrential downpour that had begun to fall as soon as I reached the village of Trentwell. It didn't help that I had absolutely no idea where I was going, except that Jack had mentioned that his rental cottage looked out over a small cove. There were only a few lanes where the houses met that description, so I had hoped it wasn't going to be too difficult to find. Now, with all the rain, my plan to find his house without an address seemed seriously stupid.

Forked lightning flashed through the sky, as dramatic and dazzling as a knife scything through the dusk of early evening. I slowed down almost to a standstill as the deep baritone of rumbling thunder echoed not far behind it. The rain was attacking the roof and bonnet of my car in a miniature machine-gun burst of ferocious wet bullets, and combined with the heavy-clouded dusk, my visibility was reduced to just a few metres.

'This is ridiculous,' I muttered, realising I was going to have to abandon my mission. Given the conditions, I should just turn around and head back home. A moment later I glimpsed a gap in the hedgerow, and pulled in to a nearby driveway to make my turn. Directly in front of me, lit in the twin spots of my headlights, was Jack's car, parked at the end of a long drive, outside a small stone cottage. I turned off my engine and lights and stared through the downpour at the cottage. It was the type of place they take photographs of and make into jigsaw puzzles. Bay windows flanked the front door, and there was a rustic homely charm to the roughened local stone walls. I could see no lights on inside, but given the weather he was unlikely to be out, although he *had* mentioned that the deserted beach was good for jogging. Perhaps I could drop off the jacket without having to see him at all? I got out of the car and ran to the front door, getting saturated in the process, even though I'd only covered a distance of less than five metres. Beside the oak door was an old-fashioned metal pull which I tugged on, although if a bell rang inside, its peal was lost in the backdrop of thundering rain. I hadn't bothered grabbing a jacket, and the thin shirt I'd worn for work was quickly plastered to my body like a second skin, while the rain continued to effectively jet-wash me, as I stood shivering on Jack's doorstep.

'Please be out, please be out,' I muttered, already scoping the exterior of the house for somewhere dry to leave the jacket and note, when suddenly the door opened and Jack was in front of me. My first thought was the sort of sound usually made by men when looking at lads' magazines. I make no apology for it whatsoever. I'm engaged, I'm committed to someone else, but I am also *not blind*, nor am

I immune to what I'm sure was just a purely hormonal reflex action. Jack was naked from the waist up, and the old faded jeans that he must have hastily pulled on over his still-damp body, were sticking to him in places where I had no business looking. But I looked anyway.

'Emma,' he said with a surprised smile, holding the door wider in welcome. 'Come in.'

I shook my head, and droplets sprayed around me like a wet dog. 'No, that's okay, I can't stay. I just came to bring you something. Hang on, it's in the car.'

A well-defined muscled arm reached out into the rain and took hold of my wrist. 'Well unless it's a dinghy, it can wait until the storm dies down. Now come inside before you drown on my doorstep.'

Short of snatching my arm out of his grip, there was little I could do but allow myself to be gently tugged across the threshold. The hallway was dark and narrow and it was almost impossible not to be overwhelmed by the intoxicating cocktail from our damp skin and whatever gel he had just used in the shower.

'This way,' he urged, as his hand slid down from the delicate bones of my wrist and linked comfortably with mine. I followed him wordlessly down the passageway, wondering how much more spectacularly I was going to fail in my plan to keep my distance from this man. So far, within minutes, he was leading me by the hand into his dark home, half naked, with my clothes clinging to me so revealingly they might as well not be there at all.

The kitchen was a warm cosy cavern, all beams and stone walls, with an old-fashioned Aga throwing out welcoming waves of heat. Instinctively I moved towards it. The only source of light were the last grey shards of the day, splintered by lightning bolts, visible through glass double-doors which looked out over a small garden and the sea beyond.

'Wow,' I breathed, as the entire sky was lit by an enormous strike which appeared to disappear into the rising swell of the waves, 'that is an incredible view.'

'It is,' he commented, his voice stirring the tiny hairs on the back of my neck. I shivered involuntarily.

'You're cold,' he observed, and I saw his eyes fall to my soaking wet shirt. He plucked a warm folded towel from the Aga, but instead of just passing it to me, he stood before me and swept it around my shoulders like a matador with a cape. He should have let go of the towelling edges, or I should have taken a step backwards. But neither of us moved. I heard a slight rasp in my breathing and felt a crazy, almost irresistible urge to reach out and lay my palm on the muscled wall of his chest. His eyes were fixed on mine, and I saw his pupils dilate. Caroline's warning echoed hollowly in my mind. I shouldn't be doing this, and neither should he. I found the strength to step away, and the moment I did the spell was broken. I rubbed the towel briskly over my sodden clothing, while he reached for a T-shirt that was draped over the back of a chair. I tried not to be aware of the interplay of muscles as he stretched and tugged on the short-sleeved garment, but it was hard not to stare.

'I'm sorry,' he apologised, 'I can't offer you a hot drink or anything. The power went down in the storm.' That, at least, explained the darkened house.

'That happens quite a lot around here,' I said, happy to talk about power cables, the national grid, freak weather conditions, in fact anything at all except that moment of intimacy that we were both trying really hard to pretend hadn't just happened. 'Still, at least you have the Aga to cook and boil water on.'

'Am I going to come across as a really stupid dumb American if I now say – huh?'

This was better; this was much more like the banter we'd enjoyed at lunch the other day. *This* was harmless and trivial. *This* I could cope with. I scanned the dimming kitchen for a kettle, but could only see an electric one, so I pulled a cast-iron saucepan from a nearby stand. 'I'll show you,' I promised, filling the pan with water. 'Then every cliché you've ever heard about the British and their tea drinking will be proved true.'

He laughed, and brought me tea bags, mugs, and then milk from the fridge. 'As you're such an Aga expert, would you consider helping me with these later?' he asked, pulling out a tray from the fridge which held two enormous steaks. 'I can't leave them to spoil, and who knows how long we'll be without power.'

I eyed the huge slabs of meat in amazement. 'That has to be half a cow you have there.'

'I'm an American,' he reminded me with a smile. 'Originally from a small town in Texas,' he continued, his accent broadening, to make his point. 'I can't let you Brits claim all the clichés.'

As I waited for the water, I held my chilled hands out to the radiant warmth of the range. My top still felt uncomfortably damp.

'Let me go and find you something dry to put on,' Jack offered, disappearing into the dark hallway. He was back a few minutes later with a soft grey sweatshirt, bearing the logo of Harvard University, which he held out for me. I ran my finger over the insignia and raised my eyebrows in admiration, 'The Texas boy did good,' I said with a smile.

'I had supportive parents, and great teachers,' he replied

125

modestly, and I liked the way he didn't claim credit for his academic success, even though I'm sure he had earned it.

I shook open the sweatshirt and slipped it over my head, trying to ignore the fragrance of him, which lingered deep within the fabric.

'I can turn around,' he offered chivalrously, as I began to unbutton my wet top beneath the roomy sweatshirt.

'No, that's okay,' I assured him, yanking reluctant buttons through holes that didn't want them to leave. He watched with mild amusement as I proceeded to attempt to wriggle out of the shirt in a series of inelegant contortions, which involved diving down the neckline and up the copious sleeves of his top. I was getting a little hot and flustered, and there was every possibility that I was now stuck inside the stupid shirt.

'Need some help?' he offered politely, his lips twitching.

'No. I'm fine,' I insisted, and then winced as a muscle twanged painfully in my neck. I gritted my teeth in determination. 'I saw this once in a film... it looked much easier than this.' I also didn't remember the actress grunting quite as much as I was doing.

'*Flashdance*, I believe,' he replied smoothly.

I stopped my contortions for a second and looked up at him. 'I'm impressed.'

'I told you, I like movies.' He had. I'd forgotten that. Finally I was free from my troublesome garment, and heaved a huge sigh of relief as I pulled the wet shirt out from beneath the Harvard top.

'But, if I remember it correctly, the girl in the movie was actually taking off her *bra*,' Jack stated.

I gave a small satisfied smile, reached up my sleeve and

pulled out the wet lace undergarment, like a magician producing a rabbit.

'Now *I'm* impressed,' he said.

We sat at his small kitchen table sipping our tea in the dwindling light, and watching the storm as it raged around the cottage. It felt as though we were ensconced on a safe island or in a harbour, protected not just from the elements, but also from all other dangers and worries of the world outside these walls. Jack made me feel safe whenever I was in his company. That had to be tied up with him rescuing me, didn't it? Yet that didn't quite explain this curious feeling, as though I'd just found my way home after a really long journey.

Sheridan. The name rang in my head like a tolling bell. His home was with *her*, not me. I put my mug back down on the table with a little more force than necessary, causing him to turn back from his study of the lightning to look at me.

'Do you have storms like this in Texas?' I asked, clumsily forcing the conversation to remind us both of his home and life elsewhere.

'I don't actually live in Texas any more. We moved to New York when I was a child.'

'And is that where you live now?' I asked artlessly, all pretence of subtlety thrown out of the window to join the storm. He studied me for a very long moment before answering, and I guessed he'd been interviewed by enough professional journalists to easily recognise a probing question when he heard one. And let's face it, mine was hardly ingenuous.

'I grew up in New York City and lived there for most of

my adult life. Then, a few years ago, when the books started becoming successful, I bought a small ranch in upstate New York, and that's where I live now.'

It was rapidly growing too dark to see anything in the kitchen, so Jack pulled a box of candles from a cupboard beside the sink. I heard the scratch of a match, before he picked up our conversation. 'And what about you? Do you and Richard plan on staying in this area after you're married?'

I swallowed a little uncomfortably at his question. Was there an implied criticism in it, or was I just being overly sensitive? 'Yes, well, it's where our families and friends live, it's where we work.'

He nodded, but again I thought I could see a glimmer of disappointment at my answer. It made me angry; he had no right to judge me, to judge *us*, for being provincial. There was nothing wrong in that.

'So how long have you two been engaged?'

'Just since Christmas.'

He lifted a candle and positioned it on the window ledge by the sink, providing just enough illumination for me to see his look of surprise. 'That recently? I somehow got the impression you two had been together for much longer.'

'We've been together since we were teenagers, but we broke up for quite a while. I went away.'

Jack continued the task of placing the lit candles at strategic points around the room. The flickering flames cast dancing shadows on the rough stone walls, making the room look like an enchanted grotto.

'So where did you go when you were "away"?' he asked, clearly no longer interested in discussing my relationship.

'London to begin with, and then my job took me to Washington for eighteen months.'

He turned to face me, with a look of surprise. 'I take it you don't mean your work at the bookshop?'

I smiled at the thought. 'No. I was in marketing. *Am* in marketing,' I corrected, hating the way I had recently started to refer to my chosen profession in the past tense.

He looked at me curiously, waiting for me to continue. 'I've had to take a little... career break... a sabbatical, I suppose you'd call it.' I paused, feeling, as always, uncomfortable when I had to explain this. 'My mother hasn't been very well recently, so I moved back home for a while to help my father look after her.'

There was admiration and understanding in his eyes. 'Until she gets better?' he questioned.

I paused at his words. 'Actually no, until she gets worse. Or at least bad enough that my dad will finally be able to accept what is happening to her, and let her go.' I looked up, trying hard not to let the tears spill over. My words might sound tough, but *I* certainly wasn't, and never more so since the car accident. 'It's Alzheimer's,' I said, only the words were a bit muffled, because somehow – and I don't remember how it happened – I was being comforted in his arms and my mouth was against the wall of his chest.

He offered no words, and I was really glad that he hadn't trolled out some well-meaning and ineffectual platitude. For a man who made his living using words, he certainly knew when they weren't required. I really liked that. Eventually, feeling more than a little embarrassed, I pulled away.

'So,' I asked, with a false cheery smile and tear-stained cheeks, 'do you still want me to have a go at cooking those steaks?'

I rummaged around in the drawers of the range in search of a griddle pan, while he began to make a salad. We worked together in companionable silence, as though this was just one of many meals we had prepared together. That was the strangest thing: that none of this – as unfamiliar as it might be – felt *strange* at all. A couple of times I glanced up and caught him looking at me with an expression that was difficult to define, but the closest I could get to it was a kind of pleasantly surprised mystification. I felt the same.

I wanted to ask him if he cooked at home with his wife, not because I was interested, but just because I thought one of us should at least acknowledge our absent partners, but somehow the right moment never identified itself. We ate at the kitchen table by the light of the candles. I had burned the steaks slightly, but Jack was way too polite to say anything other than that was just the way he liked his meat. He opened a bottle of wine, but I only had one small glass, saying that I would soon have to drive back home.

'I don't think you should leave until the storm dies down,' Jack said solemnly. 'The coastal road isn't lit and it's downright lethal in the rain.'

An image came to mind of another darkened road we both had reason to remember well. Survivor and rescuer, we shared a long and meaningful look. 'I can't be back late,' I said. 'My parents are in permanent panic mode whenever I'm driving these days.'

'That's understandable. Couldn't you call them?'

'Richard will be phoning me from Austria later, and I don't think he'd be too pleased to know I was still out.' What I really meant was *out with you*, and I think Jack realised that.

'But he wouldn't want you driving when the roads weren't safe?'

'Of course not,' I replied, springing to my fiancé's defence. There was no polite way to say that Richard would probably

130

think my safety was more in jeopardy in Jack's company than on the roads. I was suddenly overwhelmed by a tidal wave of guilt.

Jack must have sensed my discomfort, for he reached across the table and patted the back of my hand, the way you'd soothe a fretting child. 'Don't worry. We'll get you back home, one way or another.'

Then he seemed to suddenly remember something. 'Earlier on, when you first got here, you said you'd brought me something,' Jack suddenly remembered. 'What was it?' I quickly withdrew my hand from beneath his, as his words reminded me of the purpose of my visit. I felt like I'd just been doused with a bucket of ice-cold water.

'I've left it in the car. I'll just get it,' I said, pushing away from the table and heading for the front door, before he had a chance to stop me. It was still raining, but nowhere near as ferociously as before. I was back in seconds, handing him the rain-speckled brown paper package, which I had loosely rewrapped. There was a smile of curiosity on his handsome face, which froze slowly when he saw his own jacket. Wordlessly he walked back to the kitchen, and by the light of the candles he read the note Amy's mother had written. 'Can you give me their address?' he asked solemnly. 'I'd like to write back.'

'Of course.'

He looked at the folded leather jacket and I wondered if, like the dress I had worn on that fateful night, his jacket was also destined to be discarded. Some objects remain for ever tainted, however well you manage to remove the surface stains from them.

We were silent for a long time. When Jack next spoke, it was to ask a question. A question that, with hindsight, should have been preceded by a warning klaxon.

'There's something that's been puzzling me about that night, something Amy said. What was it that she was referring to when she thanked you for forgiving her?'

I frowned in genuine confusion at his words. 'What are you talking about?'

'Don't you remember,' he said encouragingly, 'just before the ambulances arrived, Amy thanked you for being a good friend and forgiving her. It seemed so important to her, that it made me curious.'

'I... I don't know,' I said, slowly shaking my head from side to side. I'd forgotten her words until that moment, and something inside me clenched and tightened at the memory. I was aware Jack was still studying me. 'I don't think she knew *what* she was saying,' I said, my voice not quite steady. 'But that's hardly surprising, is it? She was barely conscious, nothing she said made sense. They were just meaningless words.'

'I'm sorry,' apologised Jack, as he saw my look of distress. Suddenly I was back there, kneeling on the wet tarmac, looking down at my horribly injured friend, holding her hand... not for a moment really believing that this was going to be the last conversation we ever had.

For the second time that night Jack's arms wrapped around me in comfort. The sob seemed to come from somewhere deep within me, from a well I had tried to seal – not very effectively, as it turned out. He held me gently while I cried, and there was a release in being able to be this way with him because, unlike with Richard or Caroline, I didn't need to worry about *his* pain, *his* loss, or *his* feelings, I could just allow the tide of grief to take hold of me and wash me up when it was done. My hands were trapped between us, lying on his chest and I could feel the strong and steady beat of his heart against my palm. Still holding me against him, one hand moved up to my hair, gently smoothing it against the curve at the back of my neck. Gradually the torrent of tears slowed down to a trickle. I raised my head from his chest and the large damp patch I had left on his T-shirt. 'I'm sorry,' I whispered. Even my voice sounded broken and hurt.

'Sshhh,' he soothed, and then with no warning, no sign, or hint that it was about to happen, his head lowered and his lips gently brushed mine.

We sprang apart as though we'd been electrocuted. My gasp of shock cleared all other emotions away as though a bush fire had seared through them. My eyes blazed with fury. Was that what this had all been about? Had he only been comforting me so he could take advantage of my vulnerability? How could I have misjudged him and the situation so badly?

Then I looked at him properly. He looked as shocked by what he had done as I did, and almost as horrified. He held out a hand towards me in a gesture of someone trying to ward off something wicked. As though somehow all of this was *my* doing.

'What the hell—?' I shouted.

'I'm sorry. I didn't mean to do that. I don't know what I was thinking.' There was probably some sort of insult tied up in that, but I was too angry to pick up on it. 'I wasn't trying to take advantage of you, please believe that, Emma.'

I shook my head, looking at him as though I had never seen him before, as though he was a stranger. Which, in reality, was pretty much exactly what he was. I looked around frantically for my bag and plucked it up.

'Emma, please,' Jack implored, his hand still outstretched

and his face anguished. 'I don't even know how that happened. I didn't want to kiss you. I *don't* want to kiss you.' Did he really think anything he was saying was making things better?

'Good to know,' I said bitterly, 'but it doesn't change a damn thing.'

I spun on my heel and headed for the door.

'Emma, wait,' Jack cried. His hand fastened on my wrist, turning me back towards him. 'Let me explain.'

'Save it,' I spat out. 'I don't know why you did that, and I don't even care. But whatever this... this *friendship* was, you've just gone and ruined it.'

There was a tight ball of pain in my chest, and I could feel it burning like a comet with anger as I looked at him. 'I thought you understood me. I thought we were becoming friends, that I could trust you.'

'I do, we are, and you can,' he answered. I shook my head and saw that I was now at his front door without realising how I got there. But he was following close behind me, so that when I turned to deliver my parting words, I almost crashed into him. 'I owe you a lot, Jack. I won't ever deny that. But what you did just now... well that just crossed the line, as far as I'm concerned.' If my words meant anything at all to him, he hid it well. 'So thank you for saving my life, enjoy the rest of yours, and if you have any decency at all, why don't you do us both a favour and stay as far away from me as possible.'

I was out of the door by then. I could hear from the crunch of gravel that he was still following me. I jumped into my car, my heart hammering crazily as I risked one glance to where he stood, watching me with an agonised look on his face. My hand was shaking so much it took three attempts to finally slot the key into the ignition.

Illuminated in the beam from my headlights, I saw the planes of his faces cast into shadowy relief. His eyes looked bleak as he ran his hand across his mouth, and my own lips tingled treacherously at the memory of the feel of it. Guilt rose like bile in my throat, bitter and acidic. I thumped down hard on the button to lower my window. 'Richard was right about you,' I said through the gap. Jack winced as though I'd cut him. 'What the hell were you thinking? You and your wife might go in for all that open relationship crap, but *I* certainly don't!'

I sped backwards down his drive, tearing up the turf beside it in my haste. I should have been paying better attention, but my eyes were fixed only on the stunned look of shock on his face.

CHAPTER 7

The good thing about rage, the kind of blind, blood-filled rage that I was feeling as I left Jack's home, is that it gives you something tangible to focus on. And while you're busy fuelling it and feeding it with all the clever and scathing things you should have said, if only you'd thought of them at the time, then you don't have to worry about digging deeper and uncovering the thing that is *really* eating away at you.

But, like the storm the night before, my anger could only last for so long before it burned itself out. And by the light of day when the red mist had lifted, I realised that much of my reaction to Jack's touch had come from guilt. I'd allowed him to get close to me, confusing the debt I owed him with a fast pass to friendship and trust. And Richard's own reaction to Jack had only made me stubbornly determined to prove him wrong. But aside from Jack's heroism on the night of the accident, what did I really know about him? Nothing. I'd lied on the phone to Richard that night, and I couldn't remember *ever* having done that before. I blamed a cold for the rasp in my voice, hearing my dishonesty buzzing down the phone lines between us like a malevolent mosquito. I didn't mention visiting Jack. Of course, that was only a lie by omission, but I knew I was splitting hairs with that one.

It was only when I began to unravel the scene in Jack's

kitchen, winding it up like a ball of unpicked yarn, that I realised everything had started to spiral out of control with his question about Amy. Such an inconsequential thing, but once voiced it could never be unasked, and it was going to keep nagging away at me until it was answered: What *did* Amy believe I had forgiven her for? I could think of absolutely nothing she had ever done that required an apology. And even more bewildering, why on earth did my good friend, with her generous spirit, open heart and joyful approach to life, think she'd done something to hurt me? Nothing was less likely to be true.

But now that Jack had opened the door to the memory, all I could see when I closed my eyes was Amy gripping my hand on the cold tarmac of the road, as though I was a priest absolving her during her final moments, and the relief on her face when I had told her everything was all right.

I tried to tell myself there was no hidden intrigue or mystery to her words. Amy was just as likely to be apologising because she'd ruined a pair of shoes she'd borrowed... or something equally mundane. *Really? That was what was on her mind in her dying moments? Some damaged designer sandals?* I shook my head angrily at the voice of doubt, which for some reason was speaking in my head in a soft American accent. Damn him. Why the hell hadn't he just kept his stupid questions to himself?

There was only one other person who had known Amy as well as I had; one other person who might just be able to tell me what I needed to know.

'Caroline McAdam.' Her voice was clear and professional, with a sing-song intonation.

'Hi, Caro, it's me.'

Her tone softened and warmed, and the smile that I knew she was making was as clear as if I was standing in front of her. 'Hey, sweetie. How are you doing?'

Good question, and not one I really knew how to answer right then. 'I'm fine,' I replied, because that was what she was expecting to hear. 'I was just wondering... are you free for a quick cup of coffee?'

There was a slight pause, and I could visualise her, sitting at her window-side desk in the estate agency, glancing at her watch and maybe even biting her lip the way she always did when considering something unexpected.

'Yeah, I guess I can pop out if it's only for a quick one.'

I got to the coffee shop first, ordered us two cappuccinos, and found a small table by the window. I saw her walking towards the café through the glass and waved, smiling at the wide beam she sent back in return.

She carefully undid the lid of her frothy drink, and I let her take a sip before I launched into the reason I had dragged her out of the office in the middle of the morning. We didn't have much time.

'Caroline, I have something I need to ask you.'

She looked up and delicately licked away the small milky trail on her top lip.

'That sounds serious,' she observed.

'I... I don't know. It might be.'

A small furrow appeared between her brows. 'So, what's up?'

'Caroline, how much do you remember about the night that Amy died?'

I watched her face spasm, and I hated myself for having to do this to her, but there was no one else I could ask.

'I take it you don't mean about the hen party?'

I shook my head sadly. 'The accident,' I confirmed quietly.

She shook her head, as her eyes shifted away from me, staring out of the window. 'Not much,' she admitted. 'It's all a blur after we left the party. I remember Amy feeling sick, I remember the deer in front of us and then... it's all kind of greyed-out until I was sitting in the back of the ambulance.'

I'd known her memories of the night were sketchy, but I had no idea there was so much she was missing. 'So you don't remember finding Amy by the road?'

Caroline looked back at me in shock. '*I* found her? I thought that Jack did?'

Her words had an almost visceral effect on me. I reached across the table and took hold of her hand. '*You* were the one who got to her first, hon.'

Caroline looked stricken at the revelation. 'I did? It's all just gone. I can't remember it at all.'

I knew then that it was almost pointless asking my next question, but I asked it anyway. 'So you don't remember what she said, while we were waiting for the ambulance?'

Caroline's eyes widened into huge blue marbles in shock. 'What do you mean? How was she talking? She was unconscious.'

I shook my head sadly. 'No, she wasn't. She was awake... well, kind of... God, Caroline, it was awful to see her like that and not be able to do anything to help her.'

Caroline's eyes had filled with tears, and I hated myself for giving her an image that I knew was going to keep her awake at nights, just like it did to me. 'Caro, the reason I'm bringing this up is that I've remembered something Amy said, something really strange, and I wondered if you knew what she meant.'

Caroline shook her head, still grappling with the awful image of our friend being conscious after having been hurled through the windscreen of her car. 'What did she say?' she asked, her voice a hoarse broken whisper.

'Well, at first I thought she was just sort of babbling... but now, I'm not so sure. There was something really important she was trying to say to me; it was something about her being glad that I had forgiven her and that I was a good friend.'

Caroline looked directly at me, her eyes two bright blue sparkling jewels. 'You *were* a good friend,' she affirmed.

I shook my head. 'No. It was more than that. It was like she was thanking me for being so understanding. Have you got any idea at all what she was talking about?'

Caroline reached for her drink, her hand shaking so much that the froth swayed from side to side within the plastic container. 'No. I haven't got a clue.' She drank deeply from her coffee, as though to burn the taste of the lie from her mouth.

'Caroline,' I said probingly, 'are you certain you don't know? You can't think of anything Amy could have said or done that was worrying her?' The question sounded ridiculous on my lips.

Caroline's cheeks flushed slightly, yet another curious sign, but she didn't waver. 'No, of course not. Nothing you're saying makes any sense. Are you sure you didn't imagine the whole conversation? You *had* just hurt your head, after all.'

That made me mad, and I really hadn't wanted to get angry with her. 'I didn't, because it wasn't just me who heard her, Jack did too.'

That silenced her. She looked down and began to fiddle with the coffee container again. 'I really don't know what she meant.' She looked up at me, her eyes brimming with tears, and I knew my own questions had been pushed aside by a much more overwhelming realisation. 'I can't believe she was still conscious...'

I had a horrible afternoon. And now I had a new portion of guilt to add to my fast-growing mountain; I had hurt Caroline and thrust the night of the accident right back into the forefront of her mind. I was definitely to blame for the despondent set of her shoulders and her decidedly weary stride as she walked back to work after hugging me goodbye on the pavement.

I almost asked Richard about Amy's curious comment when he called me that night, but he was in a rush and was phoning from the hospital after a student had been stretchered off the slopes with an ankle injury, so the timing was all wrong. I guessed it could wait until he got back. My sleep that night, perhaps not surprisingly, was disturbed with nightmares, senseless jumbling scenes which all featured Amy desperately trying to tell me something that I couldn't understand. But the one that ripped me from sleep with a torn and strangled cry was a true gothic horror tale. We were in the church and somehow – in that weird way of dreams – it was the day of my wedding as well as being Amy's funeral. The altar was decked in wreaths, and as the organ began to play the opening strains of the wedding march, I noticed with horror that Richard, who was waiting expectantly at the head of the aisle, was standing beside a shining black coffin. The church doors were flung open and a white-gowned figure began to walk to my waiting fiancé, and no one but I seemed to notice that the coffin was still positioned precisely where the bride should stand. The approaching figure was a soft focus blur of white lace, and it was only when she finally held out her hand and took Richard's that I saw beneath the gauzy veil that I wasn't the one about to join him in marriage, it was Amy. I opened my mouth to scream, to shout that there had been some dreadful mistake, but no one could hear me, despite the fact I was yelling so loudly my voice was becoming hoarse. But the wood was solid and the padding thick; the coffin I was lying within held my dream-self imprisoned as tightly as though I was already buried many feet beneath the newly wedded couple.

I awoke drenched in sweat, panting in thick throaty gasps. It was the worst nightmare I could ever remember having. And even when I'd had a drink of water and lay back down on to the damp pillows, the images refused to disappear. I'd never been much of a one for believing that dreams mean anything, and I certainly didn't think they were prophecies, but this one had been so vivid, so intense.

I didn't put it together slowly, one small piece at a time. Instead it came to me in one complete and horrible picture. There was a moment when I knew no turmoil and then I blinked and suddenly there it was. For one minute I thought I was going to be sick, actually physically sick. I swallowed several times and could taste something revolting in the back of my throat. I had to be wrong. There had to be some other explanation. I'd just woken from a nightmare, it was four o'clock in the morning and I wasn't thinking clearly. That had to be what was going on here. Anything else was simply unthinkable.

But sometimes the unthinkable, however horrible it is, just happens to be true. All the clues had been there all along, but I had just refused to see them. It had taken Jack's question to light the fuse, and then the trailing spark had snaked its way inexorably to a huge keg of dynamite which, if I was right, was about to blow my world apart.

I saw it all now, in a horrible collage of images and memories: Amy holding my hand on the side of the road after the accident, whispering her apology with her final breath; Richard's work number hidden among Amy's belongings, and the way he'd been so grief-stricken at the funeral and distraught in the following weeks.

But on the other hand there was Richard. *My* Richard, who I'd known and trusted my entire life. The man who on Christmas Day had told me that there could never be another woman in the world for him but me, and who then, in front of both sets of our parents, had got down on one knee and produced a small velvet ring box and asked me to marry him. Of all the memories I wished I could ignore, that was the one that kept coming back and slamming into me like a bulldozer.

I had no appetite for food the following morning, but sat at the kitchen table, topping up my caffeine levels, just in case I needed further assistance in climbing the walls, which I was already scaling quite well. As dawn was breaking I had finally resolved to hold off doing or saying anything until Richard returned the following day. This was one conversation that definitely needed to be held face to face and certainly not over some dodgy mobile connection.

Across the table, my mother sat carefully shaking out a crackling golden waterfall of cornflakes into a bowl. She liked to feel she was still independent enough to make her own breakfast, which I suppose you could say she did, if pouring out cereal qualified. Her head was bent low, as she tackled the task with all the painstaking concentration of a five-year-old. In the morning light I noticed a fine network of grey threads among the auburn strands and made a mental note to make her a hairdresser's appointment when I got to work. That was the kind of thing my father would never think of organising, the kind of weight I was meant to be lifting from his shoulders.

A wave of loss came up from nowhere and side-swiped me with its intensity. Where had she gone, my *real* mum, not this dressing-gown clad woman sitting in her kitchen, who looked just like her. Because I really *needed* her now, wherever she was. I needed her wisdom and good advice, and most of all I really needed her to tell me what the hell I was supposed to do next.

She looked up from her task and smiled at me, and just for a moment I thought she was back. But then she spoke. 'Do you happen to know where they keep the milk these days?'

I shook my head sadly. She asked the same question every morning. I got slowly to my feet, feeling and moving more like someone fifty years older. 'I'm not sure, Mum, let me check in the fridge for you.'

To say that I wasn't functioning at maximum efficiency at work that day would be an understatement. I gave the wrong change to three different customers, and only two of them pointed it out; I ordered a hundred copies of a new title instead of ten; and then spectacularly managed to spill a cup of coffee over a box of new deliveries. Frankly, by the end of the day I was lucky I still *had* a job. Thankfully, Monique was understanding, and despite swearing at me, *in French*, which was a true indicator of how annoyed she was, she wisely and considerately left me alone. However, an hour before closing time she came up to me with a solemn request. 'Emma, will you do me a huge favour and piss off home now,' she said pleasantly, 'while I still have a business left.'

I couldn't really blame her, I thought, as I gathered my bag and car keys and headed for the rear exit. I saw him immediately, a second or two before he noticed me. He was leaning casually against the side of my car, idly looking around at the dingy and deserted loading bays behind the high street shops. The door clicked behind me, and his head turned in my direction. I stood motionless at the top of the two shallow steps and briefly considered turning back and begging Monique to let me stay for the last hour.

As I approached my car he levered himself from its side, and before saying anything he held up both hands. 'Now, before you start on me, let me say that I *do* appreciate this isn't exactly "staying as far away from you as possible", as you requested.'

'No, it isn't.' My tone gave nothing away. 'What are you doing here?'

'I'm waiting for you to get off work.'

'I don't finish for another hour.'

He gave a small shrug as though this didn't really matter, and leaned back against my car again. 'Okay, I can wait.'

I shook my head in exasperated disbelief. 'How long have you been waiting here, anyway?'

He glanced down at his watch. 'Not long. An hour or so, maybe.' I looked around at the insalubrious surroundings behind the shops, with scattered rubbish and broken wooden pallets stacked high beside overflowing and smelly refuse bins. It wasn't a pleasant place to have spent part of his afternoon.

'Go home, Jack,' I said wearily, pushing past him and opening my car door.

He must have picked up something from my tone, because any trace of banter left his face. 'I came to apologise. I was way out of line the other night. You had every right to be mad at me. You've had more than enough to cope with recently, and the last thing I want to do is cause you any further distress. My behaviour was totally unacceptable, and I can't excuse what happened. You were just so sad, and I was holding you, and comforting you, and then...' His voice trailed away.

In light of everything else that was going on in my life, Jack's behaviour and the attempted kiss had slid right down the scale of things that were worrying me. But he still didn't deserve to be completely let off the hook. 'So kissing other women is your go-to reaction when they need cheering up, is it?' My tone was scathing. 'You must have one hell of an understanding wife.'

His brow furrowed. 'I don't have a wife.'

More lies. I seemed to be surrounded by them suddenly. 'To Sheridan, my friend, my lover, my inspiration and my wife. For ever, Jack.' I blushed slightly as I said the words, not realising I had memorised them until I heard them tumbling out of my mouth.

'*Bitter Revenge*,' said Jack with a sigh of understanding.

'It was on the dedication page.'

He nodded. 'You must have an early edition. It's not in the later reprints.'

I was quiet for a long moment.

'I *was* married, once, a long time ago. It didn't work out.' He gave a laugh that sounded more than a little bitter. 'But none of that excuses my behaviour, I know that. *I* might be a free agent, but I should have been respectful of the fact that you're not.'

'Yeah well,' I said, getting into the driver's seat. 'The jury might still be out on that one.'

I leaned out of the vehicle to grab the handle and slam the car door shut, but Jack's reactions were faster than mine. With lightning speed he placed one hand on the frame and grabbed hold of the edge of the door. Even so, he only managed to prevent it from shutting on his hand by a split second.

'That is a really *excellent* way of losing your fingers,' I said, angry that the close shave had made my heart trip and race in panic. He crouched down beside the open door.

'What did you just say?'

'I said, even little children know better than to put their hands in the way of a slamming car door.'

There was a sharp intensity in his eyes and more than a hint of impatience in his reply. 'Not about the fricking door. What did you mean just now about the jury being out?'

I swung my legs out of the car, forcing him to straighten up and step back as I got out of the vehicle. 'Just that I might have been accusing the wrong man of cheating.'

I'm not sure what reaction I was expecting from him. He was the first person who I had even voiced the suspicion to out loud, so maybe everyone was going to stare back at me in the way that made me feel as though I was a defendant on the stand, and he was the prosecutor.

'Are you sure? Because Richard didn't exactly seem the type.'

'He's a man, isn't he?' I said bitterly.

'Ouch,' murmured Jack. 'Not all men cheat, Emma. Some of us can be trusted.'

I sighed, and tried to remove the bitter edge to my words. 'Well, right now I don't know *anything*, for sure,' I admitted.

'So you've not spoken to him about it? You have no substantial evidence?'

This man had been watching way too many courtroom dramas.

'No. We've not spoken yet. He's not back until tomorrow.'

'Then hear him out,' Jack replied, far more reasonably than I was expecting. 'Give him the chance to tell you *his* side of the story.' I nodded in reluctant agreement. It was what I had already decided to do.

His voice lightened, trying to bring some much needed light relief to the moment. 'And then, if he *has* been fooling around, I'll give you some tips on how to get away with the perfect murder.'

'*Bitter Revenge* again?'

He looked pleasantly surprised to learn I knew the plot of his debut novel.

'You've read it?'

I nodded, and before he started thinking that I'd gone out and bought it because of the curious connection I felt towards him (which, of course was *exactly* what I had done), I added, 'You get to read all sorts of strange things when you work in a bookshop.'

'Again, ouch,' he replied with a mock wince. He paused for a moment, considering. 'What are you doing now? This afternoon. Have you any plans?'

Torturing myself with the image of two of the people I trusted most betraying me didn't seem a very admiral admission. 'Going home,' I replied.

'I was going to check out a location not far from here for research. Do you feel like coming with me and working out the best way to dispose of a body in a lake?' He must have read the hesitation on my face. 'Could come in handy if you decide to embark on a career in homicide,' he pressed, with a definite twinkle in his eyes.

It was, without doubt, one of the craziest and most beguiling invitations I had ever received, and perhaps just the distraction I needed. 'Okay, why not.'

He placed a strong guiding hand in the small of my back and led me over to where his car was parked in one of the empty bays. 'I bet this is how dumb heroines get themselves murdered in your books,' I declared, climbing into the passenger seat, after he'd held open the door for me. He grinned, and pulled out a length of seat belt for me to clip into the holder. For a man who was happily discussing the best way of killing someone, he really was extremely safety-conscious.

As we drove to one of the lakes featured in the book I'd sold him, I scanned its thick glossy pages, more fascinated by the bold entries he had scribbled in the margins in thick black ink than the actual text. "Dismember? Rate of decomposition? Autopsy possibility?" I quoted, shutting the book and leaving it resting on my knees. 'Have you never thought of writing something a little more cheery?'

He laughed and took his eyes off the road for a moment to face me. 'Death sells,' he said with a disarming shrug. I guessed he knew what he was talking about; his last three books had all ridden high on the bestseller list. 'And sex, of course. That sells pretty well too.'

Unbelievably I blushed. I was a grown woman, who had happily surrendered her virginity more than a decade ago, yet I still turned a warm, rosy shade of pink just hearing him say the word.

We found the lake easily enough and only had to stop once to ask directions in a tiny rural hamlet from an elderly man walking his dog. I could tell the man's thick regional accent had been largely indecipherable to Jack as he told us our best route, accompanied by energetic windmilling arm gesticulations. As we pulled away from the well meaning pensioner, Jack smiled and waved at him gratefully, saying softly in the privacy of his car, 'Now that man needs sub-titles. I have no idea what he just said. Was he even speaking English?' I laughed and without thinking about what I was doing, I reached over and patted his bronzed forearm where it was resting on the steering wheel.

'Don't worry. I've got it.' It should have been a perfectly inconsequential action, except something strange happened when my hand touched his arm. Every nerve ending went into sensory overload as his bare skin with the soft dark hair connected with my fingertips. It was a purely involuntary reaction, totally outside my control. Perhaps much like the almost-kiss the other night had been. I saw Jack's knuckles tighten reflexively on the wheel in reaction to my touch.

The lake was a local beauty spot, and actually far too pretty a place to ever dump a body. It was ringed by a thick forest of trees and undergrowth, except at one end where a plain of large flat rocks formed a gently sloping platform to the water's edge. Jack parked his car in a narrow track and we followed a trail of quaint hand-painted arrows which led us to the lake. A light breeze eddied around us as we emerged side by side from the track, and fell into step towards the gently rippling water. The moss-covered ground beneath our feet was soft and uneven, and I gratefully took the arm Jack held out in support when he saw me struggle in my heels.

'Sorry,' I said, nodding down at my footwear, 'I normally wear my other stilettos for rambling.'

'No problem,' he said, glancing down and then frowning as he saw the heels of my shoes sinking into the earth, which was still waterlogged from the recent storm. He nodded towards the large flat expanse of rocks about twenty metres away. 'Let's head over there, shall we?'

I plucked one foot from the earth, accompanied by a noise which resembled a squelching burp. 'That was my shoe, not me,' I clarified.

His smile was gently teasing, making him suddenly look much younger than his thirty-six years. 'Sure it was,' he replied.

We struggled on for a few metres, as I concentrated very hard on not pitching face forwards into the mud.

'It would be easier if I carried you,' Jack offered, after I'd frantically grabbed hold of his arm as I lost my footing.

'No way,' I said, looking up briefly from the muddy ground. 'I can manage.'

Jack shook his head, 'You're stubborn,' he observed, watching me struggle on.

'It's been said,' I commented, thankfully placing my first foothold on to the solid rocks at the head of the lake.

'I'm sorry, I hadn't thought about all the recent rain. Are they ruined?'

Before I could answer he dropped to a crouch before me and slid one hand around my ankle. 'Take them off,' he requested, and was it my imagination, or did his voice sound a little deeper and huskier than usual? I did as he requested, resting my hands on his shoulders for support as he relieved me of the two muddied shoes.

He took them from me and went to the lake's edge and swirled the heels in the water, turning away from me as he undertook the task. By the time he had cleaned them and walked back to me, all vestiges of mud and intimacy were gone from my shoes and his face.

We stood shoulder to shoulder surveying the lake as the sun began to descend behind the trees, bringing a mysterious reddened glow to the water's surface. For a second it looked horribly like a sea of blood and I shuddered involuntarily at the image. Jack turned to me with a look of concern. 'Are you cold?'

I shook my head. Although the breeze was strong enough to make every leaf speak in whispers to its neighbouring tree, there was no real chill to the air. 'No. I'm fine.'

'Do you want to go back to the car? I can always come here by myself on another day.'

'No. Don't be silly. Besides, you can't speak "local", so I doubt you'd ever find this place again.' He laughed, and the sound reverberated around the clearing like a welcoming echo. 'You do whatever it is you have to do... I'm happy to just sit and wait.'

He looked like he might protest further, but the light was beginning to fade and that seemed to decide him. He left me for a few moments and returned carrying the type of camera used by people who are just one click away from being a professional photographer. In his other hand he carried a tartan blanket which he spread out flat on the rocky surface. It looked a little too much like a bed for my liking, so I ignored it.

'I shouldn't be more than a few minutes,' he promised. 'I just want to walk around the lake and take a few pictures.'

'Careful you don't fall in,' I warned as he began to walk away. He stopped and looked back at me over his shoulder.

'What would you do if I did?'

The answer sprang to my lips without conscious thought,

tying me to him in ways I couldn't begin to understand. 'Save you, of course. Just like you did me.'

Jack was actually a good deal longer than just a few minutes, and eventually I did drop down on to the plaid blanket, as I watched his progress around the lake's perimeter. It was peaceful there, with only the rustle of nature and the call of the occasional bird to break the silence, but it was going to take more than a serene location to lift me out of my inner turmoil. I had a head full of unanswered questions on a spectrum which ranged from *Had my fiancé actually been sleeping with my best friend?* to *How is it possible to love one man and feel so mysteriously connected to another at the same time? Did I feel this way because Jack had saved my life?* In and among those knotty issues were scattered other little gems, like *Had Caroline suspected anything about Richard and Amy?* and *What the hell was I going to do if it's true?*

Jack's reconnoitre of the lake was as thorough as an army manoeuvre. Despite the wet and slippery surface, he never once looked anything less than sure-footed as he athletically moved up and down the bank, working out something that I'm sure I would one day recognise within the pages of his next novel. Although he was too far away to talk to, I liked the way he would pause every so often and glance back at me, with a smile or a wave. Even when he wasn't beside me, he had a curious way of making me feel like he still was.

He took a great many photographs of the lake and the surrounding foliage, before coming back to the rocky plain and joining me on the rug.

'Did you get what you wanted?' I asked. 'Will you use this place in your book?'

'Maybe. It depends, I'll have to see where the story takes me.'

'Have you always wanted to be an author?' I gave a little laugh. 'Does everyone asks you that one?'

He smiled. 'Yes. That and "Am I going to be in your next book?"'

'So? Am I?'

He laughed, and I liked the warm resonance in the sound. 'You'll just have to wait and see.'

I shifted on the blanket, enjoying the feeling of the late afternoon sun on my face.

'And what about *your* career hopes and dreams?' he asked, flipping my own question back to me.

'Is this research for your plot, or are you genuinely interested?'

'Genuinely interested, of course.'

And perhaps he was, because he sat and listened carefully as I spoke of my old job, of how it had taken me from London to Washington, how it had left me eager to travel more.

'Do you miss it? Working in a bookshop must seem pretty quiet after that.'

I considered my answer carefully before replying. 'Quiet, yes. But certainly not dull. Working with Monique could never be that.'

He laughed, and I saw the glint of amusement as he clearly remembered my eccentric employer. 'Now *she* could definitely be a character in my book,' he said.

I smiled fondly. 'I owe her a lot. She's been more like a mother than a boss to me this last year.'

Jack picked up a nearby stone and skilfully skimmed it across the lake, achieving an impressive five bounces before it disappeared beneath the glassy surface.

'Did something specific happen to your mother to prompt you to move back?' he probed gently. 'If you don't mind me asking.'

I was puzzled, I thought I had explained all that to him the other evening.

'I understand about her illness, but couldn't you have stayed in London, kept your job? It seems like a lot of sacrifices to have made.'

Something bristled a little at his question, even though I know he didn't mean it unkindly.

'I haven't left marketing for ever,' I said, although I could hear an inner voice echoing inside my head with the question *Really? It kind of feels like you have.* 'I just needed to be permanently based around here, more instantly on call, for now. Actually it was because of my dad rather than my mum. He's stubborn and proud and won't ask for help, not from me, Richard, or the medical profession. He even tried to keep her symptoms hidden from everyone for the longest time.' I gave a small laugh which held no humour. 'Then, last year, it all got too much for him and he ended up in hospital.'

Jack's face was full of concerned sympathy.

'We thought at first it was a heart attack, but thankfully it wasn't. But it so easily could have been. That happened on a Saturday. On the Monday morning I went into my boss's office and asked for a long term leave of absence.'

'That was a brave thing to do.'

'I don't feel brave,' I admitted, my voice small. 'But I couldn't have lived with the consequences of staying in London if something had happened. To either of them. At least now, I can help on a daily basis, and Monique is pretty amazing about my hours. No job in London would let me be so flexible.'

Jack nodded in understanding.

'You know the really crazy thing about all this?' I asked, aware I was about to share with him something I had never before admitted. 'The one person who would be absolutely horrified with what I've done, with what I've left behind, is my mum. Well, Mum as she was, not as she is now. She was all about reaching as high as you can go, making the most of your potential, always looking for the next big goal. It's what made her such a fantastic teacher.' I paused. 'I think she'd be disappointed to know how things have ended up.'

'I don't think *anyone* could ever be disappointed in you,' said Jack.

It might, quite possibly, have been one of the nicest things anyone had ever said to me.

He shifted slightly on the blanket, bringing us closer together, so that every time he breathed in, his shoulder jostled against mine. We stared out over the darkening lake, lost in our own thoughts.

'So come on then, let's have it. What exactly happened between Tuesday evening and now which has made you question your fiancé?'

I sighed deeply. I'd been hoping that he wouldn't ask, but I guess it was partly my fault for having mentioned it in the first place. 'Nothing has happened in the last few days. I've just put together a whole load of things that didn't make any sense and now... well, now I think they do.'

'So tell me,' he urged. I drew in a deep cleansing breath, tried to marshal my thoughts, and for the next twenty minutes I shared it all with him. It was cathartic and crystallising, and as I heard the story unfold from my lips, I became even more convinced that I had reached the only logical conclusion.

Surprisingly, Jack differed in his opinion. 'And that's it? That's all you've got?'

'Huh?'

'A phone number, a shapshot, a garbled apology and a very weird dream. And that's what's made you decide they were having an affair.'

'I, well... I... yes. Isn't that enough? It sure sounded conclusive to me.'

Jack shook his head gently. 'I can't believe I'm saying this, because – and I'm going to be frank here – your fiancé hasn't made the best impression in the world on me so far, but I really don't think you have enough here to hang him with. Nowhere near enough.'

I frowned, feeling torn. I wanted Richard to be innocent, of course I did. But I just couldn't shake the feeling that I had reached the right conclusion, the *only* conclusion, even if I had jumped to get there.

'Honestly, Emma, this isn't nearly so black and white as I think you believe it is. All you have here is a bunch of clues, which you've sewn up together to form a picture, but the pieces could have gone together a hundred different ways, and you'd have an entirely different scenario. Clues don't prove someone's guilt or innocence, and sometimes there aren't *any* signs to read or to miss.' He picked up another stone and skimmed it across the lake. 'Sometimes shit just happens.'

Okay, I got it now; we weren't talking about my situation any longer, we were talking about *his*.

'Sheridan?' I said tentatively, and I felt his shoulder jerk as though he'd been burned. He was quiet for a moment and I let him decide if he wanted to tell me what happened.

'I came home early from a book tour and found her

fucking my best friend.' I gave a sharp intake of breath at the bitter and brutal way he had said it. 'In the shower, in our bathroom,' he added, as though the location was somehow pertinent.

I struggled for a moment to know what to say, trying to find just the right tone of empathy or sympathy. So God knows what possessed me to say, 'I've never had sex in the shower.'

There was a moment of stunned silence, which I filled by groaning over and over in my head *Did I actually just say that?* But it turned out that it was the perfect response, for nothing else at that moment would have made him turn to me with that look of amazed surprise, or have made him laugh so hard that he actually looked like he was in pain.

When eventually he had control of himself Jack said almost curiously, 'Nobody has been able to make me laugh as much as you can in a long, long time. You're an intriguing woman, Emma Marshall, and you continually surprise me.' I bit my lip, not sure how to respond to his words. Fortunately, he didn't seem to expect me to. 'For your sake, I really *do* hope that this thing you're worried about with Richard and Amy is nothing at all like my own situation, that it's all just one big misunderstanding.'

His words filled me with a sudden wave of panic. I guessed I would know the answer to that, one way or another, by the following day.

CHAPTER 8

There were two things I had worked out by morning: that you definitely *don't* need eight hours sleep a night, because I seriously doubted if I'd had eight hours in total over the entire week, and I was still functioning – well, sort of. The second thing was that it doesn't matter how much you prepare or rehearse whatever it is you want to say, some situations never go the way you had planned.

The coaches from Richard's skiing trip weren't due to return until six o'clock in the evening, but I got to the school car park an hour before that. I reversed into a corner space, half hidden beneath the boughs of a tree. It wasn't long before the car park began to fill with a procession of vehicles filing into the spaces around me. Despite the pleasantly warm early evening, I remained within my car, unlike the parents who were standing around in eager clusters, waiting for the return of their children. At just after six, the two coaches came rumbling down the school drive, scattering the groups of parents like ants. Richard was the first to alight from the lead coach, looking a little dishevelled and tired, which wasn't surprising after a twenty-hour journey. He quickly scanned the car park and saw my car beneath the tree. He gave a broad wave and a smile, then pulled out the clipboard tucked beneath his arm and began his final duties as tour leader, making sure each child was ticked off

159

the list as they were collected, and went home with the correct passport.

At last Richard shook hands with the coach drivers, retrieved his holdall from the baggage compartment and trotted over to where I was parked. He opened the passenger door, jumped into the seat and managed to kiss me on the lips in one virtually seamless manoeuvre. I didn't push him away, but I didn't exactly respond either, a fact which he didn't seem to notice. 'Hello, beautiful,' he said, settling himself back in the seat and smiling at me warmly. I tried to smile back, but it felt false and forced. 'Sorry that took ages,' he apologised. 'You've been waiting a long time?'

'Not too long,' was all I offered in reply. I switched on the ignition, but before I could start the engine, Richard leaned across and turned it off again.

'Hey, what's the rush?' he said, holding his arms out to me. 'Come over here, woman.' There was a time, really not so very long ago, when those words would have brought a warm smile to my lips, and I'd have gone willingly into his arms. I tried to conjure up that feeling as he pulled me closer and, now that we had the car park to ourselves, proceeded to kiss me in a way which he certainly wouldn't have done had there been lingering parents or students still around. 'God, I've missed you,' he murmured against my lips. Eventually, some of my reticence must have got through to him, for he pulled back and asked uncertainly, 'Is everything okay? You seem a little... *off*.'

You have no idea, I thought. I shook my head and pasted another faux smile on my lips. I had no intention of getting into our discussion while we were still in range of the school's CCTV cameras. I'd already picked out my perfect location, and it wasn't here.

'Just tired,' I said, and that certainly wasn't a lie. 'I've not been sleeping too well recently.'

He tightened his arms around me in a hard squeeze. 'That's because I've not been beside you,' he said, dropping his voice as he promised, 'But we'll fix that tonight.'

Despite having a collection of anecdotes from the trip that he wanted to share with me, Richard still thoughtfully asked first about my mum and dad, before launching into his stories. That's what made all of this so impossible to believe: how could someone who so obviously cared about me, and every aspect of my life, do something so unthinkably cruel? It was so out of character.

He was busy regaling an amusing story of how he and two other teachers had accidentally got locked out of their rooms after some late-night sampling of the local beer, when he suddenly noticed that I had driven past the exit which would take us to his flat.

'Hey, Emma, that was our turn-off.'

I took my eyes briefly from the road to look at him. 'I thought we might go somewhere quiet first, just for a while.'

He frowned in puzzlement. 'It's quiet in my flat.'

What I really wanted to say was *Somewhere neutral and isolated, somewhere I can scream at you, should that be the way things go, without anyone calling for the police.*

'Yes, I know,' was what I actually replied, 'but I thought it would be nice to go for a walk, maybe stretch your legs a little, after your long journey?'

'What I'd *really* like is a nice hot shower and a back rub,' he said hopefully.

Well, that certainly wasn't going to happen. 'Come on, Richard,' I said in what I hoped was just the right sort of inviting tone, 'let's go for a walk, we won't be long.'

He studied me carefully, before settling back into his seat, a doubtful expression in his eyes, which meant that he was just beginning to realise that something might be wrong. Welcome to the party.

I was heading for Farnham Ravine. It was a dramatic scenic area some fifteen miles from our home, and was a favourite summertime spot with hikers and day-trippers alike. Tall pines flanked the edges and sides of a steep rocky ravine, and in one of her earlier paintings my mother had perfectly captured the rays of dazzling sunlight piercing down through the lacy network of branches. Richard was quiet for most of the drive, and when I glanced over at him I discovered why: he was *asleep*. For some reason that made me incredibly and irrationally angry. We reached the small visitor parking area, and I slammed a little harder on the brakes than was strictly necessary, which brought him awake with a grunt.

'We're here,' I announced, unclipping my seat belt and surveying the car park, which was empty except for our vehicle. Good. No one around to disturb us.

Richard peered out through the windscreen, and rubbed his eyes as he read the welcome sign. 'Farnham Ravine? What are we doing here?'

I didn't answer, but got out of the car and headed towards a sign directing visitors to the footpath. I could hear the crunch of Richard's footsteps on the gravel surface behind me, but I didn't slow down, forcing him to jog for a moment until he caught me up.

'Emma? What's all this about?'

I shook my head but didn't reply, just quickened my pace. I was just this side of being out of breath when I eventually turned to face him. We had travelled only a short distance along the rough dirt footpath; to one side of us was an imposing battalion of tall pines and to the other was the steep rocky drop to the foot of the ravine, some thirty metres below. Now that the moment was finally here, I didn't know where to begin, which was insane because I'd been practising this for days.

'Emma, what on earth is up? You're beginning to scare me now.'

I took a deep breath in, and then released it slowly. 'It's about Amy,' I said, carefully studying his face for a reaction. I saw nothing except genuine bewilderment. Could it be that I might actually be *wrong* about all of this?

'What about her?' The wind was gusting along the path, gently lifting his dark blond hair from his forehead. Part of me instinctively wanted to reach out and smooth it back into place. Another part of me wanted to slap him. I gripped my hand at the wrist, unsure as to whether I could trust it not to end up doing either of those things – or both.

'There was something she said to me… on the night she died. When she was lying on the road and we were waiting for the ambulances to arrive.'

There it was. The reaction I had been intently looking out for. His eyes flickered for a moment and he swallowed visibly. 'What did she say?' There was a thread of something in his tone that I couldn't identify; it wasn't exactly guilt, but it was certainly apprehension.

'She thanked me for forgiving her.'

'Why?'

'I was hoping *you* could tell *me* that.'

He ran his hand through his hair, causing even more disarray than the wind had done. 'How should I know? She was *your* friend.'

'Was she?'

His eyes flew to mine, his expression confused and angry. 'What sort of a stupid question is that? Of course she was. You three girls were like sisters. You did everything together, you told each other everything. Why ask *me* this?'

'Well, it looks like we possibly didn't tell each other *quite* as much as everyone thought.'

Was that relief I saw on his face – that I didn't know what Amy had actually meant? Perhaps. Like a warrior in a battle, I continued to charge on. 'Because I think Amy may have been sleeping with someone, maybe with someone she shouldn't have been...' I paused, not for dramatic effect, but because the words were just so damn hard and painful to say. 'And I think it might have been you.'

I had worked out about fifty different ways the conversation might go from there. But I hadn't once considered the way things actually went down. Richard's face froze for a moment and then his stunned and impassive expression dissolved into one of someone in agonising pain.

'Oh God, Emma. I'm so sorry.' His words struck me like a physical blow, and I staggered backwards, fortunately in the direction of the trees, and not the steep drop-off. I was vaguely aware of his hand reaching out to grab hold of me, but I backed further away, as though retreating from a monster.

'It's true?' I said in shock. 'Are you telling me it's *true*?'

I saw him nod just once, before his face contorted in despair. My knees felt suddenly weak, and a wave of nausea threatened to choke off my words before I could get them out. 'How could you do that? How could you do that to me? To us?' He shook his head, already knowing there was nothing he could say to answer that accusation. He took an unsteady lurching step towards me, and I screamed at him, 'Stay away, don't come anywhere near me.'

'Emma.' My name sounded like it was being ripped out of him. I shook my head violently as the image of him and Amy naked together was suddenly projected into my mind upon a screen of red hot rage. I swallowed down the bitter taste of bile in my mouth.

'Why, Richard? Why? Wasn't I enough for you?'

'It wasn't that,' he groaned in protest.

'Then what? Were you bored? Felt like a change? What did she give you that I couldn't?'

'Nothing. It wasn't *like* that.'

My eyes were blazing like hot coals as I rounded on him. 'So what *was* it like? Because I can't think of a single thing that could possibly justify you destroying everything we have so you could screw around with *my best friend*.' And, as I said the words, I felt the knife slice through me, not once but twice, because the betrayal was dual-edged. The next question came out on a whisper. 'Were you... were you in love with her?'

'No. No, of course not. It's *you* I love. Amy was... a mistake, a terrible stupid mistake. It wasn't even an affair, it was just sex – it was just one time.'

'Is that supposed to make me feel *better*?' I thundered. 'Because it bloody well makes it worse.'

Richard looked around in desperation, knowing he'd said the wrong thing even as the words were leaving his mouth. To be honest there was nothing he *could* say that was going to stop the noose from tightening around his neck.

'So tell me.' The words were spat at him, as though they'd come from a serpent.

'What?' he asked helplessly. 'What do you want to know?'

'Everything.'

His eyes were blue pools of torment. He had nowhere to go, no defence he could possibly offer, and no way of avoiding answering my questions. He tried one last evasion. 'Why, Emma? Why? Can't we just find a way past this? I did a terrible, stupid and weak thing, but dissecting it isn't going to help.' His choice of words was particularly apt, because that was what this was starting to feel like: a post-mortem following the death of our relationship.

'Tell me,' I demanded.

He turned away from me as he began to speak, unable to look me in the eye as he ripped the skin from my body with his words. 'I guess it all started a couple of years ago—'

'What?' I cried out, my voice like a demented harpy. 'You've been sleeping with her for *years*?'

'No, no. I told you it was just one time. What I meant was that we started getting closer a few years ago. After you'd gone away. After we broke up.' He glanced over at me, but my eyes were narrowed in bitter anger; I could scarcely bring myself to look at him. 'At first we were just friends, we went out with Caroline and Nick most of the time, just as mates. But as time went on...'

'You fancied her,' I said bitterly.

He ran his hand through his hair. 'No, not at first. She was just Amy, your old friend. I couldn't even think of her that way. Couldn't think of *anyone* that way. I was still in love with you.'

'I'm so touched.' My voice dripped sarcasm like venom.

'Time went on, and I started seeing other people, but nothing came to anything. Because of you.'

'You're breaking my heart,' I said viciously, and then had to look away suddenly, because the truth of it was, that was precisely what he *was* doing.

'Amy understood me. We got on well, we shared the same sense of humour, but I knew... well, I suspected, anyway...' His voice trailed away, and he sounded embarrassed as he finished, 'I knew she liked me. I knew she wanted something more.'

Amy. Her face appeared before me like a mirage. I had known her for most of my life; I'd shared secrets, hopes and fears with her. I had trusted her. And yet she had broken the cardinal rule of friendship, the sacred code: she had gone after her friend's ex.

'I resisted for a very long time.'

'Well bravo to you.'

He ignored my interruption. 'But eventually, when it looked like you were *never* going to come back, things began to... *develop* between us.'

It didn't matter how many euphemisms he used, I was still getting the full ugly picture in glorious technicolour. 'So you got with her when I was in London?'

'No. Well, almost. Things might have happened then, I could see that, but then you came back home. And I realised what I'd really known all along: that it was *you*, it had always been you; I couldn't love anyone else, because my heart was yours.'

'So she just got a different part of your anatomy?' I sniped.

Richard winced, as though he'd been shot, but still continued. 'We cooled everything off immediately, as soon as you came back. We just went back to being friends, nothing else.'

'And you didn't think any of this was important enough to tell me when we got back together?' I fired on him angrily.

'You and I agreed that we didn't need to tell each other details of the other people we'd dated.'

'That's because I thought they were nameless strangers, *not* my best friend.'

'And it wasn't like we dated, well not properly. We just kissed a few times and—'

'Enough!' I shrieked, already having enough trouble getting the unwanted visuals out of my head. I certainly didn't need him to elaborate.

We were silent for several minutes. Richard was hoping that I'd finally heard enough of the ugly tale, while I was just trying to summon up the strength to hear it through to the end.

'So when did you fuck her?' I don't know what shocked him most: the way I had phrased it, or my need to know it all.

His voice was hesitant, guilt in every syllable. 'It was last year, after you got me to arrange a date for her with that prat at my school.' He looked up at me, expecting acknowledgement perhaps. All he got was a glittering stony stare. 'Well, she went out with him, but the guy was a real bastard. I told you I hadn't wanted to set it up.'

Richard was very lucky there was nothing near enough for me to throw at him right then, because he had come perilously close to making it sound that I was in some way partly responsible for what had happened. He continued in a rush, 'Anyway, things got really ugly, and she ended up calling me in floods of tears.'

'Why?'

'I don't know why. Because I was the one who'd set her up? Because I was her friend? I don't know. You don't know how many times I've wanted to turn the clock back and have her call someone else.' I braced myself for the final avalanche to bury me, as Richard completed his story. 'It was late. I went to comfort her, we had a few drinks and then... well...'

He didn't finish. He didn't need to. I got it.

'Afterwards, we both felt terrible. We both knew it had been wrong. Amy knew all along that I loved you, that it was you I wanted to be with.' He looked at me beseechingly, but got nothing in response. My heart felt like a petrified lump of stone buried in my chest. 'She begged me to let her tell you. She wanted you to know how sorry she was.'

I shut my eyes, but the pain was still there behind my closed lids.

'In the end, I convinced her that *I* should be the one to do it. I was the one who had betrayed you most. It was my job to beg you to forgive me.'

'And yet you didn't,' I said coldly.

'I couldn't,' he answered, his voice a broken whisper. 'I couldn't risk losing you, couldn't risk the thought that you might leave me. So I lied. I lied to you, and I lied to Amy. I told her that you said you would forgive her, but only on condition that the two of you never spoke about it. Ever.'

So. The mystery was finally solved. That was what she had meant as she lay dying on the road. That was why she was thanking me. I looked at the man who had betrayed me in the worst way possible, and knew that he'd been right to be afraid that this would be the end of us. Because it most certainly would have been. And now it was.

He saw my actions, and gave a moan that sounded wrought with pain. 'No,' he cried, as he watched me begin to twist the engagement ring from my finger. 'No, Emma, please.'

I looked up and saw he was crying. Strange. My eyes were dry; it was the complete reversal of our first break-up.

'Please no,' he begged, bridging the distance between us and trying to hold me. I gave one final twist and the diamond was off my finger. I held it in my palm towards him.

'Take it.'

He shook his head.

'Take it, Richard. I don't want it. We're over. Done.'

'Don't say that,' he pleaded, as tears rolled down his face. 'Give me another chance. I will never, ever, do anything to hurt you again for the rest of my life.'

The hand that held the ring remained rock-steady, although inside there wasn't a single piece of me that wasn't ripped to shreds. 'It's too late. You gave me this ring just weeks after sleeping with another woman. You told me I was the only person in the world for you, while you could probably still remember the scent and taste of her.' I thrust the hand bearing the ring closer towards him.

'Take it,' I commanded for a third time.

'I don't want it. It's yours.'

I looked into his eyes and something inside me just snapped. 'You don't want it?' He shook his head. 'Well neither do I.' And with that I closed my fist around the large diamond ring and hurled it with all my strength out into the ravine. It fell in a tumbling arc through the sky, its facets catching the last rays of sunlight as it plummeted like a shooting star on to the rocky ground far beneath us.

There was shock and horror on his face at my actions. To be truthful, I was a little horrified myself. 'Do you know how much—' He broke off, which was just as well, or I might actually have pushed him over the edge to join his bloody ring. He took a step closer to the precipice, which was foolish, I thought, giving my current state of mind, and looked down solemnly on to the vast rocky terrain. 'We're never going to find that now,' he declared.

I didn't feel a reply was warranted, but I did ask a question. 'Do you have your phone with you?'

He looked stunned and confused, but nevertheless put his hand into his pocket and retrieved his mobile. He held it out to me, in much in the same way as I had just held out his ring.

'I don't need it. You do,' I said abruptly. He frowned, still slow to realise my intentions. I met his eyes one last time. 'You'll need to call one of your friends, or a cab company, or anyone you bloody well like.' He still didn't seem to get it, not even when I started to walk away. 'I'm going, Richard, and how you get back from here is not my concern. In fact nothing about you is going to be my concern, ever again.'

In the days following our break-up Richard employed every conceivable method to get in touch with me. He phoned, he texted, he emailed; he even sent me a letter. Short of sending a carrier pigeon, he used just about every means of communication possible. It did him no good; I tore to shreds anything that couldn't be eliminated by simply pressing a *Delete* button. I suppose it was inevitable then that his only remaining option was to turn up in person at the bookshop. He was dressed in his work suit and wearing the tie I'd bought him for Christmas. The gift exchange hadn't been entirely equitable last year: I'd bought him a cashmere jumper and a tie, and he'd given me a diamond solitaire that had cost him three months' salary. I still felt a little guilty about that. Perhaps I should suggest he throw the jumper off the ravine, to square things up a little?

'Hello, Emma,' he said cautiously, loitering near the shop's doorway.

I met his gaze coolly. 'Richard.' That was all he got from me, no hello or greeting, just his name. He seemed to think that was enough encouragement, and took a step towards the counter.

'What are you doing here?'

He tried the smile, the one I'd always said was so irresistible, but it seemed as though I had finally found some immunity. Richard saw the impassive look on my face, and read it well. He cleared his throat in a way which I knew meant he was really nervous.

'I came to buy a book.'

It wasn't even worth rising to the bait. This wasn't my business or my shop, so I could hardly throw him out and yell at him to go away.

I raised a hand to indicate the stacks of books around us. 'Knock yourself out.'

My attitude clearly had him flummoxed. He must have been anticipating Furious Emma, Vengeful Emma, or even Distraught Emma. Couldn't-Give-a-Shit Emma clearly hadn't factored into his plans.

He maintained the pretence that it really was a book he was after, by pulling some volume from the shelves and opening it at a random page. He looked at it unseeingly for a minute or so, then interrupted the silence of the shop. 'You haven't answered my calls.'

I stopped pretending to be checking deliveries off an invoice, and laid down my pen. 'No, I haven't. And I'm not going to. I have nothing more to say to you, I said it all the other day.'

'Well, I still have things *I* want to say. I need to explain.'

'I don't want to hear it. We're done, Richard. It's over.'

There was a rustling noise behind me and I knew that Monique must have just come into the shop. I didn't doubt for a minute that she'd been listening to our entire conversation from the back room, and had waited for just the right moment to make her entrance.

172

'*Bonjour, Richard, comment ça va?*' she said coolly, squeezing my hand surreptitiously beneath the counter as she passed me. Richard looked up in confusion, not knowing her well enough to know that she only reverted to her native tongue when she was exceedingly happy or furiously angry. And she certainly wasn't smiling today.

'Bon... er... hello,' he replied, as wrong-footed as she had known he would be.

'Can I help you with your purchase?' she enquired, extending a many-ringed hand to him to take the volume. 'It is a fascinating book, *non*?' Richard looked down for the first time at the weighty hardback he was holding, and saw it appeared to be an encyclopaedia of European drainage systems. 'Er, I'm just browsing,' he said rapidly, sliding the book back into the wrong place on the shelf. 'Actually, I came to have a word with Emma.' His meaning was pointed and obvious, and I knew without doubt that Monique understood perfectly that she was now supposed to excuse herself, to allow us some privacy. He really didn't know her at all.

Monique threw back her arm as though she was a magician presenting me from a box which had been empty just a second before. 'And here she is!' Richard looked from me to my boss, and realised he was outmatched. It was like watching a highly devious Parisian cat toying with a field mouse. Monique was going to remain exactly where she stood, which, at that precise moment in time, was directly between us.

Richard glanced at the clock on the shop wall, and I knew he only had an hour for lunch, and was going to be pushing it to get back in time. He had no alternative but to talk in front of Monique.

'Emma, we can't just leave things where they are. We need

to discuss everything, calmly and rationally.' He flicked a quick glance at the third person in the shop. '*Privately.*'

'You can speak freely in front of Monique.'

Monique smiled and gave a Gallic shrug. 'Don't mind me. I hardly speak much of the English anyway.'

I quickly turned away to look out of the shop's side window to hide my smile, and caught a glimpse of a very familiar car. Oh no. This was about to get even more uncomfortable.

'Did you get the flowers I sent?' Richard asked me suddenly, and I looked back at him, with a flash of remembered anger. The bouquet had been huge, so wide that it had taken several hefty shoves before I finally managed to push it all the way into the wheelie bin. I told him this, and felt nothing at his responding look of helpless despair.

'You binned them?' he asked disbelievingly. I guessed they must have cost him a small fortune, but still, not as much as the ring had done.

'Yes, well I did consider driving to the cemetery and putting them on Amy's grave' – his face whitened at the coldness of my voice – 'but then… well, frankly that didn't seem appropriate either.'

He came up to the counter then, and ran his hand distractedly through his hair. 'Emma, you've got to help me. I just don't know what to do here.'

'You could buy a book,' suggested Monique innocently. I don't think he even heard her. His eyes were begging me, and despite myself some shred of compassion, which I thought I had thoroughly stamped out, stirred deep within me.

I was saved from answering by the tinkling of the shop's bell, announcing a new customer. I looked up and knew I'd been right to recognise the car. We were truly in an actual

174

living breathing French farce. All we needed now was a scantily dressed maid, and we'd have cracked it.

'Hello, Jack.'

His eyes swept each of us, assessing – fairly accurately, I imagine – the scene he had just interrupted. I heard a small sigh from my boss, which managed to sound coquettish and delighted all at the same time. From Richard there was just a single word 'Monroe', which could have been a greeting, or an accusation. Given the glower on his face, I thought the latter was more likely.

Ignoring the other occupants of the shop, Jack directed his attention and welcoming smile at me. 'Hi, Emma.' I smiled back, trying to decide if the situation had just got better or a great deal worse.

'It is a pleasure to see you here again so soon, Monsieur Monroe.'

I heard Richard's hissing intake of breath and wondered what had possessed Monique to poke the already angry tiger with such a sharp stick.

'*Again?*' Richard turned his obviously displeased look directly at me. 'Does he make a habit of this then?'

Jack took a warning step closer to the counter, so that between him and Monique I could barely see Richard. The testosterone was circling thickly in the air, like a miniature cyclone.

'It's a shop, Richard. People come in; they buy books, take them home and read them. It's not a difficult concept to grasp.'

I thought I saw a vague twitch of Jack's lips, and was extremely grateful that he, as yet, hadn't lowered himself to respond directly to Richard's rude accusation. 'And incidentally, in case you've forgotten, let me remind you – *once*

175

again – that who I do or do not see, is no longer any business of yours.'

Jack leaned back against the counter, now almost completely obscuring me from Richard's view. He picked up a catalogue from a stack by the till and appeared to be casually browsing through the titles, but that was only if you were either blind or stupid, and couldn't see that his real intention was to position his body as a shield between me and Richard.

'Well, I don't like it,' Richard declared, shooting Jack the sort of look that a hundred or so years ago had men reaching for their duelling pistols. My admiration for my new friend's tolerance level grew even greater, as he looked up equably and said, 'Really? I find reading quite diverting actually. But perhaps that's just because of my profession.'

I'd only seen Richard get close to hitting someone once before, in all the years I'd known him, and that situation hadn't been nearly as tense as this one was rapidly becoming.

'Listen, I am trying to have a private conversation here with my *fiancée*,' he ground out.

'Ex-fiancée,' I said, embarrassed that I had virtually shouted out the correction, as I frantically tried to pour some water on the flames before they properly ignited. '*Ex*-fiancée,' I repeated, a good deal more quietly. Jack's eyes went straight to mine, a hundred questions in them, most of them, in some form or other, seemed to be asking if I was all right. I gave a small imperceptible nod, but still his eyes remained on me.

From the edge of my field of vision I saw Richard glance from Jack to me, and knew he'd missed nothing of the unspoken concern on his face and my answering silent reassurance.

'Oh that's marvellous,' he declared with an angry derisive

sneer, which made it clear that it was anything but. 'Absolutely fucking marvellous!'

He turned on his heel and stormed out the door, slamming it so hard behind him that for a moment I thought he'd actually broken it off its hinges. The stunned silence in his wake was eventually broken by Monique.

'I may have to revise my opinion of that young man. He actually swears quite well, for a beginner.'

CHAPTER 9

I had only just fallen asleep, after what seemed like hours of tossing and turning, when my mobile phone buzzed impatiently on the polished surface of my bedside table. Thin early morning light was beginning to pierce through the gap in my curtains, and I had to peer several times at the phone's display to read it was only six-thirty in the morning. I blinked to clear my vision and read the caller's ID. *Caroline*. Automatically my heart skipped a beat. No one called at this time of day unless it was serious.

'Caroline?' I answered, feeling my stomach already clenching in preparation for more bad news.

She cut straight to the point. 'You *broke up*? You broke up with Richard and you didn't think to tell me?'

'Caroline, it's six-thirty.'

She steamed on ahead as though I hadn't spoken.

'What the hell were you thinking of?'

'Richard told you,' I said with a sigh.

'No, he bloody didn't! What the hell is wrong with the pair of you? I got a text late last night from some stupid girl – who I don't even know that well – from the rugby club. Apparently Richard was in the bar there last night, drinking like there was no tomorrow, and spreading the news about the two of you to anyone who'd listen. I've been sitting here for hours waiting until it was a reasonable time to call.'

I was going to point out that, in my opinion, that time was still several hours from now, but she didn't give me the chance to speak.

'I can't believe, Emma Marshall, that we've known each other for over twenty years, and *this* is how I had to find out.'

When Caroline eventually paused for breath, all I could think was, *Terrific, our break-up is now a juicy item of hot local gossip.*

'Why the hell didn't you tell me?' Caroline shot out accusingly, her lungs obviously back to full capacity. It really was way too early for this kind of conversation.

I gave just one word in response. 'Amy.'

'What's Amy got to do with any of this?'

Like an earthquake, I could feel a rumbling and tearing as the ground our friendship had been built on slowly began to rip apart. I closed my eyes and saw a lifetime of memories tumbling end over end into the shadowy depths of the chasm.

'Amy and Richard.'

Just hearing Caroline's gasp as I said their names was proof enough. 'But you already knew, didn't you?' I said bitterly. 'I guessed as much the other day, so don't bother denying it.'

'I... I...' Caroline, normally so assured and confident, seemed to be having difficulty in forming a reply. 'I didn't know for sure.' She paused and continued in a whispered confession, 'I didn't *want* to know.'

'Why the hell didn't you say anything to me, Caroline?'

'Because I couldn't be *sure*. Amy never said anything to me, and I could have been totally wrong... I just knew she'd been seeing someone, and that she was being strangely secretive about it.'

I closed my eyes, as though I could shut out the pain of betrayal which was facing me every way I turned. 'I can't believe you didn't say anything, Caroline, you're supposed to be my best friend.'

'I couldn't,' she said on a moan. 'I couldn't hurt you like that.'

'And *this* isn't hurting me?' I challenged bitterly.

Another long silence. Caroline was the first to break it. 'Look, we need to talk about this properly, face to face.'

'No, we really don't.'

'Emma.' There was hurt rejection in her voice, and I guessed this conversation hadn't gone at all the way she had expected. 'Emma please, let me help you try to sort this out. You can still be pissed at me, I don't mind, but don't shut me out. I'm your friend. You need me.' Her voice dropped to a whisper and I heard a tremor in it now that her anger was spent. 'I need *you*.'

And she was right, on both counts. We needed each other and she *was* still my friend – at this rate the only one I had left – now Amy and Richard had both spectacularly been snatched from me. But it was too soon, too early in the morning, and I was still much too raw.

'I don't want to talk about this, Caroline, I really don't. Not with anyone, not yet. There's nothing to sort out here. Richard and I are done. This can't be fixed.'

There was another long silence at the end of the line, and I could hear the low rumble of Nick's voice in the background and knew I probably had him to thank for not receiving this phone call any earlier.

'Give me a few days, Caroline. I need some space to get my head together. Please. I'll phone you when I'm ready to talk. Please, just leave me alone until then.'

I lay back against the pillows after the call, knowing there was no hope now of getting back to sleep. As much as I wanted to turn to Caroline, I couldn't ignore – or forgive – the fact that she'd suspected Richard was the man Amy had been seeing, and yet she'd said nothing to me. Not one word. She'd let me carry on planning a wedding, a life and a future, knowing all the while that everything I was building could well be sitting on a lie. The three people who I trusted more than anyone else in the world had each betrayed me, in one way or another, and the burning taste of bitter deceit seared my throat whenever I thought about it.

I opened my bedroom curtains on Saturday morning, really grateful that it was my day off. Even the weather had improved, with the sun making a long overdue appearance. I dressed in jeans and a light-weight V-necked jumper and applied just enough make-up to ensure that no one could easily tell how little sleep I was actually getting these days.

Feeling cowardly, I delayed going downstairs until I heard my father's car drive away. My parents' life largely followed a blueprint these days, which my mother gained a great deal of comfort from, which in turn comforted my father. This was a part of their Saturday ritual. They would journey to the large supermarket in the next town, where my mother would push the trolley and pull random and bizarre items from the shelves, which my father was mostly successful in returning unseen before they reached the checkout. Still, he missed the odd item, which explained the occasional jar of quail's eggs or exotic condiment which sometimes turned up in the cupboard. After shopping they would go out for lunch to the same restaurant, where my mother would spend a good fifteen minutes studying the menu before ordering the exact same dish that she had chosen the week before, and the week before that.

The day stretched ahead of me like a rolling desert highway, but I couldn't settle to any one task. I tried to lose myself in the book I was reading, looking for escape in the pages of mystery and intrigue in a much easier world, where if someone did something you didn't like, you shot them. Simple. Several hours later I finally admitted defeat and shut the book, with a sigh. The storyline was complex and none of it had gone in. I flipped it over and studied the author portrait on the back cover. It was a different photo this time, taken in a studio. I traced a finger over the thick dark hair, then shocked myself by idly wondering what it would feel like to run my hands through it. There was a glint in the golden-brown eyes staring back at me, as though he knew exactly what was going through my mind.

'Oh screw it!' I declared, jumping to my feet. I didn't stop to consider my motives, afraid of what that kind of scrutiny might reveal, and went in search of my jacket and car keys.

I scribbled a note for my parents. *Caroline phoned. I'm going out. May be back late.* Okay, so it wasn't a lie, but it was certainly an interesting version of the truth. There was one lie I was definitely guilty of telling though, and that was when I'd said to Caroline that I didn't need to talk about what had happened. Because I did, rather badly, as it turned out. But it had to be with someone impartial, someone sympathetic, someone who appreciated exactly what I was going through, because the same faith-shattering treachery had also happened to them.

I had a perfectly rehearsed opening greeting when I pulled into Jack's drive a short time later. *'Hi, Jack, I hope you don't mind me dropping in unannounced, but if you don't have any plans for tonight, I'd like to buy you dinner, to thank you for everything you've done.'* I figured that sounded perfectly acceptable. Buying a meal for someone who'd saved your life was just a nice gesture.

I arrived at Jack's house just as he was returning from a run along the crescent-shaped cove which lay beneath his house. I saw him leave the beach and start heading up the flight of steep stone steps which led to his back garden. I started descending the uneven steps which were roughly carved out of the rock face. He smiled broadly, scarcely out of breath, as I approached. He was dressed in running clothes and a Harvard vest top, which advertised the fact that he'd once been a member of their running team. I was impressed, but not surprised.

'Emma,' he greeted, and there was genuine delight in his voice. I smiled a little shyly in return, forcing my eyes to his face and away from the sheen of perspiration which glistened on his muscular arms and body, making the vest cling against him. The man had been running, for God's sake, he was entitled to be sweating. I felt a little uncomfortably warm myself as I tried to remember what I was doing there.

Jack reached for a small towel which he'd left at the base of the steps, and passed it across his face and the back of his neck. One dark lock of hair was left out of place, and I was surprised at just how much I wanted to reach up and straighten it.

'I'm sorry, I shouldn't have just come by announced,' I said. 'I'm interrupting your jog... run... whatever it is.'

His eyes twinkled. 'Not much of a runner?'

'Not unless I'm being chased or am fleeing from a burning building.'

He grinned, and I felt the tight knot of tension inside me

begin to slowly unravel. I always forgot what easy company Jack was, how effortlessly the banter flowed. It continually took me by surprise how relaxed I felt with him.

'Do you feel like taking a walk?' he asked, inclining his head towards the empty beach behind us.

'Absolutely,' I said, 'as long as you're sure I'm not intruding.'

'Of course not. I was hoping to see you again,' he confided, falling into step beside me. 'I've been worried about you since that episode at the bookshop.'

I felt a warmth on my cheeks which could have been from the effort of matching my stride to Jack's, or maybe from the realisation that I'd been in his thoughts. Was that a good or a bad thing?

We walked in companionable silence along the deserted beach, following the trail of footprints he had left in the sand. There was something wonderfully peaceful and calming in the quiet isolation of our surroundings. Eventually we reached the far end of the cove and sat down by the boundary where the incoming waves changed the colour of the sand from gold to caramel. The breeze was a little stronger now, making my hair whip about my head like auburn streamers around a maypole. I kept trying, unsuccessfully, to tuck it behind my ears and once, on looking up, I saw Jack watching me with a curious look on his face. For no reason at all my pulse began to quicken, and my lips felt suddenly dry. Jack shifted slightly and turned to stare out to sea.

'Rough week?' he hazarded, his eyes fixed on the horizon.

'I've known better,' I replied.

He turned to look at me. 'Feel like talking about it?'

I shook my head. 'I thought I wanted to, or even *needed* to. But you know what, now that I'm here, I just want to leave it all behind, like a heavy bag I can pick up later. Right now I don't even want to *think* about it, much less talk. It's all too much: Amy first and now this with Richard.'

He nodded, understanding me probably better than I did myself.

'Caroline thinks I'm wrong, that I *should* talk. But then she's always been that way, she'll work a problem through from every angle until she finds a solution.'

'It's not a bad strategy. Have you done that with her?'

I felt a little ashamed as I replied, 'No. Not really. We're not exactly on the best of terms at the moment. I kind of blamed her for not telling me she suspected what had been going on.'

His brow furrowed at my words, and I could see my answer troubled him. 'You've both been through something so terrible and tragic, something only the two of you can really understand. Maybe now's not a great time to be shutting her out of your life. And, as far as not telling you, well, she probably thought she was protecting you.'

'I know, you're right. It's just that everything feels so raw and exposed. I guess my emotions are still all over the place.' I lowered my voice as though to keep the gulls circling overhead from hearing my guilty admission. 'Most of the time I just feel so incredibly angry.' I felt like I was confessing to a terrible crime. 'I'm angry at Caroline for keeping her suspicions a secret; I'm angry at Richard for betraying me, and at Amy too for the same reason...' The expression on Jack's face was troubled as I continued, '... But mostly I'm angry – no, furious – with her for dying and leaving us.'

'I really wish I didn't have to go back to the States in just three weeks,' he admitted. 'I feel like I'm abandoning you just when things are getting tough.' He moved closer to me and put his arm around my shoulder, seeming to understand that while I didn't want to speak about it all, I did need some comfort.

I had to purse my lips, so that *'Don't leave then'* didn't accidentally escape from them, which was a ridiculous thought and would have been extremely embarrassing to have said out loud. Obviously he was going to leave; he'd told me on the night we met that his stay here was brief. He had a home and career in America; all he had to keep him in England was research material for his book.

'It's not your responsibility to look out for me,' I reasoned, my independent streak – the one Richard had always found so challenging – forcing its way to the surface. It felt good to feel it again. It had been a while.

Jack smiled, and I knew there had been no chauvinism in his comment. 'Ah, but in some cultures you're *always* going to be my responsibility. It comes with the territory, after having saved your life. Some philosophies believe that I am for ever duty bound to look out for you now.'

'Been Googling, have you?'

'Yep. You too?'

'Yep.'

There was a lot of information out there about the links between victim and rescuer: the bond, the closeness, the inexplicable commitment and obligation. Some of it explained the strange connection I had felt with Jack since the night we met, and some of it didn't even scratch the surface.

'I'm not sure talking is what I need, anyway,' I continued, picking up the theme of our conversation. 'Did *you* have anyone to talk to after you and Sheridan… you know…?' I wondered for a moment if I'd overstepped the mark. I probably didn't know him nearly well enough for such a personal question. I should try a lot harder to keep that in mind. I wasn't sure if he was actually going to answer at all, and then a lopsided grin settled on his face.

'Oh, I talked. We both did. Not to each other, mind: to two very expensive – and now extremely well-off – attorneys. You're right, sometimes talking *isn't* the answer.'

At least Richard and I didn't have to worry about selling a property or dissolving any mutual assets. There was only one asset that we had jointly owned, and I'd sent it spiralling through the air to the bottom of a ravine.

'You know, the strangest thing is that when I try to work out just how I feel about everything that's happened with Richard, I feel more humiliated and angry than heartbroken.'

He nodded.

'I think I'm about seventy per cent angry and about twenty per cent heartbroken.'

He paused for a second. 'I know I deal more with words than numbers, but you *do* know that doesn't add up, don't you?' I looked up at his gentle teasing observation. 'What's the last ten per cent then?'

I spoke so softly, my answer was almost whipped from my lips by the bracing sea breeze. 'Relieved,' I said.

As we walked back to his house, I finally remembered to ask Jack if he'd let me buy him dinner, but he turned my invitation around and asked me to stay and share a meal with him instead.

'I've been cooking on that range of yours,' he said, as he unlocked the back door and we entered the kitchen, where the air was heavy with the smell of spicy chilli. There was an enormous pot, more of a cauldron really, on the Aga's simmering plate, a pot which held enough to feed at least a dozen passing Mexicans.

'Are you sure you have enough?' I laughed as I stepped out of my sand-caked shoes and padded over to the hob, where he was stirring the gently bubbling dish.

'There is quite of a lot,' he observed. 'I hope you're not going to tell me you're the kind of girl who only eats lettuce leaves.'

'Do I look like that's all I eat?' I said with a self-deprecating laugh, before I realised that sounded as though I was fishing for compliments. I could feel my face flush hotter than the fieriest of chillies as his eyes briefly swept my body. I suddenly wished I had worn something far less figure-hugging than the thin sweater which clearly outlined the fullness of my breasts, or the tight jeans which covered my hips and thighs like a second skin.

'It all looks fine to me,' Jack pronounced, and then turned suddenly away from me. 'I need a quick shower after my run. Are you okay on your own down here for a few minutes?'

'Sure, I'll keep an eye on the chilli.'

He wagged a finger warningly. 'Do *not* touch my chilli,' he cautioned. 'It is a work of culinary genius, as well as being the only damn thing I know how to cook.' He smiled then, in a way that made his eyes crinkle at the edges. 'Sit down and relax. Make yourself at home. I won't be long.'

I couldn't sit, and I couldn't relax, and some of that was because I didn't want to have to answer the insistent question that kept circling like a buzzard around my head: *Why the hell are you here?* The other reason was a little easier to comprehend, and had something to do with not allowing my thoughts to stray to images of Jack showering under hot jets of water just above me.

I wandered from the kitchen into the hall, surprised at just how many rooms the rental property held. The first door

I tried was a room which Jack was clearly using as his office. There was an open document on the computer screen which drew me like a magnet. Reluctantly I shut the door. I don't think his invitation to 'make myself at home' had actually included reading extracts from the book he was working on.

Across the hallway was a cosy lounge. But there was something within it that was so surprising to see that I actually gasped in astonishment. I walked towards it, and was still standing looking at it some ten minutes later, when Jack found me.

I didn't hear him approach and when he came and stood behind me, lightly placing his hands on my shoulders, I jumped about a foot in the air. It took a minute or two for my heart to regain its normal rhythm, although I suspect that could have been achieved a lot quicker if he'd removed his hands from my arms and hadn't smelled so distractingly of soap, shampoo and aftershave. Every breath I took was filled with the smell of him.

'I'm sorry, I startled you,' he apologised. 'You must have been miles away.'

That was true enough. About six hundred or so, to be precise. I turned back to face the painting and Jack did likewise.

'I always like looking at this one,' he confided, his eyes sweeping over the image of the crumbling farmhouse beside a lake. In the foreground of the painting was a willow tree, whose shadows were skilfully recreated in the water's rippling surface. 'You can look at it a hundred times, and see something different on each occasion.'

I nodded in agreement. Many of her pieces had exactly the same effect on me, and it was deeply satisfying to hear that he appreciated what he was looking at.

'I wonder where it is.'

'It's a rural hamlet in the Dordogne,' I said, my eyes still glued to it.

He turned away from the wall and looked at me in amazement, then stepped closer to the hearth to examine the signature in the corner of the frame. 'F. Marshall,' he said, the respect in his voice clearly audible. 'Your mother?'

I nodded, suddenly too choked to speak. I hadn't seen this painting in years. 'We holidayed there, about ten years ago. We stayed in a *gîte* just down the lane from this place,' I said, inclining my head towards the painting. 'Mum was up at dawn every morning, waiting for just the right light to capture it the way she wanted to.'

He studied the picture with what I felt was just the right amount of concentration. 'She nailed it.'

I smiled, at the very un-art critic summation. 'She did that.'

One of his arms was around my shoulders as we spoke, and it seemed perfectly natural to lean against him, but there was nothing I could detect in his hold except the comforting support of a friend.

'Does she still paint?'

I gave a sigh which was both sad and regretful. 'All the time. But nothing like this, not any more.' There was genuine sympathy in his eyes, and the hand cupping my shoulder squeezed gently. 'We eventually ran out of wall space at home, so she started selling some pieces through a gallery in town. She did quite well, actually.' I sighed again, and looked back at the painting. 'I always liked this one though; I kind of wished she'd kept it.'

The sun was starting its slow descent towards the horizon, and when we returned to the kitchen Jack threw open the glass doors to let in the refreshing sea breeze and lazy slanting chevrons of light. He turned down my offer of assistance as he pulled armfuls of salad vegetables from the fridge, reaching further into its confines to extract some beers and a bottle of wine. He smiled approvingly when I went for the beer.

'Definitely my sort of a girl,' he said, opening two bottles and passing me one. It was just a figure of speech, I knew that, but I raised the bottle to my lips to hide my smile.

As he chopped and cleaned the salad ingredients, I cleared a space among the accumulation of papers piled on the table, to make room for our plates. A large envelope slipped from my fingertips, scattering its contents, and a collection of colour photographs fell like tarot cards across the wooden surface. I recognised the location instantly, it was the lake we had visited; the photographs were part of Jack's research. I began shuffling them back together into a pile. Each picture was so similar it was hard to see what he'd been trying to capture with the images, and then my fingers stilled as they reached the final four photographs at the bottom of the pile, which had been hidden beneath the others. They were all of me. I opened my mouth to say something, to ask why he'd taken them, and then closed it again, confused.

I learned more about Jack that evening from the things he *didn't* say, rather than the things he did. He spoke of his father, who had passed away; their closeness and how much he missed him were obvious from his voice, which I found really moving. I've always felt you can tell a lot about a person by their relationship with their family, especially their parents; it was one of the things I'd always loved about Richard. I shook my head as though to get rid of an annoyingly persistent insect. I had to learn to stop doing that, to stop relating everything back to him.

Jack was good company; amusing and intelligent and also very skilful at diverting the conversation away from anything too personal. Of course, he had every right to guard his private life, I'm sure a lot of people in the public eye did the same, but it was still frustrating. By the end of the meal, I was full of chilli, buzzing slightly from two beers and had told him probably far more than I should have done about my relationship with Richard, and had gained practically nothing in return.

When Jack went to the fridge and held up another beer with a questioning look, I shook my head. I was driving later and two was definitely my limit. He took one for himself, flipped the top and raised the bottle to his mouth. I found my eyes drawn to the long column of his throat as he swallowed deeply. I stared, strangely mesmerised by the muscles moving beneath the tanned skin. He caught me studying him, and I felt a hot flush creep into my cheeks.

'What?' he asked, slowly lowering the bottle from his lips and leaning back against the countertop.

I opened my mouth to speak, but nothing came out. *Say something*, my brain screamed at me. *Anything. Don't just sit there gaping*.

'I was just wondering...' My voice trailed away. I had no idea where I was going, or how to finish my sentence.

'What is it, Emma? If there's something on your mind, just ask.' I gulped noisily, as though I was the one who had just drained half a bottle of beer. Were all crime writers this direct and intuitive, or was it just a Jack thing?

'Well... you've talked about your work and your life in America, but you've never mentioned if there was anyone special in it... anyone waiting for you back home?'

I winced inwardly. I should have asked about his book, his favourite food, or how much he made in the last tax year! Anything would have been preferable to prying shamelessly into his personal life. Jack smiled at my cringing discomfort and there was a mischievous glint in his eye.

'Well there's Fletch, my Labrador, he's kinda special, getting a little wobbly on his back legs now, but he's twelve so it's to be expected. And then of course, there's a couple of horses who—'

I balled up a serviette and threw it at him.

'Okay. Okay I get it. I'm being nosy and intrusive. I'm sorry. Forget I asked.'

He bent to pick up the cloth, but there was no censure in his eyes as they met mine. 'There *have* been a few women in my past,' he admitted, 'but no one I regret having let get away.'

There was an open honesty in his words and face, and I was totally unprepared for it, and for the fleeting twinge of envy I found myself feeling for the nameless women who had passed in and out of his life.

'You've never thought about remarrying?'

'No, never. I no longer believe in marriage,' Jack said firmly, and there was a discernible tightness in his voice, which I regretted causing.

'What? Like it's a myth, or something?' I joked.

The tightness dissolved as his low rumble of laughter filled the room. 'You're funny,' he complimented, and something inside me swelled at his appreciation.

'I'm here all week.'

He took another sip from the bottle in his hand before continuing, 'I've gone down the marriage road once; I don't see myself doing it again.'

'Been there, done that?'

'Got the T-shirt,' he completed. There was a rueful look on his face. 'It didn't fit.'

Well. There was no room for ambiguity on that one. I gathered up our dirty plates and went to rinse them at the sink, unsure why his words had affected me. This man, with his damaged past, wasn't mine to cure or save – that would be someone else's responsibility. For some reason the realisation made me sad.

'Now, I've got one for you. Why *relieved*?'

It took me a moment to realise he was picking up the threads of our earlier conversation. 'You've waited *three hours* to ask that?'

'I'm a patient man, I don't believe in rushing things. I like to take my time.'

My pulse quickened a little at his unintentional *double entendre* and the ridiculous way I'd misinterpreted his words. I looked up to answer him and saw an amused glint in his eye, and suddenly knew better. Words were his tools, and he knew exactly what he was doing with them.

'Well?' he prompted.

'Things moved too quickly with Richard and me. And that wasn't just *his* doing, it was both of us.' At least I was honest enough to admit that. 'When I came home we fell right back into our relationship as though the years apart had never been. And that was wrong, because we weren't the same two people we'd been before. We went from nought to sixty in a matter of weeks.'

I looked up to see if I was boring him, but Jack just nodded, encouraging me to continue. 'Richard proposed at Christmas, in front of our families, down on one knee... the whole thing. It was completely unexpected and romantic and

I just got swept along with it all.' My voice was so weighed down with regret it dropped almost to a whisper. 'But it was too soon. I just wasn't sure.'

I snapped my lips shut as though I'd said something shameful. It was the first time I'd voiced that private thought out loud. At the time I'd been swept along by friends and family who were so delighted we were engaged that I'd had no room, no space, no chance to say *Can't we just think about this for a little longer?*

'You can't get married to please your family or friends,' Jack declared knowingly, and somehow I could tell that once more our past histories were crossing and merging.

'I know that.'

We were both quiet for a moment, the room feeling suddenly overcrowded now that both Richard and Sheridan had dropped in uninvited.

'Enough of this,' Jack announced. 'I'm meant to be cheering you up, not getting us both crying into our beer. How about a movie? There's a stack of DVDs in the other room. Why don't you pick something out for us to watch, and I'll light a fire.'

He hadn't been kidding when he said he was a fan of old movies. There had to be over two hundred in the box he passed me. I could spend the rest of the evening just trying to choose. I kneeled on the floor with the box before me, while Jack laid kindling and logs in the fire basket.

'I can't pick. What would you like?' I asked, glad his back was to me because my attention had been split between the box of films and the interesting way his muscles moved beneath the thin material of his T-shirt.

'Anything. You decide. Or just do a lucky dip.'

I did as instructed. '*Charade*,' I declared, holding up the thin plastic case for his approval.

'A European woman who falls for a mysterious American. Interesting choice.'

I got up from my knees and passed him the box with the picture of Audrey Hepburn and Cary Grant on the cover. 'I haven't seen this in ages, and I adore her voice.'

He slid the disc into the player, before turning back to face me. 'I prefer yours.'

I didn't know what to say, so decided not to say anything at all. Jack sat down at one end of the two-seater settee, stretching out his impossibly long legs in front of him. The seat was easily wide enough to accommodate us both, yet I hesitated and turned to a solitary armchair beside the crackling fire.

He patted the vacant cushion on the settee beside him in invitation. 'Come and sit here.'

I don't normally respond well to being told what to do. I have a stubborn streak in me that's a mile wide. I like to be in charge, I like to make my own decisions. Jack looked up from the comfortable cushions; his expression revealed he knew exactly what I was thinking.

I sat down beside him.

There are worse things than falling asleep in someone's house when you've been invited round for dinner, and one of them is to do so with your head resting in your host's crotch. Unfortunately, I did both.

I was dreaming. We were in France, in the *gîte* near the old farmhouse, and my mother was anxious to go and paint, but I kept insisting that first she should brush my hair for school. It was the usual crazy kind of dream, the type that makes absolutely no sense.

One minute we'd been watching Cary and Audrey chasing around Paris, trying not to fall in love or get themselves killed, then the warmth of the fire, the beers from dinner, or just the fact that I hadn't slept properly since I-don't-know-when, overcame me. I didn't wake with a start, quite the opposite. My eyes opened gradually, focusing on a curious metal shape directly in front of my face. I blinked slowly, baffled as to what it was and what it was doing on my pillow. The pillow, which incidentally felt weirdly contoured and not terribly comfortable. The metal shape confused me: it was like one of those magazine puzzles of an everyday object photographed from a weird angle. From where I was lying it looked just like the pull tag on a zip.

Sleep left me in an instant as I bolted upright from his lap, smacking him painfully in the jaw with the back of my head. Several swear words filled the air (I'm not sure who they came from), and we were both still rubbing our individual areas of impact as I scrambled to my knees.

'Oh God, Jack, I'm sorry,' I said, truly mortified.

'For what? Using my lap as a pillow, or for trying to break my jaw?'

He stopped rubbing the injured area, and there was indeed a large red mark where my head had connected with his face.

'I must have nodded off,' I said, which was hardly an Einstein-worthy observation. I looked over at the television and saw only a blizzard of white grainy snow. 'The film's finished?'

'Nearly two hours ago.'

'Why didn't you wake me?'

'Well, to begin with I thought you were just... getting comfortable...'

The flush started at my chin and didn't stop until it had reached my hairline. 'Then, when I realised you'd actually gone to sleep, it seemed a shame to disturb you. You looked like you needed the rest.'

'I'm so sorry,' I repeated.

He reached over and patted my shoulder in a friendly chummy fashion, not in the way you'd expect a man would do to a woman who, only minutes earlier, had had her face buried in his groin.

'Don't worry about it.'

I glanced at my watch and saw it was after midnight. 'It's so late. I should go.'

'Not without a coffee first,' Jack said. 'I want to be sure you're wide awake before you get behind the wheel of your car.'

He left me to prepare the caffeine fix, and I sank back down on the settee, still cringing inwardly when I thought of how I'd snuggled up so intimately against him while I slept. I ran my fingers across the cheek which had nestled against him, and could feel the grooved indent from the seamed fly on his jeans. Rubbing furiously at the creases, I went to check out the damage in an oak-edged mirror hanging on the wall. My face definitely looked squishy from where I'd been lying, and my hair on that side was messed up and a little tangled. Strangely, on the other side of my head, the long auburn strands were perfectly straight and tidy, pushed back from my face and lying without a lock out of place behind my ear, almost as though they'd been smoothed and stroked into position.

The caffeine did the trick, although I swallowed it fast enough to burn my throat as it went down. Jack had wanted to follow behind me in his car to make sure I got home safely, but I insisted that it really wasn't necessary.

'You've drunk more beer than I have. You shouldn't be driving at all,' I told him, as I slid my arms into the sleeves of the jacket he was holding out for me. He reached behind my neck to free my hair from the collar, his fingers scraping along the sensitive skin.

'I think a guy my size can manage three beers and not pass out drunk on a settee,' he teased.

'I wasn't drunk, I was asleep,' I protested, as he fell into step beside me on the short walk down his drive. I pulled the keys from my bag as we drew to a stop beside my car. The night was bright and starry and so quiet that I could hear the faint sound of the sea slapping against the rocks on the beach.

We faced each other in the darkness, both looking strangely awkward and uncertain as to how the evening should end. I made the first move by reaching up and resting my hands on his shoulders and lightly touching my lips to his cheek. 'Thank you for a lovely evening,' I said, pulling away, 'I really feel much better now.'

He smiled gently and then reached for my hands in the darkness, startling me. I held my breath, as a thousand butterflies took up residency in my stomach. His eyes flickered as he looked at me and there was clearly something on his mind.

'Emma... I wanted to say...' His voice tailed off, but his face revealed more than he realised. His warring thoughts were plainly visible, I saw them clearly; I also saw the precise moment when he changed his mind completely about whatever he intended to say.

'Yes?' I prompted. Jack paused, and I knew without a single doubt that this had not been his original question.

'Are you free on Friday afternoon?'

I was desperate to say, 'No. Not *that* question. *Ask me the other one, the one you've just rejected.*' But of course, I couldn't.

'Possibly, why?'

'I want to take another look at that lake before I leave and I probably wouldn't be able to find it without you.' As there was a state-of-the-art satnav sitting in his hire car, we both knew that wasn't entirely true. 'We could always get something to eat afterward; I think I saw a restaurant not far from there last time. If you want to... of course.' He sounded strangely nervous and unsure of himself. 'Will Monique give you the afternoon off?'

Of all the things I was unsure of in my life at that time – and there were plenty of them – that at least was easy to answer. 'Absolutely,' I confirmed. In fact, if she knew who I was going with, she'd probably offer to pick up the tab at the restaurant.

Jack opened my car door and delivered three parting instructions: 'Drive safely and get some proper sleep, and make up with Caroline,' he said, as I slid into the driver's seat.

'Okay.'

'I'll pick you up from your house at around four on Friday.'

'It's a date,' I confirmed, and then panicked in case he thought that's what I believed it was. 'I mean... it's not a date... that's just a figure of speech... I mean—'

'Goodnight, Emma,' he said softly, closing my car door.

It was hard to tell in the dark, but as I reversed out of his drive, I was pretty sure he was smiling.

CHAPTER 10

The shop was unusually busy on Monday and by the end of the day there was a dull nagging pain at the base of my spine and I was tired and irritable. As I pulled on to our drive I was looking forward to the prospect of a quick dinner and a very long soak in a deep bubble bath. Only I couldn't get my car in its usual space, because that spot was occupied by the last thing I wanted (or expected) to see there. Richard's car. 'What the hell,' I muttered, as I pulled up alongside it and glanced within. Empty. So he was already inside.

A fleeting movement at the window caught my eye, which meant someone had heard me pull up. No chance now to make a hasty retreat and drive the streets aimlessly until he'd gone, which had been my gut reaction.

I should have been expecting this, I thought, sitting in my car and quietly fuming. It was almost inevitable, given how my parents had reacted to the news of our break-up. I'd put off telling them for days, but once I knew our broken engagement was public knowledge, I'd had no choice but to sit them down one night after our evening meal and effectively break my mother's heart. To watch her face crumple as I explained as slowly and patiently as I could that Richard and I had decided we would no longer be getting married, was every bit as terrible as I thought it was going to be.

'We've decided that perhaps we may have rushed into

things a little,' I'd said gently, wondering if the lie sounded as false to them as it did to me.

My father, sitting on the settee beside my shocked and dismayed mother, hadn't accepted such a vague explanation. 'But you've known Richard for twenty-five years, how is that rushing?'

Thanks for that, Dad. I had reached over to take hold of my mother's hand, wondering if this was how torn and desperate parents must feel when they tell their children that they're getting divorced. My mum certainly looked as bereft as a child on hearing that her world was about to be torn apart.

'I think we may have rushed into *the engagement*,' I clarified. 'We really hadn't been back together long enough to make that kind of decision. I think we've both changed a lot while we've been apart. We aren't the same people we were when we were teenagers.'

My mother had nodded mutely back at me, which might have meant that she understood, except her eyes were confused and awash with tears.

'When you really love each other, then how long you've been together isn't the issue. Your mother and I got engaged after only three months.'

Again, Dad, thank you.

'Maybe you'll change your mind?' my mum had asked in a tragically hopeful voice.

'I don't think so, Mum.'

'Everyone has the odd tiff,' she had said, as though enlightening me to a world I might never have glimpsed before. 'It's probably just a little touch of cold feet. That'll be what it is.'

Cold feet. Cold heart. Cold everything, actually, Mum.

My father hadn't bought the version of the truth which I had so carefully rehearsed, but at least he had enough good sense not to pressure me further.

'I had an outfit and a hat, and everything,' my mum said sorrowfully. 'You two are just so perfect together. Everyone says so.'

I couldn't hold it together for much longer, and thankfully we were almost done. And then came my father's parting question: 'Emma, does this decision have anything at all to do with Amy?'

I saw a racing kaleidoscope in my head: the shattered windscreen, Amy's terrible injuries and then her body entwined in hot and sweaty passion with Richard's. 'No. Not really,' I had lied, then escaped to the privacy of my room before I lost it completely.

When I dropped my bag and jacket on the hall table, I could hear the sound of voices coming from the dining room. I caught a glimpse of my reflection in the gold-framed wall mirror, and was surprised at how normal I looked. There should have been steam coming out of my ears, because I was definitely only a few degrees from boiling point.

'There she is,' cried my mum delightedly as I opened the door, and three faces turned in my direction. Two of them were smiling, but the third looked guarded and wary, with very good reason. The table was set for four, and there were covered serving dishes and a steaming casserole at its centre. Richard was occupying the chair he usually claimed during the numerous meals he'd shared with us over the years. He had a glass of lager half-raised to his mouth, and eyed me cautiously over its rim. With admirable restraint I resisted the urge to rip it from his hand, or tip it all over him, although both ideas had merit.

'What's going on here?'

I saw my mother give a nervous swallow, and my father laid his hand comfortingly on her shoulder. 'Nothing's "going on" here.' His voice was placating. 'We're just having dinner, that's all.'

I turned to stare meaningfully at Richard, just in case they hadn't noticed that someone who definitely didn't live here had joined our table. My mum shifted uncomfortably in her chair, but this time it was my ex-fiancé who reached across the table to reassuringly squeeze her hand. Terrific. Between them, they had now made *me* the bad guy.

'It's okay, Frances, Emma's just surprised to see me here, that's all.'

Surprised wasn't the word I'd have gone for, and I'm sure he knew that from the silent daggers I shot at him across the room.

'Could I have a word with you, please, Richard? Outside.' It was a wonder I got the words out as my lips were so tightly compressed. Richard got easily to his feet, and turned to smile apologetically at my parents.

'You'd better make it a quick one,' my dad advised. 'I'm just about to serve, and it's that chicken dish you like, lad.' Just the thought of food made my stomach twist in protest, or was it hearing my father talk to my ex so warmly?

Richard deliberately took his time, carefully pushing his chair back to the table and dropping his serviette beside his plate while I waited at the door with growing impatience. Why was he bothering? Surely he realised there was no way he was coming back to the table?

He followed me into the hall and I made sure the dining room door was tightly shut before rounding on him like a kick-boxer. 'What the hell are you doing here?' I spat out.

'Are you going to deck me if I say "having dinner"?' He realised quickly it was a bad moment to have gone for humour. 'Look, your parents phoned me today, and invited me over. What was I meant to say?'

'Er... "No" would have worked.'

'How could I, when your dad said your mum was really upset about... you know... you and me?'

'There is no "you and me". Not any more. Remember?'

He went on as though I hadn't spoken, 'Then when he told me she hadn't been sleeping properly because of it, what was I supposed to have said?'

His explanation stung, but it also rang painfully true. Even Richard wasn't so insensitive that he'd have come round without an invitation. But why hadn't Dad said anything to *me* about how my mother was coping?

'And then,' Richard continued, with somewhat less confidence, 'I thought that... maybe... *you* might have asked them to call me? That you wanted to make the first move...?' My eyes widened in disbelief, but before I could say a word, he quickly added, 'But I see now, that wasn't the case.'

I shook my head despairingly. This was probably all my fault. If I'd just told my parents the *real* reason why I'd broken things off with Richard, my dad was more likely to have approached him with a shotgun than a casserole dish. But they both still thought we'd only had some stupid row, or that I had a case of pre-wedding jitters. Now, unless I threw him bodily from the house and risked upsetting them even more, I was going to have to stomach an evening sitting across the table from him.

'Come on, you two, it's getting cold,' came the summons from beyond the panelled door.

'This is not over,' I hissed, turning on my heel and

gripping the door handle. But he also reached for the brass knob, his fingers covering mine as he stepped close behind me. For just a moment we stood on the edge of a déjà-vu chasm of memories.

'No, Emma. It's not,' he confirmed on a low promise. 'It's not over at all.'

It wasn't the best of meals, but it wasn't the worst either. No one stabbed anyone with an item of cutlery, or emptied a piping hot dinner into anyone's lap. That's not to say I didn't think about it, though. Richard's recent school trip occupied most of the conversation, which was fine with me. The less opportunity we had to speak to each other, the less likely we were to end up in a slanging match.

I hated being so defensive and prickly in my own home, hated the feeling that he was invading my personal space. There were boundaries and he wasn't respecting them, and that wasn't going to change if my well-meaning parents kept trying to matchmake us back together again. It was hard to ignore their expectant and hopeful expressions throughout the meal. They were like scientists studying a polar icecap, eagerly anticipating the first moments of a thaw. They were in for a long wait.

When the oven timer pinged and my father disappeared to get the apple pie and custard (another Richard favourite, Dad really *was* pulling out all the stops) an awkward atmosphere fell over the table. Although Mum listened attentively to conversations, she wasn't much of a contributor since her illness. But her chaperoning presence meant neither Richard nor I could say exactly what we wanted. Instead we spoke through our eyes and in our body language. When my father returned I was sitting ramrod straight in my chair, as though awaiting the arrival of an executioner instead of dessert. By the time the plates were cleared I had a colossal headache, and wanted nothing more than to retreat to the sanctuary of my room.

'Coffee anyone?'

Richard opened his mouth to accept, and then caught the look on my face.

'I can't, I'm afraid, Bill. I've a stack of marking I have to get through tonight.' He got to his feet.

'Oh what a shame,' said my mother with regret, 'but actually *I've* got a pile of homework to mark too before morning.'

For just a moment the wall between Richard and me crumbled to dust as we exchanged a meaningful look.

'I'll see you out,' I said, and he nodded in agreement. He dropped a kiss on my mum's cheek, thanked my father for the meal, and followed me once again to the hallway.

There was less anger in me than before, chiefly because it required more energy to summon up than I currently had left. I was running on empty.

'You can't do this again, Richard. I can't have you turning up at my work, or finding you here in my house. It's just not fair.'

'I can't get you to see me any other way.'

I sighed heavily. 'Then what does that tell you? You can't *force* me to change my mind. Not like this. If you carry on this way you're just going to make me hate you even more.'

He gasped at my brutality. 'You *hate* me?'

I shook my head in weary confusion at the slip. Was that how I felt? 'I don't know. Sometimes, yes. Yes, I do. Tonight certainly came close.'

He had the grace to look abashed. He reached out a hand towards me, but let it fall limply back to his side when I stepped back. 'I'm sorry. It's just that I don't know what to do, what to say. I don't know how to play this, to win you back.'

'It's not a game.'

'I know that.'

'There are no winners here. We all lost.'

'It doesn't have to be that way,' he pleaded, his voice throaty with emotion.

'It does. At least for now.' I thought I was firmly closing the door with my words, but he heard something hopeful hiding between the lines.

'But maybe – not just yet, I get that – but, in time... one day...?' His voice trailed away.

'No, Richard. I honestly don't see that happening.'

He shook his head, his blond hair falling across his eyes, but not enough to hide the pain in them. 'I'm not going to stop trying to get you back, Emma. I can't just walk away.' There was nothing I had left to say. 'Please don't throw away everything we had, everything we were.'

'*You* did that. Not me. The only thing *I* threw away was my damn ring.'

He gave a humourless laugh. 'Yeah. Don't I know it? I spent a couple of hours scrabbling around in the rocks and weeds looking for it.'

Despite everything I'd said about not caring what happened to him, I couldn't stop my instinctive reaction at his recklessness. 'You climbed down into Farnham Ravine after I left? Are you crazy? You could have broken your leg or your neck. What if you'd injured yourself or dropped your phone? How the hell would anyone have known you'd been hurt?'

Strangely, the fact that I was mad at him for taking such

a stupid risk seemed to please him. 'Well as you can see, I broke neither. But I didn't find your ring either.'

I shook my head at the futility of even attempting to look for it. It was long gone.

'I thought, that if... *when* you change your mind, you're going to want your old ring back.'

'I'm not going to change my mind, Richard.'

'Not just yet,' he conceded.

There was nothing left to say. We were going round in circles. I opened the door and waited for him to use it. He was almost across the threshold before he added, 'Although incidentally, if I *had* fallen, the phone wouldn't have been any use to me.' I frowned. 'No signal,' he said bitterly. 'Nothing. After I finished searching for the ring I had to walk for another hour before I could phone someone to come and get me.'

I opened my mouth to speak, and I'm still not sure if *'I'm sorry'* or *'Serves you right'* was going to come out, but in the end I said neither, as a noise from the direction of the dining room stopped me. I turned and saw the door was slightly ajar. Through the gap my mother's silhouette was shadowed against the wall.

'Goodbye, Richard,' I said, holding the door even wider.

'Goodnight, not goodbye,' he corrected.

I didn't hear her come in. It could have been that the rustle of taffeta and silk, which stubbornly refused to stay folded on the bed, masked her footsteps on the bedroom carpet. It could have been the crackling crunch of tissue paper as I attempted to encase the most expensive dress I had ever bought – and never worn – into its storage box. But most likely it was the sound of my softly hiccupping sobs which prevented me from hearing that my mother had silently joined me in the spare bedroom as I struggled to pack away my wedding dress.

I felt her lightly touch my shoulder. I turned my face until my cheek lay upon the back of her hand. Gently she pulled the strands of hair away from my face, easing them back from my damp cheeks. She ran her free hand down my hair, stroking and soothing. I closed my eyes and felt as though I was ten years old all over again.

'Move aside,' she said softly.

I shuffled up the bed and she took my place, her hands reaching out to the folds of ivory material. With a surety that made it look as though she had spent her entire life working in a dress shop and not an art department, she skilfully began to fold the metres of fabric into place. She worked silently as the gown began to compress into a manageable shape, glancing up and checking on me with a mother's intense concern that I hadn't seen on her face in a very long time.

I watched her hands as they worked. I knew them so well. They lived on in a thousand memories of my childhood. They were the ones who supported me as a toddler when I took my first step; they wiped tears from my eyes when the nightmares woke me, and placed plasters on grazed knees when I fell off my bike. Those hands, so skilled in painting and sculpture, had belonged only to me when they'd brushed my hair each night, or when they'd held tightly to mine when together we'd said our last goodbyes to my grandmother in hospital. Those hands were supposed to hold her own grandchild in them one day in the future. That possibility, as she now packed my wedding dress into its container, had never seemed so unlikely.

When at last she was done she turned to me with a sad smile. 'Don't worry, Emmie Bear, everything will work out, you'll see.'

I'm not sure what made me cry the most: her eternal optimism, the use of my childhood nickname, which she hadn't called me by in almost twenty years, or the fact that by morning only one of us would remember that this had ever happened at all.

THE END

PART THREE

The old grandfather clock in the hall chimed the hour. Was it really that late? It must be because that clock had never lost as much as a single minute since the day my father had brought it home from the auction house. He never would tell my mother how much he'd spent on it, but the guilty look on his face whenever she had asked him told its own tale. That and the fact he'd never again gone to another auction after that day.

My make-up finally complete, I sat back against the comfortable upholstery of my dressing-table chair. The room was warm, uncomfortably so, and I lifted my hair from the back of my neck in an effort to cool down. The sun was streaming through the large glass panes of my window and while I was incredibly glad it wasn't raining today, the room was fast becoming unbearable.

The sash of the old casement creaked in protest as I pushed it up to let in some much needed fresh air. I noticed several cars that had been parked outside were already pulling away, filled with family and friends who were heading for the church. Above the noise of their engines I could hear a neighbour mowing their lawn and the smell of freshly cut grass wafted into the room on an eddying breeze. The fragrance overtook the smell of the flowers sitting in a vase on top of the antique dresser.

I crossed over to the bouquet of white freesias, which I had carefully arranged in a crystal vase. I bent my head and the auburn strands of my hair mingled with the funnel-shaped blooms as I breathed in deeply. He had sent me the flowers yesterday, and they were absolutely perfect. It was a lovely gesture and so very typical of him. What made it even more special was the message he had written on the small card that had accompanied them. I pulled it out from between the long green stalks and read it again. His words brought a smile to my lips and I lightly ran my finger over his name.

I sighed, and went back to my preparations.

CHAPTER 11

I walked up the hill to Caroline's place of work with the wicker basket of muffins bumping against my hip. I had no way of knowing how this meeting would go, or what she would make of the peace offering I had just collected from the bakery. Best case scenario: she would accept my apology and we could put the whole thing behind us. Worst case: I left with a basket of muffins hurled at my head.

The bell above the door tinkled, heralding my arrival, and the three men inside the estate agents all raised their heads from their computer screens to look in my direction. One of them got to his feet, smiling warmly.

'Emma. It's good to see you again. How are you?'

'Fine thanks, Trevor,' I replied distractedly, trying discreetly to look past Caroline's boss to the desk where she sat.

'She's not in today,' he informed me, stepping back lithely, as though I might require visual confirmation of her absence. 'I take it you're here for Caroline, and not to buy a house? She's off sick. She phoned in this morning.'

The bell in my head clanged a little louder. 'Did she say what was wrong?' I asked, fixing my gaze firmly on him. Trevor looked slightly unsettled by the intensity of my question and the smile slid slowly from his lips.

'Er no... she didn't. I just assumed it was, you know... women's problems.'

'I see,' I replied, resting the heavy muffin basket on the edge of the office junior's desk. I caught him eyeing the cakes eagerly and gently slid the basket out of his reach. He grinned good humouredly.

I turned back to Trevor. 'Did she say whether she'd be back tomorrow?'

'Sorry, I didn't ask. I had clients with me so I couldn't chat.'

'Okay, no problem. I'll give her a call when I get back to the shop and see how she's doing,' I said, picking up the basket and turning to leave.

'She won't answer the phone.'

The alarm bell was clamouring appreciably louder. I turned back to look at Caroline's other work colleague, whose name I never could remember.

'I've tried to call her several times this morning about a sale she was arranging. But the phone just rings out.'

The urge to pull one of their telephones towards me and punch in Caroline's number was a real and tangible thing. I clenched my fingers into the palm of my hand as though to stop them from embarrassing me further in front of my friend's colleagues. They were already looking at me with open curiosity. I guess I hadn't been as successful as I'd hoped in keeping the panicked look off my face.

I didn't wait until I was back at the bookshop. In the five-minute walk from Caroline's place of work to mine I tried both her home and mobile numbers eight times. The guy with no name had been right. She wasn't answering.

Throughout the morning my concern continued to gently simmer. If she hadn't picked up by lunchtime, I decided I would ask Monique if I could pop out to check on her. I knew Caroline's habits nearly as well as my own. Her mobile was always kept beside her bed, and there was a telephone on Nick's nightstand. If she was ill at home there was no way she would have been able to ignore the duet of both phones ringing in her ears.

One o'clock came and went and twenty rings of Caroline's phone had still yielded no reply. That was enough. I couldn't rest until I checked she was all right. I left the counter and went into the back room to tell Monique I was going, only to find her buttoning up her coat and swirling a long silk scarf around her throat.

'You're going out?' I asked unnecessarily.

'Is that not obvious? Do you not remember, I have an appointment with that new salesman. I am going to let him take me for an expensive lunch and will let him think that this poor little French woman doesn't understand the intricacies of running a business. I will wait until we have had the brandies before letting him know the proposal he is making is screwing me under.'

'Over,' I corrected automatically.

'I know that, Emma,' she said, with a wink. Of course she did.

Monique's absence left me holding the fort, so there was no way I could check on Caroline, which had been the only thing tamping down my panic all morning. My concern was like a restless tiger, pacing back and forth in its cage. It had nowhere to go, and the longer it was contained, the more desperate and dangerous it grew.

I didn't want to bother Nick at work, but as I didn't have his mobile number I had no other way of finding out if Caroline was okay. He was bound to have been in contact with her if she was off sick, and could at least put my mind at rest. It took ages to be put through to his department and

217

when eventually his phone was answered, I was told he was unavailable.

'I need to speak to him quite urgently,' I said, hoping I was exaggerating, but afraid that I wasn't. 'When will he be free?'

'I'm sorry; he's away from the office for two days at a conference. If it's really urgent I could try to get a message to him.'

I considered this for a moment. 'No, that's all right. It can probably wait. I'm sorry to have bothered you,' I replied, trying to squash my ballooning anxiety back into a manage-able-sized container.

'Are you sure?'

'Yes, thank you,' I said, 'I'm sure.' Only I wasn't. Not at all.

By mid-afternoon I was seriously considering interrupting Monique's business meeting and asking her to come back to the shop. I knew a lot of my anxiety was down to guilt. I had turned my back on Caroline and had childishly focused my anger in a direction it had no business going. I had lashed out at her, for no other reason than the friend I was *really* angry with, the friend who had *really* betrayed me, was no longer around to blame.

I almost knocked my phone off the counter in my hurry to answer it when it finally chirped with an incoming call. I glanced at the display hoping to see Caroline's name and felt fury arcing through me as I saw Richard's instead. I pressed the button to sever the call without answering. Thirty seconds later it rang again. He just couldn't leave it alone, could he? I glanced at the clock and saw it was after four. He must have left work and be back at his flat. I wondered what it was going to take to get through to him. It didn't seem to matter how many times I told him not to get in touch, he just wasn't listening.

He rang a further three times before he resorted to texting me. *Pick up.* I considered texting back and just saying *No*, but I didn't want to get into any type of communication with him. His second text was more imperative: *I NEED TO SPEAK TO YOU. IT'S URGENT.* I frowned at the screen, and wondered if his use of capitals had been deliberate. It felt like he was shouting at me through his mobile.

I slid the phone a little further away. The third text was the charm. That was the one that had me reaching for the phone to call him back. If he'd sent that one in the first place it could have saved us ten minutes of wasted time. *Phone me back. Caroline is in trouble.*

'What's wrong? Where is she?' This wasn't the time for hellos or civility.

His voice sounded distant and hollow, and I could hear a howling wind behind his brief and terse reply. 'I'm at the cemetery, by Amy's grave. Caroline is here too. She's in a bad way. I can't get through to her. I need you to get here. Fast.'

I really was in danger of being nominated for *Worst Employee of the Year*, I thought, as I rushed to turn the sign on the door from Open to Closed, and moved through the shop at speed, switching off the lights and turning on the alarm system. I scribbled a short, almost illegible, note of explanation for Monique, which I left propped up on her desk. I should have taken the time to call her, but I didn't want to waste a single second.

It seemed as though every traffic light was stuck on red,

and every car in front of me was a learner driver having their very first lesson. By the time I eventually pulled into the cemetery car park, my anxiety levels had rocketed up like a barometer in a heatwave. I parked at an appallingly skewed angle in the bay next to Richard's car and began to run in the direction of the burial area, pulling on my coat as I went.

I hadn't set foot in this place in almost a month, not since the day I had clung on to Richard's arm for support as I'd watched Amy's gleaming black coffin being lowered into the ground, but I remembered where to go. In the early weeks, the thought of coming here had seemed far too painful, and then after I learned what had happened between her and Richard... well, also too painful.

I hadn't seen Amy's headstone before, and in fact I still couldn't see it properly, because Caroline was kneeling in front of it, her forehead resting against the cool white marble and her arms wrapped around its sloping edges. That in itself was worrying. Even more worrying was the sound of her sobs – raw, throaty and hoarse, as though she had been crying for a great many hours. Richard was on the path, standing a little way back from the grave. He was watching Caroline with true despair as he paced anxiously back and forth, his hands moving restlessly in and out of his pockets. He heard the sound of my running footsteps and spun around. In all the years that I've known him, I don't think I've ever seen him look so relieved to see me. I came to an abrupt halt on the path, trying to make sense of everything I was seeing. Richard was like a relay runner anxious to pass on the baton of responsibility. For just a single moment I wanted to turn and sprint the other way, as fast as I could back to my car, as far away from this dreadful place as I could possibly go. But of course I didn't.

'Thank God you're here.' There was genuine fervour in his voice. I ignored his outstretched hand and stepped carefully over the spongy turf, picking a path between small piles of displaced soil, a muddy trowel and an array of what looked like plant bulbs. I came up behind Caroline and cautiously laid my hand on her shoulder as though I was trying to calm a wild pony. The shuddering of her sobs reverberated up the length of my arm.

'Caroline. It's me, Emma. I've come to take you home, honey. Come on now.'

She neither stopped sobbing nor turned around. I'm not sure if she'd even heard me, or been aware of my touch. This was horribly like the time she had kneeled insensibly beside Amy on the road as we waited for the ambulance.

'How long has she been like this?' I asked, turning my worried gaze from Caroline to Richard, who had begun pacing again.

'I don't know. I'm not sure.'

'Well how was she when you brought her here?'

'I didn't bring her,' he corrected, his brow furrowing. 'I came here by myself expecting the place to be empty and I just found her here... like this.'

There was a lot to take in in that sentence. I forced myself to push to one side the fact that Richard had come to visit Amy's grave and tried to concentrate on the person who needed me most.

'I've no idea how long she's been here or how she got here. I didn't see her new car in the car park—'

'She's not driving yet,' I cut in.

Richard looked concerned to hear this, but I felt like that was the least important thing to be worrying about just now.

'I've been trying to persuade her to move away from...

221

from the grave, but she just won't let go of the damn head-stone, and when I tried to lift her to her feet, she began crying so loudly I thought someone was going to call the police and have me arrested for assault.' I could see the panicked memory in his eyes and almost felt a moment of sympathy for him. 'I've tried calling Nick, but he's not picking up.'

'He's away at a conference,' I explained.

'So what do we do now?' asked Richard helplessly.

I ran my hand down Caroline's arm, feeling the cold dampness that had seeped deep into the fabric of her coat. She really must have been here for a very long time.

'*You* don't have to do a thing. You can go. I've got it from here. I'm going to take her home.' It felt good to dismiss him, but when I glanced up I saw he'd made no move to leave. I didn't have the energy to insist or argue, so I simply ignored him and slid my arm around Caroline's waist as I attempted to get her to her feet. 'Come on, Caroline, stand up, let's get you home now.' I felt her body stiffen and her arms tightened their hold on Amy's gravestone. I heard Richard make a small noise, which translated into *I told you so*.

'Caroline, we can't stay here,' I reasoned, 'it's going to be getting dark in a while, and you're freezing. Let's go back to yours; we'll have a cup of tea and a chat. Come on.'

She shook her head emphatically, but at least she turned her face away from Amy's gravestone to look at me. I still couldn't see all of the inscription, but two words in gold lettering seemed to leap out of the marble at me. *Trusted friend.* I stiffened.

'I can't go. Not yet,' she said, her voice cracking as she spoke. 'Not until they're all in the ground.'

I glanced left and right and saw nothing but headstones. *Everyone's already there, Caroline*, I thought, then I glanced down at the incongruous gardening equipment lying discarded beside Amy's grave. Caroline reached for a large brown bulb, which to my non-gardener's eye looked just like an onion. 'When I got up this morning I saw daffodils had started to come up in our garden, and I suddenly realised Amy had no flowers growing beside her. Every flower we leave here is cut... and dead. I wanted her to have some living ones. Amy *loved* flowers.'

Yes, she did, I recalled. Although the ones she liked best were usually the type delivered in large cellophane displays from an expensive florist. 'So I walked to the garden centre and bought all of these,' she said, her hand sweeping over the scores of bulbs lying on the turf as well as several unopened bulging net bags beside them. 'Only I can't remember which ones she liked best, was it daffodils, or crocuses, or tulips?' I knew the answer to that one: Amy wouldn't have cared less, but I couldn't say that to Caroline. Not when she was looking at me with tears falling from her beautiful blue eyes, and her lip trembling like a heartbroken child.

'Snowdrops,' I answered decidedly. 'Amy loved snowdrops.' Did she? Maybe. Who knew? Anyway, this wasn't *for* Amy. It was for Caroline.

'Come on then,' I continued, dropping to the ground beside her. 'Let's get them planted.' The ground squelched unpleasantly beneath my knees as I reached for the trowel, and I felt the mud seeping through my jeans, but it was a small price to pay to give Caroline some comfort. I reached behind me for the bag of bulbs but another hand got to it first. A large male hand, which was already ripping open the netting, as he too dropped to his knees on to the muddy ground.

'Your trousers—' I began, already too late as I saw Richard's smart work clothes had just suffered the same fate as my jeans, as his knees sank into the soft dirt.

'It's not important,' he replied, his fingers gouging into the turf to make a hole, as I already had the only trowel. I eyed his bent head as he carefully placed the snowdrop bulb into the soil. Something inside me twisted and turned, and stayed with me as I thrust the trowel into the ground and set to work.

It didn't take long with all three of us working, and when the last of the bulbs had been set in an invisible orbit around Amy's plot, Caroline finally agreed to get to her feet. She wiped her dirty hands unthinkingly down the front of her cream-coloured coat, before gently touching Amy's name on the headstone with her finger.

'I'm so sorry, Amy. Please forgive me,' she whispered, the tears which had temporarily stopped while we were working beginning to fall again.

'What's she sorry for?' I asked Richard in a low voice, momentarily forgetting that I wasn't supposed to be talking to him.

He leaned his head closer to mine and I caught a whiff of his aftershave. It was an expensive brand which I'd bought him for his last birthday. 'Isn't it obvious?' he replied, his voice regretful and sad. 'She's sorry that she... that she...' He struggled to finish his sentence.

'That she what?' I prompted in a whisper, suddenly very anxious to get some greater distance between Richard's face and mine.

'That she killed Amy,' he replied, his words achieving all

the distance I could have asked for as my head shot back in shock.

It was a slow walk back to the cars. Richard took the gardening tools and bags of unplanted bulbs and I took Caroline. She was leaning heavily on me, her legs stiff and cold from what I could only guess were many hours sitting on the wet grass before we had joined her. As we walked away from the graveside she once again began to cry.

'I hate leaving her here, all alone like this. Promise you'll come back with me and visit her again, Emma,' she asked, her voice so heart-wrenchingly un-Caroline that it felt like I was talking to a stranger. I prayed the change was temporary; I couldn't face losing another person I loved, not again. She repeated her request, her eyes searching mine for a promise I wouldn't – couldn't – make.

I felt Richard studying me from his position on the other side of Caroline. He was the one to break the silence which was beginning to stretch uncomfortably. '*I'll* bring you back,' he promised, as he pulled his car keys from his pocket and pointed them at his car. 'Anytime you want to come here, Caroline, I'll bring you back.'

But of course.

As much as I had been reluctant to do so, I eventually agreed to let Richard drive me and Caroline home. 'I can drop you back here later to collect your car,' Richard offered as I climbed in beside a visibly nervous Caroline, who only let go of my arm long enough to grab hold of the seat belt and cinch it tightly across her body.

'There's no need. I'll get a cab,' I informed him, wanting him to understand that this in no way meant that anything at all had changed between us. I saw his mouth tighten into a hard line at my response. He got it.

When we arrived I shepherded Caroline straight up the stairs towards the bathroom, and decided to temporarily ignore the fact that Richard hadn't just driven off, as I had been hoping, but had followed us both into the house.

'I'll put the kettle on while you sort her out,' he said, already disappearing in the direction of the kitchen. I shook my head in irritation but said nothing. I dropped Caroline's muddy clothes into the laundry basket and hung around long enough to make sure she had everything she needed for her shower, but short of standing on sentry duty outside the cubicle, I really had no excuse not to go back downstairs. There were three steaming mugs of tea waiting on the kitchen worktop. I took one and was grateful for the reviving hot drink. I kept my eyes firmly fixed on the mug in my hand, as though if I just avoided looking at him, I might be able to pretend Richard wasn't in the room with me. Unfortunately he was having none of that.

'Nick mentioned that Caroline hadn't been coping well over the last week or so, but I didn't know she was that bad,' he began.

I took a large mouthful of tea, burning the roof of my mouth as I tried to swallow it and my guilt down in one uncomfortable gulp.

'Did *you* know?' he asked, pressing so effectively on my emotional sore point, he could almost have been doing it deliberately.

'No. I didn't. We had a bit of a falling-out, so we've not spoken that much recently.'

'Really?' His voice held all the surprise of someone who knew me and my habits really well. 'What about?'

'It's private,' I said.

'Still, it's a bad time for you two to be arguing. Surely you need each other for support?'

'There were reasons.'

He looked at me across Caroline's neat and tidy kitchen. 'Emma—'

'You really don't need to hang around here any longer. I'm going to stay for a while, maybe even overnight as Nick's away, so thanks for calling me about Caroline, but—'

'Don't do it again,' Richard completed bitterly.

'Something like that.'

He shook his head and there was a sadness in his eyes which I refused to take responsibility for. Richard waited until Caroline, wearing a thick towelling robe, had joined us in the kitchen. He hugged her and kissed her warmly on the cheek, before leaving. At the kitchen doorway he fixed me with one last look, and then, in lieu of goodbye, just said my name.

'Emma.'

'Richard,' I countered, wondering how in such a short period of time we had managed to travel so far apart that even hellos or goodbyes were now beyond us.

I gratefully accepted Caroline's offer of a shower, and as I stood beneath the hot jets, soaping off the mud from the cemetery, I wished all the stains of the day could be so easily washed away. Richard's comment that Caroline felt that she had 'killed Amy' had left me shocked and stricken with the kind of guilt that seeps deep into your bones, and runs through the marrow like a raging cancer. I'd had no idea that Caroline felt that way. None. I hadn't a clue that she was carrying the crushing weight of responsibility for our friend's death on her fragile shoulders. *Perhaps, if you hadn't so callously turned your back on her you would have known that*, a censorious voice intoned in my mind. I dunked my head back beneath the stinging jets as though to drown it out.

Caroline had left out a soft fluffy jumper and some leggings for me to borrow, and by the time I dressed and went downstairs, my own muddied clothes were already tumbling somersaults in the frothy suds within her washing machine. I gave a small sigh of relief. It was good to know the domestic goddess was back.

She was waiting for me in the lounge, curled up on the settee with her legs tucked beneath her. I collapsed on to the deep plush cushion beside her, and we turned to each other with almost identical looks of apology.

'I'm so sorry—'

'I'm so sorry—'

We broke off and looked at each other, bright blue and emerald green eyes both brimming with unshed tears. There was a long moment when neither of us spoke or moved. Then I made a sound which was halfway between a laugh and a sob, as we fell into each other's outstretched arms in an avalanche of apologies and relief. There were garbled half sentences, interrupted by unintelligible denials, and a great many tears, some from happiness, but most were because something precious, which so easily could have been lost, had just been retrieved.

Her phone rang a short while later and I knew it was Nick by the curve of her smile as she picked up the receiver. I wandered into the kitchen to give her some privacy, but I could still hear some of her end of the conversation.

'... I got a little upset today...'

I gave a small snort at her glaring understatement. She ought to know me well enough by now to realise that if she didn't tell him herself, I was going to relay everything that had happened the moment he got back from his conference. The worrying incident in the cemetery had shown all too clearly that Caroline was still suffering with injuries from our accident. She just had the type of wounds that needed more than sutures and antibiotics.

We ordered pizzas from a local takeaway (very un-Caroline) and surprisingly managed to find enough of our lost appetites to almost finish the large cheesy feast (very un-both of us).

'So, Miss McAdam,' I began, when the cartons had been disposed of, and we had returned to the cosily lit lounge. 'Richard said something very disturbing earlier on—'

'Are you two finally speaking again?' she said with undisguised delight.

'No. No we're not. Not really,' I replied, determined not to let her divert me from what I wanted to say. How was I going to put this? I shook my head. There was no easy way.

'Caroline, you *did not* kill Amy.'

Caroline gasped. 'Wow, the diplomatic corps are crying out for people like you, you know.'

'I'm being deadly serious here, Caroline. Amy's death wasn't down to you. Not at all.'

'I was driving the car,' she stated baldly.

'And it was *my* hen night,' I countered. 'Does that make it my fault too?'

'Of course not,' she refuted.

I picked up her hand and held it tightly within my own. 'She had just taken off her seat belt. And you did everything you could to avoid the accident,' I told her, recalling that her memories of the final moments before the impact were hazy. 'And afterwards, if it hadn't been for you bravely climbing out of the wreck and finding Amy on the road, well

Jack would never have known we were there, and wouldn't have stopped and well... everything would have been different.' In more ways than I could even begin to count.

I could see a familiar furrow crease her brow. It was the one she used to wear when faced with an impossibly hard problem which refused to be solved. I pressed home my point. 'Jack might have been the one who pulled me from the wreckage, but *you* saved me every bit as much as he did, Caroline. You have to believe that. I owe you my life.'

It had been a good decision to stay the night, I decided, as we prepared for bed some hours later. I suspected that half the reason for Caroline's mini-breakdown at the cemetery had been due to a long sleepless night without Nick. She had stopped taking the sleeping pills her doctor had prescribed, but so far had adamantly refused to listen to his advice to attend bereavement counselling. I'd actually found several screwed up leaflets for support groups stuffed into a kitchen drawer when I'd been looking for takeaway menus.

'There's no shame in needing help,' I said, as I unwrapped a brand new toothbrush Caroline kept for unexpected guests (incidentally, who *does* that?).

Caroline was cleaning her own teeth in the adjacent sink, and I had to wait until she'd expelled a foaming mouthful before she bargained. 'Maybe I'll go, if you will. 'Have you considered counselling? *Relationship* not bereavement. For you and Richard.'

I patted my lips on the thick fluffy guest towel and shook my head.

'That's for people who have a problem that can be fixed in their relationship. This isn't fixable. It's irreparably broken.'

'It doesn't have to be,' she continued, stepping cautiously

through the minefield of my shattered engagement. 'I know you really don't want to hear this, but Nick says he's never seen Richard like this before. It's way worse than when you guys broke up last time.' I bit my lip, but didn't reply. 'He's *really* sorry, Emma. He knows he made a dreadful mistake.'

'Good. I'm glad he appreciates that. It saves me having to keep pointing it out to him, and by the way, I thought you guys were on *my* side.' This is what we've come down to, I thought sadly: who gets custody of the shared friends.

'We're not on anyone's side. We're Switzerland.' I glowered at her reflection in the mirror. 'Okay, *I'm* on your side. But Nick's Switzerland. All right? It's not like Richard has anyone else to talk to.

'You're going to get past this, aren't you?' she continued desperately, switching off the bathroom light and padding ahead of me into her bedroom. 'People do. They find it in their hearts to forgive and then they move on.'

I ran my comb through my hair before climbing into Nick's side of the bed. There were two perfectly good spare rooms in the house, but for some reason neither Caroline nor I had considered I would sleep anywhere else except in her room. She climbed into the other side of the bed and switched off the light. Perhaps she didn't want me to see her face when she asked her final question. 'The reason why you don't want to get back with Richard, that wouldn't have anything at all to do with Jack Monroe, would it?'

The question hovered in the darkened room between us. 'Goodnight, Caroline,' I said firmly.

I lay awake for quite a while after the gentle pattern of Caroline's breathing told me she had already fallen asleep. It took me longer to drop off, and it wasn't really surprising that memories of countless sleepovers from our past were keeping me awake. Except there would have been one other person in the room, occupying a narrow foldaway bed pushed as close as possible to Caroline's divan. The memories were so vivid that I almost expected Caroline's mother to come through the door at any minute, telling us with exasperation, 'For the last time, girls, go to sleep.' My eyes grew heavy and I turned on to my side, curling my legs up in tight foetal curl.

'G'night, Caroline,' I murmured sleepily into the silent room. 'G'night, Amy.'

I saw it as soon as I looked out the window the following morning. It looked, I thought, a little shinier than the last time I'd seen it, as though it might possibly have been through a car wash.

'Your car,' said Caroline in bewilderment, staring through the front windows at the older and shabbier vehicle parked neatly beside her own, as yet unused, model. 'How did it get here?'

I'd set the alarm on my phone extra early, to give me enough time to call a cab, retrieve my abandoned car from the cemetery and *still* get to work well before the shop opened. At the very least I owed Monique an early start and an explanation.

'Ohh,' Caroline answered her own question. 'Richard. He's got a spare key, has he?'

He did. It was one of many things I'd been meaning to retrieve from his flat. There were also several items of clothing hanging at the far end of his wardrobe, a shelf of toiletries in his bathroom and quite a few books and DVDs slotted among his throughout the flat.

'Well, that was thoughtful of him,' Caroline put forward, popping two slices of bread into the toaster. 'Wasn't it?'

I gave her a watery smile but didn't reply as I savagely buttered and mutilated a slice of toast. I think that said it all.

As much as I didn't want to, I had to acknowledge the return of my car. In the end I took the coward's way out and did it by text. *Thank you for retrieving my car.* I hesitated, wondering what to add. I flexed my fingers over the screen, before allowing them to type in a quick flurry. *Can you please drop my spare key into the shop next time you are passing?* I hit Send before I could change either the message or my mind.

'There,' I said with a smile, leaning back in my seat to survey my handiwork. 'What do you think?' My mother extended both her hands, carefully considering the deep pink varnish I had just applied to her nails.

She looked up at me and smiled. 'They're beautiful, Emma, so pretty. Thank you.'

I began gathering up the tools from our home manicure, screwing lids on to various creams and lotions and slipping bottles back into a vanity case. My mum positioned her hand so that the late afternoon sunlight slanting through the window could showcase the neatly shaped and polished nails. 'Such a pretty colour, it's exactly the same shade as Magenta Sunset from the Fisher colour chart that we order from at school.'

I raised my eyes and looked at her with a sad smile. How cruel was Fate when it decided that she should be able to recall the brand name of practically every colour on a chart she hadn't set eyes on in years, but couldn't remember a thousand lost memories of her life as a wife and mother.

We both really enjoyed the hour or so we spent on her weekly manicure, but probably for vastly different reasons. Over the months, as I filed and shaped and painted, I never once forgot the memory of what had prompted me to introduce this new ritual into our lives. Richard and I had gone to visit a care home which someone had recommended as having excellent facilities for Alzheimer's patients. Of course my dad had categorically refused to accompany us, which in hindsight had been no bad thing. Not that there was anything particularly terrible about the home; the building was modern, the facilities were more than satisfactory and the staff seemed friendly and attentive enough.

But as we toured the building, past the bedrooms which though filled with photos, cushions and throws still looked like they belonged in a hospital, a feeling of immense sadness started to wash over me. We walked down a long corridor passing rooms occupied by vacant-faced elderly residents, often sitting in the dark, staring distantly at... at nothing. This wasn't the place for my mum, not now, not ever. This wasn't where my warm-hearted parent with the quick and easy smile and the irrepressible sense of humour belonged. The creative woman with the keen eye and artistic flair had no business being here. She wouldn't fit in at all.

We came to the end of the corridor and the manager, who had been showing us around, reached into his pocket and extracted a key to unlock a pair of wide double doors.

'And this day room is kept specifically for our dementia patients. We have to keep it locked as some of them have a tendency to go walkabout.'

The door swung open and I felt my heart sink as I realised I was wrong. Mum would fit right in. The aroma of incontinence was hard to ignore, but that wasn't the reason why

I didn't want to cross the threshold into the room. Suddenly my hand was gripped and squeezed firmly, and I turned to see Richard looking at me with concern. He shook his head gently and brought his face closer to mine.

'This isn't the place for her. Don't get upset.'

I had nodded back at him, my throat too tight for words, but I truly don't think I had ever loved him more than I did at that moment, just because he understood everything I was feeling without me having to say a single word.

Of course we couldn't just abandon the tour; that would have been rude. We had to at least make it look as though we were seriously considering the respite care package we had come to view. There were several residents within the day room, most of whom looked further down the road to dementia than Mum was currently positioned. But looking around at their lost and empty faces was a horrible preview that I knew was going to stay with me for a long time to come.

There were boxes of jigsaw puzzles piled upon a table, which no one was attempting, shelves full of books with no revealing gaps to indicate any had been taken down, and the baby grand piano positioned in a bay by the window had a faint layer of dust upon it. The room, like the people in it, seemed to have lost its purpose. I could hardly hear the manager's words over the noise of a wide-screen television with the volume blasting out so loudly I was surprised no one's hearing aid had blown a fuse.

I turned away, and that was when I saw her. She looked old, way older than my mum, and was sitting slumped in what appeared to be a very sophisticated electric wheelchair. Her sparse hair was a white candyfloss bird's nest, with her pink and shiny scalp showing through. She was wearing a nightdress that looked clean enough, and a hideous green dressing gown with fresh stains down the front. She was staring far away into a distant corner of the room, at the point where the wall met the ceiling. I followed her gaze and saw nothing but cornice and plasterwork, but her eyes were transfixed as though she saw so much more. There was nothing of her; she was a jumble of bones in a dressing gown, with paper-thin wrinkled skin covering the places where flesh ought to be. *Who are you?* I thought sadly. *You're someone's daughter, someone's wife, probably someone's mum. How did you get so lost?*

I turned to walk away, my eyes beginning to fill; my dad had been right not to come today, I wished I had made the same decision. I dropped my gaze, and that was when I saw them, the old lady's shrivelled and wasted bare feet, with the prominent blue veins and gnarled toes, whose nails were finished off with a perfectly immaculate pillar-box red coat of varnish. It was the single most incongruous thing I had ever seen. Those nails were absolutely perfect. Someone had spent time and effort giving a woman who clearly went nowhere and probably couldn't even remember her life before this place, an outstanding and beautiful pedicure. Someone cared. She hadn't been cast adrift and abandoned after all.

That care home wasn't the right one for us. But that old lady with the brightly painted toenails gave me the strength and determination to keep looking at others, not for now, but maybe for the future. Something else came out of that visit too, because now whatever else was going on in my life, whatever else I was doing, I set aside the time each week to paint my mum's nails.

'Some post arrived for you this morning,' announced my father, walking past with a cup of tea in hand and the newspaper tucked under one arm. 'I've left it in your room.'

I didn't look up from my task of slicking a coat of clear varnish over Mum's nails. 'Thanks, Dad, I'll check it out when I go upstairs.'

Four letters were propped up against my mirror. I examined each in turn before dropping them back on to the dressing table: one from the bank; one mobile phone statement; a reminder about my car tax and a letter from my dead friend's mother. Linda's extravagant handwriting was instantly recognisable, even though I'd only seen it once before on the package returning Jack's leather jacket. This envelope felt too small for her to be returning anything, and I had no idea why she was writing to me. Inside the envelope was a single sheet of paper, carefully wrapped around another sealed envelope, like we were playing pass the parcel... from beyond the grave. Because of course I had instantly recognised the handwriting on the second envelope too. It was different from her mother's, untidier. There was only one word on the envelope, my name. So she'd clearly never intended for it to be posted. You'd have thought I'd have wanted to read whatever it was that Amy had to say, but I didn't. Instead I picked up the letter from Linda.

Dear Emma,

Donald and I have finally finished packing up Amy's flat. It was very difficult and emotional, and we'd been putting it off for weeks. I think if he'd had his way, Donald would have kept on paying the rent for years, and have kept the place as a shrine to her, but, well, that would have just been morbid, wouldn't it? Amy wouldn't have wanted us to do that.

Anyway, I found the enclosed letter tucked away with Amy's important papers. She obviously meant for you to have it, and I wonder if she'd intended to give it to you on your wedding day? Anyhow, here it is. I hope you don't find whatever she had to say to you too distressing. You're lucky. I would give anything to hear from her one last time.

All my love,
Linda xxxx

Linda's final sentence made me feel unbearably guilty. How much better would it have been for Amy's parents to have found a letter addressed to them in her flat, and not to me. And as for finding it distressing to read, well, I'm sure it would be. If I had any intention of reading it, which I didn't. I didn't want to read Amy's well-wishes for my wedding-which-never-was, and if she was writing about anything else... well, I didn't want to read that either. Not now. Not yet. Maybe never.

I went to my wardrobe and pulled from its depths a tattered old shoebox I hadn't looked in for years. It was held down with a broad elastic band, its cardboard lid bulging upwards under a pile of teenage mementos and souvenirs. I placed the pristine white envelope in its new resting place and bound down the lid. Then I buried the box back in my wardrobe.

'Oh look,' said Monique with false good cheer, during a lunchtime lull later that week, 'one of your men has come to see you. I am so glad. The day was beginning to drag a little.'

I gave her the sort of withering look that only employees

who share a genuine and long-standing affection with their bosses are allowed to get away with. I saw Richard climb out of his car, having parked it with uncharacteristic reckless-ness on the double yellow lines which flanked the kerb outside the bookshop.

He entered the shop wordlessly, placed my spare car key on the polished wooden counter and slid it towards me.

'Your key. As requested.'

There was nothing on his face that gave away what he was feeling. Not a solitary trace. But if you'd been there when he'd fallen out of a tree when he was nine years old, and had steadfastly refused to cry, even though his arm was broken in two places, you'd have recognised the pain he was concealing. I know I did.

I tried to swallow down a nagging feeling of guilt. Richard didn't look well. Beneath the tan he'd acquired while skiing, he looked pale and tired. I told myself I didn't care.

'Thank you,' I said, covering the key with my hand, feeling the sharp edges digging into my palm. 'You didn't have to make a special journey,' I added.

'I got the impression you didn't want me hanging on to it any longer than necessary.'

'Well, no,' I replied uncomfortably. 'Actually, there are some other things of mine that are still at your place, things I'd like to collect...' He winced, as though I'd knifed him. 'Perhaps I could call round one lunchtime in the week and get them?' I didn't have to translate that 'lunchtime in the week' was a euphemism for 'when you're not there'. I could see from his eyes that he got it.

We stood awkwardly facing each other, strangers travelling through a weird and unfamiliar territory. Frankly, it had been easier when we were still yelling at each other.

'Yes. Whatever you want. You still have your door key?'

I nodded, mentally reminding myself to leave that behind when I'd finished.

'How's Caroline?' he asked abruptly, and I could sense our mutual relief. Here at least was a neutral topic, with no hidden undertow to suck us under.

'Much better. She went for her first counselling session the other day, and she sounded quite positive about it. Nick's really relieved; he's been so worried about her.'

Richard nodded, opened his mouth to say something and then thought better of it. This was awful. Excruciating. Every sentence was a minefield. It was impossible to pick a pathway through the dismembered remains of our relationship without causing injury. Where was Monique with her acid-tongued *bon mots* when you needed her? I glanced behind me, but my boss, for the first time ever, had tactfully left us alone to talk.

'Oh, I almost forgot, I've brought you something,' Richard said, pulling a large padded manila envelope from beneath his arm.

My heart sank. After the flowers, I really hoped he wasn't going to try and win me back with gifts. He was wasting both his money and his time.

'It's a book,' he said, placing it on to the counter.

I slid my fingers beneath the flap and pulled out a large expensive-looking hardback. *Alzheimer's: A Revolutionary Understanding*. Although I'd read a great many books about this villainous disease since my mother had first been diagnosed, I hadn't seen this particular title before.

'It's new,' Richard said, as I turned it over and speed-read the back cover. 'There are some really interesting case studies in the last chapter. They mention strategies we've not tried before. I think some of them might help her.'

I laid the book back down on the counter. 'Thank you. It looks interesting. What do I owe you?'

A look of genuine pain flashed across his face.

'Nothing. Of course, nothing. I ordered it months ago, before… before everything. It's just taken a while to get here.' He shook his head as though he still couldn't believe I had offered him money. 'You don't owe me anything.'

'Well, thank you again.'

He glanced at his watch. 'I have to go. I guess I'll see you around.' He saw the look on my face. 'Or not.' He walked to the door, and then stopped. I could almost see his inner struggle as he fought down whatever it was he really wanted to say to me. 'Don't throw that book away, just because it came from me,' he asked, clearly remembering the fate of the flowers. 'At least read it first.'

'I will,' I promised.

And I did. Richard was right, the book contained strategies that could possibly help Mum. They gave me hope. What I didn't know how to deal with, what I *really* struggled to push from my mind, were the countless notes Richard had painstakingly annotated in the margins of the book. He must have spent ages writing them, and I didn't know what to make of that at all.

Caroline timed her call perfectly. She knew exactly when I left work each day and phoned just as I was gathering up my bag and getting ready to leave.

'Hi. It's me,' she announced, then plunged straight in. I guess she wanted to catch me off guard. Mission accomplished, my friend.

'Do you know what day it is today?'

It was a stupid question. Of course I knew. Important dates like that stick in your brain. 'Yes, yes I do.'

'Well I was wondering...' My not-quite-so-certain-of-herself friend let the question hang in the airwaves between us. I remained silent.

'I've bought some flowers.'

'That's nice.' I wasn't being deliberately sarcastic, but then, I wasn't exactly being sincere either.

'Will you come with me after work so that we can lay them together?'

I sighed. I'd known that this, or something very like it, was going to have been the purpose of her call.

'No, Caro. I don't think so.'

'But it's her *birthday*,' she protested sadly.

'I can't, Caroline. I just can't.'

'You have to forgive her some time, Emma. You can't keep this up. I *know* you.'

'Well, maybe I can. Maybe I'm just not as nice a person as you.'

'Yes, you are,' she defended loyally.

'Go without me,' I requested. 'I'm sorry, but it's still too soon for me.'

'Well, all right.' Caroline had caved with very little real argument. I guess she hadn't really thought that I would say yes. 'But I'm going to tell her the flowers are from both of us,' she said with a small challenge in her voice.

'Okay, whatever.'

I stood staring at the calendar on the office wall, long after Caroline had hung up the phone. My eyes were fixed on the two black numbers in the square grid.

'Happy birthday, Amy.'

CHAPTER 12

There was warm sunshine and a tree-ruffling breeze outside my window on Friday afternoon as I changed out of my work clothes and into something more suitable for visiting the lake. It's not like it's a date, I told myself fiercely as I pulled on a pair of black trousers and reached for just about the only thing I hadn't yet tried on. It was a soft angora jumper with a deep cowl neck. The jade colour complemented the red in my hair, and brought out the green of my eyes. The one decision that *had* been easy to make was my foot-wear. Definitely flats.

I pulled the clip from my hair and brushed it until it fell in a waterfall of burnished copper on my shoulders. I had just finished applying a slick of gloss to my lips when his car pulled up outside. My heart began to pound, and my mouth felt suddenly dry. It was absurd, but I felt like a nervous teenager about to go on her very first date.

It was strange to see Jack standing in the hall of my parents' house, politely shaking my father's hand. He looked up with a warm smile when he heard my descent on the stairs, and I hoped the clatter of my feet was loud enough to mask the sound of my breath catching in my throat as his eyes met mine.

There was an odd feeling of worlds colliding as Jack and my father exchanged their greetings. This was new and alien territory for me. Richard had been like a member of our family for so long that I scarcely recognised the feeling of fluttering anxiety as my family and personal life crossed paths, and all I could do was stand back and hope that everyone would like each other. I needn't have concerned myself on that score. Jack was charming, modest and respectful when my father haltingly expressed his long-overdue gratitude to our visitor.

'We owe you everything, Frances and I,' he said humbly. We all turned as my mother walked silently from the kitchen and came to stand beside him. 'There are no words that can express it adequately. If it hadn't been for you, we would have lost her. You saved all of us, when you got Emma out of that car.'

'It was my pleasure.' Jack's soft American accent made his reply sound both warm and sincere.

'She means the world to her mum and me—' My father's voice was choked with emotion.

'Dad,' I interrupted, finding his honesty with a total stranger both touching and unexpected. 'You'll embarrass Jack if you keep going on like this.'

'Not at all,' Jack interjected smoothly, lifting his hand to briefly cover mine where it rested on the wooden banister. 'I understand perfectly how you must feel. Losing Emma would be unthinkable.'

A silence fell over the hallway. I swallowed so noisily that I'm sure all three of them heard it. 'And this is my mother, Frances.' I hastily filled the void with a totally unnecessary introduction.

Jack extended his hand and after a moment or two of awkward hesitation, my mother placed hers within it. 'It's a pleasure to finally meet you, ma'am,' Jack said, his smile warm and genuine. 'Emma talks about you so fondly all the time, that it feels like I already know you. I was really hoping I'd get the chance before I go back to the States to tell you how much I admire your work. There's a wonderful piece of yours hanging in my rental home. Emma tells me you painted it in France and it is, without doubt, one of the most captivating paintings I have ever seen.'

His words hit just the right note with my mother, who seemed to suddenly relax in his company – which was particularly unusual with strangers – and swell with pride at his compliment. Was it his admiration that had pleased her, I wondered, or was it that he'd said he was soon returning to America? Because she certainly *hadn't* looked happy a moment earlier, when his hand had briefly covered mine. If my personal life was ever divided into teams, there was very little doubt whose side Mum would be cheering for.

'I like your parents,' Jack said when we were in his car and pulling away from my house. 'They seem like really good people.'

'They are.' I fidgeted slightly in my seat, still feeling uncomfortable about what had happened as we were leaving. 'I'm sorry about just now... my mum, she gets muddled quite easily.'

His hand left the wheel and gently patted mine. 'It wasn't a problem,' he assured me, returning his hand to the wheel, 'don't give it another thought.'

But I couldn't help it. The thought was there. Constantly. Today's incident just served to underscore it. As far as my mother was concerned, nothing would ever really be right again until the day she saw Richard and me get married.

Jack had been helping me into my coat, when my mother

had spoken for the first time. 'Are you one of Richard's friends?'

There was an awful moment when I looked hopefully at the ground, to see if a hole might just have appeared. Unfortunately, all I saw beneath my feet was beige carpet.

'No, Mrs Marshall,' Jack replied gently, 'I've only met him a few times and don't know him that well at all.' He looked down at me with a kind smile. 'But I *am* one of Emma's friends.'

My returning smile was full of apology and thanks.

'You know who this is, Frannie,' my dad interceded. 'I told you earlier. This is Jack Monroe, he's the gentleman who helped Emma and Caroline after the accident.'

My mother nodded, as though this was an interesting but somewhat trivial fact, and not what she really wanted to talk about at all. 'And will you be going to their wedding, Mr Monroe? Emma and Richard's wedding?'

I looked at my dad, who shook his head helplessly. She knew that we had called things off. Or at least she had done just the day before.

'Mum,' I began, 'you remember that Richard and I—'

'She'll make such a beautiful bride,' Mum interrupted. 'Of course, they had to postpone it; that was only right. But I think they've waited long enough now. Don't you?'

Dad looked uncomfortable and I felt vaguely sick with embarrassment. Jack, however, seemed quite unperturbed by the bizarre conversation. 'Emma will indeed make a beautiful bride, but I'm afraid I won't be around to see it. I'm not going to be here much longer, and I'm actually not a big fan of weddings.'

The knife slid in and then twisted in the wound, as Jack's comments cut deeper than he could ever have realised. From behind Mum, my dad mouthed an apology to us both, as he gently took my mother's elbow and steered her back to the kitchen. They were almost at the doorway when her final comment rang into the hall. 'Who was that nice young man with Emma? Was he a friend of Richard's?'

'She's not always that confused. That's what makes it so frustrating,' I said. 'You just never know how she's going to be from one day to the next. It's so hard on my dad.'

'And you too,' Jack observed sympathetically.

I shrugged. 'They've been married for nearly forty years, and the thought of not having her around terrifies him.'

'Yes, she's clearly a big fan of marriage. *Your marriage* in particular.'

'I guess most mums want to see their daughter happy and settled, but with mine it's become almost an obsession.'

Jack was silent for a moment, concentrating on his driving.

'And, of course,' I continued, 'she really loves Richard.'

'Don't we all?'

I gave a loud snort of laughter which was neither ladylike nor refined. He took his eyes from the road and flashed a quick grin at me, which made me feel warm in places a smile didn't usually reach.

'What will she do when she realises that your marriage isn't going ahead?'

I sighed, all laughter evaporating at his question. 'I don't know,' was my honest answer. 'I hope she'll accept it, and that it's not going to make her worse. I couldn't bear that, to be the catalyst that tipped her over. I couldn't live with myself if that happened.'

His fingers flexed tightly on the wheel, and he seemed to be carefully considering his words before speaking. 'Just don't let yourself get sucked back into a relationship with him, if it's only to please your parents.'

I didn't reply. He took his eyes off the road for much longer than he should have done. There was no smile on his face at all this time. 'Emma, you can't be serious. That would, *without doubt*, be the worst thing you could do.'

'It would make a lot of people happy,' I said with a sigh.

'Are *you* one of them?'

'No.'

'Then, don't do it. Don't even think about it. Take it from me; don't marry someone to make other people happy. It just doesn't work.'

I suspected that Sheridan had suddenly joined us in the car. Oh yes, there she was in the back seat, sitting right next to Richard. There were suddenly far too many exes for anyone to cope with, and I was determined that neither of them was going to ruin my afternoon with Jack.

We drove on with the surprisingly warm April sunshine filtering through the windscreen. The car was a warm and safe cocoon, taking me far away from the emotional endurance test my life currently resembled. I was happy to let it.

'What will happen with your mom when your dad can no longer cope alone?' Jack asked, returning to a subject I thought we had finished with.

'I don't know. I've looked at a couple of residential places, but Dad won't consider them, not even for respite care.'

'What about home care? Could you get someone to live in to help? Would your father go for that?'

I sighed. 'I don't know. Maybe. Richard and I looked into it a while back, but even with our combined salaries, it wasn't something we could afford.' I gave a humourless laugh. 'And somehow I don't think his offer to help still stands.'

'Then how about me?'

'Pardon?'

'I could help you. I'd like to.'

His words were so completely unexpected, they took a second or two to register. And in those moments I caught a glimpse of another life. I saw my father, unbroken by exhaustion and worry. I saw him going out to play golf, or popping down to the pub with his friends, all the things he was no longer able to do. I saw too the changes it could make to my own life. I could go back to London, resume my career. Become a daughter to my mum, instead of a carer. I saw it all, and then I slammed the door on those reckless dreams.

'No. Absolutely not.'

I don't think my words surprised him, although he breathed in sharply when I laid my hand on his upper arm. 'Please don't think I'm not grateful, Jack. It's really generous of you, but it's not something we could ever accept.'

'What's the point of being successful and earning more money than I can possibly spend, if I can't help other people?'

'That's what charities are for.'

'I already give to charity. That's not why I offered.'

'Then why did you?' Perhaps my question sounded more confrontational than I intended, but I really wanted to know the answer. He took a long time before replying.

'Because I care about you, about what happens to you. I want to make your life better.'

'Thank you for the offer, Jack. I really mean that. But no.'

Jack took his eyes from the road for a moment. 'Just promise me this: if the time ever comes when you *do* need help, you won't do anything stupid like rob a bank, or take three extra jobs... or get married, just to fix things.'

I wanted to ask him which of those options he thought

was the worst idea, but I think I already knew the answer.

Jack must have sensed my need to drop the subject, because he skilfully took our conversation in a totally different direction, and spent the next twenty minutes relating an amusing anecdote about something that had happened on a book tour of the Far East. But it was his evocative description of the country and the people which captured me most, making me yearn to book myself on the very next flight to Shanghai.

'Your life is so very different from mine,' I said, my voice sounding unintentionally wistful.

'In what way? Explain.'

I sighed, not wanting to sound as though I was moaning, just observing. 'In just about every way imaginable. You do a job you clearly love, and you're very good at it.' Jack shrugged modestly. 'You travel; you get to see the world. You aren't tied down by responsibilities.'

We had reached the turn-off for the lake. 'Here?' he asked. I nodded. He hadn't needed me to navigate at all and I wondered, not for the first time, why he had asked me to come today.

'You could have all those things too.'

I gave a long exhaled breath and shook my head regretfully. 'I don't think so. Not for the time being, anyway.'

His mouth drew into a line, and I think my answer may have disappointed him slightly.

'You shouldn't give up on the things that are important to you. Your family matter and you want to do right by them, but you shouldn't give up on your dreams, they're what make you *you*. Sure, you have responsibilities, and commitments, but then everyone has those.'

'Do you?' I asked unthinkingly.

He paused for just a moment before replying. 'Yes, of course I do. Really important ones that I can't ignore – that I wouldn't *want* to ignore.'

I twisted in my seat, my curiosity aroused. Who or what were the commitments he was referring to, the things that had brought such a serious tone to his voice? But he was done with sharing. He unclipped his belt and reached for the door handle.

'We're here,' he announced with a smile.

Jack held his hand out to me as we approached the lake. For just a second I hesitated, before placing my palm against his and allowing his fingers to firmly twine around mine. He was a tactile man, that was his nature, and by now I should know better than to attach too much importance to his frequent physical contact. But that was easier said than done, when my heart had a habit of leaping and my lungs constricting whenever his skin touched mine.

We circled the lake twice and I was grateful for his supporting arm when the ground was uneven or slippery, and even when it wasn't. Jack seemed preoccupied, perhaps lost in a twist or conundrum within his plot, although I suspected there might be more on his mind than just the perfect murder location.

I watched him closely as he stood at the shore of the lake, knowing the image of him silhouetted against the water was going to stay with me long after he returned home. He'd be gone from my life in less than two weeks and I honestly didn't know how that made me feel. What I did know was that after today I would never again visit this lake. It was too tied up in memories of him.

I spread the blanket we had brought from the car on to

the same flat rock as before, and waited for him to join me.

'It must be very strange spending your entire life plotting crimes and how to get away with them,' I observed when eventually he sat down beside me on the tartan rug.

'You'd be surprised at how liberating it can be,' he replied with a smile. 'I like to think it makes me a better adjusted human being.'

I raised my eyebrows. He looked at me for a long moment, and I once again felt he was on the verge of telling me something, standing on the edge of a precipice and then deciding not to jump. He looked back at the lake. 'There's something about this place...'

He had his back to me, and I noticed how his hair took on an almost blue-black sheen where the sun caught it. I let myself stare, because he couldn't see me. I picked up one of the large flat pebbles from the ground beside us and began toying with it nervously.

'It doesn't feel like the sort of place where a life should end,' I began, not sure if I was talking about his book or our own reality, maybe both, 'but more where something could begin.'

I felt my heart race, knowing how much I had just given away with my words. Had he even understood what I was trying, very clumsily, to convey? Did he have any idea of his effect on me? I think he must have done, because his hand slid across the blanket between us and covered mine. My breath caught in my throat.

'There is something about you, Emma, that manages to get to me in a way no one else has been able to do for a very long time.'

'I don't know what it is – if it even *has* a name,' I replied, my voice dropping to a whisper as though my words were a guilty secret that the trees might pass on, 'but I think I feel it too.'

He nodded slowly, and I don't think my response was exactly a surprise. 'I want to be honest here, Emma. Because I'm past the age of playing games and not saying it how it is. There's something here, something between us, and I don't know if it's because of how we met, or if it's just a physical thing, but it definitely feels real.'

'I know. And it scares the crap out of me.'

He gave a humourless laugh. 'Not the most flattering thing to hear, but given the circumstances, I understand the sentiment. But you have enough complications in your life right now, you don't need another one.'

Jack stood up abruptly and held out his hands to draw me to my feet. But he didn't release me when I stood in front of him, just looked into my face for a long moment, as though he was trying to imprint it into his memory. So I could one day turn up within the pages of his books, or was there another reason? I didn't realise a small frown line had been drawn between my eyes until his thumb gently tried to erase it from my brow. His voice was soft as he broke the spell of the moment. 'I'm sorry, Emma, today was meant to be a pleasant distraction for you, not something else for you to worry about. Perhaps you should just forget we had this conversation?'

He bent to collect the blanket, and while he wasn't looking I picked up the large flat pebble I had been playing with. I wanted something to remember from this moment; something tangible and solid. Silently I slipped the stone into my pocket.

I was quiet on the short drive to the restaurant, going over everything he had said in the dwindling daylight beside the lake. By the time we reached the cheerfully lit gourmet pub there was only one thing I knew with absolute certainty: the things he had said were already indelibly scored in my mind, and nothing, not now or in the future, was ever going to make me to forget them.

The restaurant was charming, all oak beams, stone walls and rustic charm. We were shown to a secluded table beside a window, lit by a spluttering red candle in a glass.

There was an elderly couple seated nearby, leaning close to each other across the width of their snowy white table-cloth, their wrinkled, age-spotted hands unashamedly entwined. I felt an unexpected pang of envy at their intimacy. I missed that; I wanted that feeling back again, and I was pretty certain now who I wanted it with. Impossible dreams, the type that had no foothold in reality, but still they refused to go away.

'It's been a nice afternoon, Jack. Thank you for inviting me.' I sighed. 'I think I needed to get away from everything.'

'It's good to see you looking more relaxed,' he said with that smile of his that always made my pulse rate skip a little. I wasn't the only one affected by his charms; the waitress had most definitely been staring at him when he'd held out my chair, with his customary good manners. She'd briefly glanced my way, her face full of appreciation and a look which so clearly said *Well done!* that it was hard not to smile. Women were always going to do that: look at him that way, flirt a little perhaps, try to get his attention. Yet when we were together, I had never once felt that his focus was anywhere else except entirely on me. Jack had everything you would ever want or look for in a man, the whole package. He was a glossy magazine's tick list of every woman's composite ideal. Was it really so surprising that I was starting to fall—

'What can I get you both to drink?'

Did I just think '... to fall'?

'Would you like to see the wine list?'

'... to fall'?, as in '... in love'?

'Emma?'

But I wasn't falling in love with Jack. Was I? This was just some passing infatuation, physical attraction. It couldn't be love. Well, could it?

'Emma, is something wrong?'

I jumped, as though I'd just awoken from a trance, to find both Jack and the waitress studying me with open curiosity. 'A glass of house white, please,' I said, delighted that I hadn't lost the ability to speak coherently, even if I had apparently taken leave of the rest of my senses. Could I actually have done something so stupid as to fall for someone who was about to permanently disappear from my life, was practically allergic to commitment, and still scarred by the betrayal of his ex-wife? How was *any* of that even possible, when only six weeks ago I'd been about to marry someone else?

Jack was speaking, but once again I'd been too distracted to hear him. 'Sorry,' I apologised, shaking my head as though I could reposition all the errant thoughts scampering through it into a far corner of my brain. 'What did you say?'

He looked at me thoughtfully. 'Are you sure you're feeling all right? You're not sick, or anything? You look a little... odd.'

'No. I'm fine, absolutely fine,' I lied.

He reached across the table and covered my hand with his. 'It's going to get easier you know, in time. It isn't always going to hurt this much.' He had taken my hand in his so many times before that I should have been immune to his touch, but as his fingers curled around mine, something felt different. A pulse began to pound in my throat as he looked at me. His dark tawny eyes were suddenly serious.

'I still don't like the thought of leaving so soon when things are still so difficult for you.'

What I wanted to say was *'Stay then. Finish your book here. Finish all your books here. You have the most portable profession in the world. You don't have to leave.'* All of which would have been completely ridiculous and more than a little insane. So what I *did* say was, 'You saved my life, Jack, but that doesn't make you for ever responsible for it, or me. You're off the hook now.'

There was a bitter sweetness in his smile as he replied, 'Somehow I think I'm *always* going to feel kind of responsible for you.' His voice was strangely serious. 'Even from the other side of the world.'

There really wasn't anything I could say to that, but I stored his words in a far recess of my mind, for later examination.

'*Could* you stay longer, I mean, if you wanted to?' I felt the flushed heat of a blush creep over my cheeks as I tried to make my question sound entirely inconsequential.

'Not really,' he admitted. 'I've got business in New York, and the tenancy on the Trentwell house is up at the end of the month.' He almost left it there, but then added cautiously, 'And, as I mentioned earlier, I have a... commitment... a responsibility to someone back home. I *have* to go back.'

I swallowed, determined not to let him see the effect his words had on me. There it was then, he had a 'commitment'. There *was* someone he was going back home to, I'd suspected that there might be. So this was the end of it; in fact tonight could very well be the last time I ever saw him. I felt the sharp jab of tears behind my eyes and furiously blinked them away. If this *was* the last time, I was determined not to squander it on thinking of all the things that might have been.

I hid what I was feeling behind the teasing banter which always seemed so easy between us. I laughed when he pretended to find the British fare on the menu totally bewildering. 'Shepherd's pie, ploughman's, bangers, and toad in the hole? What is wrong with you people?' I toasted the future with him and tried not to let the sadness in my eyes show that his and mine were clearly going in two very different directions.

We left the restaurant by a rear door, finding ourselves in an outdoor seating area beside a river. The sun was very low in the sky and would soon be setting, and its dwindling rays made the flowing water sparkle and glisten like bubbling mercury.

'Do you feel like taking a walk before we go?' Jack asked.

I nodded, and fell into step beside him as we travelled the length of the patio until we reached a short flight of wooden steps leading down to the towpath. Jack took my hand on the damp and slippery treads, and then kept hold of it as we walked along the path. The temperature was noticeably cooler than it had been earlier, but I didn't feel the chill at all with my hand in his.

There wasn't another soul to be seen on our side of the river, and on the other bank there were just open fields. It felt private and isolated, as though we were much further than just a few minutes' walk from civilisation. As the shadows grew and the trees cast intriguing silhouettes around us, I felt like we were disappearing into our own private world, a world where all the rules were different.

There was a bridge up ahead, a wooden-railed old-fashioned affair. There was no reason for us to take it. There was nothing we needed to reach on the other side, and yet when we came to it, we both turned to climb its short flight of steps. The trees on both banks were heavy here, their branches low enough to graze Jack's head as we stepped on to the planked decking. When we reached the centre of the bridge, we stopped by unspoken consent and watched the river give up its fight with the night, as it turned from silver to inky black. There was a gentle breeze blowing, which ruffled my hair away from my face, but I let the red strands billow wherever the wind took them, as I braced myself against the bridge railing and looked back along the length of the river. The moon was out now, impatiently pushing the last fingers of daylight away.

We didn't speak for a long time. Words seemed superfluous in this moment of perfect harmony. I was the first to break the silence. 'It's so peaceful here. I'd like to stay for ever.' I expected him to laugh at such a fanciful statement, but he didn't. 'You should have brought your camera,' I continued.

He moved from his position at the rail to stand in front of me. 'I don't need it,' he said, his voice low. 'I think I'm always going to remember this moment... and for all the wrong reasons.'

I don't remember his head lowering, nor his arms going around me, and that's a shame, because I knew sometime in the future I was going to want to replay this moment over and over again. All I knew was that one moment Jack was standing in front of me, and the next I was in his arms, my mouth moving beneath his as I was swept along by a primeval force, giving in to the most amazing kiss I had ever experienced.

I was tumbling in freefall, mindless of where I was or when I would crash back to earth. His body fitted perfectly against mine, every contour finding its counterpart as we merged into one. I heard a groan, and it might have come from either of us as the kiss defied our need for oxygen and continued to transport me from reality into a red velvet haze, where I knew nothing except the complete rightness of feeling this man's mouth and tongue matching and meeting mine.

He didn't break away abruptly or all at once, but released my mouth slowly with a series of shorter lingering kisses, which made even breaking apart deliciously erotic. He kept his hold on me, but arched backwards so that he could see my face. Neither of us was breathing properly, and I could feel our hearts hammering against each other through the walls of our chests, speaking to each other in an ancient rhythm.

'I know I shouldn't have done that,' Jack began, his voice ragged and not quite controlled, 'but I won't apologise or lie, because I'm *never* going to be sorry that I did.'

I tried to speak, but my lips didn't seem to want to perform anything so mundane, all they wanted was to be joined with his again.

'Perhaps it was wrong of me to take advantage of you like that. But just once... just one time... I had to know what it would feel like.'

There was so much wrong in his last sentence I didn't know where to start. 'You didn't take advantage... you didn't.' My ability to communicate articulately seemed to have vanished along with the fire in his eyes. 'I *wanted* you to kiss me.' I could almost hear my last shred of pride slip through the planks of the bridge and fall into the water below. 'I've wanted it for a long time.'

Jack closed his eyes briefly. I really thought he was going to give in and kiss me again, but then with a strength and determination I hated him for finding, he gently increased the distance between us. The tremor I felt running through him was the only indicator I had that he hadn't wanted to release me at all.

'This is wrong,' he said, not quite meeting my eyes as he spoke, 'for both of us.' I tried to shake my head in denial, but he stilled the movement by capturing my jaw in his hand. Very tenderly he drew his thumb over my lower lip, which was still swollen from his kiss. 'You've been through too much and you're vulnerable and confused. You don't know which way to turn, and I'm an unnecessary complication that you just don't need right now.'

'But—' I could hear the defeat in my voice long before my brain had the good sense to realise this was a fight I wasn't going to win.

Jack shook his head sadly. 'It's much too soon for you, and far too late for me.' His arms flexed and he eased me further away until the last bit of body contact between us was broken. 'I'm not what you need in your life right now, Emma. But God help me it's taking every last ounce of strength I have not to drag you back into my arms and obliterate the memory of every other man whose lips have been on yours.'

I looked up at him with eyes that weren't ashamed to plead. What I felt was written all over my face and a revealing pulse was throbbing erratically at the base of my throat. There was no question what I wanted. None at all. I heard him groan softly as he looked at me, before he determinedly forced himself to look back at the river.

'You don't need to be starting something now with me.

Something with an end that's staring you in the face. You've had too many endings in your life recently. I won't be another one.'

I could have tried arguing, I could have begged, but a small kernel of self-preservation finally kicked in, saving me my last vestiges of dignity. 'What did you mean about it being too late for you? Because you're about to leave?'

He turned away from his study of the river and looked at me, and there was a sadness in his eyes as he replied, 'No. That's just geography. What I meant was that *you*... are too late for me... ten years too late, in fact.'

Ten years. That was when his marriage had ended. I could feel the spectre of Sheridan and what she had done rising from the darkened river like a water sprite, killing the moment more effectively than any ghost could have done.

There was nothing left to say, and Jack turned on the car's stereo on the drive back, attempting to fill the gaping chasm that had split open between us. It might not have been very mature of me, but rather than hide behind a façade of meaningless conversation, I pretended to fall asleep, and he pretended to believe me.

CHAPTER 13

The memory of my time with Jack followed me like a stalker in the days that followed. Just when I thought I had shaken it, I would look up from whatever I was doing, and there it was again. Phantom memories I could well do without haunted me, and kept flooding into my mind at inappropriate moments. They materialised on my Saturday afternoon walk through the forest, when the leaves blew in the breeze and suddenly it hadn't been my mother by my side, but Jack, and the forest had fallen away and I was back on the bridge, lost in his arms.

They followed me to work, appearing unbidden and making me falter in mid-conversation, forget what I was doing and stand vacantly in an empty room, running my fingers over my lips, remembering his kiss. Monique dealt with the matter with her usual stylish aplomb.

'I may sack you this week,' she said conversationally over coffee one morning. I burned my lip trying to swallow down the hot mouthful I had just taken.

'Pardon?'

'Nothing personal,' she assured me, giving me a charming smile and a small shrug, 'but you are now bloody useless at your job.'

It wasn't exactly the best performance appraisal I'd ever received. But it also wasn't entirely inaccurate.

'Sorry,' I said, to cover the transgressions of the last few days and the ones I felt certain were still to follow. 'I'll be better soon. In a week or so,' I assured her.

'What, when he goes back to the States, you think that will fix things? That all these feelings you have for your American author are just going to magically go away when he leaves?' I stared at her with eyes as wide as marbles, for I'd said nothing at all to her about my feelings for Jack. 'What, you think I am now so old and blind I have forgotten the ways of the heart? I am French,' she announced proudly. 'I could not possibly forget.'

The evening with Jack had felt so very much like an ending that his call a few days later was totally unexpected. But not as unexpected as his opening comment.

'Toad in the hole... that can't possibly be a *real* toad, can it?'

'I beg your pardon?'

'It's just been troubling me, that's all. I mean, why would anyone want to eat a toad? For a start I think they're poisonous.'

'No, Jack, it's not a real one.'

'Hmm, I thought as much.'

There was a long moment of silence, making me think this bizarre call was at an end. Then his voice returned. 'So do you know how to make it?'

'Yes, I do. Would you like me to make it for you before you leave?'

'Are you free on Saturday afternoon, say around four?'

'I am.'

He paused. 'I spent longer trying to invent this ridiculous excuse to call you than I do outlining the plot of an entire thriller.'

I smiled. 'Well done. It didn't sound contrived at all.'

His chuckling response merged with the purr on the line as he hung up.

'I'm sorry. You think *what*?' Caroline's voice was loud enough to make several customers at the nearby tables turn their heads.

I pulled my chair a little closer to hers, lowering my voice. 'I think that I may be falling... have fallen for Jack.'

'Ridiculous!' she said, dismissing my declaration in a one-word summation.

'No, it's not. It's how I feel. How I think I've felt for weeks, only it took me a while to recognise it.'

'Look,' said Caroline, and I could see she was making a real effort to talk in a calm and measured tone, when I suspected that what she *really* wanted to do was give me a good hard slap across the face. 'What you think you feel for Jack... well, it's just not possible. He's a good guy, a *great* guy, a really *heroic* guy. But he's not the type of man people like us end up with. He's like a character in a book, he's all glamour and gloss and excitement. But he's not *real*. Not in the way that say Nick is.' She paused, clearly wondering if she should finish that sentence. '... Or Richard.'

'Richard. Oh yes, he's *just* the kind of man every woman dreams of finding. The type who sleeps with your best friend behind your back. He's your perfect partner.'

'Emma, it was only one fucking time.'

My head shot up in shock. It was rare to hear Caroline swear. Of the three of us it had always been Amy whose colourful language would have given Monique a good run for her money.

Caroline sighed, shook her head and tried another tack.

'Look, you said yourself that Jack is against marriage?' I nodded. 'And he hinted there was someone he had to get back to in the States?' I nodded again. 'And you think he might still be hung up on his ex-wife?' One more nod, much sadder this time.

'Well,' she said, giving a long drawn-out sigh, 'I take it all back, the guy's an absolute catch. Go for it!'

I hated it that she was being sarcastic, but when the facts were all laid out as baldly as that, I could see she had a point. I sighed and leant a little closer to the table. It was lunchtime and the coffee shop was crowded. Although we'd managed to get one of the few booths at the rear, I was still aware that we could easily be overheard by those on the surrounding tables.

Caroline took a bite of her sandwich before looking at me with an expression of pure despair. 'It must have been one hell of a kiss,' she said.

'It was,' I admitted. 'But that's not why I feel this way.'

'Isn't it? Look, Emma, you scarcely even know the guy. You met him less than two months ago. You can't be in love with someone who's little more than a passing acquaintance.'

She sat back in her seat, clearly satisfied she had scored a winning point.

'I'd known Richard *all my life* and thought I was in love with him. And where did *that* get me?'

Caroline sighed, realising she was losing ground with that argument. 'So tell me again exactly what Jack said to you after the kiss, when he dropped you back home.'

'That's just it,' I said, shaking my head, as confused now as I'd been five days ago. 'He acted as though absolutely nothing had happened. As though the bridge, the kiss, what he said after simply hadn't occurred.'

Caroline pursed her lips, as though trying to decide whether or not to voice the next question. Then she went for it. 'And you're *absolutely sure* that they really did?' I looked at her scathingly. She cracked first. 'Okay, okay. Don't look at me like that. I had to ask. You've been through a lot recently and you *did* hit your head in the accident—'

'That was seven weeks ago, and I most definitely did not dream this up or imagine it. I couldn't have. It was the most mind-blowing kiss I've ever had.'

Two elderly women sharing the table nearest to ours looked up with interest at my last comment, which admittedly had been said a great deal louder than it should have been. I smiled benignly in their direction, and pulled my chair closer to the table.

'So when are you seeing him again?' she asked. There was a note of helpless resignation in her question.

'On Saturday. I'm making toad in the hole.' Caroline's head shot up. 'Don't ask,' I advised. 'So, do you think I should tell him how I feel, or is that just looking for trouble? Do I bring up what happened the other day? Do I ask him about it? Or just leave things as they are?'

'That's a lot of questions. Give me a minute.'

I sank back down on the black leather padded seat as I waited for some words of wisdom and guidance. I was out of my depth and needed Caroline's sensible level-headed advice. Caroline with her long-term relationship, solid values and high moral fibre.

'Okay, I think I've got it. Do you want to know what I *really* think you should do on Saturday?' I leaned expectantly towards her. 'I think you should sleep with him.'

I'm not sure who was more shocked, me or the two old ladies on the next table. Me, I think.

'Pardon? What did you just say?' The old dears both set their cups back on their saucers; I guess they wanted to get it straight too.

'Sleep with Jack. Have sex. Scr—'

I interrupted her before one of the blue-rinse ladies had a heart attack on top of her English muffin. 'I understand the terminology.' I looked at her in confounded disbelief. 'Who *are* you? And what have you done with the real Caroline?'

She gave a slightly sheepish look from beneath her fringe. 'I know it might sound a little unorthodox—'

'You reckon?'

'—but hear me out, because I think this might actually be the best thing – for you and Richard, that is.'

I was going to have to ask my elderly eavesdroppers for clarification on that one, because I clearly didn't understand *anything* that was being said here.

'Let me get this straight. You think I should... *make love...*' I deliberately used the one description she had intentionally not included, 'with Jack, someone I think I'm developing real feelings for, and that doing this is somehow going to sort out my relationship issues with Richard, who – unless you've forgotten – cheated on me?'

'Precisely,' Caroline said, giving a satisfied nod.

I shook my head, wondering if they'd put something stronger than just beans in today's coffee. 'Caroline, you are officially crazy. What you're saying is completely ridiculous.'

My old friend pulled a face, as though her solution was so glaringly obvious she couldn't understand why I didn't get it. 'Look, right now you won't even entertain the idea of getting back with Richard, will you? You're hurt and angry with him. Justifiably so. And the way I see it, nothing is going to change until you can get past what he did, or maybe... *until the scales are balanced.*'

Nothing she was saying justified her outrageous suggestion. 'Think about it, Emma, if *you* did the same thing... well it would kind of cancel out what Richard did. You couldn't continue to be angry with him, if you'd done the same thing. You'd be back on a level playing field again.'

I looked at her in despair. 'Caroline, I cannot, *will not*, have sex with Jack to get even with Richard. What kind of a person would that make me? And besides which, you're disregarding my feelings for Jack.'

Caroline sighed again, and conveniently chose to ignore my last remark. 'All I'm saying is that sleeping with Jack might be exactly what you need right now.' That point I couldn't argue with. 'Jack is like a hot and intense holiday romance. I admit that you and he clearly have some sort of spark or attraction going on, and I know you think what you're feeling is love, but you have to know that in reality, *it's not*. It's all in your head, it's all make-believe and tied up with him being a hero and saving you. He saved me too, remember – in a way – but you don't see *me* going around thinking I'm in love with him. Well, do you?'

I gave a small sound of disgust, but didn't reply.

'Emma, really, you have to trust me on this. In the cold light of day these feelings that you think you have for Jack just won't stand up. But you've got yourself so lost in this impossible attraction that you can't see clearly any more.' Her words shredded me like knives, but I wasn't about to let that show. 'So maybe if you and Jack... do the deed,' she added much more coyly, having only just become aware of our OAP audience, 'well, it will get him out of your system. Purge him out.'

I pulled a face. She was making it sound as though my feelings for Jack were some sort of unpleasant disease which I needed to eradicate.

'And then, when it's done, you'll see the difference between having a quick fling with someone you're infatuated with, and a lasting relationship with someone you love.'

I just stared at her.

'And you get to have sex with a really hot guy,' she added, as though that was sure to be the clincher.

'Amazing,' I said, and she was so pleased with her idiotic proposal, she didn't even realise I was being sarcastic.

'I know,' she declared. '*You'll* stop obsessing about Jack, *he'll* get a holiday quickie, and you and Richard will be able to find a way to get back together again. It's a win-win-win situation.'

Both the old ladies were nodding their heads wisely as though Caroline was the UK's answer to Doctor Phil.

'Caroline. You're nuts. That is the worst advice I've ever heard. Stick to selling houses, because you're never going to make it as a relationship counsellor.' She looked crestfallen at my rejection. 'Plus, you seemed to have overlooked the biggest and most insurmountable problem in your plan.' Caroline waited expectantly for me to finish. 'Jack doesn't want any sort of involvement or complication, not even a meaningless "quickie". He's made that perfectly clear.'

I dropped my coat and bag over the banister when I got home that evening and followed the smell of cooking into the kitchen, expecting to see both of my parents pottering around as usual. But the room was in darkness, the only light coming from the glass oven door, where I could see a casserole was cooking. I walked through the kitchen into the adjacent lounge, which was also in shadow.

'Dad? Mum?' I called out into the silent house. Something was wrong. Since Mum had fallen ill, their lives were governed by routine and order. Spontaneity and impulsive behaviour had moved out when Alzheimer's moved in. I thundered up the stairs, but even before I had flung open their bedroom door, I already knew I was the only one home. I ran back down the stairs, almost losing my balance in my haste to find my phone. I seized my bag and took it into the kitchen, pulling out my mobile as I went. I was still dialling my father's number when I saw the note. It was propped up against the kettle.

I flicked on the overhead lights and read his neatly written script. By the time I reached the end of the brief explanation, the perplexed look on my face had changed from a frown to a scowl. *Have gone to the pub with George*, the note began, which was almost as ludicrous as having written, *Have been kidnapped by aliens, please bring ransom*. It was rare for my father to indulge in the luxury of a little male-bonding time in the local with his friends. But, bizarre as that was, that wasn't the part of the note which really bothered me. *Your mum is at the school with Richard. Dinner is in the oven. We should all be back at eight.*

What did he mean Mum was *at the school with Richard*? Had she gone wandering again, and had Richard found her? Surely that couldn't be right. There's no way Dad would be socialising over a pint if Mum had managed to get herself to the school again. So that could only mean that Richard had *taken* her to school? But why? For the life of me, I couldn't think of a single reason why he would have done such a thing, even when we *were* engaged, and far less so now. It made no sense. And worse than that, it made a mockery of my father's begrudging agreement to exclude

Richard from our family life, at least until the dust of our break-up had settled.

The more I thought about it, the madder I got. Richard was using my mum's long-standing affection for him as a tool to worm his way back into my life. It was outrageous. And if he thought that acting like this was going to win me back... well, he had another think coming. Fired up with righteous indignation, I grabbed my car keys and headed for the door.

I had to keep reminding myself to slow down as I travelled the familiar route to the school. But it wasn't easy with anger coursing through my veins like a stimulant, practically forcing my right foot to press down harder on the accelerator. Pithy imaginary conversations ran through my head as I drove, each of them cutting Richard down to size. In reality I knew I'd probably not say anything of the sort in front of my mother. It didn't matter. I was just going to find them and take Mum back home, and if he couldn't get the subtext from that, then he was even more obtuse than I thought.

The school was largely in darkness and I knew the main doors would be locked, so I headed for one of the side entrances, hearing the whirr of security cameras following my progress. I realised this plan could end badly: alarms going off, police cars arriving, and no easy explanation to offer as to why the daughter of an ex-member of staff had been caught trespassing within her old school.

I reached the door and saw the corridor beyond was in total darkness. I paused for a second with my hand on the aluminium handle. I didn't have to do this, did I? The fiery anger that had propelled me out of my house and into my car had banked down to smouldering embers of annoyance. I should probably just go back home and forget all about it. My fingers flexed around the tubular handle, then almost of their own volition pulled open the door. I held my breath. No alarm sounded, no security guard came racing down the corridor. I took it as a sign that I'd been right to come.

I didn't need the benefit of lighting to find my way around the building. Nor to know where I should look first. I ignored the passageway that led to the Technology Department and Richard's office, and headed straight for the Art Block. It was where Mum would want to go. It was where she always headed.

As I walked through the swing doors, I could see that several rooms were brightly lit in the suite of art classrooms and staff offices. I took a steadying breath, steeling myself for what was sure to be an unpleasant scene, whichever way it went.

'Excuse me, can I help you?' The voice came from behind me, and I must have jumped a foot in the air; I certainly hadn't heard anyone approach, or emerge from any of the rooms. I'd been so focused on liberating my mother from Richard's care, I'd been deaf and blind to anything else. Despite the enquiry, the tone was sharp and suspicious and they didn't sound like they wanted to help me at all. Unless helping was a euphemism for throwing someone out. 'The school is closed and this is private property.'

I turned slowly, unsure of how much trouble I was in.

'Emma! For goodness sake, I didn't realise it was *you*.' The person, who only a few seconds ago had sounded like they might be about to hit me over the head with a sculpture, now enveloped me in her arms in an enormous hug. 'What on earth are you doing walking around in the dark like that? You gave me a proper scare. I didn't know you were coming too tonight. How are you, sweetie? We've all been so worried about you. Such a tragedy.'

I nodded, a little distractedly. Janice's presence took even more wind out of my sails. She was a warm and friendly woman, who liked nothing better than a nice gossipy chat. When Mum had run the department she'd been her assistant, and I knew they had been good friends as well as colleagues. For that reason alone, she deserved more of my attention and courtesy.

'I'm doing well, thank you.' Janice patted my hand consolingly, and I knew the empty ring finger hadn't gone unnoticed.

'Such a shame you had to postpone the wedding,' she said, and I think there was a question behind the seemingly innocent statement. Did that mean Richard hadn't told anyone at school that our wedding was more than just postponed?

I decided to go with a noncommittal 'uh huh', which thankfully she didn't pursue. I flicked a glance over my shoulder at the lit art room behind me, expecting that at any moment Richard and my missing parent would emerge, to make my discomfort complete.

Janice misread my look. 'They're in C4, the large art room,' she advised. 'You can go on through and join them.'

I hesitated, wondering what to say, and how much of it was likely to be the hot topic of conversation in the staffroom by break time tomorrow.

'Er, what are they doing, Richard and Mum?'

Janice looked a little surprised at my question. 'The same as usual.'

That didn't really help. I hoped if I just stayed quiet long enough she might elaborate; Janice wasn't a woman who really went for silences. She didn't disappoint me. 'I always think this is such a lovely thing for him to do.'

I gave a wan smile. Richard doing lovely things was a

concept I'd been struggling with recently, but it wouldn't do to tell her that. 'I guess it is.'

'Oh absolutely. And you just know how much it means to her.'

'Oh yes, of course.'

'It always bring a little lump to my throat though, you know.'

Okay, that was enough, I just wasn't going to figure it out without asking. 'I'm sorry, Janice, just what *exactly* is Richard doing here with Mum?'

'Taking her round the art exhibition, of course. As usual. Isn't that why you've come too, to join them?'

'The art exhibition,' I said, on a long sigh of comprehension. It was something Mum herself had instigated, and she'd worked long and hard to raise private sponsorship for a small exhibition gallery to be built on the side of the art rooms, where each year the students' work was displayed.

'You said, "as usual"; do you mean Richard has done this before?'

Janice frowned, clearly confused that I appeared to know so little about what was going on. Welcome to my world, Janice. 'Oh yes, he's brought her for the last three years now. But they always come late in the evening, when school is closed and everyone's gone home. I don't even come out of my office any more until they've gone. Your mum gets upset when people greet her and she doesn't remember them. And I don't want to cause her any more distress, especially when I know how much she loves looking at the work the kids have done.'

I stood in the corridor feeling smaller than any child who went to school there. Richard had done a really nice thing, secretly bringing Mum here over the years. And the fact that

274

he'd never told me about it, or looked for thanks, just made me feel even more of a heel, if that was possible.

'Didn't he tell you anything about it?' I shook my head dumbly and saw Janice's gentle answering smile. 'That's so very Richard, isn't it? He's such a nice thoughtful young man. He's a real keeper, isn't he?'

I truly didn't know what to say, especially as I had thrown my 'keeper' back almost as cavalierly as I'd thrown away his ring.

'Go and join them,' urged Janice, giving me a gentle shove in the direction of the exhibition area. 'I'll just go back into the office – don't want your mum seeing me.'

I waited until she had disappeared and shut the door behind her before proceeding down the corridor. From the doorway I stood watching Richard and my mother in the room beyond, through the glass doors. The walls were covered with paintings and charcoal sketches and there was a large display area with pottery exhibits. Richard was following Mum as she walked slowly around the exhibition, carefully studying each piece in turn. He appeared to be listening intently as she pointed out details that caught her eye. I had no idea if what she was saying was sensible, if she was in one of her lucid moments, or if it was all a meaningless jumble. It was impossible to tell from Richard's face, because he was listening and smiling, patiently standing beside her, asking her questions I could only guess at, but which seemed to evoke an animated response, lighting her up with an enthusiasm I hadn't seen on her face in a very long time. I took one last lingering look at the two of them together before turning and silently walking away.

CHAPTER 14

I'd been putting it off for quite some time, the way you put off making a dental appointment, despite a nagging tooth-ache, because you just *know* that despite the dentist's best assurances, it *is* going to hurt. But I had finally run out of excuses. It was time to clear the last vestiges of my presence from Richard's flat.

Monique clearly applauded this decision, providing me with an extended lunch break and an enormous cardboard box to transport my belongings out of Richard's life. 'It is time you close the door on this chapter of your life, Emma,' she advised with charmingly mixed metaphors.

'I know. But every time I try, Richard just keeps jamming it open with his foot.'

'Then you must stamp on it,' she suggested, tempering the words with a disingenuous smile, '*then* it will close.'

I did the familiar drive to Richard's flat on autopilot, wondering as I turned into the residents' car park if this was the last time I would ever visit this place. Probably. I pulled into Richard's empty parking bay and hefted the cardboard box out from the back seat. Working on muscle memory my fingers automatically punched in the code on the keypad at the entrance. The block was quiet; the residents were mainly young professionals who were most likely at work at this time of day. That was good; I didn't really want to bump into any of Richard's neighbours while I was severing these final ties. My footsteps echoed hollowly on the linoleum-covered stairs as I climbed up to the third floor. I slid the door key into the lock, reminding myself that I must remember to remove it from my keyring before I left, and leave it behind.

There was a vague musty smell in the air as I opened the front door and stepped into the flat's small hall. I sniffed and my nose wrinkled at the combined odours of leftover takeaways and a room which hadn't seen an open window in quite a while. I glanced into the kitchen and grimaced at the dirty plates stacked on the worktop, despite the fact that there was a perfectly good dishwasher just below them. Richard hadn't entirely reverted to student living, but he wasn't far off. Not my problem. Not any more. I resolutely turned away from the dirty crockery. I positioned the card-board box more securely on my hip and headed for the bedroom. I had only taken a few steps when I heard it. I froze like a startled fawn and turned my head slowly in the direction of the sound, as though if I moved too fast even the bones in my neck might give my presence away. A second later I heard it again, and this time I could tell precisely where the noise was coming from. Richard's bedroom. There was someone here in the flat with me, someone who had even less business being there than I did. Too late I remembered the fliers that the local police had circulated some months before, warning residents about the spate of daytime burglaries in the area.

I felt my heart begin to race and my mouth went instantly dry in panic. Any moment now the bedroom door could burst open and whoever it was who had broken in would find me. I heard a scraping sound of something moving across the wooden floor in Richard's bedroom. Were they coming? Did I have time to reach for my phone and call the police? No, of course I didn't. I had to get out of there. *Run*, my brain told my unresponsive legs, which were frozen in fear where I stood. No, they'd hear me too easily and would be upon me before I got halfway to the front door. I had to creep out silently and hope the noise of the opening door wouldn't be heard. I took one slow tentative step backwards and knocked into a framed poster Richard had hung in the hall. It fell from its flimsy nail and crashed to the floor in a cacophony of breaking glass.

Shit! Run! I told myself, just as a voice cried out from behind the bedroom door.

'Who's there?'

My heart was still pounding crazily when Richard threw open the door, wildly brandishing a tennis racquet.

'Christ, Emma, I thought you were a bloody burglar.'

'Likewise,' I replied, my voice still shaky, even though the threat of danger was gone. 'And what were you planning on doing with that?' I asked. 'Challenge them to a match?'

He looked down at the racquet in his hand and shook his head, before throwing the inadequate weapon into the lounge. It landed with a small thump on the patterned rug, right beside Richard's jacket and bag which appeared to have been carelessly discarded on the floor.

'What are you doing here anyway?' I challenged, not pausing to recognise that *I* was the person who didn't belong there, not him. Amazingly, it was only then that I noticed something that should have been glaringly obvious. Richard was wearing just a faded old T-shirt and a pair of boxer shorts, and the room he'd just emerged from was in total darkness, with the heavy blinds drawn shut to keep out the spring sunshine.

I reached out and flicked on the hall light, stepping closer towards him as I noted the unhealthy pallor of his face and the thin layer of perspiration on his brow. He squinted in the light and I immediately snapped it off. 'Sorry. Have you got another migraine?' I asked. He nodded dully, as he reached out to hold on to the door frame for support. 'You should be in bed,' I advised solemnly.

'I *was* in bloody bed, until I was woken up by someone trying to ransack the place,' he said. His eye fell to the large cardboard box which I had dropped on to the hall floor. 'But I see you weren't here to take my possessions, just yours.' His voice sounded pained, which could have just been the headache, or maybe not.

'Look, I'll just go,' I said, bending to retrieve my box. 'I only came during the day because I thought this would be easier – for both of us – when you weren't home.' A thought suddenly occurred to me. 'Where's your car anyway? I wouldn't have come in if I'd seen it outside.'

'I left it at the school,' he replied, and I saw the effort it was costing him to stand and talk to me. He really did look terrible. 'One of the guys at work dropped me back, my vision was going weird and I didn't think I should drive.'

I knew Richard's migraines; he'd suffered with them for years. They were largely manageable, as long as he took his medication at the first signs. Only rarely were they severe enough to disturb his eyesight and force him to take to his bed. This was clearly a bad one. The worse ones were usually brought on by stress. Perhaps it was hardly surprising that he had one now.

'Go back to bed,' I said firmly. 'I'll let myself out. I'll come back another time.'

He turned back gratefully in the direction of his darkened

room. 'You might as well get whatever it is you've come for,' he said bitterly as he walked jerkily to the double bed, as though even the movement of his limbs caused pain in his pounding head.

'You're really bad, aren't you?' I questioned, scarcely noticing that I had followed him into the bedroom as he slowly lowered himself back down on to the mattress. There was something about the way he was sitting there on the side of the bed with his throbbing head in his hands that made it impossible for me to leave. 'Did you take your pills?' I questioned.

He shook his head, and then winced as though he really regretted having done that. 'No. I just wanted to get straight into a darkened room and see if I could sleep it off.'

I gave an exasperated sigh, and sounded entirely like a girlfriend as I said, 'Why on earth not? You *know* you can never shake these off without the pills.' I turned on my heel and headed for the bathroom. 'I'll get them.'

Nothing had changed or been moved in the bathroom since the last time I had been there. The shelf of my shampoo, conditioner, face cream and body lotion was exactly as I had left it. My spare dressing gown was hanging on the back of the door and a couple of my hairclips sat on the edge of his bathtub. I was everywhere. No wonder he was doing such a terrible job of letting me go.

I pulled open the mirror-fronted medicine cabinet and reached automatically for the shelf where he kept his migraine medication. The box was there, but when I pulled out the foil blister sheet, all the holes in it had already been punctured and it was empty. With the box in hand I returned to the bedroom.

'There are none left. Where's your new packet? You *did*

get your last prescription filled, didn't you?' It was surprising how easily I was managing to slip back into the role of nagging girlfriend.

Richard had laid back on the crumpled pillows during my absence, his face pretty much the same shade as the white bed linen. 'No. I kept meaning to, but I never got around to it.'

'Richard,' I said, my voice rising slightly in irritated exasperation.

He flinched at the increase in decibels. 'Yeah, well, I've had other things on my mind lately.'

I may have hesitated for a second or two, but not for much longer. I didn't really have an option here, did I? Without waiting for permission, I opened the top drawer of the bedside cabinet where I knew I'd find the prescription. I plucked the small green sheet from Richard's belongings.

'What are you doing?' he asked, his aching head clearly not firing on all cylinders.

'Filling your bloody prescription for you,' I replied, preparing to go. He turned his head slowly on the pillow to look at me, carefully, as though his neck was lying on a surface of broken glass.

'Thank you,' he said weakly.

I didn't know what to say or how I felt about seeing him like this, so sick and vulnerable. I think that's what made my voice so unnaturally brusque. 'Go back to sleep. I won't be long.'

There was an annoyingly long queue in the pharmacy, and by the time I let myself back into the flat I knew Richard's headache was probably a roaring giant beating a club on the inside of his skull to get out. I managed to find a clean glass in the kitchen, no small achievement, and filled it with icy cold water before returning to his bedroom. To keep the light from bothering him, I had shut the bedroom door when I left, and I hesitated now on the threshold, not sure if I should knock and risk disturbing him, or walk right in. It was ridiculous, because despite our break-up, this place still felt very much like my second home. I curled my hand around the door handle and pushed it slowly down. Richard was asleep, but not in a peaceful, relaxed kind of way. In his restlessness he had thrown off the covers, and they were now twisted into a tangled origami knot beneath his legs. Even in the darkened room I could see a glistening sheen on his exposed torso, for he'd discarded the T-shirt which was now lying on the floor in a damp and unpleasant ball. I didn't know what to do for the best: leave him sleeping or try to get him to swallow the pills? His head was moving restlessly from side to side and occasionally a spasm of pain crossed his face. Pills, I decided.

'Richard, I'm back.'

He made no reply, but his brow furrowed as though he'd heard my voice.

'Richard, open your eyes. You need to take these.' I pressed out two of the pills into my palm, but there was still no sign from the bed that he'd heard me.

'Richard, it's me. Can you hear me? Wake up and take your pills.'

I know he recognised my voice then, because his expression changed and he mumbled something which may very well have been my name, if it had been spoken underwater, with a mouth full of cotton wool. I put both the pills and drinking glass on to the bedside table and crouched down beside the bed. If anyone had told me that I would be here, in Richard's flat, looking after him like this, I'd have called them crazy. But what was I supposed to do? Just leave him suffering and walk out?

I slid my hand beneath his neck and gently raised his head off the pillows. With my free hand I picked up the two small white tablets. His lips felt hot and dry as I gently parted them with my fingers and slipped both pills on to his tongue. I had touched those lips a thousand times, I'd felt them on practically every inch of my body, but the intimacy of this moment made me so uncomfortable I could actually feel my face begin to flush. This felt beyond inappropriate, especially given the way things were between us. I reached for the glass of water and held it to his mouth.

'Swallow, Richard.' Obediently, still more asleep than awake, he did as I asked. When I was sure the pills were gone, I tilted the glass once more to his parched lips. 'Drink some more,' I requested and obligingly he took several small mouthfuls of the refreshing liquid. Suddenly his hand came up and covered mine, so unexpectedly that I almost dropped the entire glass of icy water all over him. That would have been one sure way to wake him up, I guess. His fingers moved across the back of my hand in a slow caressing movement. He's asleep. He doesn't know what he's doing, I told myself as I removed the glass before trying to slowly slide my hand out from under his.

'Don't go, Emma.' His voice was thick and muzzy, spoken from the depths of a dream. I lowered our conjoined hands until they rested on the wall of his chest before I finally managed to inch my own away from his without waking him. I stood for a long moment with just my fingertips left resting on his upper body before finally breaking our contact.

'Shhhhh...' I said, my voice sounding like I was soothing a toddler. 'Go back to sleep.'

He did.

I cleared the flat, of me. I went systematically from room to room removing every last trace of everything I had unthinkingly left behind over the last twelve months. When I had collected everything except the clothes inside his closet, I cleaned the flat. I told myself I was just doing it to pass the time, not because I cared about how the place looked or how its occupant chose to live within it. By the time I was done, the kitchen surfaces were once more clear and the dishwasher was thrumming through its cycle. The late afternoon shadows had lengthened and I had no real reason to remain. Yet it felt wrong to just walk out and leave.

When Richard still showed no signs of stirring, I eventually decided I would have to risk waking him by retrieving the final items left behind in his bedroom. I tiptoed into the darkened room, and eased open the wardrobe doors. I worked quickly in the semi darkness, using just the light coming from the hall, as I plucked my few items of clothing from their hangers and slid open the dresser to remove the small collection of underwear I had kept there.

When the bedside light behind me was suddenly switched on, I almost dropped the well-laden cardboard box I was carrying from his room. I had no idea he was awake or how long he had been watching me. Richard levered himself up into a sitting position, resting against the pillows.

'How are you feeling?' I asked.

He ran a hand through his hair, making it look even more dishevelled than all his tossing and turning had done.

'Better,' he said, then his eyes went from me to the large

box that I was holding. 'Worse.' There was no point in pretending I didn't know what he meant.

'I've made you a sandwich and there's fresh water in the jug,' I said, nodding at the tray I had left beside the bed.

'I thought...' he said, his voice trailing away.

I shook my head. 'No, Richard. Nothing has changed.'

'But you stayed.'

'Just until you woke up. I'm going now,' I said, moving toward the door as I spoke.

'Is this about that American—'

My sigh was weary. 'He's not the issue.'

'But you still care about me, Emma. I *know* you do.'

I looked at him sadly. His headache might have improved, but he still looked far from well. But I couldn't afford to let him think that what had happened today was anything more than just basic humanity.

'Not enough, Richard. Nowhere near enough.'

I saw him looking sadly at the overflowing box in my arms. 'You're really not coming back?'

I could feel unexpected tears thickening my voice. 'No, I'm not.'

He turned his head away from me, and I think we were both glad of the dim light that kept our faces in shadow.

'I've just been fooling myself all this time, haven't I? I kept thinking that if I proved to you how incredibly sorry I was, if I could make you understand how much I love you, that you'd give me another chance. I know I don't deserve it, but it's the only thing that's kept me going.'

I could think of nothing to say that we hadn't already been over far too many times before. I waited until I reached the door before I turned back to face him.

'I honestly don't know if I could have forgiven you for

cheating on me, if things had turned out differently, if the accident hadn't happened,' I admitted, with an honesty that surprised me as much as him. 'But what I *can't* forgive you for, is what you've taken from me.'

His look of total bewilderment confirmed he had no idea what I was talking about.

'Amy,' I said quietly.

He jerked and I saw his throat move convulsively at her name.

'You took Amy from me with what you did. You took her memory from me.' My tears were falling now, and I didn't give a damn if he saw them or not. 'I should be grieving for my best friend but, thanks to you and what you did, I can't. I can't think of her at all without seeing the two of you together, kissing... touching...' I shuddered and Richard looked ripped raw at my reaction. 'Because of you, I can't mourn her or even *think* about her without getting angry, without feeling betrayed. And I don't think I'll *ever* be able to forgive you for that.'

It felt more like an ending than our actual break-up had done. And, as I drove home with the box of my life with Richard jiggling and rattling on the seat beside me, I had finally believed Richard's parting words: 'I won't put pressure on you any more, Emma. I'm not going to keep trying to win you back, or get you to change your mind.' I had nodded gratefully, feeling both the freedom of a huge weight being lifted from me, yet strangely a simultaneous sensation of panic as the door to our story clanged shut with noisy finality. 'But just know one thing: when you change your mind – and you *will* change your mind – I am going to be right here waiting for you.'

My parents were both out when I got home, for which I

was grateful, because I really didn't want to have to explain the box I carried in my arms like a miniature casket. It didn't take long to slip my belongings back where they belonged, back into my life and out of Richard's. I was about to shut the wardrobe doors when my eye fell on something tucked away in the back. There was still one last thing that needed to be done.

I reached for the shoebox and dragged it out on to the bedroom carpet. I released the elastic band holding the lid in place, and there it was. Waiting for me. I hadn't been ready before, it had been too soon. But now I was.

I sat down on the floor, my back against the divan of the bed, and picked up the small white oblong. My heart started to pound and my fingers were shaking as I turned the envelope over and broke the seal. It was time to let her speak, for the very last time. The time had finally come to read Amy's letter.

Dear Emma,

That sounds weirdly formal, doesn't it? But then this whole thing is really strange. Here I am writing you this letter, knowing all the while that I am never, ever going to give it to you. Crazy, huh? I'm certain you wouldn't want to read it anyway. If you don't want to talk about it, then the last thing you want is to see it set out on paper in black and white (blue and white actually, as I don't have a black pen!).

But I have to write this down, I have to get it all out of my head and on to paper, maybe then I can lock the memories (and this letter too) in some secret place and actually begin to move on.

I don't know how you do it, I really don't. I look at

you sometimes when you're smiling at me, or hugging me goodbye, and I search your face and your eyes for a trace, a hint... anything... of what I'm sure you must be feeling. But there's nothing to be seen, nothing at all. You are either the world's very best actress ("... and the Oscar goes to Emma Marshall...") or (and I suspect this is probably the case), you are the best, kindest and most forgiving person in the entire universe. An angel... no, more than that, a saint. Well, some sort of celestial being, anyway. No one else could have found whatever it is you drew upon when you decided not to a) have me stoned in Hallingford High Street, b) hire a hit man to take me out, or c) (worst of all options) shut me out of your life and never speak to me again.

Let me just say one thing from the very start, I deserve all of the above – and more. Don't think I don't know that, because I do. I don't know why you don't hate me. I hate me. Anyone who ever hears what I've done (although I hope to God no one ever will) would surely think I am the most despicable creature to ever crawl out of a pit and walk among decent people. People who know how you're meant to act and behave in this world. People who know that you should absolutely, categorically, never, ever, ever sleep with your best friend's fiancé. Okay, so he was only your boyfriend at the time, I know that, but I don't think I can get off on a technicality. What I did was terrible. Horrible. I am a horrible, horrible person, whose only redeeming feature is that I happen to be best friends with someone so truly great that she will forgive me for making the biggest mistake of my whole stupid life and allow me to hold on to a title of which I am no longer worthy. And if the only thing you ask is that I never mention it, not once, not ever, then I have to respect that. I guess that's the only way you can move past it, if it's never voiced out loud.

I can see that works for you, because – from the outside at least – everything looks great between you and Richard. Thank God. And I really, really mean that. I want you to be happy. Blissfully, joyfully, laughing all day and night, and they-lived-happily-ever-after happy. You deserve that. Both of you do. And – not that this in any way excuses me for my betrayal – I don't think that you've always felt that way since you came home. I know how hard it must have been for you to put your career and whole life on hold, and come back here to help your dad look after your mum. See, that's another example of just what a good person you are. I'd like to think I would do the same thing for my own parents, but if I'm honest (and I promised myself I would be here), then I don't think that I would.

Sometimes, even recently, I thought I could see something on your face that looked, I don't know… kind of lost or… overwhelmed by everything. Caroline thinks you have pre-wedding jitters, but I'm not so sure. I thought you looked that way even before you got engaged. Now, with hindsight, I don't know if I allowed myself to think that some of that uncertainty and confusion was about Richard. Did I do that? Was I that stupid? Probably. If there is one thing that this whole miserable situation has taught me, it's that you must really and truly love him (and me too) to forgive us for hurting you so deeply.

I guess Richard told you everything that happened that night? You obviously know that what we did was not in any way at all premeditated or planned. It was nothing we wanted to happen. There! I've gone and done it again. I've lied, and I'd promised myself there would be none of that in this letter. Let me clarify. Richard one hundred per cent never wanted or planned for it to happen. Give me a stack of Bibles and I will swear to that. But me... well, there was a time... when you were living abroad, and we'd lost touch with you... well, there's no way to dress this up. I started to let myself think that... maybe, just maybe, Richard and I might... you know. But it was me, just me, getting things all mixed up and confused (as usual). It was only in my head that he had those sorts of feelings for me. Just me living out some stupid silly little fantasy that I should never ever have allowed to grow. In reality I know the truth, I always have; Richard has never loved anyone but you.

He cried, did he tell you that? The very moment we had finished... you know... he started to cry – hey, who knew I was that bad at it? Sorry. It's nothing to joke about. I've never seen a man cry like that before. I've never seen someone so torn apart with guilt and shame, but then I think I came a pretty close second on both of those emotions.

I've done some stupid, thoughtless and irresponsible things in my life (I don't have to list them – you witnessed most of them over the years!). But this thing... this sin, crime, betrayal, is the worst of them all, and if we live to be little grey-haired old ladies sitting in our rocking chairs in the retirement home, I still don't think I will ever be able to understand how you let us get past this.

I love you, Emma, with all my heart. I am beyond

sorry that I took something so precious as our friendship and almost destroyed it. Thank you for saving it, for saving me. I promise you this: I will never, ever do anything to hurt you again for the rest of my life. You have my word.

Friends for ever, Amy xxxxxxxxxx

'Do you prefer this one?'

I pulled back the curtain and studied Caroline in the dress she had just tried on. I pulled a face and shook my head. 'Not as much as the others. Try the blue one on again,' I suggested, lifting it from the pile draped over my arm and passing it to her.

It was Saturday morning, the shops were crowded and the music in the changing rooms was giving me a headache. Girly shopping trips together were more a feature of our teenage years, but Caroline had been surprisingly persistent in persuading me to join her.

'Please, Emma. I need to get a really special dress for my birthday, and I don't want to shop alone,' she had pleaded over the phone.

'Take Nick,' I'd suggested, knowing he would probably be just as enthusiastic at the prospect as I was.

'I can't,' she'd whispered down the phone, which I guess meant he must have been within earshot.

'Why not?'

There were shuffling sounds as she moved to a position that offered her more privacy. 'He's been dropping hints for days now, about making it a big celebration evening. And I really think this is going to be *the night*.'

'The night for what?'

Her voice fell to an excited whisper. 'I think he's going to propose, Emma, on my birthday. We always said we'd wait, save up more money, but since Amy... well I think it's made him rethink. So you see why you have to come, I need you to help me pick out something fabulous to wear.' Of course I'd said yes, and tried really hard to ignore the small stab of jealousy that had slid between my ribs at her words. I had no right to begrudge her the excitement of something she'd been wanting and waiting for almost her entire adult life. Just because my own engagement and wedding plans had ended in disaster, I could never be so selfish as to deny her this. We'd both been through a terrible time; Caroline deserved this happiness.

The curtains rattled and she stood before me in the blue dress. Her hair was dishevelled from the many outfits that had passed over it, she was shoeless and was wearing stripy woollen socks, perfect under her jeans and boots, but not really suited for the silky strapless dress, which fitted her slender frame as though it was custom made. She looked stunning.

'That's the one,' I told her with assurance. She smiled broadly, looked back into the mirror and nodded happily. 'If Nick doesn't propose to you in that dress, then I'll marry you myself.'

Our hunt for the perfect dress had kept us focused for the morning, but as I stood beside her in the queue for the checkout, Caroline raised the subject of my own plans for later in the day. I should have known that she would.

'Are you still going to see Jack this afternoon?'

I shuffled forwards as the queue crept closer to the tills. 'I think so,' I replied.

'You don't sound sure.'

I shrugged, trying to feign a nonchalance I didn't feel. 'No. It's not that. It's just going to be weird, that's all. It's going to be my last chance to say goodbye to him.'

'It's probably going to be your last chance to do... anything else... with him too,' Caroline advised solemnly, as she extracted her credit card and passed it to the assistant.

'God, not that again. You're obsessed. It's not going to happen, and especially not if he's about to disappear out of my life in just a few days.'

'Maybe he'll change his mind and stay longer,' Caroline suggested, wincing slightly as the price of her purchase appeared on the small display on the till.

'I don't think so. He said something about only having had a three-month option on the lease to the house.'

Caroline watched as the assistant carefully folded her dress in tissue paper, before pulling a large glossy bag from beneath the counter. You got the good stuff rather than the plastic carrier bags when you spent as much as she just had. 'I could always check the other estate agents in town on Monday,' she suggested, 'see who's handling the property and if the lease can be extended.'

I shook my head. 'There's no point. He's going back to the States, and he's not going to change his mind. Just leave it.'

By the time I had fought my way out of the multi-storey car park and driven back to Hallingford I was ready to call it a day, but Caroline was unusually insistent about stopping for a quick drink and a sandwich before we went our separate ways.

'My treat,' she promised. 'It's my way of saying thank you for dragging you around the shops all morning.'

She'd phrased it so artlessly, I didn't even see through her ploy. We had ordered our sandwiches and were already sipping our drinks when she looked up and exclaimed, 'Oh my goodness, look who just walked in.'

It was like the hammiest acting from a second-rate amateur dramatic production. I looked up and saw that Nick and Richard had just entered the pub. Coincidence? I don't think so. I turned to Caroline with a glower, all good humour gone.

'Caroline McAdam...'

'What?' she replied, with feigned innocence. 'I didn't know they were coming here. They were playing squash at the Sports Centre, the last I heard.'

I saw Nick do a very poor version of a double-take as he pretended to be surprised to see his girlfriend at the exact same pub he had 'randomly' selected. He took hold of Richard's arm and nodded in our direction. I saw Richard's face pale and his mouth tighten. I knew him well enough to recognise that his reaction, at least, was genuine. If it was a set-up (and could that really be in any doubt?) he certainly wasn't part of it.

Nick said something, to which Richard shook his head, but despite that Nick began to head towards us, leaving Richard very little option but to follow.

'Well, this is a surprise,' said Caroline, still in absolutely no danger of ever getting nominated for any type of acting award.

'I had no idea you were going to be here,' her boyfriend said, and I just knew that they'd rehearsed those words several times earlier, to make sure they said them just right. And yet still they came out all wrong.

'I'm sorry,' said Richard, looking genuinely uncomfortable

as his eyes met mine. 'I meant what I said the other day. I didn't know anything about this.' *Him*, I believed. 'I'll go,' he volunteered, already turning to the door.

I saw the look of frustration that passed between our two matchmaking friends. Clearly they hadn't factored on Richard actually being the bigger person here. And then, before I realised I was going to do it, I stopped him.

'Richard, no, don't go.' All three of them looked shocked at my words, but no more so than I was myself. 'There's no need. It's a small town, we're not going to be able to keep avoiding each other. Our paths are bound to cross... *accidentally*,' I looked pointedly at Caroline as I said that. 'We can at least be grown-up and civil when they do.'

There was truth in what I said, but I think my softening was more down to the promise Richard had made me at his flat than to Caroline's meddling. If Richard had finally realised and accepted that I needed space, I could at least be reasonable.

It wasn't the most comfortable half-hour the four of us had ever spent, and I don't think Richard and I directed a single comment to each other, but spoke instead through Caroline and Nick, as though they were United Nations interpreters, fluent in the language of awkward ex-lovers. I chewed my sandwich and swallowed my drink fast enough to give me indigestion, but at least Richard and I had been able to spend thirty minutes in the same room without either of us sniping, yelling or hurling recriminations at each other. It was quite a milestone. Caroline certainly thought so, as she walked me to my parked car.

'See,' she said, linking her arm through mine, 'that wasn't so bad, was it?'

I was still quietly simmering. If it wasn't my parents, then it was her and Nick that we had to contend with. At this rate I would have to spend my entire free time with Monique, because she was the only person left who didn't want Richard and me to get back together. Then I realised that wasn't entirely true, there *was* one other person who wasn't on board with the plan. Jack. But he was going to leave in five days, so he didn't count.

'Don't do that again, Caroline,' I said earnestly, after kissing her briefly on the cheek. 'I know you mean well, but we just need everyone to butt out of our lives.'

'I'm sorry. It's just that I want you guys to get back together so badly. There's been so much awful in our lives, I just want there to be a happy ending.'

'Maybe this story just doesn't have one,' I said sadly. 'You can't force me to change my mind about Richard, or forgive him, or trust him again. Nor can you thrust me into a one-night stand, hoping it will make me appreciate everything I once had. I know what I had, and I also know that for now, those feelings have gone.'

'But not for ever, surely? In time ...'

I reached for the car door and opened it. 'Richard isn't a bad man,' I said, finally acknowledging the truth that had been following me around like a shadow for days, 'he's a good man who did a very, very bad thing.'

I was nervous as I drove, which if I stopped to think about it was kind of ridiculous. The meeting was my idea; it was long overdue and important things had to be said. The choice of venue... well, that one wasn't down to me.

I parked my car in the small car park, glancing around at the numerous empty bays surrounding me. Good. No one else was here. At least we could talk undisturbed. I pulled on a warm jacket and wound a long soft scarf around my neck before getting out of my car. It was late April, but still cool.

My feet crunched noisily on the gravel path. There were rows of bright red tulips lining the path, standing and swaying in the slight breeze like a military guard of honour marking my route. I smiled a little at the fanciful notion and then sobered as I rounded the corner and saw that I was almost there. My heart began to beat faster and my mouth suddenly felt way too dry to summon even a greeting, much less speak of all the things I knew would have to be said today.

I left the path and watched my boots instantly disappear from view in the grass which, even this early in the season, had begun to grow. I walked on, keeping my eyes firmly fixed on my feet slicing through the brilliant green blades, rather than on my destination. I drew to a halt and finally raised my eyes. I reached into the deep pocket of my jacket, allowing my fingers to fold around the item I had placed there before leaving home. I pulled it out and finally, I spoke.

'Hi, Amy. I got your letter.'

The breeze fluttered the single sheet in my hand, like a white flag of surrender. It was a good analogy. I took a step closer to the headstone and brushed away a smudge of dirt that was marring the pristine perfection of the white marble. Not that Amy would have worried. Housekeeping had never been her forte. The thought made me smile and relax in a way I had believed it would be impossible to do in this place.

'Do you mind if I sit down?' I asked Amy, as I dropped to the ground beside her final resting place. The grass was a little damp and I could already feel it seeping through the

297

denim of my jeans. But a little discomfort was a small price to pay.

The flowers Caroline had laid here on her last visit had withered and died, and I reached out to remove them from the place where our friend lay.

'So, I bet you're surprised to see me here today? I don't blame you. A few weeks ago this would have been the last place on earth I wanted to be.' The wind swirled in a small restless eddy, blowing the hair from my face. 'I guess you probably think the same thing,' I added, smiling slightly. I had to believe that in this world or the next Amy would have retained her sense of humour. It was one of the things I had always loved most about her. The thought pulled me up short, like a match being struck in the darkness, allowing me a brief glimpse of the truth before it fizzled out. I *did* love Amy. Alive. Dead. Friend. Confidante. Bridesmaid and Betrayer. I loved her regardless. I always had done, and I always would.

I smoothed out her letter, laying it over my crossed legs. Random words and snatches of sentences caught my eye as my fingers swept over the page, flattening out the creases. ... *beyond sorry... biggest mistake... forgive us...* I stared down silently at Amy's last message to me. I didn't need to read it again, I'd already memorised every word.

'It's a good letter,' I said, directing my comment to the ground below the marble plinth. 'A couple of spelling mistakes here and there... but I can forgive you those,' I joked. Amy's grasp of grammar and spelling had always been somewhat haphazard and creative. I slid my fingers across the grass until they grazed against the gravestone marking her existence and departure from the world. 'That's not all I forgive you for, Amy.'

I paused for a long moment, desperate to hear more than just the rustling leaves or my own breathing. I didn't believe in ghosts, or the hereafter, but I would have given anything at that moment to see her, hear her and touch her. I closed my eyes and saw her face in my mind; she was smiling and her beautiful blue eyes were alight with laughter and life.

'Oh Amy, I miss you so much.'

Amy waited patiently for me to hunt for a tissue in my bag before I felt able to continue. I blew my nose noisily, and then crazily apologised out loud to my lost friend and her neighbours. No one seemed to mind.

'So, I came here today to tell you it's okay. It really is. I know you thought I already knew about... about what happened with you and Richard. But I guess you probably know now that he never told me anything. You can see everything from... over there... can't you?' I was stretching my own beliefs to the absolute limit here, but for myself as much as Amy, I had to trust that somehow and somewhere she could hear my words.

'Things are much clearer now, now I've had time to think them through. I know you never for a moment intended to hurt me... or Richard... in any way. You'd never do that to me, I know that. But it happened, and I think I know why. You loved him, didn't you? You loved him too.' Somewhere I imagined the spirit of Amy gasping at my revelation. 'Perhaps I always knew there was something... just a hint maybe, that you liked him. Well, maybe more than liked. Not that you ever acted on it when we were dating. But when I left, when I told Richard that I thought we'd reached the end of our story. Well... I can't blame you. And I was gone for so many years. Years he spent waiting for me, and all the time you were waiting for him.' A small sob escaped me, sounding raw and broken. 'God what a waste. What a mess we made of everything.'

Amy didn't argue.

'And then, after all that time, he finally saw you. The real you. How did that feel, Amy? Did you feel guilty because of me? You shouldn't have. I'd told him I was never coming back. I never wanted him to wait for me. But he did, didn't he? I wish you'd had someone to share it with. But you couldn't speak of it to anyone, could you? Not even Caroline.'

A magpie swept down from the sky, startling me when it landed on the grass beside me. One magpie, just one: one for sorrow. The black-and-white intruder fixed me with a long and knowing stare, and just for a second I imagined it understood everything I was saying. Stupid. I shivered and the spooked bird took to the sky once more before disappearing into the trees on silent sweeping wings.

'And then I came back. I hadn't wanted to, I think we all knew that. But Mum needed me... and Dad needed me more. And Richard was there, and it was all so easy, and comfortable, to slide right back into things all over again. That must have really killed you, mustn't it—' I gasped in shock as I realised what I'd said.

'Sorry,' I apologised to my friend and those in the surrounding plots. 'Terrible choice of words. But I know now how much it must have hurt you. You were so close, so almost where you wanted to be, with the person you always wanted to be with. And then, it was all gone. Snatched away from you.'

I paused, wondering if I should continue with what I was about to say. Amy had always been a good listener, and these days her ability to keep a secret wasn't even in question.

'I know mistakes can happen when you follow your heart,

like they did that night with you and Richard. I understand that… because it's happening to me too. Well, not exactly the same thing, of course, but I've got myself tangled up in something that's not going to end well. It can't. And now I understand a little of what you must have been feeling. Being close enough to touch the thing you want, and knowing all the while that it's never going to be yours.

'I don't suppose you've got any advice for me on this one, have you?' I asked her sadly, as a single tear trickled down my cheek and landed with an audible plop on Amy's letter. The solitary sparkling jewel of moisture had settled, of all places, squarely over her looping familiar signature. It felt like a sign, but if it was, I didn't know what it meant.

I smiled sadly. 'Guess I have to figure this one out on my own, huh?' I asked my silent friend.

Slowly I unfurled my legs and rose to a crouch beside Amy's marble headstone. I reached out and gently traced the gold edged carving of each letter of her name with my fingers, as though I was saying goodbye in Braille. I leaned in and laid my lips against the cool marble of her name, feeling closer to her at that moment than I had done since the night when we'd lost her.

'Everything is all right with you and me, Amy. There's absolutely nothing you need to worry about. Sleep peacefully my beautiful friend.'

THE END

PART FOUR

I looked away from the mirror when I heard the opening of the bedroom door. Caroline's head popped through the gap.

'Hi, sweetie, how are you doing?

I smiled; just seeing her familiar face calmed me. 'I'm fine,' I assured her, although the pulse beating visibly at my throat revealed that might possibly be an overstatement. 'Where's Nick?' I asked.

'Downstairs, having his ear chewed off by some cousin of yours from Devon.'

I pulled a face. 'Tell him I'm sorry.'

'Do you want me to hang around?' Caroline offered, glancing around the room at the cellophane-covered dress, the underwear draped across the bed and the shoes neatly lined up waiting for me to step into.

'No, I'm good. Go down and rescue that poor man of yours.'

Caroline smiled and turned back towards the door. 'Oh I almost forgot,' she said, walking back to the dressing table, and giving my shoulder a gentle squeeze. She pulled two small square envelopes from the pocket of her jacket. 'These arrived a little while ago.'

I took them from her outstretched hand and glanced briefly at the handwriting. I didn't recognise either of them. I didn't have time to read any more cards right now, they were going to have to join the sizeable collection downstairs.

'So,' continued Caroline, a little uncertainly, 'see you at the church, then?'

'I'll be there,' I said softly.

Caroline left, still looking back at me over her shoulder with undisguised love on her face. I took the two thick vellum envelopes to place beneath the paperweight I kept on my dressing table. I lifted the large glassy-smooth pebble, the one I had collected from the shore of the lake, and slid the cards beneath it. My fingers lingered for a moment, running over the silky grey veined stone, remembering...

CHAPTER 15

I was nervous as I unloaded the supermarket bags from my car and walked to Jack's door. This would be the first time I'd seen him since the night of our kiss, a thing he seemed to have been able to instantly dismiss, but which had stayed with me, in graphic detail, for every waking moment since.

He opened the door with an easy smile and an apology. 'Hi, Emma,' he greeted, his lips curling gently as he said my name. He took the bags from my hands and set them down on the hall floor. 'Sorry, I'm just talking to someone on Skype, leave those bags and go on through to the kitchen, I won't be a minute.'

I nodded my compliance as he ducked back into the room he had commissioned as an office.

'Hi, sweetheart, I'm back. Sorry about that.' I felt a lance run through me. It started at my back and pierced straight through my heart, clipping several other vital organs on its way. I put my hand out to the wood-panelled wall to steady myself. I wasn't trying to eavesdrop, really I wasn't, but as Jack hadn't closed the door properly behind him it was almost impossible not to hear his next words.

'No, it was just someone at the door... no, just a friend. Now what were you saying?' I snatched up the supermarket bags and virtually ran into the kitchen. What was I doing here? I thought, dumping the carriers down on the kitchen table with enough force I was certain to have broken every egg in the carton I'd just bought.

I had read all sorts of stupid hidden meanings into Jack's invitation today. I'd been so sure that he'd invented this whole crazy cookery ruse as an excuse to spend one more day with me. And now, when I got here he was on the internet sweet-talking some nameless woman on the other side of the world. And it was crushingly obvious that whoever she was, he cared about her; that much was clear by the warm and loving tone of his voice when he spoke to her. I'd heard traces of that sometimes when he spoke to me, fleeting glimpses of intimacy, enough to recognise it when it was directed at someone else. So why was I still standing in his kitchen like some pathetic idiot, wearing my brand new jeans and white shirt *(not too try-hard, didn't want him thinking I'd overdressed for the occasion)*, just waiting for him to say goodbye to one woman and then pay some attention to me? I didn't deserve to be treated like this. Not again, not by anyone, and certainly not by him.

Caroline's warning rang like a grim reminder in my head. Well, she needn't have worried; romance hadn't been on Jack's mind at all when he'd asked me to come here today. Apparently, the only reason I was here was to cook his bloody dinner. He'd even directed me straight into the kitchen! I should just go, I thought, already heading back into the hall. Jack was still talking on his computer and with luck I could ease open the front door and make a dash for my car before he even noticed I had gone. I took a step further into the shadowy hall.

'I've missed you too, honey. It's been far too long this time, but only another five days.'

The woman talking to him on his laptop screen said

something which I couldn't make out, and Jack responded with a low rumbling laugh. 'Of course I will,' he promised. I had to get out of there before he started intimately discussing the reunion they were both no doubt eagerly awaiting. I took a step and the old oak board beneath my foot creaked noisily, giving away my presence. Jack's head spun around.

'Everything okay, Emma?' he asked, his eyes warm and gentle as he turned away from the screen to look at me. Masochistically I tried to see beyond the breadth of him to catch a glimpse of the woman who made him look and sound so full of tender affection. I could see nothing at all except a mass of pale gold hair. A blonde, that figures.

I realised he was still waiting for a response as I stood in his hall like a cartoon character pantomiming someone stealthily trying to tiptoe away, which actually was precisely what I *was* doing.

'Yes, fine,' I said, flustered by having been caught. There was no chance now to make an unobserved exit. 'I was just… just… getting the shopping,' I improvised wildly, hoping he hadn't noticed that the bags I was referring to were already in the kitchen. 'I have to put some things in the fridge.'

'Okay,' he said with a slightly bemused smile. Perhaps my voice hadn't sounded as natural as I would have liked. 'I'm just saying goodbye here, I'll be with you in a moment.'

I knew a dismissal when I heard one. I walked back to the kitchen biting my lip until it actually hurt. What do I do now, stay or go? If I ran out of his house, like some pathetic heartbroken heroine, Jack would instantly know how badly I had misread everything about our entire relationship. He'd just been the Good Samaritan who had happened to be in the fallout zone when my world had crumbled apart. *I* was the one who had mistaken responsibility, friendship and concern for a deep and lasting emotional connection tying us together. It wasn't Jack who couldn't see the difference between a fleeting physical attraction and something so much more. That was all me.

'Hi, I'm sorry, that was really rude of me,' he said, walking in with the apology already falling from his lips. He bent down and lightly kissed my cheek. That was new. I stiffened, but I don't think he noticed for he was already crossing the kitchen and heading for the kettle.

'Coffee?'

I opened my mouth to say, *'No thanks, I can't stay'*, and instead heard my voice replying, 'Yes please, black, no sugar.'

As the water boiled Jack crossed to the table and looked down at the two over-stuffed carrier bags. 'I didn't think you would actually bring all the ingredients with you.'

He looked so calm and unfazed. Moving so easily from his lover to his dumb English friend that something inside me tightened and twisted uncomfortably.

'Well, that *was* why you invited me here today, Jack, wasn't it? You asked me to cook for you, isn't that what this is all about?'

He looked at me carefully, and I found my gaze drawn to his lower lip, and the way he had drawn it in, considering my question. It was a physical effort to wrench my gaze away from his mouth. Jack looked confused, and it wasn't an expression I was used to seeing on him.

'Is something wrong, Emma?'

'No,' I lied, looking him straight in the eye. 'Why do you ask?'

He looked uncomfortable and wrong-footed, yet another new look for him.

'You seem... prickly.'

I forced a tight smile past my unwilling lips. 'No. Just keen to get going.' Jack's eyebrows rose at my words. 'With the cooking,' I amended.

I knew he didn't believe me, but I really didn't care. I was going to go through with this silly little charade and not let him see just how much more I had thought this day was meant to be about. All I had left was my pride, and I wasn't prepared to lose that too.

He made the coffees while I made a great pretence of readying the ingredients I had brought, lining them up along one side of the kitchen table, as though I was preparing to be filmed for a television cook show.

'Do you need me to do anything?' he asked, as I hunted for bowls and utensils in the cupboards of his kitchen. I remembered seeing most of what I needed when I had cooked our steak dinner. I closed my eyes briefly on the memory. So much had happened since then, and none of it good. I carried what I needed back to the table and directed him to the other side of the room. If I was going to get through this at all, I needed far more distance between us. In fact the width of the kitchen was still nowhere wide enough. Well, in another five days there'd be an entire ocean between us. And then he'd be with her, whoever she was.

'It's best you stand well clear,' I advised, pouring flour recklessly on to the scales and momentarily disappearing behind a small white cloud. 'I'm a pretty messy cook. You should really have asked Caroline here to do this instead of me.'

'I didn't want Caroline here. I wanted you,' he answered, his voice low. It was just that sort of talk that had led me so hopelessly down the wrong track I had taken.

I cracked an egg into a cup so viciously that I was never

going to be able to fish out the pieces of broken shell that had gone in with it. I discarded it and reached for another one.

'Emma,' Jack said, crossing back across his kitchen and sliding his fingers around my forearm. 'Will you please just tell me what is bothering you.'

There was that look in his eyes which I had always thought meant so much more than it actually did. I was finally getting wise. It was about time.

'Why should anything be bothering me, Jack? You tell me,' I challenged, carrying on with my cooking as though he had never interrupted me. 'So, the oil has to be really hot,' I said, pouring a generous amount in the bottom of a roasting dish and opening the Aga door.

'You seemed fine on the phone the other day,' Jack said ponderingly.

'So hot it actually has to be smoking,' I continued, turning back to the kitchen table and picking up a wooden spoon.

'It sounded like you *wanted* to see me again,' he continued, sounding a little embarrassed.

'Beat in the eggs and milk,' I said tightly, dropping both ingredients into the flour.

'And I certainly didn't make it a secret that I *really* wanted to see you again before I left,' he confessed.

'Then beat it,' I said through clenched teeth. My hand wielding the spoon moved furiously around the bowl, slopping batter mix over the table. I hadn't lied; I was an atrociously messy cook.

'And when you first got here today, you looked happy.'

'Add the rest of the milk,' I said, waiting for him to reach the conclusion he was inexorably heading towards. There goes any last chance of salvaging my pride.

'But when I saw you in the hall just now, you looked...'
His voice trailed away as comprehension dawned like a sunrise in his eyes.

Hurt. Humiliated. Embarrassed. Take your pick, I thought.

'The person I was talking to—'

'Is absolutely no concern of mine,' I completed his sentence.

He ignored my interruption. 'Is my daughter.'

More batter slopped alarmingly out of the bowl. Very gently he reached across and took it from my hands. A wise decision.

'Your daughter?' My voice was an incredulous croak. 'Your daughter? You have a daughter?' I queried, as though I might possibly have misunderstood what he was telling me.

He nodded slowly. 'I have.'

'But... how... why... You've never said anything about her.' My words sounded more like an accusation than anything else.

'No, I haven't. Very few people know of her existence, and that's just the way we'd like it to stay. In fact, until just three years ago, I didn't know she existed myself.'

All anger drained from me then, as though a plug had been pulled. 'What do you mean? How's that possible? How old is she?'

'She's ten years old, and her name is Carly.'

Ten. She had to be Sheridan's daughter, she just had to be. Jack astutely read the question in my eyes without the need for words.

'Sheridan was newly pregnant with her when she slept with my best friend. Maybe she knew about it, maybe she didn't. I've never been entirely clear on that one. But she wanted me out of her life so completely, with no ties and connections to hold us, that she never told me about her.'

The spoon fell from my fingers and clattered noisily on to the table top, adding further to the mess I had made. 'Jack, that's horrible. How could she do that?'

He shrugged, but I could still see how it had hurt him.

'But you're her father. How could anyone hope to keep something like that a secret? Didn't you guess when the baby was born?'

'I didn't even know there *was* a baby,' Jack said bitterly. 'We had the world's fastest divorce and then she simply disappeared for the next nine months.'

'But then what happened? When she came back with a baby, you must have guessed then?'

His next words shocked me, and explained an awful lot about Jack's mistrust and aversion to marriage and commitment. 'She never came back with the baby.'

'What?'

'She left her with her sister to raise. Her sister lives on a farm and has two kids of her own, one is almost the same age as Carly. They're more like twin sisters than cousins.'

I shook my head at how unbelievably cruel Sheridan had been, not just to Jack but to her own daughter. But when I voiced those words, Jack disagreed.

'Believe me, she did the kid a favour. Her sister is totally different from Sheridan. She's warm and loving and caring. She's a great mom. Carly adores her, and her cousins are like her siblings.'

'But still...' I said, grappling to get my head around the enormity of it all. 'So how did you find out about her?'

'From Sheridan,' he said, and there was a twist to his lips as he said her name. 'She was between husbands, short of cash and her sister's farm was in danger of being repossessed by the bank. She needed me – or rather my money – to bail them out. So she had no option but to tell me about the child.'

'Oh my God, Jack,' I said, reaching for one of the kitchen chairs and sitting down, totally shaken.

'What am I supposed to do with this, by the way?' he asked, still holding on to the bowl of batter.

'Pour it over the sausages in the pan,' I answered distractedly.

While he did as I had instructed, I tried to get my head around the complexity of Jack's life. This was the responsibility he had spoken of back home. This was the commitment he had to someone. And it was one hell of a big one.

With the pan returned to the Aga, Jack turned back to me.

'So what happened when you found out about Carly? Did you apply for custody?'

Jack shook his head sadly. 'How could I? She was seven years old and her aunt and uncle were the only parents she had ever known. She'd been with them her entire life. How could I pull her away from them, or her cousins? How could I tear her whole world apart like that?'

I felt a lump like a burning hot coal lodge in my throat. I knew I'd been right in instinctively hating his ex-wife. I just hadn't known there were so many valid reasons for doing so.

'Susan and Mike – Sheridan's sister and brother-in-law – have been really great. They've let me come into Carly's life and over the last three years we've built up a really good relationship.'

I sighed and gave a shaky smile, thankful there was a happy ending to this story. 'So she knows she's yours?'

He nodded and there was a look on his face that I didn't

313

initially recognise. Then I realised what it was, paternal pride. 'She's a great kid. She and her cousins come out to the ranch and stay for a few days each month. They love the place. It's never going to be an ideal situation, but we make it work.'

I reached across the sticky table for Jack's hand. 'She's lucky to have you as her dad,' I said solemnly. He looked slightly embarrassed, but still pleased at my words.

'Let's go for a walk,' he suggested suddenly. 'The beach is lovely at this time of day and I think we could both use the fresh air.' He nodded in the direction of the stove. 'Can we leave this?' I nodded. 'Then let's go,' he said, getting to his feet and pulling me from my chair.

We walked right to the end of the cove, and he kept hold of my hand the entire way. I kept looking up at him as we walked, seeing him through new and wiser eyes. I felt touched that he trusted me enough to share his secret with me.

'So perhaps now you can see why I've steered clear of relationships, unless they were casual or undemanding, since my divorce?' he asked.

I looked up at him, trying to commit everything about him to memory. It was a film I would want to replay a great many times in the months to come, when it was all I had left of him and our unique time together. So I took care to drink everything in, from the way the wind gently lifted the thick black strands of hair from his forehead, to the way his eyes crinkled at the edges when he smiled. I felt something slowly begin to tear inside me; he was going to be almost impossible to forget.

'I've learned to be more careful now in my choices. It's much easier when everyone wants exactly the same thing.

That way no one gets emotionally attached... and no one gets hurt.'

It sounded like a cold and empty existence to me and I think he must have seen that in my eyes. 'But that's not your way, is it, Emma, not at all?' I was startled to have the conversation directed at me and was wondering how to respond as he continued, 'Even after everything that's happened with you and Richard, you still believe in finding that happy-ever-after ending, don't you?'

He wasn't mocking me, or even trying to be deliberately cruel; he couldn't know how hard it was to hear that he and I were at polar opposite ends of the earth when it came to relationships.

'Well,' I said slowly, 'my faith in its existence has been tested lately, that's true enough.' I swallowed past the small and unexpected lump in my throat. 'But I'd like to believe that someday... there'd be someone' – *you,* a voice in my head screamed out – 'who could make me a believer again.'

He nodded his head, as though he'd received a doctor's prognosis, which wasn't great news, but not entirely unexpected. 'The ring, the chapel, the wedding... you still want all that?' It wasn't so much a question, more of a statement.

I was going to deny it, but why bother? We both knew it was the truth. 'I guess I'm just an old-fashioned girl, at heart.'

He gave a gentle smile and steered me to the flight of steps leading back to his cottage. I was pretty sure there'd been a test hidden in our conversation, and I was equally sure I'd just failed it.

He climbed the stone steps ahead of me. 'Watch out on these,' he warned, 'they can get a little slippery. Just stay close to me.'

'I'm right behind you,' I said, wondering why the words

sounded so familiar and significant and then I remembered the first time he had said them to me; it was on the night of the accident, when he'd been pushing me away from the exploding car. I opened my mouth to remind him, and then suddenly my foot slipped on the worn and crumbling step and I began to fall. I scrabbled for a handhold on the surface of the wall but there was nothing to grip on to. Jack spun around, his face horrified. His hand reached out to grab me, but it was too late. This time he couldn't save me, and I flew backwards off the steps, landing with a breath-stealing thump on not just the sand, but on something sharp and hard that was hidden beneath its soft surface.

'Emma!' Jack cried out, jumping from the steps and rushing to my side. 'Are you okay?'

I gave a sound which was supposed to be a laugh but which sounded perilously like I was about to cry. I'm not a baby, but it really hurt.

'Are you hurt?'

'Just my pride,' I lied. There was no way I was going to say anything about the rock or whatever it was that my bum had connected with so painfully. He held out his hand and pulled me to my feet. I tried to turn my wince of pain into a rueful grin. I don't think he was fooled.

'Goodness, are you all right?' An elderly couple who had been taking an early evening walk on the beach had rushed over to lend their assistance. It really was beyond embarrassing.

'I'm fine,' I lied once again, somehow managing a more genuine-looking smile for the anxious newcomers.

'Do you need us to call for help?' asked the woman, already pulling a mobile phone from her pocket.

'No, no, no. I'm just a bit winded, that's all. Please don't worry about me,' I reassured her.

'We'll be fine, thank you,' Jack reiterated, and the couple seemed to accept our word and headed back down the beach. Jack waited until they could no longer hear us before turning to me. 'What have you done, and how bad is it?'

'I'm fine. I was more shocked than anything.'

'Emma Marshall, don't lie to me. I'm the guy who pulled you out of a car wreck; I know when you're hurt or not.'

There was no point in lying. He was going to find out in a minute when he saw me limp up the steps. 'I think there was a rock or something where I landed on the sand.'

Jack looked at the damp sand which, embarrassingly, still held a perfect impression of my behind. He kicked the area with the toe of his boot and revealed a large sharp jagged stone buried a few centimetres beneath the surface.

'Shit,' he muttered. He turned to look at the rear of my jeans. 'How bad is it, are you bleeding?'

'No, of course not. I've got enough natural padding back there to cushion the blow.'

He didn't smile as I had hoped.

'Bruised?'

I shrugged. 'Probably.'

'Show me.'

'No,' I said, horrified. He raised his eyebrows as though he was daring me to challenge him. 'This is just a kinky attempt of yours to see my arse, isn't it?' That *did* make him smile. 'Look, let's get back to the house and let me have a look at it, before we start deciding who else should be allowed a peek.'

My progress up the steps was slow, but I adamantly refused his offer to carry me. I think he only let me get away with that for fear that holding me in his arms might actually hurt me even more. Of all the areas to have injured in my fall off the steps, why couldn't I have twisted an ankle or sprained a wrist like any sensible person, why did it have to have been my bum? Eventually we reached the warmth of his kitchen and he shut the door firmly behind him.

'Okay, Emma,' he said, having watched me limp painfully across the tiled floor. 'That's enough. Are you going to show me your fanny now or not?'

Despite the throbbing pain from my rear end, I burst out laughing. 'No, Jack, I'm not. And I really have to warn you that that word has a totally different meaning over here, and asking a question like that is likely to get you either slapped or arrested, possibly both.'

He looked a little taken aback, but quickly recovered. 'If you're not going to show me—'

'Which I'm not,' I completed.

'Then at least go and have a hot shower. It'll help to take the sting away and bring out the bruise. There's a full-length mirror in there, so you'll be able to assess the damage.'

'You seem obsessed with getting me undressed,' I said flippantly, and then ruined my sassy answer by blushing as I said it. 'But if it makes you happy I'll have a shower and check out what I've done, just as long as we're clear that I'm the only one who gets a look. Okay?'

'Okay,' he reluctantly agreed. 'I'll make us some tea while you shower. You'll find clean towels in the cupboard at the top of the stairs.'

'Thanks,' I said, and hobbled out of the kitchen.

On a scale of one to ten, my bruise scored about an eleven. I winced as I eased down my jeans and lacy briefs and surveyed the damage, looking over my shoulder into the mirror at the bluish-purple discolouration. It was roughly the size of a saucer and covered most of one buttock and inched on to my lower back. And despite what Jack had said, I didn't think I needed that shower to bring it out, it was doing that quite well all by itself. Nevertheless, I dropped my shirt and bra on to the rest of my clothes on the floor and turned on the dial inside the cubicle. I winced as the hot jets ran over the damaged skin, but after the initial sting, it began to feel a little more comfortable. There was a rack inside the double-size shower, and I couldn't resist taking a small handful of the shower gel, which smelled so reminiscently of Jack, and smoothing it over my naked body. I closed my eyes and let the water fall on to my head, losing myself in an x-rated daydream where I wasn't alone in the steamy closet, and that he was behind me, his strong fingers running along my slippery limbs, his mouth claiming mine beneath the cascading water.

The noise of the bathroom door opening made me jump so much that the bottle of gel slipped from my fingers and clattered noisily on to the cast-iron tray.

'Are you okay?' Jack called through the door's opening.

'Don't come in,' I cried out in panic, instinctively trying to cover myself. 'I'm naked.'

I heard his small chuckle. 'I always find that best for showering.'

I dropped the hands that were ineffectively trying to shield my breasts from view. 'Very funny.'

'How are your injured bits?'

'Colourful,' I replied, 'but the shower is definitely helping.' It was completely unsettling to be having this conversation with him while totally nude, and only a metre or so away.

'I've brought something to help.'

My hands instinctively flew back up to cover me, but the

319

small gap through which he was talking didn't widen. Just his hand came into view, as he placed first a tall bottle of lotion of some kind and then a steaming cup of tea on to the tiled floor.

'If you need help with the cream...'

'I have a lousy sense of direction, but I think I can find my own backside,' I joked.

'Okay then, see you downstairs.' I heard his footsteps disappearing down the wooden floored hallway. He hadn't even attempted to come in. It was respectful, courteous and completely honourable of him. It was also somewhat disappointing.

The tea was reviving and welcome, and despite a rather pungent initial aroma, the lotion Jack had left was noticeably soothing as I rubbed it over the injured skin. I borrowed a comb to smooth the tangles out of my hair, and as I cleared a circle in the steamy mirror, I saw that only my waterproof mascara remained from the make-up I had so carefully applied before leaving home. I gave a small shrug and bent to retrieve my clothing. If the prospect of my undressed body hadn't been sufficient to entice him, then what hope had there been for a little eyeshadow and lip gloss?

He was waiting patiently for me at the bottom of the stairs, and as I descended the treads I saw he was carefully studying my gait for a limp. Thankfully I was much more mobile after my shower.

'You seem to be moving easier.'

I nodded. 'I'm fine. It really is just a bruise, albeit a horrendously big one.'

He looked worried at my words. 'I'm so sorry. I should have gone behind you on those steps.'

'Then I'd have taken us both down,' I reasoned. I sniffed the air, smelling something burned and charred.

'We killed the toad,' Jack declared solemnly.

I laughed at his words, and noticed for the first time how dark the hall had become. At some point while I'd been in the bathroom, the grey clouds which had been gathering all afternoon had turned into a thick grey blanket covering the sky. It was raining hard.

'It's not your fault I fell. It's mine. I should have listened to your warning.'

'I don't think you're very good at following orders,' he said ruefully. 'Now I'm going to be haunted for months by nightmares of what dreadful injury you were concealing from me.'

'Oh, for goodness sake—' I exclaimed, suddenly turning my back on him. 'You're not going to rest until you see it, are you? Go on then, look, if that's what it takes to satisfy you that I'm not mortally wounded.' I pulled my shirt free of my jeans and undid the top fastening on my waistband. 'But I have to warn you... it's not pretty.'

The hall was silent except for the falling rain battering against the windows and the soft purr of my zip. I didn't need to do more than lower the waistband of the jeans a few centimetres for the bruise to be visible.

I heard his sharp indrawn hiss of breath as the dark discoloured skin came into view. I was showing far less than I did when wearing a bikini on the beach, but there was something very intimate in holding up the back of my shirt and pulling down the jeans to allow him to study my exposed body.

'I'm so sorry,' he repeated, his voice much huskier than before. I felt a small tug on the waistband as his hand took

321

hold of the fabric and inched it lower, until the denim no longer covered me. I felt his fingers move slowly from the garment and brush against the undamaged skin of my lower back, and then dip lower and run against the top seam of my lacy briefs.

I sucked in a mouthful of air as though I was drowning, and heard the roughened raggedness of his own breathing. He paused, and I knew he was waiting for me to stop him. I did nothing. His fingertips ran just beneath the light elastic at the top of my underwear, following a path around my hip bone, lingering to stroke the sharp contour and then moving around on to the softer skin of my lower abdomen. I looked down at the strong fingers slowly circling and caressing my flesh. I leaned my entire weight back against him and heard him groan softly. Very slowly he turned me around. His eyes were heavy as his mouth lowered to my lips and his tongue searched for, and found, mine in a rush of desire that swept me along like a tidal wave. The kiss was so overwhelming and intense that I was numb to the pain of the pressure of the banister rail behind me, and then the wall as we stumbled back against it. His body pressed powerfully against me as his kiss took me with him through a blazing inferno which scorched and branded me as his.

I was flying, falling, lost, my only anchor to this world were the lips devouring mine and the strong shoulders on to which my hands were fastened, gripping and holding him against me. His lips released me and moved to the column of my throat, searing the skin I willingly offered with a blazing trail of kisses. I murmured his name, my hands journeying from his shoulders into his thick dark hair, finally knowing the feel of it between my fingers. He raised a hand and pushed the shirt from my neck, allowing him access to the sensitive skin of my shoulder. The thin strap of my bra was eased aside as he gently bit the delicate flesh and my knees literally felt incapable of holding me up a moment longer. I didn't think that they'd have to. But I was wrong.

The fall in temperature happened so quickly, I didn't even see it coming, and at first I didn't register the climate change. The fire storm became an ice blizzard, as Jack slowly froze and then determinedly levered himself away from me, bracing his arms against the wall on either side of me. The dying embers of passion were still blazing in his eyes, but when I leaned forward, lips parted, inviting him to claim them again, he moved further away. The swirling clouds of desire began to clear and I looked up at him in confusion.

'Jack?' I asked hesitantly.

In reply he just shook his head. 'I can't do this.'

No bucket of ice-cold water could have been as effective as those words were at putting out the fire. But I still didn't know why he'd said them. My eyes spoke the question my throat was suddenly too constricted to ask.

'Don't...' Jack said hoarsely. 'We can't...' For a writer he was being far from articulate. 'This is all wrong.' I got the meaning of that one all right.

'Why? Why is it wrong?' I had found my voice, even if it was a shaky parody of itself.

He ran his hand distractedly through his hair, following the same pathway my own fingers had taken only moments earlier. 'You know why.'

I shook my head. 'I don't.'

He sighed and pushed away from the wall, staring out the window at the falling rain; that's when I knew I had lost him, when he wouldn't even look at me as he spoke.

'I can't do this with you.'

'Can't, or don't want to?'

In answer he swivelled back to face me, grabbing my hand and laying it against his chest, letting me feel the thundering pounding of his heart beneath my palm. 'Does that feel as though I don't want to?'

I shook my head again, aware that my eyes were beginning to fill with tears, and not ashamed to let him see them.

'Then why? Is it Sheridan? Is she the reason?'

He looked genuinely shocked and also slightly horrified at my suggestion.

'What? No, of course not. Why would you even think that?'

This wasn't the time or the place for that one. 'Jack, why then? Why are you pushing me away? Surely you know by now that I want this?' I threw my last piece of pride down at his feet.

'That's why I have to stop it.'

I was broken and confused and he was making no sense.

'I want you, Emma,' he admitted, his voice raw, 'more than I've ever wanted anyone else in my entire life.' His declaration should have filled me with joy, if only it hadn't been delivered in such a dire and terrible way. 'But what I said the other night on the bridge hasn't changed... and nor have I.'

'Don't *I* have any say in this? What about what *I* want?'

'I know what you want,' he replied, and despite everything I still felt my cheeks ignite at the implications. He looked back at the rain.

'You want someone who will be there for you. Someone who can commit. Someone who isn't about to disappear to the other side of the world. Someone who isn't me.' His voice deepened as he went on, 'You have to know that stopping

324

this now is the last thing I want to do. I can't even look at you without wanting to sweep you into my arms and carry you up those stairs to my bed. But I can't be that much of a bastard. I'm stopping for *you*, not me.'

'You don't know what the hell I want...' I said bitterly, hands shaking as I zipped up my clothing, '... or what I need.'

'Whatever it is, it's not me.'

There was nothing left to say. I had laid my feelings out as plainly as I knew. And he'd turned me down. 'I have to go,' I said, hoping, even at this final moment, he might protest or try to stop me.

He turned away from the window and nodded. This couldn't be it, could it? After everything that had happened between us, was this how it was really going to end?

I pushed past him and flung open the door. The rain was pounding the ground with a ferocity that stung my skin as I ran down the drive to my car. *Stop me, call me back*, I silently pleaded as I ran past his own car. *Do something, do anything, don't let me go*. But he never intervened, never moved at all from his position in the open doorway. I flung open my car door, grateful I'd left my bag and keys inside it earlier. I paused for just one last long look at him. Our eyes locked. He didn't disguise the pain and regret in his, but he also didn't move.

I got into the driver's seat, slammed the door and reversed out on to the road faster and more recklessly than I should have done. My falling tears and the pouring rain, which the wipers were struggling to control, were a double hazard. I was lucky not to meet any other vehicles as I drove erratically away from him. I wasn't concentrating enough to be behind the wheel, and two miles outside Trentwell I snapped on the indicator and pulled over to the side of the road. I stared sightlessly through the curtain of rain falling on the windscreen, seeing nothing except his face, his eyes. I couldn't leave it this way. I'd never even told him how I really felt about him. Would that have changed things? Would it have made a difference? Was I really going to be able to live the rest of my life without knowing the answer?

I furiously wiped the tears from my eyes with the back of my hand and turned the ignition key. The engine roared into life. Performing an illegal U-turn in the empty road, I headed back to his house. I didn't have a plan in mind, there were no clever or wise words that might make him change his mind. I was working on nothing here except a primitive instinct that was pulling me back towards him, as surely as though an invisible cord was stretched between us, compelling me to return.

The light was fading fast as night and the rain washed the last rays of daylight away. I drove mindlessly through the downpour, never stopping to consider how I would feel if, or when, he turned me away once again. By the time his driveway came into sight my heart was pounding as though I had run the last few miles, instead of driven them. This was it. My final chance.

It was a miracle that we didn't crash into each other. It was *his* reactions that must have prevented an accident, not mine. All I knew was that as I turned on to his property I was suddenly dazzled by the bright intensity of two headlights bearing down on me as he sped down his drive. I slammed on the brakes as he swerved abruptly to one side, coming to a halt half on the lawn beside the driveway. The pouring rain kept obscuring my vision, which meant I saw Jack throw open his door and begin to walk towards me in a series of disjointed snapshots, as the wipers swept across my screen.

His eyes were locked on to mine as he strode through the sheeting rain, his shirt plastered to his arms and body like a second skin. My hand fumbled for the door handle and I virtually tumbled out of the car as I made my way to him, pulled by a force more powerful than gravity. Tears were probably still running down my face, but they were lost among the raindrops. I covered the last metres between us at a run and he caught me, his arms capturing me and lifting me up against him. My legs left the ground and curled around him as he walked blindly back to the house. His lips never left mine as he carried me, eliminating the need for words and speaking their own language, which my own fluently answered. Nothing else existed for me in those moments; I couldn't feel the rain or the cold, my world had become just this man, his arms holding me against him, his tongue matching mine and the hardness of his body pressing intimately against me.

He stopped just once as we reached the front door, which in his haste he hadn't bothered to close properly. I liked the urgency that implied. He took his mouth from mine just long enough to look into my eyes as he gave me one last, totally unnecessary, chance to change my mind. 'Are you sure? Because once we go in, I don't know if I'll be able to stop. There won't be any going back, Emma.'

He got his answer as my mouth returned to his, my hands tightening on the back of his neck as he kicked open the door. My fingers were already undoing the buttons on his shirt as we climbed the stairs, pulling the wet fabric from his muscled shoulders as he carried me into his room. He lowered me gently on to the mattress as I reached hungrily for his belt. He was naked before I was. He took more time tugging my own wet clothing from me, savouring each moment before I impatiently pulled him towards me.

It was unlike anything I had ever known or experienced before. I cried out when he entered me, unaware that tears were falling as he took me somewhere I hadn't even known existed. He called out my name as his body shuddered in orgasm, filling me and completing me. I came right behind him.

CHAPTER 16

'That might just possibly be the worst bruise I have ever seen.'

I slowly opened my eyes. I was lying face down in a tangle of twisted sheets, each knotted snarl reminding me of our bodies, rolling and entwining on their surface throughout the night. I had a sudden flashback of his hands gripping fiercely on the cotton bedcovers beside my face, as he had gradually lowered his body inside me, at a pace so tantalisingly slow it had pushed me over the precipice of lust and desire into a world of undiscovered sensations.

'That's not the most romantic morning greeting I've ever heard,' I mumbled sleepily into the pillow.

Jack was lying on his side, propped up on one elbow, staring down at my prone body, which was exposed to the elements and his scrutiny. He bent down, lifted my hair to one side, and kissed the sensitive skin on the back of my neck.

'You're right. I'm sorry. Good morning.' His voice was a seductive purr as he moved his lips to whisper against my ear, 'Last night... you and me... it felt... there *are* no words...'

It was quite a feat to rob an author of the ability to string together a coherent sentence. I smiled into the feather pillow. 'That's better,' I mumbled approvingly.

'But that is still one God-awful bruise.' The pillow swallowed my small laugh.

Jack set his lips to a much more interesting activity than speech, as he dropped a trail of feather-light kisses down the curve of my spine, stopping only at the very edge of the tender, damaged skin. Very gently he kissed the injury, his tongue grazing me and provoking a very natural chain reaction to begin deep within me. 'Better?' he asked, his lips still against my flesh. I groaned softly in reply, and the sound encouraged him. Very gently he turned me over.

I saw the desire reignite in his eyes as they travelled the length of my body, stopping on the swell of my breasts and then moving down past the narrowness of my waist to my long legs, which were already beginning to part in readiness.

'So, anywhere else that's hurt?' he asked, his voice a low sexy throb.

'There may be some other areas that need your attention,' I murmured huskily.

'I'll see what I can do,' he promised, his head lowering. The room fell silent except for the raw ragged sounds of our breathing. It was a very long time before either of us was capable of speech.

I must have dozed, because the morning light coming through the window had shifted its path across the bed when I next opened my eyes. My head was on Jack's chest, and his fingers were slowly threading through the strands of my hair, winding and twisting them to hold me captive against him, as if there was ever the slightest danger of me wanting to be anywhere else. I curled closer to the curve of his body, feeling the strong and steady beat of his heart beneath my head, and the warmth of his limbs tangled with mine. I should have known that a moment of such complete and utter contentment was too perfect to last.

Jack bent his head and kissed my forehead. 'At the risk

of being accused of being unromantic again, can I just say that I'm absolutely starving.'

It occurred to me then that we hadn't done anything as prosaic as eating for a very long time. As though the thought of food had woken it from its slumber, my stomach made a very noisy sound of agreement.

'And I need to keep my strength up, if I am going to spend the rest of the day making wild and passionate love to you.'

'Is that what's on the agenda?'

'It's certainly on mine,' Jack confirmed with a sexy smile.

He wasn't going to get an argument from me. I levered myself reluctantly from his body, but before allowing me to move away, Jack ran his hand lingeringly down my arm from shoulder to wrist. 'And we need to talk, Emma, and when you're lying here naked in my arms, I can't concentrate on anything except how much I want to make love to you again.'

I turned and swung my legs off the bed, a very content and satisfied smile on my face. I looked around the room for my clothes – any of them – and then smiled secretively as I recalled Jack pulling them off me and carelessly discarding them. The missing items could be anywhere: stuck on top of a wardrobe; in a far corner of the room; or even hanging off the ceiling light. It wasn't as though either of us had been paying much attention at the time.

'Here,' said Jack, passing me a shirt that was lying over the back of the chair. I shrugged happily into the pale blue garment which still smelled vaguely of him. The shirt was enormous on me, and I had to roll up the sleeves at least three times before my hands emerged from the cuffs, but at least it was long enough to just about cover my modesty, given my missing underwear. Jack pulled on just a pair of jeans, and as I padded barefoot down the stairs behind him it was a real struggle not to reach out and run my hand over the tessellating muscles of his back as he moved. He was like an exquisite piece of art, or a beautiful sculpture, which I'd suddenly been given permission to touch.

The Aga's heat ensured that the kitchen was warm and even wearing nothing except the thin shirt, I still didn't feel cold. As we waited for the kettle to boil, Jack pulled me once again into his arms, and bent down to kiss me. The roughness of his cheek was another new sensation to explore, as my fingers travelled over the dark bristle.

'I still can't believe that this... us... has actually happened,' Jack breathed into my hair.

'You can't?' I questioned, leaning back to see his face.

There was a half-smile on his lips. 'And yet, I don't know why. Because I've certainly been having some fairly graphic dreams about it for the last few weeks.'

I felt the heat in my cheeks, but I didn't lower my eyes.

'Mr Monroe,' I said, trying to sound like a shocked Austen heroine, which was tricky to pull off when I was pressed against a very firm and obvious part of his body. A part which I couldn't recollect any character in Miss Austen's books ever having mentioned.

'You have no idea,' he said, nuzzling my neck. The kettle boiled, but we both ignored it. 'I'm just sorry it's taken us this long to get here, and that we've got so little time together before I leave.'

Suddenly I was very glad that I wasn't looking at him as he spoke those words. Practicalities and reality hadn't even begun to pierce the bubble I had happily been floating in for the last twelve hours. Maybe I was just being naïve, but it hadn't occurred to me that after the night we'd just shared, Jack would still willingly walk out of my life.

'Can you... can you maybe stay a little longer?' I tentatively asked the skin just below his collarbone.

'I wish I could, but it's just not possible.'

There was a very long pause, when the only sound in the kitchen was the gentle hum of the fridge and my hopes crashing to pieces on the floor.

Very gently, Jack lifted my chin with his hand until I was looking directly into his eyes.

'This wasn't just a one-night thing for me, Emma. You *do* know that, don't you?' I nodded dumbly, unsure the path our conversation was taking. 'We'll find a way to make this work,' he promised softly. 'We'll still see each other. I can manage to get over here every three months or so, and then we can make arrangements for you to come out and visit me...'

'A long-distance relationship,' I said quietly, looking past him at the jewel-bright sunshine razoring through the glass doors, and trying very hard not to let him see the moment when all of my dreams were crushed and shattered by his words. I don't know what I'd been hoping for, or expecting... No, that's a lie, I *did* know what I'd been hoping for, and it definitely hadn't been a long-distance transatlantic relationship. I had wanted it all: commitment, a promise, a future.

'I know it'll be difficult,' Jack continued, his arms clasped behind my back, 'but if we both try hard enough, we'll make something of it.'

I tried a smile, which didn't feel entirely natural. That there was something real and powerful between us was undeniable. But I was only now starting to realise that we had very different ideas of where it should go next. Jack's view of the future might have differed from mine, but one thing I could never accuse him of was not being intuitive or being able to read me well enough to know when something was wrong. 'That's not going to work, is it? It's not what you wanted?'

I felt the sharp sting of tears and tried to blink them away, but I had to be honest with him. 'No. Not exactly.'

He looked sad for the first time that day, and I hated that I was the one who had put that expression on his face. 'We both knew this could never work out that way. It's what scared me about ever letting this happen. You have commitments and family that you can't abandon, and so do I. Perhaps it might have been better if we'd never—'

I silenced him by placing my fingers against his lips. 'No. Don't say that. Don't even think it.'

We smiled sadly at each other, and I fought hard not to let what I was feeling show on my face. There *were* compelling reasons that kept us on either side of the world, but whose were the most valid? What Jack was offering me was so much more than what he was usually prepared to give, and so much less than what I wanted from him.

'I don't want to lose you,' he said softly, the tenderness in his voice almost my undoing.

'Then stay,' I said, knowing how unfair I was being, asking him to leave the daughter he had only recently found.

'Come with me,' he countered. I shook my head in denial, even while visions of what could be were flashing through it like glorious excerpts of something you'd been longing to see. 'We could work something out, Emma. We could. Think about it, seriously, and then...' he paused and kissed me so expertly that any coherent thought was impossible, '... then just say "yes".'

I loved the intimacy of preparing our breakfast together, loved the fact that he couldn't walk past me without a brief kiss or a lingering touch, and even from the other side of the kitchen I could feel his eyes on me as I prepared scrambled eggs at the stove and made toast. When our hunger was satisfied, at least for food, I went to tidy up the mess I'd made, but Jack caught my wrist as I passed his chair, easily stopping me.

'Leave it,' he instructed, 'I'll do it later. Right now I'd much rather do this.' He got out of his seat, towering above me in my bare feet. Effortlessly he lifted me up and sat me on the edge of the kitchen worktop, evening up our height difference. Jack's arms slid behind me, as mine wound around his neck. His fingers coiled through my hair, holding me close, as he kissed me with increasing intensity until we were both breathless.

'I can't believe we only have four more days together,' I said regretfully, my lips against the side of his neck.

'Not even that long,' he replied sadly. I shifted in his arms and pulled back to see his face. 'I've got meetings scheduled in London over the next two days. I can't put them off. I've booked into a hotel for a couple of nights.' I must have made a pretty poor job of hiding my disappointment at being robbed of the time I thought we'd have. Jack looked equally unhappy.

'Come with me,' he urged suddenly. 'My meetings won't take all day, and even if they do' – his voice dropped in timbre – 'we'll still have the nights.' We shared a secretive intimate look that new lovers the world over would instantly recognise.

'All right,' I agreed rashly. Two days and, even more enticingly, two nights, with him? I'd have been a fool to say no.

Jack's smile took on a new depth as he pulled me closer to him once more. I was lost in our kiss, and the delicious sensations running through me as he slowly began to unbutton my shirt. His hand moved leisurely over my heated flesh, cupping my breast as his fingers found the hardened nipple. I groaned against his mouth, and his answering sound almost obliterated the distant banging noise of someone hammering on the front door.

I froze in his arms, but he didn't allow me to move back. 'Ignore it,' he growled. 'They'll go in a minute, it's probably just the postman or someone.' His tongue silenced my reply as his mouth returned to mine. The knocking persisted for a minute more, and a tiny voice tried to cut through the red haze of desire to remind me that today was Sunday, and there *were* no postal deliveries. I ignored both the voice and the impatient rapping sound, concentrating only on the warmth flooding through me as Jack reached under the shirt to pull me closer against the hardness of his body beneath his jeans. The knocking stopped.

'See. I told you they'd go,' he murmured.

My hands, which had been fastened upon his arms, reached down to the clasp of his jeans. I caught a fleeting passing shadow in my peripheral vision which, thankfully, stilled my fingers on the zip. The pounding was back, but this time it was much closer, its source now evident from the large angry figure of a man hammering on the glass doors.

Every worst nightmare I have ever had was encapsulated in the next few minutes of my life. Jack and I sprang apart so suddenly that my nakedness was easily visible to the figure standing a few metres away behind the glass doors. My hands were shaking as I hurriedly covered myself with the edges of the open shirt.

'Why aren't you answering your fucking phone?' Richard's voice was an angry roar, clearly audible even through the doors. Jack was already striding towards them, while I remained in a motionless shocked daze on the worktop.

'What?' I said stupidly, when the shock which had robbed me of speech allowed me to talk. Jack was still unlocking the doors as Richard continued to yell at me through them.

'Your phone, Emma! Where the hell is it? Why aren't you picking up? I've been trying to reach you for hours!'

The click of the releasing lock was lost as Richard torpedoed into the room, not even looking at Jack and heading straight at me like a raging bull. I scrambled off the worktop, still dazed and confused as Richard charged in my direction. He was stopped a metre or so from me by Jack's hand which fastened menacingly on his arm. Richard turned on him, with matching ferocity. 'Get your fucking hand off me!' he spat out.

After a brief and terrifying second, when the whole situation could have rapidly exploded into violence, Jack did as Richard wanted. He did, however, quickly cover the distance between us, ensuring that he could easily intervene if Richard looked as though he intended to hurt me.

But that wasn't what he was here for, I knew that now. As the numbing terror which had first gripped me began to abate, a cold foreboding ran through my veins.

'Why haven't you answered your phone?' thundered Richard again, almost spitting into my face with fury.

Because it's still in my bag, which is on the front seat of my car, where I left it last night in my hurry to fall into Jack's arms and be carried to his bed. That was the reason, though not one I was going to offer him.

'What's wrong?' I fired back at him anxiously, but Richard wasn't rational or sensible enough to answer me straight away. 'Your dad is going frantic trying to get hold of you.

He thought you'd spent the night with me!' he said bitterly, throwing an ugly and disgusted look at Jack, before turning back to me. 'I guess he hadn't realised you were the type to screw around.'

There was an angry sound and Jack's hand was back, this time shoving forcefully into Richard's shoulder, pushing him backwards. 'That's enough,' he said, his voice more terrifying for its low warning note than if he'd been yelling like Richard.

'What's this all about? Is it because I didn't come back last night?' I felt the guilt spear me like an arrow. It hadn't even occurred to me at the time to think about my parents and how they would worry when I hadn't returned. I'd been so selfishly lost in Jack, I simply hadn't even considered them. I was mortified at my thoughtlessness.

'It's not *you* being missing that's concerning anyone,' Richard spat out venomously, 'it's your mother.'

There was a moment when no one spoke or said anything. I felt like I was teetering on the edge of an abyss, as the ground beneath my feet began to crumble away. Unthinkingly I reached out to Richard and grabbed the material of his shirt sleeves in both hands.

'How long has it been?'

He shook his head. 'No one knows. Your dad woke up at six o'clock this morning and she was already gone.'

I gave a small moan of despair. 'Where have you looked?'

'Everywhere. We've looked everywhere. We all know the drill.' I saw him flick a disdainful glance at Jack, who had suddenly become a complete outsider in this unfolding drama. 'We called the police two hours ago. They're organising a search.'

My hands left his arms and flew up to cover my mouth. Jack's shirt gaped open, and I saw Richard's eyes skim me,

338

a look of raw pain clearly visible on his face. I gripped the garment's edges tightly in one hand as I spun from him and ran to the hall. 'I'll be one minute,' I shouted as I pounded up the stairs, not really sure which man I was addressing with that remark.

I was half sobbing as I scrabbled beneath the bed, frantically looking for my missing clothes. Jack joined me moments later, pulling me to my feet and handing me the items I'd been desperately searching for. I yanked on the clothing, my mind spiralling through every disaster which could have befallen my lost parent, while all I'd been thinking about was myself.

'They'll find her,' Jack reassured me, holding my shirt out. I grabbed it wordlessly from his hands, and rammed my arms into the sleeves. In far less time than it had taken to get me out of them the night before, I was back in my clothes and racing downstairs, my heels thundering noisily on the wooden treads.

Richard was waiting in the hall beside the open front door, an unreadable look on his face. 'They've set up a control point for the search at the edge of the woods.'

I nodded dumbly, heading towards the open door. Suddenly my steps faltered, as I turned to my former fiancé in panic. 'Where's my dad? Is he still at home?'

Richard grabbed hold of my arm and began to propel me outside. 'No. He's with some police liaison woman at the search HQ. He refused to stay at home; he said it made him feel useless, that he had to be involved. Your neighbour is waiting at your place in case Frances comes back alone.'

I shook my head again and tried really hard not to cry. Not once, not ever, had she made it back home under her own steam. We'd always had to go out and find her.

'And the school has been thoroughly checked, because you know how much she likes to go back—'

For the first time there was a look of sympathy in Richard's eyes. 'It was the first place I went,' he assured me. 'She wasn't there. But I called the head and some guys from the department and they've gone back and they're going to stay there until... until we find her.'

I looked at him in gratitude. 'Thank you.'

He shook his head, looking at me as though he'd just seen someone he almost recognised hiding behind a mask. 'Come on. We're wasting time here.' Interesting choice of words. 'We have to go.' He began to walk briskly towards his car, which was parked behind mine in Jack's drive.

Jack. I suddenly turned back to the house. I hadn't even said goodbye, I'd just walked out. I hesitated, as Richard looked back at me impatiently. He was already beside his car, the door open. I looked back at the house and felt something tearing me clean down the middle. And then Jack was suddenly at the door, pulling it closed behind him. He had put on a sweatshirt and boots and his car keys were in his hand.

'You're coming?' I asked, not realising my voice would come out on a note of such disbelief.

'Of course, I'm coming,' he responded, giving me a ghost of a smile which I couldn't return.

'Emma!' Richard's summons was imperative and urgent.

'Go,' urged Jack, as I turned and began to run to my car, 'I'll be right behind you.'

I've never been involved in a search party before, so I've no idea if this was par for the course, but the sheer number of police cars, sniffer dogs and volunteers filled me with despair.

Not to mention the helicopter which was already circling overhead. I parked my car haphazardly on a gravelled area with about twenty other vehicles and ran to where Richard was waiting.

'They're just beyond the brook,' he advised, not bothering to slow his speed walk, not that it mattered, I was already running.

'And Dad?'

'He's there too.' I nodded, trying to pull myself together before I saw him. He would be in pieces and the last thing he needed was for me to be the same.

'How did you know where to find me?' I gasped out as we rounded a small copse and the brook came into view.

'I phoned Caroline. She told me where you'd be. I guess it was inevitable that I'd be the last to know.'

There was nothing I could say, and it wasn't the time to think about Richard's shock or his bruised ego. This wasn't about anything except finding my missing parent, safe and well.

Several makeshift tables had been erected, upon which they'd laid out large ordnance survey maps of the area, held down at the edges by stones to stop them blowing in the wind. Although the sun was out, there was still a sharp coolness to the air from last night's storm. What had Mum been wearing when she'd walked from her bedroom, down the stairs and out of the front door? Was she out in these conditions in just her nightwear? Had she pulled on a coat, or was she wandering somewhere lost, barefoot and freezing? How long does it take a person to get hypothermia? Wordlessly I shook my head in denial and raced towards an adjacent police car, from which my father shakily emerged, a bright red blanket draped around his shoulders.

I could see he was crying even before I flung myself into his outstretched arms.

'Oh Daddy,' I cried as I fell against him, somehow reverting to the name I hadn't called him by in over a decade.

'Emma, Emma, Emma,' my dad replied, his voice as shaky as the hand which smoothed down my hair as he held me against him. 'Where is she? Where has she gone? Where's my Frannie?' I gently pulled back from his hold and looked at him worriedly. He looked like he'd aged about twenty years since the day before. I glanced over at a kindly-looking uniformed woman waiting beside the police car, who I assumed must be the liaison officer.

'Now don't you worry, Bill. I told you, we're going to find her for you. You just have to trust us. We know what we're doing here.'

I didn't doubt her words. I glanced around me and back at the tables and a group of officers, who were listening intently to instructions being delivered by a tall grey-haired man, who I guessed must be the detective in charge. As well as the uniformed officers there were four policemen with sniffer dogs, who were each being passed my mother's pink cardigan. It was what she'd been wearing the last time I'd seen her. I gave a small helpless gasp as each dog in turn inhaled deeply of her scent and then began to pull vigorously on their leads, anxious for the search to commence.

'I'm just going to go over and talk to the officer in charge,' I said to my dad, squeezing his hand.

'The volunteers are all gathered over there,' informed the liaison officer, pointing to a large crowd of people gathered some distance away from the tabled area.

My jaw fell open in surprise. 'Who *are* all those people? Where did they come from?'

'They're our neighbours, and friends,' said Dad sadly, receiving a comforting hand on his shoulder from the liaison officer, who I suddenly decided I liked very much indeed. She was just what he needed right then.

'I should go and join them,' he said, taking a few shaky steps away from the car. My look of horror was mirrored by Richard, who had been standing to one side while I spoke to my father.

'No, Bill,' said the policewoman gently. 'Remember, we agreed that wasn't such a good idea. You need to stay here at the car with me, then when we find Frances I'll be able to drive you straight to her, rather than having to track you down from somewhere out in the field.'

My dad gave an answering nod. Thank God he was willing to listen to the officer, because he scarcely looked strong enough to support himself right now, much less go hiking over the fields searching for his missing wife. He looked over at Richard. 'Thank you for bringing Emma to me, lad. I knew she'd be all right if she was with you.'

I looked across at Richard, waiting for him to lash into me with his words and the truth. Wasn't it exactly what I deserved?

'Yes. She was with me all along, Bill. I told you I'd bring her back.'

'Why don't you two go and join the volunteers?' suggested my dad's new police companion. 'They're going to be assigning search areas and you'll need to hear what you have to do.'

We nodded our agreement and walked swiftly across the rough grass to the accumulated crowd in silence.

'Thank you for saying that,' I said gratefully, as I scanned the crowd looking for, and finding, a tall solitary figure who was standing a small distance apart from the others. I began to turn towards him.

'Yeah, whatever,' Richard replied bitterly, moving to join the opposite side of the crowd.

Before addressing the group at large, the officer in charge took me to one side and quickly ran through the progress of the search so far and how they proposed to proceed. I hoped that Jack, who was standing beside me, with his arm comfortingly around my shoulders, was listening, because I struggled to decipher anything that was being said from the depths of the panic which was threatening to consume me. From the officer's words I did manage to work out that while the group of gathered volunteers tackled the vast rural and wooded area close to our home, numerous policemen were conducting door-to-door enquiries and searching gardens. He informed me that no road accident victims had been brought into any of the local hospitals in the last six hours, which I supposed was meant to comfort me, but just made me worry that Mum might still have been struck by a vehicle in the dark, and be lying injured beside the road. I suddenly saw an image of Amy in my mind, and glanced up at Jack. From the way he gripped my hand in comfort, I knew he was thinking exactly the same thing.

I realised pretty early on that the police didn't really expect any of the volunteers to actually find my mother. The dogs and handlers already had a head-start on the long snaking chain of volunteers. Nevertheless, we followed instructions and fell into place behind the small group of officers who remained some fifty metres or so ahead of us. In a slow-moving procession we crossed the rough open grassland, which was still sodden from the rainfall of the previous night, every pair of eyes staring fixedly at the ground.

The tracker dogs were haring forward at considerable speed, so I guessed they'd not managed to pick up a trail. Or did that mean the exact opposite? I suddenly wished I'd paid closer attention to all those forensic crime shows on television, because I really had no idea what any of us were looking for as we scoured the ground for some nameless clue, which I probably wouldn't recognise even if I saw it. Perhaps Jack, given the nature of his writing, had a better grasp of what was going on, but despite the fact that he was walking beside me, his hand firmly gripping mine, it felt as though there was a deep chasm opening up between us.

With each stumbling step I took over the long wet grass, I could feel the heavy weight of guilt prising me from him like a crowbar. If I hadn't stayed at his house, would Mum still have gone missing? Had she found my bed empty and left the safety of our home to go looking for me? Or, going back to the very beginning, if I'd just stayed with Richard, if I'd never broken off our engagement, would that have changed the events of today? They were impossible questions, and I was so afraid that if I opened my mouth to speak, I was going to ask them out loud; it seemed safer to remain silent.

'It's going to be all right. We're going to find her,' said Jack eventually, bringing my hand up to his lips and kissing my knuckles as though to seal his promise. But even his touch, which I'd always been helpless to resist, failed to comfort or reach me this time. This was the flip side of the happiness I had felt last night. This was the price tag, and suddenly the cost felt far too steep.

'You don't know that. You *can't* know that. She could be anywhere. She could be lying unconscious in a ditch... she could be hurt… someone could have taken her…' Each possibility was more horrible than the last, and a look of concern crossed Jack's face at my torment and his inability to ease it.

'Emma! Emma!'

I spun around at the familiar voice, calling me from some distance away. It wasn't what I'd been praying for; it wasn't someone telling me that Mum had been found, safe and well, but it was the next best thing. I broke free from Jack's hand and ran back over the grass to Caroline and Nick who were making their way towards the group of volunteers, both carrying large flat objects which were impossible to identify from so far away. Whatever it was she was carrying, Caroline laid it down on the grass and ran to me.

I fell into her outstretched arms with enough speed to knock the air from both of our lungs. She let me cry for a minute into the quilted material of her jacket before delving into her pocket and producing a folded tissue which she passed to me.

'How are you holding up?' she asked, scrutinising me carefully when I'd finished noisily blowing my nose.

'I'm okay. Or I will be, when we find her.'

Caroline nodded, but there was a small worried expression on her face. She looked over my shoulder, as her attention turned to the figure who had followed me.

'Hi, Jack.'

I turned, and saw that his fleeting smile of greeting was tempered by a look of anxiety at my distress.

'Don't you worry about me, I'll manage both trays,' interrupted Nick, bringing some much-needed normality to the moment with his gentle sarcasm. He had picked up whatever Caroline had been holding, and was now manfully struggling to carry two enormous trays of take away beverages, bearing the familiar logo of our local coffee shop.

'Here, let me,' said Jack, stepping over and relieving him of one of the trays.

'Thanks,' said Nick gratefully. 'I'm Nick, by the way, Caroline's partner,' he added by way of introduction. 'I'd shake your hand, but...' He nodded toward the loaded tray in explanation.

'That's okay. I'm Jack.'

'He knows who you are,' a voice cut in sharply. I jumped. I hadn't seen Richard leave his place in the line of volunteers and join us. There was an ugly moment, which fortunately Caroline rescued by going over and hugging Richard in greeting. I saw her whisper something furiously into his ear before she stepped out of his arms, and his lips tightened stiffly in reaction to her words.

Surprisingly, it was Nick once again who brought the awkward moment to a close. 'Shall we pass out these drinks to the volunteers then, before they get cold?'

'Yes, of course, why don't you two guys do that?' suggested Caroline, effectively dispatching Nick and Jack off on a mission. There was a long uncomfortable moment when only the three of us remained, staring at each other.

'Do you two want to have a word in private—' Caroline began, only to be cut off by Richard and me crying out, '*No!*' in complete unison. It was the first time we'd been in agreement about anything for weeks.

Richard took one last look at me, his face giving away none of his emotions, before announcing sharply, 'I'm going back to the line.' I could tell from the set of his shoulders as he stomped away that he was lividly angry and desperately hurt in equal measure.

'Richard found you at Jack's then?'

'Oh yes,' I said bitterly, as we briskly walked back to rejoin the volunteers.

Caroline took my hand and squeezed it. 'I'm sorry. He was absolutely desperate trying to find you, and your dad was going crazy. I had to tell him.'

'No, it's okay. I understand,' I replied.

'It wasn't awkward, or anything?' she asked.

In a few terse sentences I recounted the moment when Richard had come perilously close to catching a private porno of his ex-fiancée having sex in the kitchen with another man.

'Shiiit!' exclaimed Caroline on a low drawn-out exclamation. She was quiet for a moment, considering. 'Still, *Project-Make-Richard-Jealous* certainly appears to have worked,' she concluded.

I raised my head from my study of the grassland, to refute her words and tell her the reality had been nothing like that, only to find that Jack had silently joined us, empty coffee tray in hand. It took just a single glance at his frozen shocked face to know he had clearly heard everything Caroline had just said.

Fortunately, our attention was diverted at that moment by a helicopter circling overhead. It hovered for a moment or two above the assembled crowd before swooping off in the direction of the forest.

'It has to be bad if they've brought in a helicopter,' I said grimly.

'Not necessarily,' commented Nick, who had just finished distributing his own tray of drinks. 'It's just another of their resources. It's good that they're taking it seriously.'

I stared at the retreating aircraft, far from comforted to realise that the search was escalating into a full-blown police

348

operation. And if I needed further evidence of that, I saw it in the ambulance, blue lights flashing, which had just joined the parked vehicles at the edge of the field.

I felt all colour drain from my face. 'Have they found her?' My voice was a terrified whisper. 'What's the ambulance for?'

'I'll go and find out,' promised Jack, kissing me briefly on the cheek before running off to the line of police officers who were now some distance ahead of the rest of the crowd.

'He really does seem to care about you,' Caroline said quietly, when he was gone.

'I can't think about that now. I can't think about anything. Not until Mum's found.'

'I know,' she said, reaching down and squeezing my hand. I curled my fingers around her own gloved ones, and felt an unfamiliar hard edged object pressing against the wool on her ring finger. My eyes went to hers, but she just shook her head gently, dismissing her own monumental news. 'That can also wait until after your mum has been found,' she said softly. I don't think I have ever loved or valued her as much as I did right at that moment.

Jack was back in just a few minutes with an update. He'd run there and back, yet was barely out of breath. 'The ambulance is just there as a precaution, for *when* they find her.' I think we all noticed his deliberate emphasis on *when* rather than *if*. 'They've not had any luck yet in the streets near your house, so they're widening the search. The hospitals still have no news… which is good.'

None of it sounded good to me. It all sounded terrible. And it was about to become even worse, as Caroline noticed the arrival of a large sign-written van which pulled up beside the ambulance. 'Terrific. Bloody vultures. Doesn't take them long to get wind of something, does it?'

I peered back at the van, which bore the insignia of the local television station, and saw three people pile out of it. One was carrying a camera, and another a long sound boom. 'Must be a slow day for news when a frightened lost woman, suffering from dementia, makes the six o'clock,' I said bitterly.

'I guess it's because of the wedding and the crash and everything,' Caroline hazarded, and I knew she was probably right. Our private and personal tragedy had been all over the local papers for several weeks, and now this new horrible instalment just added to the story.

Our progress was slow, but eventually we reached the edge of the dense forest, and the officers efficiently broke the large group up into smaller segments, giving us each a pathway to follow. Mum had now been missing for at least nine hours, and it was hard to concentrate on anything except how cold, tired and hungry she must be, wherever she was.

Jack took my arm as we entered the forest, where the ground was uneven and slippery with mud. I glanced back over my shoulder and saw Caroline and Nick close behind us on the path. Suddenly a fleeting movement caught my eye and when I peered through the trees I saw Richard, heading back towards the car park area at speed.

'Where's he off to in such a hurry?' asked Nick, to no one in particular.

I shrugged, and turned my attention back to not being hit in the face by the many low overhanging branches in the forest, as I followed Jack's broad shape down the slippery slope. The police had thought it unlikely that Mum would have ventured into the forest, but I knew better. Painting a vista through a curtain of branches had been a trademark feature in many of her pieces of work, and even though she no longer painted anything like that, she still enjoyed long walks through the forest, whatever the weather. This was *just* the sort of area that would have attracted her.

We had one unpleasant moment as we ventured deeper into the shadowy forest when somehow the news team and some reporters from the local paper and radio station managed to locate us among the trees.

'Could we just get a brief statement from you, Miss Marshall?'

I shook my head and turned away.

'Is this something your mother has done before? How is your father coping at the moment?'

I lowered my head and increased my pace, trying to outrun them with their intrusive questions.

'Is she a danger to herself? Or to anyone else?' asked a sharp-voiced female reporter. I froze and could feel the fury crystallising on my face as I began to turn around. Jack quickly intervened. He caught my wrist and met my glance with an almost imperceptible shake of his head. 'I'll get rid of them,' he said quietly, stepping past me to stand directly in front of the small pack of journalists, effectively creating an imposing wall with his height and breadth.

'Look, guys, I know you're only doing your job, but now is not the best time for a comment. I'm sure later on, if Mrs Marshall is still missing, we're going to really need your help and support in getting the public involved in the search. But right now, let's just be decent human beings here and give the family a little space.'

With slightly embarrassed nods, the band began to disperse and head out of the forest and back to the field. The sharp-voiced female reporter was the last to go, and before she did she turned her full attention on Jack, her eyes narrowing. 'Are you Jack Monroe, the author?' she fired in eager anticipation, her eyes glittering at the prospect that a visiting celebrity might somehow be involved in the unfolding story.

Jack shook his head and lied incredibly convincingly. 'No. I'm not. Although I get that quite a lot, so I guess we must look alike.'

'Thank you,' I said gratefully when Jack resumed his position in front of me on the path, after checking the journalists had definitely gone. 'I hadn't thought that we might need to have them onside later.'

'Well, let's hope we don't,' he added grimly. 'Either way, it never pays to piss off the press.'

A short time later, we had a heart-stopping moment when I thought we had actually found something. We were much deeper in the forest by then, where very little natural light succeeded in piercing through the canopy of trees. The path was narrow and beside it was a steep embankment, at the bottom of which ran a vigorously flowing stream.

'Watch your step here,' cautioned Jack, extending his arm in case I needed to hold on to it. I glanced down the embankment and saw something small and yellow at the very base of the slope. Something that looked to be the exact same colour as my mum's favourite scarf. I caught hold of Jack's sweatshirt sleeve and pointed wordlessly towards the foot of the embankment.

'What is it?' he asked, bending his head closer to mine and following where I was indicating.

'There's something down there, something yellow... I think it's Mum's scarf.'

Without stopping to consider the dangerous descent, Jack left the path and began to climb down. The sides were steep, with very few handholds and his feet slipped several times on the muddy surface, causing the breath to catch in my throat until he had once more gained purchase.

I peered as far over the edge as I could, without going down the embankment myself, in a far less controlled manner than Jack was doing. Caroline and Nick came to stand on either side of me, Caroline linking her arm through mine. Jack disappeared from view behind a thicket of bushes, and I felt a moment of panic. What if it wasn't just her scarf down there? The undergrowth was thick and bushy, plenty dense enough to conceal a body.

Jack climbed back up the slope so silently I didn't even know he was there until the foliage rustled and he hoisted himself back up beside me. He shook his head regretfully, holding in his hands the bright yellow item which had caught my attention. It was a child's toy dog, the yellow fur thread-bare in places and saturated from its time in the stream. I held out my hand and took the sodden item from him, as tears began to course down my face.

'I know this sounds stupid, but when I was a little girl Mum and I had a favourite story she would read to me. It was about a boy who'd lost his favourite cuddly toy, a dog.' My voice cracked. 'It looked just like this one.'

Jack enfolded me into his arms and I wept noisily into his sweatshirt, while Caroline and Nick stepped to one side and tried very hard to pretend they weren't there at all. Jack had just quietened the sobs down to hitching whimpers when the sound began. It pierced the late-afternoon hush with a strident familiar two-tone wail. A siren from one of the emergency vehicles was sounding. My head jerked away from Jack's chest like a snared animal. A second siren joined its voice to the first, and then three long klaxon-like sounds from a car's horn, repeated over and over again.

'Something's happened,' I exclaimed, pulling out of his arms and already turning. 'We have to go back.'

I think all three of them cried out for me to slow down or to be careful, but I ignored that wisdom and began to run with pounding strides back towards the field. Jack caught up with me easily, and as soon as the path widened enough, he took my hand and we ran together, our feet flying over the muddy surface until it finally gave way to grass and the ambulance was at last visible in the distance. All along the length of the forest other rescuers were also emerging from the trees, drawn out of the wooded area by the summoning sirens.

It must have been a bizarre sight from the search HQ, to see the ramshackle group of volunteers running en masse towards them, led by a tall man holding the hand of a frantic-looking young woman. As we got closer I saw the police liaison car had just been repositioned closer to the ambulance and my dad was being helped out of it by the grey-haired chief detective. He bent low to hear a question my father must have asked, and then pointed back in my direction.

There was a stitch piercing my side like a knife blade, but I ignored it as the roaring sound of two vehicles approaching at speed joined in with the symphony of sirens. I glanced away from my father and looked towards the road. The first vehicle was a marked police car, its siren blaring and its blue lights glowing brightly. The second vehicle was a complete surprise. It was Richard's car.

The police car slewed to a screeching halt, in the type of manoeuvre they usually only get to perform on skid tracks. Stopping beside it, in only a slightly more sedate fashion, came Richard's vehicle.

Richard jumped out and ran around to open the passenger

door. I still couldn't see very well, but this time it was because the tears were already streaming down my face. I raised my hands and furiously brushed them away from each eye, not even noticing that at some point Jack had released my hand and I was now running alone.

Very carefully and gently, but then he'd always been that way with her, not just today, Richard held out his hand beside the open car door and helped my mother to her feet.

I pushed and barrelled past a gathering circle of people to reach her. My father beat me to it, enveloping her in his arms and holding her so tightly it looked as though he would never let go. He turned and saw me standing there, my face awash with tears of relief, as was his own. 'Emma,' he said gruffly, opening one arm out to me. I flew into the space he'd created, my whole body shuddering with relief. My mum, sandwiched tightly between her two emotional family members, looked a little startled and bemused at our behaviour.

'Where have you *been*, Mum? We've all been so worried,' I cried at last. My father still appeared to be some time away from coherent speech or sensible questions.

My mum looked genuinely puzzled and glanced curiously at the gathered audience who were sharing our emotional reunion, before asking simply, 'Have you? Why? I went out for *you*, Emma.'

It was what I'd been fearing all along. She'd gone looking for me. I reached up and pulled a small twig free from her hair, noticing for the first time that there were several smudges of dirt on her face.

'You went to find me?' My voice was hoarse with guilt.

'No. Not you,' corrected my mother, as though I was once again a small child, who'd just said something charmingly endearing. '*Your ring.*'

355

My father and I looked at each other in bafflement. Mum gave a small tutting noise, as though it was extremely tiresome having to deal with people who just couldn't keep up. 'Your *engagement* ring,' she said, slowly and loudly enough that surely everyone in the crowd must have been able to hear. 'I went out to find your missing engagement ring.'

For the first time I turned away from my mother and looked at Richard, who was standing a short distance away, his eyes fixed on all three of us. The question was there on my face, I didn't need to voice it. He'd had years and years of reading my facial expressions, so he knew what I was asking.

He nodded; a look of similar incredulity on his face. 'Yeah, I know. But that's where I found her; she was at the bottom of Farnham Ravine, searching for our engagement ring.'

There were several gasps of amazement from people in the crowd, and I clearly heard my father's shocked exclamation, 'Oh, Frannie.' Me, I was just too shocked to speak. I took a shaky step towards Richard.

'In the ravine?' My voice was a hollow ghost.

He nodded.

'At the bottom? Had she fallen?'

He shook his head. 'No, thank God, but that's what I thought when I first saw her there. But I was wrong. Turns out she just climbed down. She told me she's done it before.'

I thought of the painting hanging in our lounge. Yes, she had done it before, but that had been years and years ago.

'How... how...' I shook my head as though that would help me to make sense of what I was hearing. 'I don't get it. How did she know to go there? And how did you figure out that's where she was?'

Richard shrugged. 'I'm not sure how I worked it out. I

think searching through the grass reminded me of looking in the ravine for the ring... and then I remembered your mum overhearing us in the hall the other week... and well I just followed a hunch... and... she was there—'

I hadn't intended to do it. If you'd asked me only minutes earlier, I'd have said that nothing on earth would have *ever* persuaded me to do it again. But as the picture became clear, as I realised Richard had made the connection no one else had even considered, and by doing so had undoubtedly saved Mum's life, I just couldn't help myself. I flew into his arms and his own tightened around me, literally lifting me off the ground. 'Thank you, thank you, thank you,' I sobbed into the curve of his neck.

His arms remained tightly fastened around me, and I could hear the emotion in his own voice. 'I'm just so glad I found her in time. I couldn't bear to have lost her either, Emma.'

As Richard held me against him, I was vaguely aware of a whirring clicking sound which rose above the excited chatter of the crowd. When he eventually released me, I realised the noise was the continual shutter clicks from several professional cameras which were pointed directly at us. The moment of our emotional embrace had been captured, and was probably already being earmarked as the money shot for their next edition. Not to be outdone, there were at least a dozen or more camera phones clicking away. From the edge of the crowd I could see one of the journalists hadn't wasted a single moment, and was already doing a piece to camera. Although I couldn't hear everything being said, one phrase carried clearly above the crowd, as the reporter smiled into the lens and described the 'miraculous rescue by the woman's future son-in-law'. My glance flew to Richard, and then back to the reporter. I opened my mouth to correct her, and then realised the camera was still rolling. 'And here are the daughter and her heroic fiancé,' she continued smoothly as the camera swivelled towards us. 'You must both be so happy.' All words of correction and denial died on my lips, as I stared blankly at the glowing red light which I knew meant they were recording.

'We are,' said Richard, reaching down and taking hold of my hand.

Behind us the liaison officer was now guiding my parents to the ambulance, gamely running interference with the pack of journalists.

'Mrs Marshall,' hailed one of them, 'just one last question: why didn't you tell anyone where you were going?'

My father raised a stilling hand to the reporter, and I could see how anxious he was to get my mother out of the mêlée and into the hands of the medics. But amazingly Mum seemed virtually unaffected by her ordeal, and if anything was relishing the interest from the assembled crowd. She clearly had no idea that every last one of them had gathered there today to search for her.

'I wanted it to be a nice surprise for both of them. Emma's been so distraught lately, and I know how sad she must have been when she lost her ring. So I just thought I'd go and get it for her.' *Just!* I still had no idea how she'd managed to get to the ravine, or climb down the steep descent without breaking her neck.

A microphone was suddenly thrust through the crowd into my face. 'This question's for the happy couple: when is the wedding?'

I could feel the weight of a hundred eyes upon me. I tried to look beyond the microphone-wielding reporter into the crowd, seeking the one face I needed to find. But there were too many people packed all around us.

'We haven't decided on any immediate plans,' answered Richard, speaking for us both, although not using the words I'd have chosen. His answer didn't do anything to correct their misapprehension. 'We're just glad that Emma's mum is safe and unhurt. That's all we're concentrating on for now.'

The police liaison officer was now at the open rear doors of the ambulance, trying to urge my parents up the shallow steps. You could almost hear the collective groan of the press.

'One last photo,' pleaded the reporters. 'One with all the family: mum, dad and the two lovebirds.' I'm sure my face perfectly reflected my dismay at that description, but Richard gave the smallest shake of his head and I knew he was right. Did I really want to be laying bare our personal life in this extremely public forum? Reluctantly I took my place between Richard and my mother, as the flashlights erupted like a firework display.

'Okay, folks, can I ask you all to back up and give us a little room here,' interceded the chief detective, as his officers firmly began to ease back the reporters and crowd. 'I'd like to thank all of you for giving up your time so generously and for helping us to achieve the best possible outcome today.' A small ripple of applause ran through the crowd and I turned to face them, smiling in gratitude, even as my eyes continued to scan desperately through the assembly. I still couldn't see him anywhere.

'One more of the engaged couple? Perhaps sharing a kiss?' called a hopeful voice from the crowd. Richard saw the look of horror in my eyes and answered for me.

'That's all for now, I think.' He put an arm around me, turning me away from the cameras. I climbed the steps of the ambulance where my mother was now being attended to by a paramedic. I turned around, and from my elevated position I was finally able to see Jack, or rather the back of his car, as he drove away in a grey cloud of displaced gravel chips.

CHAPTER 17

Despite being urged by all three of us, my mother absolutely refused to go to the hospital to be checked out. In the end, rather than distress her further, it was agreed to allow her to go home. It didn't even occur to me to question Richard's right to accompany us. Somehow, in the unfolding drama of the day, the walls separating us had begun to subtly crumble. Even the sting of infidelity and broken promises lessened their significance when the tragedy we'd been facing had turned into a triumph, thanks to him.

It didn't even seem strange when Richard took control when we arrived back home, putting on the kettle, pulling cups from the cupboard and knowing – without having to ask – how everyone took their tea.

I watched him work, my attention split between him and my parents' conversation in the adjacent lounge. I shook my head in disbelief as I overheard my mum admit to hitching a lift with a passing lorry driver to get to the ravine.

'After all those lectures she gave me as a teenager about not taking lifts from strangers,' I said in a stunned voice, as I took the steaming mug from Richard's hand. 'She could have got lost; been run over; someone could have hurt her; or she could have fallen clean down to the bottom of that bloody ravine.' I was still unable to escape the list of awful possibilities.

'But she *didn't*,' Richard countered soothingly. 'None of that happened. You can relax now. Frances was lucky today, she must have had a whole squadron of guardian angels looking out for her.'

I gave a small grateful smile. 'No. Just one. You.'

He looked embarrassed and pleased in equal measure at my words.

'Maybe now we'll be able to persuade your dad that we're going to have to find a better way from now on.'

I bent my head low over my mug, effectively hiding my face from view. His use of the 'we' pronoun hadn't gone unnoticed, and a small worrying alarm bell began to ring.

The rest of the afternoon blurred by in an endless carousel of visiting medical professionals, police officers, and the incessant ringing of our telephone. We were grateful to learn that, physically, Mum appeared to have sustained nothing more serious than minor scratches and a few bruises, all of which would have easily lost to mine in a contest. Emotionally... well that was a different matter. My father's face was a portrait of worry when he quietly told us to expect a visit from a social worker and someone from a dementia society over the next few days.

'That's *good* news,' Richard said encouragingly. 'It means we're going to be able to get you more help.' My father smiled back weakly, still looking unconvinced. I remained silent, unable to ignore this second appearance of that worrying pronoun. But there was something else concerning me even more than Richard's apparent reinstatement as an honorary family member. Jack. I hadn't been able to reach him all afternoon. I'd been trying pretty much every ten minutes or so from the moment I got back into my car, and so far the only thing I'd heard when calling his mobile was the annoying tinny voice of a recording advising me 'This person's phone is switched off.'

I saw Richard watching me closely each time I pulled the phone from my pocket, either to call or check my messages, of which there were none. With much more restraint than I'd been expecting from him, he very wisely said nothing.

By early evening I'd gone from vaguely concerned and frustrated, to angry. Jack had no idea what was going on. Surely, if I meant anything at all to him, if *last night* had meant anything, he should have been the one phoning *me*, checking on *me*, not vice bloody versa. When Richard volunteered to go and collect a takeaway for dinner, I tried Jack's number one more time, and finally heard a different sound at the end of the phone. It was ringing. I grabbed a jacket from the hook by the back door and quickly slipped out into the garden to speak to him in private. It rang six times, and with each trilling tone, my heartbeat began to race. I took a deep and calming breath. I didn't want to begin our conversation by sounding hurt and angry that he'd not been in touch.

'Hi, this is Jack.' The soft burr of his accent warmed me, and I could almost feel the tension that had been flowing through me begin to evaporate.

'Hi, it's me—' I began, hoping he'd recognise my voice as easily as I would his.

'I'm sorry. I can't take your call at the moment. Just leave me a number and I'll get right back to you.' There was a prolonged beep and then silence. He'd let it go to voicemail. For just a moment I considered hanging up, but some small persistent hope refused to be quashed in the darkness.

'Hey, Jack. It's Emma. It's eight o'clock, and I just wondered if everything was okay? I've not heard from you since you left the forest and I've been trying to reach you for hours. Call me when you get this.' Perhaps I should have added something personal to my message, but I was still hurt that he hadn't been in touch. Surely he must know I'd wanted no part in all that media craziness when Mum had returned? Why wouldn't he talk to me so I could explain?

Halfway through our Chinese takeaway, my mother's head began to droop, and my father didn't look that far behind her. It was amazing they were both still upright after everything that had happened in the last twenty-four hours.

'Look, why don't you two go upstairs to bed? I'll clear up things down here,' I volunteered, helping my sleepy mum to her feet.

'*We'll* clear up,' corrected Richard, already gathering up containers and dirty plates.

My mother nodded vaguely and headed towards the stairs, but Dad wasn't so willing.

'I think I might just stay down here tonight...' he began, a look of real concern on his face, '... just in case.'

I knew what he was worrying about; the same thought had been on my mind all evening too. 'She's not going to go anywhere tonight. She's too exhausted.'

'Still... I don't want to take any chances... not until I've installed some type of alarm on the doors.'

I sighed deeply. He didn't know it, but I was actually more worried about how everything was affecting *him*, rather than anything else. He wasn't a young man, and the last thing he needed to be doing was sitting up all night on sentry duty.

'*I'll* sleep down here tonight,' I told him. 'If I keep the lounge door ajar, I'll easily be able to hear if the front door is opened.' He still looked doubtful, but I was already gently propelling him towards the stairs. I kissed the soft wrinkled skin on his cheek. 'Go and get a good night's rest.'

It didn't take long for Richard and me to clear the kitchen, but by the time I finished wiping down the worktops, I too was yawning widely. I guessed no one in our family had got much sleep the night before, for vastly different reasons.

'You look exhausted,' Richard observed. 'Go and sit down in the lounge and I'll bring us both some tea.'

After a moment's hesitation I nodded in agreement. I needed to speak to Richard privately, without my parents around; I needed to make sure he understood the way things stood. And I realised it was something I needed to take care of sooner rather than later.

Sleep didn't creep up on me; it didn't sneak in slowly, inviting me to drift along with it. It came out of nowhere like a wrecking ball, felling me into unconsciousness with one mighty swipe. I opened my eyes, and my first thought was *Why's Richard taking so long with the tea?* Then I noticed that the room was bathed in early-morning light, and there was in fact a cup of tea on the small oak table beside me, but it had a very unpleasant-looking skin on its surface. I reached out and curled my fingers around the cup, it was stone cold. A very familiar soft snorting sound came from the other side of the room, and I froze. I knew that noise. It was one which I'd once found strangely endearing. I slowly turned my head and saw Richard fast asleep in one of the armchairs, gently snoring through slightly parted lips.

I sat up very slowly, noticing that a thick fleecy blanket had been draped over me while I slept, dead to the world. Richard again. I got to my feet, feeling the kinks in my spine groaning in a chorus of protest. The old, poorly sprung three-seater was not the most comfortable place to have spent the night, but it was probably a darn sight more accommodating than the chair where Richard now slept.

Trying to make as little noise as possible, I walked across the room, feeling the chill of the wooden floor beneath my feet. The boots, which I had definitely still been wearing when I sat down the night before, were now standing upright like a pair of bookends beside the table. There was something very intimate about the image of Richard slowly unzipping and removing them from me while I slept. How could I not have felt him doing that? Great guard I'd turned out to be, falling asleep pretty much thirty seconds into my watch.

'Good morning.'

I jumped, not realising he too was now awake. 'Morning,' I replied, running my fingers through my hair and rubbing my eyes. 'I can't believe I fell asleep.'

'Fell into a coma, more like,' Richard corrected.

'Why didn't you wake me?'

He gave me a look I recognised; it was the one he usually reserved for responding to totally idiotic comments. 'You needed to sleep. You looked absolutely terrible.'

'Gee thanks,' I said, glancing at the mirror hanging over the fireplace and seeing that I still did. Well, perhaps more dishevelled than anything else, but it certainly wasn't my most attractive look. I glanced down sorrowfully at the white shirt which had looked so much better the day before, when it hadn't been slept in, *or plastered to my body in the rain, and gently removed by Jack*. I shook my head, refusing to allow such dangerous thoughts to creep in.

Richard was folding the blanket that had been covering him, before reaching for mine. 'Thank you,' I said, nodding toward the coverings. I bit my lip, wondering if there was any way to say my next sentence without sounding supremely ungrateful. 'Why didn't you go home, Richard?'

His eyes met and held mine and there was something in their clear blue depths I didn't want to acknowledge. 'I thought somebody should stay and guard the door,' he supplied easily, 'and I don't think *you'd* have heard if anyone had taken a run at it with a battering ram, so I decided it was best to hang around until you woke up.'

'I see,' I said slowly. 'Well, thank you again.'

'Emma, you don't have to keep thanking me. That's not what I'm here for.'

I felt an icy cold shiver run over my heart, because I really didn't want him to expand on that comment one little bit. I wasn't ready to hear that. Fortunately I managed to divert both of us with my sudden exclamation. 'Mum! Is she all right? She didn't try and get out again, did she?'

Richard shook his head, and I could tell he was sorry to have our conversation derailed. 'No. She's still sound asleep. I went up about forty minutes ago and I could hear them both snoring in tandem through their bedroom door.'

I gave a small smile. I seemed fated to be surrounded by nasally-challenged sleepers. 'You weren't doing too badly in that department yourself, a moment or two ago.'

He grinned in a way that was achingly familiar. 'So you've always said, but I just don't believe it.'

'I'll record it next time—' I broke off in shocked horror. The laughter slid from his face at my comment. We stared at each other wordlessly, both lost in a country we vaguely recognised, but probably shouldn't have ventured into.

'I'll go and make some tea,' Richard said eventually, and I nodded with as much gusto as if he'd just promised to cure cancer.

'Tea would be absolutely wonderful,' I over-enthused.

When he had safely disappeared into the kitchen, I ran lightly up the stairs and splashed copious amounts of cold water on my face and cleaned my teeth. By the time I'd dragged a comb through my hair, I was starting to feel a little more presentable and much more in control.

I could hear crockery being moved in the kitchen and smell the appetising aroma of toast beginning to fill the hall. I was turning towards the kitchen when a soft knock on the front door stopped me. I glanced down at my watch, it wasn't even seven o'clock in the morning. Who could be calling on us at that hour?

If I looked crumpled and untidy, Jack was the exact antithesis. He stood on the doorstep looking immaculate and clean-shaven, wearing a dark suit, shirt and tie. Even though he was a metre away from me, I swear I could breathe in the smell of his shower gel and aftershave on a waft of air that hit me as I opened the door. Or was that just my imagination?

I wanted to throw myself straight into his arms, and it would only have needed a microscopic amount of encouragement from him for me to do so, but none came.

'Jack,' I said, my voice sounded strangely small and uncertain.

'I'm sorry it's so early,' he apologised.

'No. That's fine. I've been awake for a while now.' *Where have you been? Why didn't you call me? I needed you.* My head was suddenly crowded with all the things I wanted to say, but the only thing that managed to come out was, 'I left a message on your mobile.'

'I got it.'

Those three words told me more than a whole chapter of

explanations. I'd been reaching out to him, asking – well pleading really – for him to call me. And yet he hadn't done so. Something hard started to form in my chest, somewhere in the region of my heart.

We looked at each other, and I noticed for the first time the stiffness in his stance and a small muscle moving at his jaw. He looked tense, which was something I'd never seen before.

'How is your mother? Is she all right?'

'Yes, she is,' I replied. 'Better than we are.' I felt a hot flush flood my cheeks in case he thought the 'we' I was referring to was him and I. 'Er... I mean the family, my dad and me... you know...'

The uptight look relaxed slightly, as a small understanding smile found a gap and crept through it.

'Are you coming in?' I asked, because that's what you do when people turn up on your doorstep, even if you know, without a shadow of a doubt, that the answer they are going to give you is *No*.

'No. I'm sorry. I can't. I have to leave for London. I've got a meeting at just after nine.'

I nodded. Life went on. It didn't matter what tragedy you lived through: car crashes; missing family members; fledgling romances withering and dying before your eyes, life still carried on regardless.

'I don't suppose you can still come with me...?' His voice trailed away in a very un-Jack-like manner. I guessed we both knew my answer before I voiced it.

'I can't. Things are going to be crazy for the next few days. I'm needed here. We've got doctors and social workers and—'

'I understand.'

Do you? I thought, letting my eyes speak to him, when my throat was too frightened to. *I don't think you do. I don't think you understand anything at all, because if you did, you wouldn't be standing there, so close and yet a thousand miles away from me; you'd be holding me in your arms and kissing all the coldness away.*

'I should have phoned,' said Jack, his voice regretful. I'm not sure if he meant last night or this morning before calling round to see me. It didn't really matter; my answer was the same either way.

'Yes, you should.'

'It's just—' He stopped suddenly as the door to the kitchen swung open and Richard walked casually into the hall, his shirt unbuttoned and untucked, clearly displaying the firm taut muscles of his abdomen.

'Breakfast is ready, Emma,' he announced in a purposely relaxed tone of voice. I threw him a horrified glance over my shoulder, before my eyes flew back to Jack. His face was a frozen plateau of hard angles and ridges, as though it had been carved out of a glacier. Richard's, on the other hand, looked vaguely smug. If he'd had a thought bubble above his head, I'm sure it would have read *Payback's a bitch, isn't it?*

Jack's eyes narrowed and hardened and I knew they saw everything, from my crumpled clothing to Richard's lack of it. In a horrible parody of the scene in his own kitchen, Jack read what he thought he had just interrupted.

'This isn't what it looks like.' I reached out my hand to Jack, but he took a half step away from me. Everything I felt as I saw him recoil from me was plainly written on my face. I turned desperately to Richard. 'Tell him. Tell him why you're here. Why you stayed. Tell him nothing happened.'

Richard shrugged, in a supposedly nonchalant way, but said nothing. It probably didn't matter. I doubt that Jack would have believed him anyway.

'Jack, please,' I said, my eyes filling as I saw the look in his.

'I'm glad everything's worked out for you, Emma.' Jack's voice was tight and controlled. 'I'm glad you've got everything you were hoping for.'

'But I haven't. It's not like that.'

He smiled then, but it was cool and distant. There was no sign there of the man who had held me in his arms and changed my life in one single night.

'I have to go, Emma. Take care of yourself.' He turned from me then, and walked away.

I remained at the open front door long after his car had disappeared from view. When I eventually closed it and turned around, Richard was still standing in the hall, watching me carefully.

'That went well,' he observed mildly.

My mouth tightened in annoyance as I strode angrily towards him. I grasped on to the trailing end of one side of his open shirt, and yanked on it hard enough to hear the seam rip slightly in protest.

'Nice one, Richard. Very mature.'

He had the grace to look a little shamefaced, but I noted he didn't apologise as he tucked the shirt back into his jeans before following me into the kitchen. I sat down heavily at the table, not realising how much the scene with Jack had affected me, until my trembling hand spilled tea over the table as I reached for my cup.

Richard sat opposite looking wary, no doubt wondering

if I was actually furious enough to aim my drink all over him after what he'd just done. And I *was* mad at him for his childish stunt, but nowhere near as angry as I was with Jack at that moment. Why had he so readily believed the circumstantial evidence? Or Caroline's stupid comment? Why hadn't he known that the person who had given herself so completely to him the night before would be physically *incapable* of turning to another man? Didn't he understand anything at all about me?

'What does he mean to you, Emma?'

I kept my eyes focused on the table top, and answered with a long and painful sigh. 'It doesn't really matter, does it? Whatever I thought was there, evidently wasn't. I think he just made that abundantly clear.' I raised my head to look at Richard's carefully neutral face. 'You must be very happy.'

Surprisingly his hand came across the table and took hold of mine. Even more surprisingly, I didn't pull away. 'No, I'm not. Nothing that hurts you could ever make me happy. Even if it's seeing you being rejected by the man you replaced me with.'

Way to go, Richard. Any more salt you want to grind into that particular wound?

'But I'm not sorry he's out of the picture,' he continued. 'Caroline said he's going back to America in a few days?' I nodded mutely.

'Seeing you with him yesterday morning was the single worst moment of my entire life.'

I looked into his blue tormented eyes, and clearly saw his pain at the memory.

'I'm sorry,' I said softly. 'Whatever's happened between us, whoever is to blame, I would *never* have chosen to have deliberately hurt you like that.'

Richard's throat swallowed convulsively, and I knew he was going to have a lot of trouble dispelling the image of Jack and me together. So would I, for obviously different reasons. 'I've never felt anything like that before, such blind rage and jealousy. I wanted to lash out, to hurt someone as badly as I was hurting.' He gave a small laugh, which held absolutely no humour. 'I never really appreciated before how it must have felt for you, when you found out about Amy. I thought if I just apologised... if you understood it had all been a terrible mistake, that you'd forgive me... that we'd get past it...' He ran his free hand through his hair, looking helpless and boyish, and more like the man I once loved than he'd done in a very long time. 'But if the pain I caused you was just a fraction of what I felt yesterday...' His voice trailed away, as a whole new level of sadness welled up within me at the hopelessness of everything, and where we had all ended up.

'Except for just one thing...' His words sounded tentative but optimistic. 'Despite everything, despite knowing about you and...' he hesitated, as though the very name tasted bitter on his tongue, '... Jack, I still believe there's a way forward for us. You see, the reason it felt like my heart had been ripped out of my chest when I saw you with him, was because I still love you, very much.' His voice dropped. 'I understand your pain now, better than I ever wanted to, and I think I know where it comes from. Because I think you still love me too.'

His words sideswiped me. I hadn't seen them coming or been expecting them, but when I tried to pull my hand from his, he wouldn't let me.

'Just listen for one moment, Emma, please.' I nodded reluctantly. 'I know this whole mess is down to me, I know

I ruined things. God knows, whether you ever forgive me or not, I'm still going to spend the rest of my life regretting what I did to you. But there's only ever been one person in the world for me. And I know it's probably too soon to be saying this, but I don't want to waste any more of our lives. I want you to have this... again.'

He took his hand from mine and delved into his pocket, retrieving a small velvet-covered box and sliding it across the table to me. For the second time in the conversation I lost my footing as, like an accomplished magician, Richard pulled away the rug on which I'd been standing.

I looked at the small box with a mixture of astonishment and trepidation. 'I don't believe it. Did you actually *find* my ring in the ravine yesterday?' I asked incredulously.

His smile was regretful. 'Now that *truly* would have been amazing, wouldn't it?' He shook his head. 'I think that kind of thing only happens in books or the movies.'

My fingers were shaking as they reached for the box. Although I was afraid I already knew what it contained, I was unable to resist the lure of the small velvet container. The catch sprung open easily, revealing a diamond ring, which was an almost exact replica of the one I had thrown away.

'Oh, Richard,' I said on a long sad sigh.

'I've had this for quite a while now,' he confessed, 'ever since I realised I wasn't going to find your first one.' Carefully he pulled the ring from its slot in the jeweller's box and held it out to me. 'You see, I never stopped believing. I never gave up hope. We belong together, you and I. *I* know it, our friends know it, your family know it... and deep down, I think you do too.'

His words whirled around me like a cyclone, filling my head and making it spin in confusion.

'Richard... I... I don't know what to say.'

'It's not that hard; you just have to say *yes*, like you did before.'

'It's not that simple. Not now.'

'Yes it is.' His voice was suddenly stronger, more confident. 'Just answer me this, do you still love me?' His eyes were like lasers slicing through my protective armour and reaching the vulnerable inner core of truth. I couldn't lie, however much I wanted to.

'Yes,' I said quietly, giving the one admission I never thought I'd hear myself make. 'I *do* still love you, Richard.'

The roads were quiet, but it was early so I hadn't really expected to meet much traffic. I yawned widely, and opened the car window to let in some much needed fresh air. I hadn't slept well the night before; I'd been too tense trying to plan exactly what I was going to say when I saw him.

Two days had passed since Richard's proposal – or re-proposal, if that was even a word – and so far I had told no one about it. Not my parents not Caroline, and definitely not Jack. Not that I had any idea where he'd been or how to get hold of him anyway, because on the few occasions when I'd tried his phone it had gone straight to voicemail. This time I hadn't left a message.

Mum, and the new plans for her ongoing care, had taken up my days. It was a harsh truth, but it had taken the near tragedy of her trip to the ravine to finally get through to my dad that the kind of help she needed was more than he and I could provide alone. And it turned out there was a great deal more assistance available than either of us had realised, and none of it required her being put into residential care. At least not yet.

And there was something else that had been resolved in the last two days too. There was an answer I was now ready to give, and my heart hammered like a caged bird in my chest every time I thought of it. I was still ten minutes away from his home when my mobile phone trilled and vibrated from within the depths of my bag. I switched it on to speakerphone and smiled as Caroline's cheery voice filled my car.

'Hey, Emma, sorry to call so early, but I wanted to catch you before you left for work.'

I smiled wryly, as I wondered if I even had a job left to go to, but I didn't bother to correct her, because I didn't want her to know where I was heading this early in the day.

'That's okay. What's up?'

'Well, I don't know if this is even relevant any more, but I was talking to another estate agency yesterday, who have been handling Jack's rental place.'

My hands tightened on the wheel at the mention of his name, but my tone was neutral as I said, 'Oh yes?'

'I asked if the property was available for the next quarter. You know, just in case he wanted to extend his lease for another term.'

'And was it?'

'Afraid not, my love. In fact, it's off the letting market completely. Apparently it's been sold.'

A long sigh escaped from my lips, like steam through a valve, it was the final confirming nail to hammer in the coffin of my brief relationship with Jack Monroe. 'Oh well, it's not important anyway. He's leaving tomorrow.'

There was a long silence from the other end of the phone before Caroline's voice came back, asking carefully, 'Are you all right, Emma?'

'Me? Yes, I'm fine.' I was getting really good at lying these days. 'Why?'

Caroline again paused before answering. 'I don't know... something in your voice... you sounded kind of *funny*.'

'It must be the phone line,' I said. 'Anyway, I've got to go, Caro. Thanks for calling, I'll speak to you soon.'

By the time I reached his place I was feeling physically sick with nerves. My legs were shaking as I walked to his front door, and my stomach was flipping so violently I was really glad I had decided to pass on breakfast. He took a long time answering and when he finally did, there was no disguising the astonishment on his face when he saw me.

'Emma.' There was a question in the greeting, and I wasn't surprised, for he hadn't been expecting me, and certainly not at this time of day.

I smiled nervously, wanting to reach out to touch him, and knowing I should wait until he heard what I had come to tell him. I cleared my throat nervously.

'Hi. I'm sorry it's so early. I just wanted to let you know...' I had thought this was going to be hard to say, but suddenly, when I looked into his eyes it was actually the easiest thing in the world. 'My answer... is yes.'

His face gave nothing away, but he stepped back from the door and held it open.

'I think you'd better come in.'

THE END

PART FIVE

I almost wished I had taken Caroline up on her offer to help me get dressed, as I struggled to do up the long zip at my back, but eventually I heard it purr up the length of my spine and into place. I smoothed the fabric down over my hips and turned to check my reflection in the full-length mirror. I gave myself a small nod. It was just how I had wanted to look today.

I was spraying his favourite perfume on to the skin at my wrists when a rumbling sound from the street below drew my attention. The cars were here. I glanced at the clock. Right on time. The pulse below the sprayed fragrance skipped and began to quicken.

I could hear movement and the sound of opening doors drifting up from downstairs, and knew most people had now left to make sure they got to the church before us. I glanced around the room, checking to make sure nothing was forgotten. The thought produced a strange spasm within me. Fortunately at that moment a light knock sounded on the bedroom door.

'Come in,' I called.

CHAPTER 18

'Come in,' he repeated. For just a moment I thought I had seen his eyes light up in pleasure at finding me there on his doorstep, but when I looked again there was nothing in them except polite cordiality. He probably greeted the postman with greater warmth. Five seconds in and already this wasn't going the way I had planned.

I followed him into the hallway and then to the lounge. He didn't ask me to sit down.

'Can I get you something?'

I shook my head, already beginning to feel my nerve slipping away. If he disappeared off to make tea or coffee at this point, I was afraid I would lose it completely. I took a deep breath, desperately trying to remember what had seemed such a wonderful opening line in the middle of the night.

'I probably should have called first,' I said, hearing the thread in my voice that showed how nervous I was.

'Perhaps,' Jack conceded.

'I'm sure you're busy with packing... and everything.' I had to admit, there was very little evidence of it around us, but then it *was* a furnished rental. 'I didn't want to risk missing you,' I explained. His face was impassive. 'And as I hadn't heard from you...' I let the accusation hang there in the air, waiting for some sort of explanation or apology. He remained silent.

'Well, I have something important I have to tell you.'

'Richard has asked you to marry him. Again,' Jack cut in, his voice bitter.

I gasped. 'Yes, yes he did. How did you know that?'

'I always thought that he would.' He looked directly at me, without flinching. 'So, you've come here today to tell me you said yes.'

He was standing just a metre or so away from me, close enough for me to easily see his face was devoid of all emotion. Something inside me blew as the valve keeping the steam under control couldn't withstand the pressure.

'No, of course I didn't say yes! Are you insane?'

That certainly caught his attention. He jolted as though he'd touched a live current. But he still didn't come any closer to me. I thought the moment in my parents' kitchen, when I'd had to tell Richard that although I loved him, I wasn't *in love* with him had been bad, but that was nothing compared to this.

I looked directly into Jack's questioning brown eyes and knew he too deserved my honesty. 'Part of me is always going to have feelings for Richard. He was my first love and he's connected not just to me, but to my whole family. But I can't love him, not the way he wants, or the way he deserves. Not any more.' I could hear the tremor in my voice, and wondered if he could too. 'And do you know why that is?' I asked, on a note of despair and exasperation. 'Because I'm in love with *you*.' This was rapidly turning out to be the most unromantic declaration of love *ever*. My voice cracked slightly, as I continued, 'And just so you know, I'm an old-fashioned sort of girl, and *I'm* not meant to be the one to say that first, the man is.'

There was a long pause, during which Jack spectacularly

missed his cue to say that he loved me too. I cleared my throat and smiled nervously as I looked directly into his unreadable face. 'So, can we please just put the last three days behind us and go back to where we were? You asked me a question on Sunday, and my answer is "yes". I will come with you to America. I want to give us a chance too.' I thought I saw a subtle change in his expression, but I didn't know what it meant. 'That's if... if the invitation still stands?' I added nervously.

A silence stretched between us.

'Well, that's the problem. Because actually, things have changed somewhat.' Even in my very worst-case scenario, I had never thought I would hear him say those words. Was this still about Richard, or what he'd overheard Caroline say, or had he simply realised he'd made a mistake?

'Oh,' I responded, my voice trembling like a lost child's. I needed to get out of there, fast. I took a step backwards, my eyes fixed on the door and escape.

'You see, after thinking about it, I realise what I asked doesn't sit comfortably with me.'

Don't cry, I told myself furiously. *Whatever you do, don't cry.* I'd known all along how difficult it would be for him to commit to anyone. He'd had time to think about it, and was backing off. I should have seen it coming.

'You see, what we were discussing, well... that's just not going to be enough for me now. I want more.'

My head flew up at his words. 'More?' I asked, my voice small and uncertain.

'Much more,' he confirmed, smiling properly for the first time since I'd walked into the house. 'You see, I want to go to sleep at night with you curled up in my arms, and know that you're going to be there in the morning... for *all* my mornings. And I just don't think I made that clear enough the other day.'

'But... you don't do long-term relationships... you don't want commitment.'

'Who said that?'

'You did.'

He looked a little abashed at my reply, before nodding slightly. 'You're right, I did. But that was before.'

'Before what?'

'Before you.'

There were so many questions I wanted to ask, but the look in his eyes was suddenly making me dizzy and breathless. I felt a smile stretching across my face as Jack took a step towards me and held out his hands. As though this was a fantastic dream that I was frightened would end at any moment, I carefully placed mine in both of his. He pulled me closer until our bodies were almost touching. 'Since the very first day I met you, you've turned my entire world upside down, Emma. You've made me look closer at the man I am, and got me questioning what I want from the rest of my life and who I want to share it with.'

'And did you come up with any answers?'

He nodded, his eyes like pools I would willingly have drowned in. 'Just one. You. *You're* what I want from life, *you're* the one I want to share it with.' He released my hands and slid his arms around me, finally closing the last small distance between us. 'I love you, Emma,' he said tenderly, 'and I'm really sorry you had to say it first. I shouldn't have let that happen. But if it's any consolation at all, I *felt* it first. I've felt it for a very, very long time.'

His head lowered and his lips found my mouth and told me wordlessly that all he had said was true. When we finally broke apart I knew there were tears of happiness escaping from my eyes. He saw them and brushed them gently away with his fingertips.

'I know how much you'd be giving up by leaving with me,' Jack said.

'I'm gaining more than I'm losing.'

'Even so, I think we could balance things up a little more fairly. I think we should split our time between the ranch and here. That way we stay together *and* honour both of our family responsibilities.'

It was the perfect compromise, or would have been if it weren't for just one small detail.

'When you say *here*, do you mean in Trentwell? In this house? Because we can't, it's been sold.' His eyes were patient, waiting for me to catch up. '*You? You* bought it?'

He nodded.

'But... but... what if I'd said no? What if I'd accepted Richard's proposal?'

'Then I'd just have had to work even harder to win you back. I wasn't ever going to walk away without fighting for you.'

'But... you bought *a house*...' I was still stunned that he had done something so impulsive.

Jack shrugged, then looked suddenly serious. He pulled me back into his arms and his voice was husky as he spoke. 'I'm not going to propose to you, because I know it's too soon for that,' his eyes held a glint of humour and irony, 'and besides, everyone is doing that these days.' I gave a wry smile. 'But I *do* want to give you something,' he continued. 'Something so you'll know that I'm serious about us, that I'm committed.'

'I think buying the house did that,' I said, my voice a little breathless.

'Yes, well, you can't wear a house.' He reached into his pocket and palmed something from within it. 'I'm in this Emma, one hundred per cent, all the way, committed.'

He slowly opened his fingers, to reveal an exquisite sapphire ring.

'It's beautiful,' I breathed unsteadily.

'Try it on,' he said softly.

I picked up the ring from his outstretched hand and looked up at him hesitantly. This wasn't a proposal, he wasn't asking me to be his wife, at least not yet. So which finger should the ring go on? His smile was gentle as he saw my confusion. He took the ring from me and held it poised over the third finger on my left hand.

'It goes here,' he said, sliding the ring in place.

It was a perfect fit. Just as we were.

THE END

PART SIX

'Come in,' I called.

My breath caught in my throat as I saw him standing at the open door. He looked so handsome in his suit, the crisp white shirt setting off the soft tan of his skin. His thick dark hair was, for once, almost tamed into place. His warm golden-brown eyes went straight to my face, and there was no disguising the love in them.

Something inside me instantly calmed and quieted when I saw him. Just looking at his face could do that.

'The cars are here,' he advised, his American accent more pronounced by his lowered tone.

'I'm ready,' I declared.

'I thought we could walk down the stairs together. Make a bit of an entrance, you know?'

I smiled at the notion, recognising the sentiment behind the suggestion, and loving him even more because of it. I saw his gaze skim the room, moving past the small vase of flowers on the dresser and then return to it.

'They're pretty.' I swear it was almost as though he knew.

'Freesias,' I said, my eyes following his to the perfect white blooms. 'They're actually from Richard.'

He nodded, but there was no real surprise on his face. 'Shall we go?'

I slid my hand into the offered crook of his arm. He bent down low and gently kissed my cheek. 'I love you,' he whispered, so we wouldn't be overheard by the people waiting for us in the hall below. His words brought a tear to my eye. I blinked it away, and smiled at the face I loved so much. 'Right back at you,' I said, tugging gently on his arm.

He stopped just once before we got to the top of the stairs.

'Where's your stick?'

I smiled at his worried expression. 'It's in the hall by the door. I can manage the stairs perfectly well without it. I'm not going to fall.'

His handsome face still wore a look of concern, and his arm flexed firmly, as though preparing to take my weight in case I was wrong.

'Hold on tight to me, Grandma,' he said tenderly, bringing yet another smile to my lips, as so many emotions welled up inside me. I loved all of my grandchildren, of course I did, but Scott, who resembled his grandfather not just in looks, but in every last mannerism and character, held a special secret place in my heart.

I paused on the first tread and looked down into the expectant faces of my family waiting for us in the hall below. Our two sons, our daughter, their partners and all our grandchildren were looking up, their faces wreathed in a sea of emotions. I smiled down at them all, hoping they would follow my lead. I began to descend the staircase, taking my time, not because I needed to be careful, but to give me the chance to study the gallery of photographs that lined the wall. The first pictures were of the Trentwell house and Jack's ranch, the homes we had lived in for the first five years of our life together.

The next picture was one I had taken. It was summertime and Jack and my parents were in the garden of the home we had bought them in the retirement village. It had been the perfect compromise for everyone.

'Are you going to be okay here, Dad, really?' I had asked anxiously.

'Home isn't bricks and mortar, Emma, you should know that by now, with the amount of time you spend flying back and forth across the Atlantic.'

I had smiled and squeezed his hand tightly.

We looked up then as one of the carers walked my mother across the lawn towards us. She was splattered with splotches of paint from the art class she had just attended.

'Home is where the person you love lives,' he added gently.

The next portrait had been captured by Jack. It was of me; I looked exhausted, exhilarated and totally besotted as I smiled up at the camera from my hospital bed, cradling a small blanket-wrapped bundle. I touched the frame and was drawn back in time.

'Well?'

'Give me a minute.'

'How long does it take to pee on a stick?'

I pulled open the bathroom door, my face lost beneath the width of my grin.

'Yes?' he asked excitedly.

'Two blue lines!' I cried.

Each photograph brought with it a memory and a smile. The gallery was a living breathing catalogue of our life together: birthdays, celebrations, homes we no longer owned, holidays...

The sun had been hot and the sky a brilliant blue and Jack and I were pictured in front of the Taj Mahal, a palace built by a man for the wife he loved. Supposedly one of the most romantic places on earth.

'Emma,' began Jack, getting down on one knee before the beautiful white memorial, and taking my hand. 'Will you marry me?'

Tourists taking photographs of the palace stopped their snapping and turned towards us; some even pointed their cameras in our direction. Locals just walked on by with indulgent smiles. They saw this a lot.

'Well?' prompted Jack, his eyes warm. 'Lucky number seven?'

I smiled and shook my head and smiled down at the man I loved with all my heart, who I would continue to love until that heart beat no more.

'No, Jack, not yet.' He had a regretful smile on his face as he got to his feet. 'I really thought that this place would be the charm,' he said, pulling me into his arms and kissing me warmly. Around us the gathering crowd burst into a small ripple of applause. I guess they thought I'd said yes.

'You got close that time,' I admitted in a whisper against the softness of his lips. 'Just keep asking.'

We never did get married, even though Jack proposed a total of twelve times over the years. It became a source of amused indulgence in our family, how the man who'd wanted no commitment had continued to ask me. But I'd never needed the ceremony or the piece of paper to know that we would stay in love and be together for ever.

Each year we celebrated the day he had given me the ring, the one I still wore on my wedding finger. That had been our anniversary, the day we didn't get engaged.

I stopped beside the large colourful photograph, taken just a few months earlier, at our fortieth anniversary.

'Emma Marshall, you are and always will be the love of my life.' Jack raised his glass and invited our assembled family to join in the toast.

'To a beautiful story with a very happy ending,' he finished, fixing me with a tender smile.

'Happy endings,' our loved ones echoed back.

We came to a final stop just three steps from the bottom, on a large square tread. Someone had opened the front door in readiness for our departure, and from this position I could see out into the road beyond, to the line of four long black limousines. My eyes were fixed to the first car, so full of flowers it was almost impossible to see the precious cargo it was transporting.

I felt my lip begin to tremble, but before any of my family could come to my assistance I heard his voice, whispering softly for me alone, 'You can do this, Emma. You can. Just remember that I love you.'

I bit my lip and stood up straighter. But before moving on, I turned to the final portrait upon the wall. He'd never wanted me to put it up, but I had insisted, and won that particular battle. It had been taken a year after we'd met, and was the official photograph for the jacket of the book he'd come to England to write. There were hundreds of photographs that had been taken over the years, but this one remained my favourite. I'd been in the studio for the shoot, and in the instant before the shutter had clicked, I'd said something that had made him laugh and turn towards me. The moment had been perfectly captured by the photographer, with Jack's eyes twinkling with humour and alight with a look that was just for me.

I turned to the portrait and smiled into the face of the man I loved. I lifted a hand to my lips and gently kissed my fingertips. Leaning towards the picture, I spoke in a low whisper, but I knew that somehow, somewhere, he would hear me. 'Don't go rushing too far ahead my darling.' I pressed my fingers gently against the glass covering his lips. 'Our story isn't over yet. I'll be right behind you.'

Acknowledgements

I have come to realise there is a lot you can learn about writing acknowledgements for a book by watching awards acceptance speeches. What you don't want to do is to forget someone important. And what you really don't want to do is to ramble on thanking every single person who has ever crossed your path since you left school. And crying, like an emotional idiot. You don't want to do that either (so embarrassing). So with dry eyes but an enormous smile of gratitude I would like to thank the following people:

My wonderful agent Kate Burke from Diane Banks Associates, who is my ambassador, travel guide, passport and visa in this strange new country I am visiting.

For my brilliant editor Laura Palmer and the astounding team at Head of Zeus for the hundreds of things that are done behind the scenes, which allow me to claim all the glory (so unfair!)

For all my amazing friends who stood by and proudly applauded and have shared the excitement with me over the last twelve months, with a special nod to Debbie, Kim, Sheila, Janet, Gillian, Christine and Hazel.

Thank you and a sad farewell to two old and trusted friends. You were there when I wrote this, heard me practise the dialogue out loud, and never once laughed at the plot, criticised, or stopped purring. Minty and Chip, I miss you both.

When I look down and see how far I have come, I know I wouldn't be here at all without the love and support of three amazing people: Ralph, Kimberley and Luke. You are my story, and I wouldn't re-write a single word.

THE
STORY
OF
US

Notes for your book club

The novel opens with Emma stating that she believed she was in love with two men at the same time. Do you feel that was true? Is it even possible?

Whose act of betrayal is worse, Richard's or Amy's?

If the accident had never happened, do you think Emma would or should have been able to forgive Richard and become his wife?

Was there any one act of Richard's throughout the novel that changed your perception of him?

Emma and Jack have both been badly betrayed by people they loved. How much do you feel this contributes to the intensity and strength of their relationship?

What do Jack and Richard represent in terms of Emma's future? Did you find yourself rooting for one man more than the other? If so, why?